EXCELSIOR!

EXCELSIOR!

BY PAUL HYDE BONNER

CHARLES
SCRIBNER'S
SONS NEW YORK

TO MY MOTHER

"There in the twilight cold and gray,
Lifeless, but beautiful, he lay,
And from the sky, serene and far,
A voice fell, like a falling star,
    Excelsior!"

HENRY WADSWORTH LONGFELLOW

AUTHOR'S NOTE

Neither my wife's family, nor anyone else
for that matter, need suspect that the
people who appear in this book are repro-
ductions. From Robert Eggli down—for
"down" was the angle of his vision—they
are purely creatures of my imagination,
brought through my pencil to whatever
life you, dear reader,
may endow them with.

CHAPTER I

THE old man walked out on the terrace and looked at the lake, at the continuous line of square, solid houses which bordered the opposite shore, their faces showing white in the morning sun. They were stark now in the December chill, like gravestones placed in wavering rows along the hillside and framed by the shadow of the Uetliberg with its tapestry of dark pines. In summer it was a softer, mellower view when their surrounding trees and shrubs, in full leaf, hid at least half of the stuccoed walls.

It was a scene that meant much to him. He could remember when there were only little clusters of houses, the lakeside villages, separated by wide expanses of field and forest—Wollishofen, Kilchberg, Thalwil. For better than seventy years he had watched it change, the intervals slowly being closed as one house after another had encroached on the farmers' properties, not suddenly as suburban housing projects expand like colonies of mushrooms near other cities in other lands, but gradually, in an orderly, careful advance. For building in Switzerland is a matter of vast concern, never to be entered into lightly. Here a man builds himself a house for his lifetime, planning it in every minute detail to suit his particular taste and method of living. Thus the old man had built his own house fifty years ago on the land that he had bought from his father. He had been rich even then, not alone from his junior share in the partnership, but with the fortune of his wife whose father, like his own, was a man of means. He had built a house that he had considered appropriate for a banker of substance, a big house, a house that would have been called a palazzo south of the Saint Gotthard

or a château had it been in the canton of Vaud. He had built it
with foresight, knowing that he would have children and they
would have nurses, knowing that he would grow richer and would
wish to collect works of art, as was the custom and duty of rich
men. And just as his house had come into being in the way he
had studiously planned it with his architect, so had the children
been born and raised, and the paintings purchased and hung,
and the priceless bits of Greek and Roman statuary placed carefully so that the light would reveal the utmost of their beauty.

As he stood there with his great house behind him and the
lawns of his garden sloping down to where a solid mass of shrub-
bery screened the street below, and looked out over the city of
Zürich and the long line of the lake shore, listening to the
chorus of tolling bells reverberating in the crisp air, he thought
how sure and solid and orderly his little country was, how it had
been able, an Alpine fortress rising in the center of a continent,
to preserve the wealth and culture of a civilization which had
continually endeavored to destroy itself. Without this safe deposit, this haven where the energy of capital could be stored,
there would be no hope of revival for the Western world.

He looked at his watch. It was seven-fifteen. The first edition
of the *Neue Zürcher Zeitung* would have the news, but it would
not be news to him. He had known it at five o'clock of the
previous afternoon, as bankers since the days of the Fuggers
and the Medicis had been the first to know of great events. A
cable from his son Jacques in New York had said in the code of
the bank: JAPANESE FLEET HAS ATTACKED AND DESTROYED AMERI-
CAN PACIFIC FLEET AT PEARL HARBOR, HAWAIIAN ISLANDS. He had
at once called his son Walter, who was temporarily on duty with
his regiment at Baden, and Walter had motored over for dinner.

The two of them had dined alone. The father had sent his
sister Victoria, who had lived with him since the death of his
wife, to his daughter's house for dinner. There were many things
which he had to discuss with his eldest son that were for no other
ears, not even Vicki's. Walter had been highly agitated. The

news had seemed to him to be a fatal stroke. With the loss of the Pacific fleet the United States would be at the mercy of Japan. All of her forces would have to be used for the defense of her possessions in the Pacific, and even for defense of the Western Hemisphere. This, Walter had argued, would give Hitler a free hand in the conquest of England and the Near East. The bank should now weigh its moves on the assumption of a Nazi victory, with undisputed control of all Europe and Africa north of the Sahara. The alternatives for the movement of capital were Buenos Aires and Johannesburg.

The old man had listened attentively to his son, letting him pursue his thread of reasoning until the end. Then he had told him in blunt, unequivocal language that he was a fool, that he had better go back to Baden and play at being a soldier.

"You travel about, but you do not see," he scolded. "You read, but you learn nothing. You do not know America. Neither does Jacques, though he has become a citizen and is married to an American. Americans are a strange people with many traits I do not approve of. They are extravagant, impulsive, and often unreliable. They talk too much and act too quickly, but as producers they have no equal. The Japanese have been fools. By this sudden unprovoked attack at the very moment when they were negotiating with Washington they have asked for their own defeat. You watch what this will do to America. It will electrify them. It will unite them into one solid mass of energy which will produce new fleets, new squadrons of airplanes, tanks by the thousands. Yes, and within six months they will have an army of three million men. Every young man will be a soldier, even my grandson Robert—as it is here."

"But he is at the university, at Yale," Walter interrupted.

"Pfah! What will that matter?" the old man said with impatience. "You mark my words that he has already joined his regiment."

"He has no regiment, Papa. They do not have military service in the United States."

"Don't pick me up on details," the old man said crossly. "You know well what I mean—he will enlist, or whatever they do in America to join the army."

"But Hitler," Walter persisted, "he will be free to do what he wishes in Europe. There will be no more aid to England of guns and airplanes."

The old man banged the table with his fist, causing the glass and china to jingle and the maid to turn at the pantry door to look at her master with an expression of apprehension. Not that she was afraid for the service—that could be replaced, but she knew that fits of anger were bad for the old man. Fräulein Victoria had told the servants many times during the past year that they must take care not to anger him as the doctor had said his heart could not accept any violent emotion.

"It will be just the contrary," he shouted. "England will henceforth receive ten, twenty times as much assistance as she has had in the past. There is no longer a question of neutrality. It is war, and Congress will give Roosevelt whatever he asks. And remember this, my son. Roosevelt is a gentleman and he will not forget England because some little grinning Jap has stuck a pin in his behind."

"What shall we do, then, about the funds?" Walter asked.

"Nothing. Absolutely nothing," the old man announced. "That is, for the present. Later we shall see." He turned to see if the maid was still in the room. Finding that they were alone, he went on in a low gruff voice. "The time may soon come when we should shift some of the Austrian, Hungarian and Rumanian accounts from Buenos Aires and Rio to New York. But that can wait for events."

"Yes, Papa," Walter said meekly. He did not pursue his argument, not only because he knew that it would be futile, that his father's mind, once it had arrived at an analysis, a diagnosis, was set and unmalleable, but also because he respected his father's judgment. In all the years of his adult life he had rarely known the old man to be wrong in a forecast of international affairs.

Others too were aware of this. That is why his bank had become the fiduciary agent for the rich of the world. Individuals, corporations, trusts, banks of every country had entrusted Robert Eggli with their fortunes, firm in the belief that his wisdom and insight would protect their money from dissipation or seizure. In the process he had become a multi-millionaire—in fact, one of the richest men in Europe. But his reputation for honesty and sagacity meant more to him than his millions. He was a proud man, conscious of his own worth, fiercely jealous of this reputation.

After dinner they went into the old man's study, a handsome library lined with bookshelves which were protected by carved oak frames with copper screening in the French manner. Over the mantel was a portrait of a Milanese lady of the fifteenth century by Ambrogio de Predis, lit by a reflector. The maid followed them with the coffee tray and decanters of brandy and kirschwasser, which she placed on a low circular table by the fire. Robert Eggli went over to an immense humidor from which he took out a box of Havana cigars. These he offered to his son and selected one for himself, chopping off the end with a gold clipper on his watch chain. Then he sat down by the fire, lit his cigar and waited for Walter to pour the coffee.

"You will not need me, then, tomorrow at the bank?" Walter said.

"No, there will be no movements in the accounts."

"Will you have a cognac, Papa?"

"No, that fool Dr. Huber does not allow it."

"What does he say about your health?"

"*Ach*, he says my blood pressure is too high. He's a fool! What does he expect of a man of eighty? I still feel fine. Never felt better."

"That's good. You look well, Papa."

It was true. The old man looked surprisingly well; in fact, he looked like a man of seventy. He was small, not over five feet six, with a straight back and a thin, wiry figure. His complexion was pink, like that of a child, which accentuated the hard, bright blue of his eyes. His white hair, thinning on top, was very precisely brushed back above his small round ears. With his narrow pointed nose, sensitive mouth, and delicate, almost feminine hands, he did not look the part of a cold irascible banker. That aspect of him was more apparent in his attire. The dark blue suit was from Savile Row, like all his suits, and it fitted him correctly, easily, without demanding attention. His shirt was of grey linen, but his starched collar was white with a sheen on it, and in his grey silk tie was embedded a large pink pearl. The dark red carnation in his buttonhole completed the effect of a dandy who was self-assured.

"You will sleep in the Zollikerstrasse tonight?" the old man asked.

"No, I shall motor back to Baden," his son replied. "Hélène and the children are spending a fortnight with Frau Sieber in Winterthur. Besides, I have to be ready for reveille at six tomorrow morning."

The old man snorted. "In my day a captain did not have to attend reveille."

"There is always the fear that the Germans might make a sudden attack."

"They will not attack us," the old man stated flatly.

"Let us hope so. They attacked Russia when no one thought they would." This was a sly dig at his father who had believed that the Von Ribbentrop–Molotov pact was a clever move on Hitler's part to confine the war to one front.

"And that is when that dunderhead of a paperhanger showed his true colors. With the march on Russia he disclosed at once his stupidity and his ignorance. A great general studies his history. That is why von Bismarck was great and this Hitler a jackass. His good generals, the old Junkers of the General Staff, no longer have any use for him."

Walter looked up from his kirsch with surprise. "You think so?" he asked.

"I know so. I have received messages."

"But if he is fool enough to attack Russia, he may be fool enough to attack us."

"Now it is you who are talking like a fool."

"You mean because of the accounts."

"What else?"

Robert Eggli recalled all of this as he stood on his terrace looking out on the houses of the Enge and Wollishofen across the lake. He had an exact photographic memory which enabled him to re-enact a scene with every word and gesture as it had been originally performed. But the recall depressed him. His son Walter was now fifty, a full partner in the bank and destined to be its president when he, Robert, should die. He was privy to every secret of the firm—the only other person who possessed a key to the code book in the vault which identified the account numbers. The old man had summoned him from Baden as a test. He wanted to observe Walter's powers of inductive reasoning, to find out if this heir, this stalwart, handsome son of middle age, could face a *fait accompli* and, from his experience and knowledge of the world, rationalize its effect on the course of history. For it was on that ability, and that ability alone, that the international banker justified the confidence of his clients. Ministers of state might have the ability—a few did—but their judgments and decisions had of necessity to be swayed by political considerations which evolved from the vacuity of national emotion. Therefore ministers of state could seldom be rigidly honest, even with themselves. He knew this from his own experience. How many prime ministers during the course of his long life had consulted him, listened to his appraisal, then shrugged their shoulders with a smile, saying, "I agree, Monsieur Eggli. In all probability your prediction will prove accurate, but you must understand that if I were to guide my policies on such an assumption, my government would fall within a week."

Poor unhappy men these were who held the destinies of their

people in their hands, yet were bound and tied by the exigencies of popular will. And popular will, as Robert Eggli well knew, was as fickle and impulsive and erroneous as the whim of a child. Yet his son had reacted to the news of Pearl Harbor exactly as any untrained, ignorant *petit bourgeois*. His mind had jumped quickly to the obvious, the pat conclusion. That was acceptable. Every mind works that way. His own had performed in the same manner when he read the cable. But those first thoughts are spoken only by the fools. The wise man places them in escrow while he marshals all the factors and examines them in light of the circumstances. And the factors to be dealt with in international crises of this sort are complex, multitudinous and diverse. The processes of addition and subtraction, of placing into the calculator of the mind the correct sums in the proper order must be precisely performed if the result is to be valid. Only when the equation has reached its final q.e.d. should the answer be expressed in words for others to hear or read.

This had been the crucial test of Walter Eggli, and he had failed miserably. As the old man saw it, no single event during the course of his long life was so deceptive, so open to diametrically opposed conclusions as this unprovoked attack on the American fleet. If ever there had been a moment when a banker needed to exercise his powers of analytical thinking, it was now. He had strongly suspected that his son would prove incapable, would prefer to sound off, then to subside into filial agreement and admiration of his father's wisdom. It had always been that way, and it had not altered. Was it his own fault? Had he been too severe, too impatient, too domineering? Should he have given Walter more latitude, more responsibility? Yet how could he have done that without being certain that the results would have justified his confidence? After all, it was the money of others with which they were dealing. That was a sacred trust. The world had complete faith in the judgment of the House of Eggli. That faith was based on experience. The world had discovered that capital in the bank's hands was not only preserved against wars and depressions, but grew and prospered. There was nothing more fearful, more timid than money. One little loss and it fled in fright. And that was the end of the banker. He might as well close his doors and spend the rest of his days in idle amusement.

He wondered if Jacques were any better, if age and independence had fostered within him the quality of judgment. He had not seen his younger son for two years, not since the summer of 1939 when he had taken a moor in Scotland and had invited Jacques and his wife to shoot with him. Jacques had been forty-five at the time, and he had thought him a fairly silly man. A good shot, yes, almost as good as Lord Dunalkin, but a buffoon who drank too many cocktails and told too many ribald stories. He had become hopelessly Americanized, not in the good sense but in the Long Island–Palm Beach sense of smart-aleck irresponsibility. The fact that he had done well in Wall Street was hardly attributable to his own ability. He had, after all, the Eggli accounts to invest, which totalled a sum that even Morgan and Company would respect, and the advice that surrounded him was of the soundest. But even had he matured more solidly than Walter as a result of removal from parental dominance, nevertheless it was improbable that he could be induced to give up his adopted country and return to Switzerland.

Alone, he might have done it—that is, if the future of the bank depended on it—but Doris, his American wife, would never let him. There was nothing wrong with Doris. She was a clever, handsome girl who had done much to mould Jacques into a man of the world; but her attitude towards Switzerland and the Swiss was condescending—not patently or rudely, for she was always most charming and gracious when she visited the family in Zürich. He realized that intellectually she admired all of the Swiss traits that had made his little country a haven of order in a world of hate and confusion, but he suspected that underneath she considered the country a sort of picture-postcard stage-set, inhabited by stolid, ruminating cattle with bells around their necks. And more than that, more than her concept of dullness and quaint unreality, was the fact that she feared and distrusted her husband's complete and abject reliance on his father.

Robert Eggli's relationship with his American daughter-in-law was difficult to define. She admired him as all women admired him, because he was powerful, dominant, and male. She was attracted to him as all beautiful women were attracted to him, because he dressed himself impeccably, undressed them with his keen blue eyes, and treated them with courtly gallantry. Yet she hated him because he came between her and Jacques as a force which could, on command, take her husband from her. The old man realized all this and liked her for it. No, he thought, she would never allow Jacques to return permanently to Switzerland —not so long as he, Robert, was alive.

As for his son-in-law Hans Waldmann, the husband of his daughter Lucy, he was reliable, loyal, painstaking, but beyond that there was little to recommend him as a successor. He was too insular, too narrowly Swiss ever to acquire the banker's vision. He had the studious approach of the sound, careful lawyer, but he lacked the intuitive sense of international trends which should guide the banker in times of stress. No, he would never do; the law had constricted his vision to the potholes and rocks in the road, as if his head had been permanently lowered, robbing him forever of a view of the horizon.

Those were the three. There were no other men of the family. Oh, if Vicki had been a man! Well, thank God she was not, for being younger she would survive him, and it made him shiver to think what would happen to the bank if she ever took over its affairs. He was quite aware that everyone imagined Vicki was a cross he bore with fortitude, yet they were wrong. True, she irritated him at times with her nagging, her gossip, but she was the only one who had the courage to stand up to him, to tell him off. He admired her for that. Her mind might be erratic and dominated by emotion, but she feared no one. A trait, he liked to think, that was truly Eggli.

This conclusion brought his mind suddenly to Yvonne. He turned and walked back into the house. In his study he picked up the telephone and dialled long distance. "Give me Geneva 65-06-11," he said.

CHAPTER II

THE Baroness Yvonne de Marty was a polyglot *femme du monde* who had both shrewdness and wit. Had she been educated in any other country than England, she might well have been a modern counterpart of Madame de Staël, but the school for young ladies in London, which she had attended at the turn of the century, did not envisage a knowledge of classic literature as a necessary passport to debutante balls and eventual marriage. Nor had the finishing school in Florence demanded more than a steady plodding through *I Promessi Sposi* and an occasional flying-wedge attack on the Uffizi. Those were the Edwardian days when young ladies were groomed for bed and breeding. The objective was the capture of the prize bedfellow, or at least a suitable one. Considering the fact that her father had been a Jewish banker in the City and her mother a French actress at the Comédie Française, she had not done badly.

Her coming-out ball at the Hyde Park Hotel had been brilliant, with all of the more spectacular peerage and the Tatler set present and herself a veritable fairy princess in a gown by Worth and a new diamond *collier* by Boucheron, the gift of a very proud father. Within a fortnight she had received six offers of marriage from gangling, awkward young men, all of whom bore the subsidiary titles of eldest sons, and who had been advised by their fathers that a solid dot of Liebermann securities would greatly assist in maintaining the ancestral estates and racing stables. Feeling secure in her beauty, which was exceptional, and in her financial background, which her father had given her to believe was massive, she turned these down and waited for someone who could touch her heart and excite her passion.

Baron de Marty was not long in making his appearance. Although he had attended the ball and dutifully danced with her, he had waited with Gallic perspicacity until the noble saplings were cleared from the doorstep before making his call at the Liebermann mansion on Carlton House Terrace.

It could be accurately described as love at first sight. Henri de Marty was thirty-two at the time, and the time was the month of June, 1910. He was Counsellor of the French Embassy to the Court of Saint James's and a career diplomat. But more important as far as Yvonne Liebermann was concerned, he was a skillful and polished lover, even though he was far from handsome in the British Adonis sense. He was, in fact, quite undistinguished, being rather thickset, with bushy black hair and a prominent Breton nose. But he understood women as well as he understood the intricacies of politics. He knew that the female heart was not the commanding instrument, but merely the indicator of disturbances in other quarters, and he was a past master at creating disturbances. As a tactician he was aware that a *jeune fille* cannot be conquered by the same methods as a *femme du monde*. With virgins one started by creating an atmosphere with words, not necessarily suggestive words, or even romantic words—just a combination of words which evoked sensation, which made both the listener and the speaker forget all abstract ideas and concentrate their beings on the sensory nerves. Henri de Marty did just this on his first call, did it in his own language, which is more suitable for sensation than English, over a cup of tea. Yvonne, listening, grew all hot and tingly, thinking it was the tea or a slight touch of fever. But when the tingling continued after he had left and returned for three days every time she thought of the Baron, she knew that it was neither the tea nor influenza.

On his second call he could tell instinctively that she was ready to be kissed. His approach was so expert that she thought afterwards she must have been the aggressor. At all events, the kiss did it. She felt as if she were dissolving, liquefying, and as soon as her mind could form a thought it decided that she wanted those kisses for herself for life. On the fifth of July, 1910, she became Madame la Baronne de Marty at Brompton Oratory, which was her mother's church.

Yvonne de Marty had first met Robert Eggli at a dinner party at the hôtel of her uncle, Max Liebermann, on the Rue de Grenelle. That was in 1928, a year before her husband had died of a heart attack after a stormy interview with the Italian Ambassador at the Quai d'Orsay. She had sat next to Eggli and had been fascinated by his quiet self-assurance. He exuded a sense of authority, as if he expected both tribute and obedience. Though he spoke to her in flawless French, nevertheless his sentences had not been Gallic, but terse and unadorned with qualification. Yet underneath the stern exterior she felt the force of a powerful, *élan vital*. Years later when she had learned much about his country, she was to say that he was a pure product of the Zwingli Reformation—a proud burgher, the leader of his guild in the Protestant city-state of Zürich, which had not altered its evangelical strictness since the middle of the sixteenth century.

For his part, he was immediately attracted to her. She was beautiful, even more beautiful than she had been as a girl, with that added beauty, that fullness and grace which comes to women who have experienced the refinements and ecstasies of love. She exhibited that ease with him which indicated she was aware of the male beneath the armor, so that the words they spoke had nothing whatever to do with their basic dialogue. Before the evening was over he invited her to lunch and she accepted. The following day they went in his Rolls to the Moulin de Bicherelle, where he had reserved a little *cabinet privé*, and from that day on he had been her lover, constant, passionate and considerate.

Yvonne de Marty was awakened by the ring of the telephone at her bedside. As she reached over to pick up the receiver, she saw that the dial of her gold travelling clock showed it was half-past seven. She was annoyed. Although she had lived in Geneva for four years now, she had yet to accustom herself to Swiss early rising. "Allo!" she said sharply.

"Is that you, my dear?" It was the voice of Robert Eggli. He never addressed her by name over the telephone, nor did he allow her to mention his name.

"Yes," she said, less annoyed now that she knew it was her beloved friend. "Are you in Geneva?"

"No, but I intend to come over today. There are some matters I must attend to."

"How nice. I am really delighted. It is so long since I have seen you. When do you arrive?"

"I shall take the train which reaches Geneva at five-fifty in the afternoon."

"Good. Then I shall expect you for dinner."

"If you will be so kind."

"What would you like? Shall it be ombre chevalier and a poussin?"

"Perfect. And a bottle of the Perrier-Jouet of 1918."

"Splendid! Even two bottles if you like. It sounds as if you wish to celebrate some good news. What is it, another grandchild?"

"I shall tell you this evening. Adieu."

Yvonne de Marty hung up the receiver and lay back on her pillow of handkerchief linen edged with lace. She put her left hand to her breast and felt her heart beating rapidly, and she marvelled that the sound of his voice could still so thrill her. Even at eighty, she thought, his voice has that same timbre, that exciting, vibrant quality of power held in check. It had always seemed incredible to her that he had already been sixty-seven when she had first met him in Paris. According to the rules of human life-span, he had been an old man, far past his prime, and yet he had defied those rules by sweeping her off her feet with an ardor that was youthful and vigorous. Only in the past three years had there been any slackening in the force of his desire. Not that she cared. She had grown to love him for other qualities that were deeper, more abiding. There was a granite solidity to his loyalty that made her almost weep, it was so staunch and true. Behind the gruffness, behind the cold, rational exterior, behind the proud, stern rectitude of the Zürich burgher was a sentiment that was deep and faithful.

Was it not he, Robert, who had saved her when the double tragedy hit her without warning? But for him she would be a penniless widow, dependent on the charity of her uncle. For her father's fortune had been wiped out by the crisis of the New York Stock Exchange at the very moment when her husband had died of a stroke. Within twenty-four hours Robert Eggli had appeared at her apartment in the Avenue Foch. He had known both stories—how, she did not know—but it was characteristic of him that he always knew of events in every capital of the world before they were carried on the wires of the news agencies.

He had been more stern and practical than usual—moments of sentiment always caused him to put on an armor of defense— as he had asked her for an inventory of her possessions. He had known that the loss of Henri de Marty was the greater blow of the two, that she had loved her husband, and that her unfaithfulness had been no indicator of any diminishing devotion. She was simply one of those women who were capable of loving two men at one time, each commanding separate unrelated parts of her heart. Robert had understood that clearly and had never demanded more than his share of her affection. But the situation had changed and, like a wise banker, he had taken prompt steps to gain complete control of the enterprise. He wanted her, he needed her, and the moment had come to acquire ownership. Knowing him, she had realized at once the nature of his inquiries, and she was quite content to let him effect her rescue and thus the title to all of her heart.

She remembered now so vividly that scene in her little salon of ivory and gold *boiserie*. Robert Eggli had paced back and forth, his hands clasped behind his straight back, his blue eyes contracted by concentration, while she sat on a *fauteuil* in a black peignoir and recited the list of what she owned. There was the apartment in Paris, a château near Saint-Lô in Normandy with some sixty hectares of farmland and park, and a villa on the Côte d'Azur. The upkeep of these would take more than the income of the twenty-five million francs which Henri de Marty had left her. And of course there were her jewels. She had no idea what they were worth, but they ought to realize a tidy sum. When she finished, Eggli continued his pacing for some minutes in silence before he sat down facing her.

"My dear Yvonne," he said, "you must excuse me if I seem crude and brutal. But you know me for what I am—a Swiss. We are not given to fine phrases and diplomatic ways of speaking our thoughts. We say what is on our minds, which is honest even if it is not gallant. I am fond of my wife Matti. She is a good woman, a good wife and a good mother, but she is now an old lady, not as old as I in years—she is sixty-five and I am sixty-eight—but much older physically and mentally. Our life together these days is one of respect and affection. It is many years now since it has been more than that. Since a year you have given me generously of the kind of love a man needs if he is to be healthy and complete. I have come to rely on that love. It is something that means much to me—very much. I do not wish to lose it. Whether I do or not is for you to say. If it were in my power, I would offer you marriage; but that I cannot do, now or ever. Not even in the unthinkable circumstance of the death of my dear wife would it be possible. What I propose to offer you, with the very great hope that you will accept, is my loyal love and affection as long as I am alive. As a proof of my sincerity, I would settle on you in your name, for you and your heirs, a sum which will give you an income in dollars, which at the present rate of exchange should be the equivalent of ten million francs a year. With this money you should be able to lead the life to which you are accustomed, maintaining the château in Normandy and the villa at Cannes should you choose to do so. The only condition with this offer is that you do not give any part of your love to any other man. Perhaps you are thinking me silly, but there is no escaping the fact that I love you, that I am jealous, and that I carry with me always a profound pride in my possessions. I want you for myself. I do not wish to share you with anyone."

Yvonne rose from her chair and came over to him with outstretched arms. "My dear Robert," she said, "you are the most wonderful friend that any woman ever had." Then she fell on her knees before him, buried her face in his sleeve and wept. He stroked her hair gently until she finally lifted her face and looked at him. "Never fear, Robert," she said, "I shall love you always and no other. While Henri was alive I loved him too. He was a fine man, Robert, never forget that; but he is gone and now I have only you, my dear." She took one of his hands and pressed it in both of hers. "You believe me, don't you?"

"Yes, I believe you, Yvonne," he answered, but his face remained stern and she knew there was yet something that he had to say. "There is one caution, however, which I must give you. There are no secrets in this world. Sooner or later my family will learn that you are my—friend."

"Mistress. Say it, Robert. I am not ashamed of the word."

"At all events, they will find out, or they will guess, that it is my money on which you live. Behind my back they will say that I am a silly old man who has lost his head to a beautiful French woman with a title."

She smiled and asked, "And does that bother you?"

"Not in the least," he replied sharply. "I ignore their gossip. What they say as long as I am alive is of no importance. It is only after my death that they may start trouble. They will fear that you will make some claim on my estate. Even though you would not do such a thing, they might well attack you, believing it their best method of defense. To avoid this there must be some document between us, some statement which will indicate clearly and legally that you have been provided for and therefore waive all future rights to anything in my estate."

"But of course!" she said, rising to her feet and pointing to her delicate Louis XIV writing desk in the corner. "Write it, my dear Robert, and I shall sign it now, at once."

For the first time at that meeting he dropped his cold business-like air and laughed. "You are too hasty, Yvonne," he said. "Would you sign your life away before you have received a sou?"

"I trust you implicitly, Robert," she said, looking at him with gratitude and affection. "I would sign anything you asked me to."

The pleasure her words evoked was evident in his face, although he did not thank her. "The first step is to effect the settlement of the principal," he said, rising to his feet. "That must be done in such a way that gift taxes are avoided. When that has been arranged, you will receive from some banking house —probably one in Paris, though not your uncle's—a statement of the securities you own and the cash available. If you are as smart as I think you are, you will allow my bank to direct the investment of your funds as long as you live. The preservation of capital in the times in which we live is not a simple matter. You have seen what has happened to your father's fortune in the New York market. It may interest you to know that the House of Eggli has not lost one cent there, either for itself or its customers. We liquidated all of our holdings in Wall Street last July."

"Poor Papa," she said, "this is going to kill him. His pride will never survive it. Never fear, Robert. What has come so generously from you shall remain in your hands."

"That is good. I am glad to hear you say that."

"What is more," she said fervently, "as soon as this money is mine, I shall make a will leaving it to your children."

"You are not required to do so much."

"To whom else should I leave it? To Uncle Max or his children? No, Robert, it is right that it should return to your descendants."

The stern look had returned to his face, the mask which hid his emotions from all but her, and he kissed her hand awkwardly and left her.

Twelve years had passed since that meeting in Paris, twelve years during which she had remained faithful to her pledge. Not that it had been difficult, for other men no longer tempted her. There had been many candidates for her affection, which was inevitable in the case of a beautiful and desirable woman with money enough to lead a life of luxury. Most of the men who had pursued her hotly were, she knew, after her money. They saw her as a lonely widow, and they were the sort who shunned working for wealth if it could be acquired via the boudoir. They neither amused nor interested her. Her marriage with Henri de Marty and her friendship with Robert Eggli had given her a taste for men of action, men who were not afraid of ideas or of giving battle. More and more during the years in Paris had her coterie of friends become the acquaintances and associates of Robert— bankers, industrialists, diplomats, and ministers of state and their wives.

After the death of Frau Eggli in 1935, Robert had dropped all pretense concerning his mistress. At dinner at her flat on the Avenue Foch he had sat at the head of the table, and he would accept no invitation in Paris unless she were invited. Thus his children soon learned that what they had heard as gossip was indeed fact. Jacques and Doris had been the first to meet her at a dinner at the house of Jules Cremier, the steel magnate, and they had been both surprised and delighted to find her a lady of charm and poise. Having listened to the stories of Walter and Hélène and Tante Vicki, they had gained the impression that she was a flashy courtesan out of a novel by Colette, whose title of Baronne had been assumed for the purpose of finding more important mines of ore. They realized—at least Doris did—that the Zürich appraisal had been colored by the puritan concept of a woman who lived with a man out of wedlock, above all a French woman, as being a species of cocotte found in the foyer of the Bal Tabarin. On her last visit to Zürich in 1939 Doris had tried to convince her brother-in-law that the picture he had painted was not true to life, but her arguments had fallen on unheeding

ears. They did not want to believe that their father's lady friend
was anything but a designing slut, who was out to rob them of
their heritage.

All this had been relayed to Yvonne in recent years, since
Robert, foreseeing a European war and his consequent inability
to visit Paris when he wished to, had urged her in 1939 to move
to Geneva. The bankers and wits of French Switzerland, who
liked to refer to the sober Zürichois as bumblebees because of
the harsh buzz of their dialect, took great delight in describing
to Yvonne the picture which Zürich had painted of her. She was
not really amused, although she laughed at their stories. It nettled
her to be classed as a kept woman, a tart. In Paris her position
had been accepted without question. There the love affairs of
ladies were respected and understood. The Genevois like to think
themselves as emancipated as Parisians. In a cautious, limited
way they received her in their circles, but they still retained a
strong taint of Calvinism, not as pronounced as the stark puritanism of Zwingli's Zürich but existing none the less. She was
afraid, too, that all the talk might injure Robert, might serve to
destroy confidence in him as the great banker. She welcomed his
visits because she loved him, but there were no dinner parties,
no lunches together in public restaurants. His visits were clandestine, in the privacy of her little house on the Rue de Glacis de
Rive. She had proposed this and he had not argued, because he
knew that it would not be circumspect within the borders of the
Confederation.

Yvonne pressed a button on her night table that signalled to
her maid. At least the dinner must be perfect, she thought, with
ombre chevalier poached and served with sauce mousseline, followed by a roast poussin and a salad of endive.

CHAPTER III

I AM quite sure that something must have happened. Something important," Tante Vicki said. It was the evening before and they were drinking their coffee after dinner. She had waited for this announcement until the children, Rudolph, a student at the university, and Christine, at high school, had gone to their rooms to study. Both had been skiing over the week end, leaving much work to prepare for Monday's classes.

"I think you exaggerate, Tante Vicki," Hans Waldmann said. He was a big heavy man with a bald head and horn-rimmed glasses, a prosperous lawyer who worked hard because he enjoyed his success—not that he needed the income, married as he was to Lucy Eggli, the daughter of the great banker. "It is not unusual for Grosspapa to have a private talk with Walter. After all, Walter is the next in command at the bank. Also, you must remember that Walter is on military service, which means that such talks have to take place on Sunday evening at home and not at the office as they would otherwise."

"No, Hansli, you may be a smart man, but this time you are wrong," Tante Vicki persisted. "I could tell by the way Robert spoke when he told me that I was to have dinner here because he wished to be alone with Walter." She turned toward Lucy. "You know how he is, Lucy, when something is troubling him, his mouth set in a straight line, his eyes hard like the blue sapphires in that necklace Matti always used to wear at New Year's. It was something important, something to do with the war, you mark my words. Was there anything on the radio at six o'clock?"

"Nothing startling," Lucy Waldmann answered. "Always Rommel and Wavell in the desert."

"Maybe he has word that Hitler will attack us," Tante Vicki said.

"God forbid!" Lucy exclaimed.

"That danger has passed," Hans said reassuringly. "Will you have a kirsch or a cognac, Tante Vicki?"

"Just a drop of cognac," the old lady answered. "The doctor says it's good for me."

"And you, Lucy?" Waldmann asked his wife.

"Nothing, thank you."

Hans poured a thimbleful of cognac in a liqueur glass and took it to Tante Vicki, then poured himself a kirsch.

"What makes you think the danger has passed?" the old lady asked. "How does one ever know what that madman will do?"

"It would gain him nothing to conquer Switzerland, now the Nazionalrat has passed a law that in the event of invasion all bank accounts automatically become the property of the army," Hans explained.

"But suppose he captures the army?" Tante Vicki argued.

"Before he could do that, one or two pilots of the Air Force would be deputized to fly to England or Portugal with all the authority governing the accounts, and the Nazis would find nothing here but a plugged-up tunnel on the Saint Gotthard. That would make it impossible for them to supply Il Duce with the coal and petrol he needs to carry on the war."

Lucy made no comment as she sipped her coffee. She was thinking that her father and Walter might well be discussing the question of an inheritance for that Baroness who was now living in Geneva, but she would not express the thought. The subject of the Baroness was taboo, on her husband's orders. She would like to meet that woman. Ever since Jacques and Doris had defended her she was curious to learn what manner of person it was who could capture and hold her father. She must have qualities far above the average, of that Lucy was sure. Her father disdained mediocrity in all people. That was why he had always been so rough on his sons. He suspected them of being little men. True, he admired smart, fashionable women, probably because they were such a contrast to the dowdy Swiss, but beauty and chic would not be enough to hold him beyond one evening. And he put up with his sister Vicki, even admired her because she said what she thought. Yes, somehow, sometime, she must contrive to meet this Baroness de Marty in order to judge for herself who was right—Doris, or Hans, Walter, Hélène and Tante Vicki.

The house of Hans and Lucy Waldmann in the Scheideggstrasse, which was in the Enge quarter of Zürich, was in every respect different from that of old Robert Eggli in the Riesbach section. Not only was it on the opposite shore of the lake under the Uetliberg, but it was modern and severe, whereas the old man's mansion was rich and ornate. Both Lucy and Hans were studiously interested in art. They collected carefully, cautiously, the works of the nineteenth-century impressionists and moderns, relying on their own judgments and never on that of dealers. Whereas the father had bought masterpieces ranging from Van Eyck to Gainsborough, because he considered that a man of his position should be surrounded only by the works of classic masters, the Waldmanns declared that they cared nothing for the names and reputations of artists and were solely interested in the quality of the picture, which was of course a pose. The room in which they were drinking their coffee and liqueurs with their Aunt Victoria was almost monastic in its simplicity. Like a museum, its cream stucco walls and oyster-colored hangings of monk's cloth and fireplace framed in travertine became an unobtrusive frame for paintings by Renoir, Cézanne, Redon, Hodler and Paul Bodmer. The rugs on the polished parquet floor were Moroccan, with white grounds on which were black geometric patterns. Only the furniture was a concession to antiquity. It was mainly eighteenth-century Swiss, of fruit woods highly polished, and the forms were a subdued recognition of French cabinetmakers. They were the only part of the décor of which Tante Vicki approved.

"I think you will find," Hans held forth pontifically, "that Papa and Walter are merely discussing banking affairs. It is quite normal that they should wish to be alone. The affairs of one's clients are most confidential."

"Do you suppose it could be that woman?" Tante Vicki asked, not having listened to what Hans had said.

Waldmann cleared his throat ostentatiously to signify that the subject was distasteful.

The old lady ignored him. "God save us! Maybe she has turned out to be a spy for the Germans."

"I am sure that Papa would not discuss her with Walter," Lucy said, glancing at her husband who was frowning ominously.

"Don't be too sure about your father," Tante Vicki said. "He is not like Hans who prefers to stop his ears and close his eyes when anything unpleasant is mentioned. If Robert has made up his mind to tell his son that this woman is going to have a baby, and that . . ."

"Really, Tante Vicki!" Hans exploded. "I must ask you to remember that the children are upstairs and the door to the hall is open."

"And do they still believe that it is the stork who brings the babies?" the old lady asked indignantly.

"One should not make jokes about it," Lucy said.

"Who is making jokes?" Tante Vicki exclaimed. "I am quite serious. It has always been my suspicion that one day she would produce a child and insist that it was Robert's heir."

"Gotteswillen! This is preposterous!" Hans said, rising and closing the door to the hall.

"You must remember, Tante Vicki, that Grosspapa is now eighty," Lucy said. Unlike her husband, she had no wish to change the subject, though she disapproved of it.

"And what difference does that make?" the old lady argued.

"It may not be his, but don't forget that Robert is still a very active man. At eighty he is worth two of the young men one sees about nowadays, spindly creatures who spend their energies chasing golf balls around the fields, shooting roebuck, and thinking of bed as only a place in which to sleep. Besides, as I say, who knows who the real father of the child is? It might be any one of a dozen men in Geneva. If she says it is your father's, how can he deny it? And he wouldn't, even if he suspected it might not be, because he would be so proud to boast that he had produced a child at his age."

"It seems to me, Tante Vicki, that we are jumping to a great many conclusions," Hans said stuffily. He had resigned himself to the fact that he could not get her off the subject of the Baroness de Marty except by the tactical means of the barrister. "In the first place, there is no evidence that any child has been born"—he could not bring himself even to refer to the Baroness—"and secondly, we have no knowledge of what Grosspapa and Walter are discussing."

"The fact remains that this woman is living right under our noses—" Tante Vicki started to say.

"Geneva is hardly 'under our noses,'" Lucy interrupted.

"Any place in Switzerland is under the nose of a Swiss," the old lady insisted. "Only last week Marie Rappart was here, staying with old Frau Lange, and she told me confidentially at tea that she had been invited to lunch at the house of some Englishman and his wife, and who should be there but *that woman!*"

"You mean to say she is invited?" Lucy asked.

"By English people," Tante Vicki answered. "The English judge only by titles. They would invite anyone who called herself Baronne or Comtesse, whether they were entitled to it or not."

"I must agree with you there," Hans said, seeing his chance to steer the conversation into safer waters. "I have noticed that the English put great store by titles. I remember when I was in London in 1938. There was a chap . . ."

"What did Marie Rappart think of her?" Lucy asked, interrupting her husband and causing him to scowl again.

"She said she was fascinating," Tante Vicki replied. "But then you cannot rely on Marie's judgment. She likes everyone. Everyone is always sweet and pure and kind in her eyes. She did tell me one interesting thing. She said the woman speaks English without an accent. Now I find that very suspicious."

"Why should she not speak English?" Hans asked gruffly. And then suddenly realizing that his question might be interpreted as a defense of the Baroness, he added, "That has no relation to morals."

"But she is a French cocotte," Tante Vicki said, confirmed in her belief that Yvonne de Marty was from the *coulisse* of the Folies-Bergère.

"She was born and brought up in London," Hans announced flatly.

"Are you sure, Hans?" Lucy asked, incredulous.

"I am sure," he answered.

"*Gotteswillen!* So you know the woman!" Tante Vicki exclaimed.

Hans Waldmann's face turned beet-red. He was furious with his wife's aunt. "I do not know her. I have never laid eyes on her," he snapped angrily.

"Then how can you be so sure about where she was born and brought up?" the old lady asked.

"I have made certain inquiries," Waldmann said, not happy about confessing that he had done so.

"So! You have made inquiries." Tante Vicki was delighted to find someone who really knew something about the woman. Although no facts could alter her own preconception, nevertheless she was eager to hear them even if they were to be discarded.

"You never told me this, Hans," Lucy said, quite annoyed with her husband.

Hans Waldmann was alarmed now. If it should reach the ears of his father-in-law that he had checked on the past life of the Baroness de Marty, all hell would break loose. Just why he was so afraid of the old man, he had never been able to figure out. But he was, just as they all were. Of course he had good reason to step with care as far as Robert Eggli was concerned. He was after all the bank's Zürich lawyer, and the fees from this source alone constituted a handsome income. But fees or no fees, he knew that the wrath of the old man was something he dreaded. "Now listen to me, please," he said in a tone of sudden genial confidence. "It must never be repeated that I have inquired into this matter, not even to Walter or Hélène. You understand that I did it for the sake of the family. Someday I may be called upon to protect our interests and it is better to be forearmed in such a case."

"Do you think I would be fool enough to tell Robert?" Tante Vicki said.

"Naturally you would not tell him," Hans said pleasantly. "It is not for that reason I am warning you. I know that neither you nor Lucy would willfully destroy me. Just remember that it is not only the direct statement that convicts. It is also the chance remark, the unimportant observation which might cause someone to ask, 'So! How do you know that?' Then you hedge and say, 'Someone told me, but I can't remember who it was,' or 'Why, it's common knowledge.' And in the end people put two and two together and say, 'It must have been that fox Hans who has been doing some detective work.'"

"But you could have told me," Lucy said, still piqued at being denied a wife's privilege of knowing her husband's secrets.

"Enough of this nonsense," Vicki said impatiently. "What did you find out?"

"I have your promises?" Hans asked unhappily.

"Naturally," the old lady announced.

"She was born in London, the daughter of a well-known Jewish banker named Jacob Liebermann," Hans said. "As a young girl she married Baron Henri de Marty, a French diplomat. With him she lived in Cairo and Washington and finally in Paris. He died of a heart attack in 1929, and in that same year her father lost all his money. Just when or where Grosspapa met her, I do not know, but it was probably shortly after the Baron's death."

"When she had set herself up as a cocotte," Tante Vicki added.

"Did de Marty leave her a fortune?" Lucy asked sensibly.

"As far as is known he left her something, but one would hardly call it a fortune," Hans replied. "She has a modest house in the country, a villa on the Riviera, and an apartment in Paris."

"Where, like Violetta, she entertains her lovers," the old lady interjected.

"Aha! Then why did she come to Geneva in 1939?" Lucy asked.

Hans smiled knowingly, as if his wife had hit on the very core of the matter. "That is what many people would like to know," he answered cryptically.

"We would like to know," Tante Vicki said, to make the question more specific.

"And so would the Gestapo," Hans said, enjoying the disclosure.

"The Gestapo!" Lucy exclaimed.

"So! Just as I have always said, she is a spy," Tante Vicki announced with satisfaction.

"The Gestapo have taken her apartment in Paris," Hans said. "One of their important officers is living there."

Lucy would have liked to ask her husband how he knew all this, but she refrained, fearing that he would refuse to tell, which would leave her aunt with the impression that he was in league with the Gestapo.

"She is spying for the Bolshevics no doubt," the old lady said. "They tell me that Geneva is full of Russian spies."

"More likely it would be for the British," Waldmann said.

"Ach, yes," Tante Vicki agreed. "The British would do just that, employ an immoral woman with a fake title."

"But the title is not a fake," Lucy insisted. "Hans has just told us that her husband was a real baron."

"That I refuse to believe," the old lady stated. "It is just a story they told Hansli to make him feel better about his father-in-law."

Waldmann lifted his hands in a gesture of defeat. There was no use arguing with the old lady. She would believe what she wanted to believe.

"Poor Grosspapa," Lucy said. "Can't someone warn him?"

"I shall not do it, if that's what you mean," Hans said firmly.

"But I shall," Tante Vicki announced. "It is my duty."

Hans looked alarmed. "But Tante Vicki, you promised me that you would say nothing of what I told you."

"Nor shall I," the old lady said. "Furthermore, I don't believe a word of it. I shall tell him that it is common gossip he is keeping a woman who is an English spy, and that unless he watches his step he will ruin his bank and end up in jail."

"But is it common gossip?" Lucy asked, worried by the turn of events. "I certainly never heard that story before this evening."

"Of course it is," Tante Vicki insisted. "It is what Marie Rappart was trying to tell me in a tactful way. Didn't she say that she had met her at the house of English people? What else are English doing in Geneva if not spying?"

"I would think this over carefully before I spoke to him, if I were you," Hans cautioned.

"And let him ruin us all?" the old lady said.

"He knows what he is doing," Waldmann said with conviction.

"But does he know that she is a spy?" Tante Vicki asked.

"If she is, then you may be sure he knows it," Hans replied.

"I don't understand it. You mean that he is using her for his own purposes?" Lucy asked.

"I did not say that," her husband answered her, annoyed at having words put in his mouth. "All I wished to say was that you can rely on Grosspapa not to be caught in a situation which might jeopardize the bank and his clients."

"Then why did you make your inquiries?" Lucy asked.

"Because I wished to learn what sort of a person we might have to deal with if anything should happen to your father," Hans answered truthfully.

"You could have saved yourself the trouble," Tante Vicki snapped. "You could have asked me. I could have told you. She is a cocotte!"

"Yes, Tante Vicki, I know that is your view," Waldmann said wearily, hoping that the matter was closed.

Lucy sighed. "Oh, dear," she said, "it is all very confusing."

"There is nothing to worry about as long as Grosspapa is alive," Hans assured her.

Tante Vicki rose to her feet with a spring. "It is time for me to go home. I told Tobald to bring the car at ten." She kissed her niece. "Adieu, Lucy dear. It has been such a pleasant evening. I enjoy a good talk better than a game of skat."

"Good? I thought the talk depressing," Lucy said.

Tante Vicki turned to Hans. "A spy as well as a cocotte. Don't forget that."

CHAPTER IV

WALTER was furious with himself as he drove back to Baden, and he attempted to assuage his anger by driving his three-litre Bentley as if he were competing in an international road race. It had been ten-thirty when he had left his father's house in the Sudstrasse and the streets of Zürich had been almost void of traffic. Now, on the open road, there was nothing to impede him but the skim of dampness which shone on the pavement under the glare of his headlights. In normal times there would have been many cars returning to Zürich after a Sunday in the country, but gasoline was heavily rationed these days, being allowed only for errands which had to do with the defense of the Confederation. As an officer of the army he could get sufficient to take him occasionally from his regiment to his home. His father, too, because of his age and the importance of his banking activities to the security of the state, could obtain enough for his use in town. But at this hour of night, on a broad cantonal road, he could count on meeting no vehicle other than an occasional bicycle. He drove relentlessly, shifting into third before each curve and swinging the car around with a screeching of tires on the wet pavement.

Why had he behaved so stupidly? he asked himself. Why had he allowed himself to express his first thoughts, which were always silly and emotional? With anyone else in the world he would have kept his mouth shut until he had had time to weigh the matter carefully, and would then, in all probability, have come to the identical conclusion of his father. He was not really stupid, certainly not as stupid as his father thought him, but there was something about the old man which affected his glands, made

31

him appear as awkward and dull as a schoolboy. At his age—he
was now in his fifty-first year—he should have sufficient control
of himself to meet anyone, no matter how brilliant and clever,
on equal terms of self-assurance. And as a matter of fact, he
could and did. With his colonel, with all the great bankers and
industrialists whom he met in the course of the year, he was
calm, collected and sufficiently intelligent to command their
respect. It was only with his father that he behaved like a frightened ignoramus. It was disgusting and infuriating, because he
had no one to blame but himself. Certainly he could not blame
the old man for thinking him a fool. He had been a fool, a
bloody fool. And he knew well what his father had been thinking—that this son of his did not have the capacity, the acumen,
the calm power of analysis necessary to manage the affairs of the
bank.

But who was there, he wondered, beside himself who could
take over if his father died? Not Jacques certainly, who had
become an American citizen and would never consider transferring his family from New York to Zürich. Who else then?
Hans Waldmann? Possibly. The old man liked Hans because
he was cautious, solid and trustworthy, but he was also aware
that Hans had a restricted cantonal vision which made him
suspicious of everyone who did not speak Zürichdeutsch. He
had heard his father say that he was like his namesake, ready to
fight anyone who came from beyond the Zürichberg. That was not
the mentality for an international banker, though it was useful
enough for legal advice on tax matters.

What angered Walter most was that he had lapsed into this
infantile fright at the one moment when he was expected to
present a truly adult attitude. It had obviously been a kind of
test. His father, knowing that the Jap attack would have vital
repercussions on world history, had purposely summoned him to
Zürich to determine if he, his oldest son, had the capacity to
appraise this news correctly. The old man had probably made
up his mind in advance to alter his will in the matter of partner-

ship succession on the basis of Walter's performance. Oh, God! Had he lost his last chance to be the head of the firm? Not that he presumed for a moment that he could ever equal his father, but he could be a good, sound banker whom the clients would respect. Well, he had muffed it, thrown it out the window on a shot of adrenalin!

A beam of light suddenly flashed across the road in front of him as he rounded a curve at about eighty kilometers an hour. A car was coming out of a side road on his right and had not seen his lights because the curve had deflected them. He leaned on the horn, but it was too late. A truck rolled out onto the highway, turning to head towards him. There was not enough space to brake his car on the slippery curve. He made an instantaneous decision and swung the steering wheel hard to the right. His car leapt over the grass, then arched like a hunter as the front wheels shot into space and fell forward, the headlights swinging wildly across a panorama of leafless fruit trees. Walter clung to the steering wheel as he felt the car turning over. He was quite relaxed; the tensions of his anger and self-pity had vanished. He let himself revolve with that delicious dizziness he used to achieve as a child when he rolled down the terrace of his father's lawn. Then he realized that the car had ceased its motion and that he was lying, head down, huddled into a ball against the door opposite the driver's seat.

He tried to move, but in his tight tunic with his booted legs above him, it was almost impossible to get a leverage. Besides, the slightest movement of his shoulders produced a cracking sound which he realized was the broken glass of the car window. Carefully he screwed his head around to see just how he should start trying to extricate himself. The dash light was still on, and he could make out from the glow beyond the door window above him that the headlights were shining. Thank God the engine stopped, he said to himself. My boot must have hit the switch as I was rolling around. He felt a trickle of warm liquid on his cheek and thought at once it was escaping gasoline. He sniffed.

There were no fumes. Then he heard the voices and the sound of feet scrambling down the bank.

"Are you in there?" a gruff peasant voice with an Appenzeller accent shouted.

"Yes, I'm here," he called.

"Good," the voice answered. Then to the others it said, "He's not dead, thank God. He speaks."

"Are you hurt?" the voice asked, and Walter could tell that it now came from the open window above him.

"No, I'm not hurt, not that I'm aware of," he answered. "But I don't dare move on account of the broken glass."

A torch lit up the inside of the car, which must have disclosed his boots, because someone said in an awed, frightened voice, "*Gotteswillen!* It's an officer!"

Walter was getting impatient now. "Listen to me, you fellows," he said in a tone of command. "Do as I tell you. Open that door on top, and one of you hold it while the other gives me his hands. That way I can pull myself up without cutting my back on broken glass."

"Yes, sir. We shall do that at once, sir," the voice said respectfully, then started giving orders to his companions. From the way he spoke, Walter guessed that they were soldiers.

It seemed a very long time that they rattled and pried at the door. Finally with impatience, for he was beginning to get very cramped and uncomfortable, he called to them to try and pull him through the window.

"Perhaps that is better," the leader answered. "The door will not open. The fall has bent it."

There was a lot of noise and scraping against the body work above him before he felt hands tapping his knees. "Give me your hands, please, sir," a voice said, and the light of the torch flashed again into the car. He reached around his legs until he had grasped two large hands with skin as rough as sandpaper.

"Put your head forward, sir, so as not to hit the instrument board," the voice cautioned. "Now, up we go!"

He let his arms be pulled up while he stuck his chin into his chest and slid his legs around sidewise.

"Your hands are now on the doorframe, Captain," the voice said. They had noted his rank as his shoulders had come into view. "Perhaps it is better now if you pull yourself up, if you can."

Walter, with an effort, got his legs unfolded and under him. His boots crunched on the broken glass that lay on the grass under the window. Slowly he straightened his knees and pulled himself upright until his head and shoulders protruded through the door which was now on top. From the light of the torch and the reflection of his own car's headlights, he could see his rescuers. There were about eight soldiers in all; their leader, the man with the Appenzeller accent, a sergeant, was shining the torch on him with a worried look on his face.

"Get the first-aid kit," the sergeant ordered one of the men. "It's on the back of the driver's seat." The man scuttled away up the steep bank into the darkness.

"Don't worry about that," Walter said. "I'm all right. Just get me out of here."

The sergeant took a crumpled red bandana handkerchief out of his hip pocket. "Perhaps you had better wrap this around your head, Captain," he said, handing it to Walter.

"Why should I do that?" Walter demanded crossly. "Here, give me a hand while I climb out of this wreck."

"You are bleeding badly, sir," the sergeant said.

Instinctively Walter put his hand to his head and felt his hair soaked with warm blood. "Ugh!" he exclaimed, looking at his hand which was crimson. He glanced down at his tunic as he felt warm drops falling from his chin, then took the proffered handkerchief and mopped his face. "Come," he said, "give me a lift."

The sergeant and one of the soldiers leaned over and gripped him under the armpits, then heaved him up until he could sit on the sill of the door window. Pulling his legs out of the car, he jumped down onto the grass. The first stab of pain went through him, making him realize that he was more bruised and sore than he had imagined.

The soldier who had gone to fetch the first-aid kit returned out of the darkness and the sergeant suggested that Walter sit down on the grass in front of the car where the headlights would allow him to put a bandage on properly.

"Were you and your men in the truck that came out of the side road?" Walter asked as the sergeant wrapped his head in yards and yards of gauze.

"Yes, sir, but I never saw your lights."

"Where are you going?"

"To the depot at Dietikon. We have a load of supplies."

"Take me there as quickly as possible. I shall telephone to Baden for someone to fetch me. Come, that's enough bandage." He held out his hands. "Help me to my feet. My legs seem a little stiff."

The sergeant and a soldier raised him from the ground. "You had better see a doctor straight off," the sergeant advised. "That head needs some stitches."

"So! Is it as bad as that?"

"Yes, sir."

Walter started to walk, but the pain and the stiffness made him stumble. "You men will have to give me a hand," he said.

"Maybe we should take off your boots, Captain," the sergeant said.

"Not now. Just help me to your camion. We can see about the boots when we reach Dietikon."

Two of the soldiers put his arms around their shoulders and virtually carried him up the steep bank with his feet barely touching the ground. When they reached the truck, two other soldiers climbed into the cab and pulled him up into the seat beside the driver. He realized then that he did not have his cap.

"Someone go back to my car and fetch my kepi," he commanded.

"I have it here," said a soldier who was standing on the road.

"I found it in the car." He handed it up to Walter, but it was smashed beyond repair. Walter dropped it on the floor of the cab, realizing that even if it were new he could not wear it over the mass of gauze which covered his head.

The sergeant ordered his men aboard and climbed into the driver's seat beside Walter.

"Has anyone turned out the lights of my car?" Walter asked.

The sergeant turned his head and looked down at the orchard below the bank. The lights of the Bentley were still shining. "Franz!" he shouted. "Quick! Run down there and turn out the lights of the Captain's car."

At the ordnance depot in Dietikon which was on the outskirts of the town, they carried Walter into the orderly room and sat him down by a telephone. The sergeant had wanted to call the medical officer who lived in Dietikon and was on call for any emergency at the depot, but Walter insisted on having his own physician. Dr. Hüppli was not only one of Switzerland's most famous diagnosticians but was the Eggli family doctor, having married one of Walter's cousins on his mother's side. The doctor himself answered the telephone.

"Rüdi," Walter said, "I am sorry to wake you at this hour, but I have had a little accident."

"Who is it, for God's sake?" the doctor asked gruffly.

"It's Walter. I have smashed up my car—the Bentley—and I have a cut on my head."

"Where are you?"

"I am in Dietikon, at the ordnance depot. The soldiers brought me here."

"A cut on your head? Is it clean or lacerated?"

"I don't know. I haven't seen it. The soldiers have covered my head with bandages, but it's bleeding right through them."

"Anything else? Any bones broken?"

"I don't think so. I can move every limb, but they are very sore."

"Listen, Walter, have they transportation at the depot to bring you into Zürich?"

"Just a minute, I'll ask the sergeant." He turned to the orderly on duty. "Tell the sergeant to come here at once." The soldier ducked out of the room and came back in a few seconds with the sergeant. "Have you a car here to take me to Zürich?" he asked.

"There is the camion, Captain," the sergeant answered. "We are not allowed to use the staff car without Lieutenant Meyer's permission."

"Yes, Rüdi, there is a car here," Walter said into the telephone. "Shall I come to your house?"

"No, go directly to the Chirurgische Poliklinik in the Rämistrasse. I shall meet you there," the doctor said and hung up.

"Get me the staff car, Sergeant," Walter commanded. "You can tell Lieutenant Meyer that you did it on the orders of Captain Eggli."

The sergeant clicked his heels, saluted, said, "Very good, sir," and did a rightabout-face.

Walter opened his eyes only to shut them again quickly because of the strong light of the sun on the window. On the second try he opened them only slightly, just enough to make out that he was in a white hospital room and that his wife Hélène was sitting in a chair by the foot of his bed reading the Neue Zürcher Zeitung. He waited until his mind could recollect all the events of the night which had led to his being in a bed in the Poliklinik, aching everywhere except in the head, where he most expected it, before he spoke. He wondered how many hours had elapsed, that Hélène, who had been at her cousin's, Frau Sieber in Winterthur, should be here at his side. It immediately crossed his mind that he must be more critically injured than he had imagined to cause her to come to Zürich. She was not what one would call an affectionate wife—that is, she had never displayed any signs of deep emotional involvement as far as he was concerned. He was, in fact, convinced that she only stuck to him because of his fortune—his father's fortune—and the children. No one had ever told him explicitly about her affairs, but that had not been necessary; he knew about them. The latest one with Tony Venturi had been going on now for three years, discreetly enough during her semi-annual visits to Lugano. Discretion in Switzerland was an arbitrary custom. It was a matter of how one acted the role, not what one did. There was no use trying to be clandestine, for among those Swiss who revolve within a certain milieu, the ones who take their holidays at St. Moritz, Lugano, Pontresina or Flims, the discussion of private lives is a major relaxation.

That Hélène had always been an enigma to him was the reason she had fascinated him ever since the first night he had danced with her at the Grasshopper Ball. Even then, at the age of eighteen, she had stood out among the other debutantes like a chamois in a field of sheep. There had been something alert, burning, vital about her, with her grey eyes taking in, weighing the possibilities of each awkward, earnest youth in a smiling cynicism which seemed to say that she was looking for something far superior to anything Zürich could offer in the line of young men. This attitude of supercilious amusement, of condescension, of slumming in pastures foreign to her taste had at once annoyed and intrigued him. Had she been born and raised in Basel or Berne he would have understood and accepted it, but she was as cantonal as he, born in Thalwil and raised in Zürich. Therefore, according to his code, she had no special right to put on airs. He had pursued her relentlessly for five years—"dogged her" would be the word—until she had consented finally to become his wife, which she had done with a smile and a pat on the back of his hand, as if to say, "All right, now you can have your bone." His father had considered it a suitable match.

Without moving a muscle that might rattle the bed linen and cause her to lift her eyes from the paper, Walter looked at her and thought how really stunning, how smart she was in her artificial un-Zürichois way. No wonder men fell for her, she was so well turned out, so soignée, and had such a quick, alert mind. Her only failing as far as he was concerned was that she did not care a centime for him. It might be even worse than that, she might even think him an awkward, bumbling dolt. He had suspected that for a long time. Not that she did not give him credit for certain areas of sound thinking—she did not agree with her father-in-law that he was a fool—but she thought him obsessed by an inferiority resulting from an incurable parental fear. This in a woman's eyes, or at least in her eyes, was worse than stupidity because it was weak, unmanly. And yet with all her contempt for him, here she was, sitting patiently at his bedside, waiting for him to regain consciousness.

He wondered if he had been under the influence of an anesthetic or merely asleep. He took stock of the messages issuing from his bone and muscle. His head was still bandaged; he could feel the tight bands across his forehead, but it did not ache, nor was it sore. The muscles of his legs ached and one hip bone pained where it bored into the hard mattress of the hospital bed. The new sensation, the one which was unfamiliar, not being related to anything he could recall of the accident, was a pain in his chest as if his ribs were being held in the grip of iron bands. He moved his hand up and felt through the coarse nightshirt the rows of bandage around his chest and over his left shoulder.

Hélène heard the rustle of the sheets and lowered her newspaper. "I thought you would never come to," she said, not unpleasantly.

"What time is it?" Walter asked.

She looked at her wrist watch. "Eleven-fifteen. How do you feel?"

"All right. A bit sore. What is this on my chest?"

"You broke a collarbone."

"Anything else?"

"Ten stitches on your scalp."

"Did they need to give me an anesthetic for that?"

Hélène smiled. "Don't you remember? Rüdi gave you a sleeping pill after he'd sewn you up."

"No anesthetic?"

"No anesthetic."

"Funny." Walter rubbed a hand across his eyes. "I can't seem to remember a thing after getting into the staff car at Dietikon. Was Rüdi waiting for me here?"

"That's what he told me on the telephone. He called me at Jacqueline Sieber's after they had put you to bed."

"When was that?"

"It must have been about three this morning."

"When did you come over?"

"On the four-thirty train."

"And came right here?"

"I went to the house first to get you some things—toilet articles, pyjamas and some Nescafé. I got here about half-past five. Would you like some breakfast?"

"Have you had yours?"

"Yes, the nurse brought me a nice breakfast at six-thirty. What would you like?"

"Just café au lait."

Hélène got up and pushed the bell button which was hanging on a cord from the bedpost near his head. "I'll ask the nurse to bring some boiling water and hot milk," she said. "I'll make you Nescafé. The hospital coffee is undrinkable."

The nurse was a plain-looking buxom girl with bright red cheeks, kinky brown hair and eyeglasses. After listening to Hélène's order, she came over to the bed and looked down appraisingly at Walter. "You feel better, don't you, Herr Captain?" she said, grinning at him.

"I never felt too badly," Walter growled. The smirking condescension of this peasant annoyed him.

"Ho!" the nurse exclaimed. "They tell me you were in quite a state of nerves when they brought you in here." She lunged out of the room, closing the door behind her.

"What does that fool mean?" Walter asked testily.

His wife shrugged her shoulders. "I have no idea. I was not here. Rüdi intimated that you were a little excited. That's why he gave you the barbiturate."

"Ugh!" Walter grunted, trying to remember but failing.

"Had you been drinking?" Hélène asked.

"Drinking? Good God no, not with Grosspapa!"

"You were with your father? Where? In the Sudstrasse?"

"Of course."

"How would I know? What brought you in from Baden?"

"He called me to come in for dinner. He had something to discuss with me."

"This?" she asked, showing him the headlines in the *Neue Zürcher Zeitung* which announced the attack on Pearl Harbor.

A flush of color came over Walter's face as he remembered, for the first time since he had spun off the road, his annoyance with himself for his too hasty analysis of this new development. "Yes," he admitted angrily.

His wife put the newspaper back on her lap and stared at the front page, as if rereading it. She realized now what had happened, and it was not at all what she had supposed after hearing Rüdi Hüppli's story. She had thought that her husband had been on a party with his brother-officers and had managed to get himself very drunk, which would not have been too difficult, he having no head for alcohol. Yet she had, oddly enough, been cheered by the news. A feeling of relief and encouragement had come over her once she had learned that the wounds were not serious, and she had made up her mind to go quickly to him. The knowledge that her careful, hesitant Walter who had always been frightened of what people might say or think about him, who never made a move or uttered a sentence without measuring its effect, who was afraid to laugh for fear of being thought frivolous, had actually gone on a bender and cracked himself up seemed too good to be true. Maybe, she had said to herself as she watched his bandaged face while he slept, he has finally grown up, rid himself of the shackles of insecurity in a bottle of champagne.

But now that bright bubble of hope had burst. It was not the release of alcohol but his father who had caused him to crack up— that keen, dominating old man in whose presence her husband visibly disintegrated, shrank to imbecility and childhood. She knew how Walter hated himself for this cringing weakness, and she also knew that he was powerless against it. The old contempt rose up in her, like bile in her blood.

The nurse came in with a tray on which were two pitchers, one of hot water and the other of hot milk, a cup and saucer, and some slices of mealy wartime bread. "Where is the Nescafé?" she asked, putting the tray on the bed table.

Hélène got up and fetched the can of Nescafé from the top drawer of the dresser. She handed it to the nurse. "Well, Walter, I shall be going home. I must be there when the children arrive. They were taking the ten o'clock from Winterthur."

"I thought you were going to make the coffee for me," Walter said sadly.

"The *Fräulein* can do that better than I can, can't you, nurse?" Hélène answered, with a brittle smile.

"Nothing to it," the nurse said.

The telephone rang and the nurse picked up the receiver before Walter could reach for it. "Yes, sir, she's right here," she said and handed the receiver to Hélène.

"Yes?" Hélène asked guardedly, then her face burst into a smile. "Ah, Grosspapa! Do you wish to speak with Walter?"

"I have nothing to say to him," the old man's voice said. "How is he? Is he badly hurt?"

"No, nothing serious, a broken collarbone and a cut on his head, that's all. Rüdi gave him a sleeping pill and he has only just awakened."

"He drives too fast—like a silly young boy. I've always told him it would happen someday. So he cracked his head, did he? Well, that is the least valuable part of him—for you at least, Hélène."

Hélène laughed flirtatiously. "Now, Grosspapa, you must not say such things. The day will come when we will all need it."

"God help you! Tell him that I am going to Geneva and that I'll see him when I get back."

"Very good." She put the receiver back on its hook and turned to Walter. "If there is anything you need, have the nurse telephone me," she said, taking her long mink coat from the back of the chair and throwing it over her shoulders.

"What did Grosspapa have to say?" Walter asked, feeling the skin of his scalp tighten so that the stitches hurt.

"He just wanted to know if you were going to live."

"Is he coming to see me?"

"No, he's going to Geneva. He told me to tell you that he'd see you when he gets back."

"Do you have to go?" Walter pleaded.

"Yes, I must," she said energetically. "I promised Willi and Margi I would give them all the news of you."

"Give them my love," Walter said. "And tell them to come and see me after school."

"Adieu," Hélène said, giving him a polite wave of the hand as she opened the door and swept out.

"What, no kiss?" the nurse said when the door had closed.

Walter did not answer. All the hope that he had known when he awoke to find Hélène at his side had vanished.

CHAPTER V

MR. EGGLI and I will be back around four o'clock to pick up the chrysanthemums," Doris Eggli said to Morton, the aging butler, who was holding the car door open for her.

"Yes, ma'am," Morton said and added, "and the brace of pheasants. Don't forget them."

"Quite right, Morton. I'm glad you reminded me." She got into the driver's seat and the butler closed the door, but she opened the window for a final instruction. "Oh, Morton, Master Robert wants his ski boots sent to him. He forgot to pack them when he went to New Haven in September. You'll probably find them in his closet."

"They're in the tack room, ma'am. I saw 'em there and wondered had he forgot 'em."

"Have you his address at Yale?"

"Yes, ma'am." The old man smiled, a rare gesture for him. "He always writes to Maggie and me about once a term."

"Well, I'm glad to hear it. That's more than he does for his parents. Send him the boots, Morton, parcel post."

"Yes, ma'am. And Miss Evangeline, will she be back this evening?"

"I don't think so. She's lunching with us at the club. If she is coming back, I'll let you know when we pick up the flowers."

"And the pheasants."

Doris laughed. It always amused her to note how devotedly Morton protected the interests of her husband. Personally she was fed up with pheasant. It was now the fifth week end in a row that Jacques had gone over to the Southside on Saturday

45

afternoon to shoot, and the deep freeze in their flat on Park Avenue was bulging with birds. Roast pheasant with bread sauce and currant jelly and a fine old Burgundy was Jacques's idea of heaven. She longed for the season to end and a return to veal and lamb and beef. "I wish he'd let you keep them," she said sadly.

"Don't worry, ma'am. Mr. Eggli give me and Maggie a brace for ourselves."

"Friday night, then, as usual," she said, winding up the window and putting the car in gear.

Their house in Upper Brookville on Long Island was a solid brick Georgian affair, framed in boxwood and dogwood, giving it an air of dignified, luxurious gentility. Built thirty years before by a prosperous corporation lawyer, it had acquired a patina of age, so that now, with the trees bare and the lawns uncut, it looked as if it had authentically existed since the eighteenth century. Jacques Eggli had bought it ten years ago as a summer residence, because it was situated in that part of the world where the bees of finance did their swarming. For some years Doris had blocked the move as she had an inherent distrust of the North Shore. All her life until her marriage she had summered with her family near Narragansett in Rhode Island, and she had been brought up to believe that the portion of Long Island which centered its life around the Matinecock Club was too ostentatiously wealthy, that the outward and visible displays of net worth there were considered more important than evidences of intellectual magnitude. Her father had been an architect and classical scholar who, though successful enough to own a house in Murray Hill and another in Rhode Island, firmly believed that money as an end in itself was a coarse and ungentlemanly aim. Thus it had been that Jacques' efforts to settle near the Matinecock Club had been thwarted until her father's death.

Once the decision had been made and the house and property purchased, Doris had accepted her fate gracefully. She had by then learned that Jacques was not an intellectual and that nothing she could do would ever make him into one. He was a banker to the bone, feeding and fattening on the surreptitious ways, the methods of weighing men against balance sheets, optimism against facts, future prospects against past performances, and, above all, on the propensity to limit trading and information to an exclusive inner circle, who could be relied upon to keep all secrets from the world at large, particularly brokers. In the United States, Jacques had soon learned, this inner circle of bankers expected its members to play as they played. The games were strictly limited to golf, bird-shooting and salmon-fishing. Hunting and polo might, under certain circumstances, be tolerated, but generally speaking these were sports looked at askance as belonging to inherited, non-active wealth. Yachting was acceptable only if you were known to have started your career on State Street, Boston.

Jacques conformed, not because of any snobbism or desire to climb higher on the banking ladder, but because he felt happier, more content when taking on the protective coloration of the flock with which he flew. When he had arrived in New York at the age of twenty-six to do his apprenticeship in the banking house of Spears, Wetherell and Company, who were the correspondents of Eggli and Company of Zürich, he had never had a golf club in his hand. But as soon as he discovered that it was a game which all the partners and associates of every house in Wall Street indulged on their week ends, he at once joined a minor club in Scarsdale for the sole purpose of taking lessons. Being a natural athlete who played good tennis and skied well, it was not long before he broke 90. It was then that he had suggested to Mr. Wetherell it might be wise for him to join a good golf club on Long Island.

Doris thought about this quality of adaptability of Jacques's only obliquely as she drove along the winding road to the club. She was really thinking about their son Robert, who was a junior at Yale and whom she adored to the point of worry without cause. She had always hoped that he would finally emerge a true Davenport like her father, gentle, introspective and inquiring; but the hope had vanished as early as his fifth form at St. Paul's

when it had become all too evident that he was a replica of the
man he referred to with affection as "Grosspapa." The proof lay
in the clarity and method of his thinking. Unlike her father and
herself, he had no dim areas in the scope of his ability to acquire knowledge. All subjects—languages, history, mathematics,
science and philosophy—were relatively easy for him, so that
he was able to maintain presentable marks with the minimum
of work. He read quickly and retained. Physically he was taller
and broader than his grandfather, but the china-blue suspicious
eyes and the delicate, almost feminine mouth were the same.
A big American body supporting a narrow Swiss mind, she said
to herself, then blushed and stamped on the accelerator. She
did not really believe that her husband's mind was small. That
was an unjust thought. It might be called circumscribed, limited
to finance and dirty stories, but it was not a whit smaller than
the minds of any of the dollar-incrusted, red-faced, jocular men
she would be meeting in five minutes. To label it Swiss was
particularly unfair. There was certainly nothing small about old
Robert's mind, which observed the globe from an Alpine pin-
nacle, appraising and judging people and events.

With all the vast, diametrically opposed differences of milieu
and upbringing, she and Jacques had led a good life together.
She never dwelt on the subject, but she was aware that the
reason for the success of their marriage had been her ability to
flatter his ego, to build him up to a feeling of self-sufficiency and
power, thus compensating for the inner doubts which had been
stamped into him by his father. Today, as an American citizen,
a respected member of the banking community, and a man of
wealth and position, he had an assurance and gaiety that was
remote from the suspicious, insecure boy she had married twenty
years ago.

The European war had brought them one blessing. It had prevented them from making their annual pilgrimage to Zürich. Not
that she disliked the city or Jacques's family, but she dreaded
the spectacle of his disintegration in the presence of his father.
It was like watching him return to the nursery. In an instant,

at the moment of meeting, the old man would wipe out all the labor of her married years. Jacques would visibly shrink as he stammered and stuttered before the man who could dominate him completely—the man whom he admired and feared, whom he loved and hated. In theory she too hated old Robert for doing what he did to her husband, yet, oddly, she could not help liking him, even with the hate still in her heart. There was some compelling quality about him which captivated her in spite of herself. It was not just his courtly manner, which women found flattering. There was something else, something conveyed by his calm, studied gaze at her, by the touch of his delicate hand on her arm that sent delicious little shivers up her backbone. She sensed how the Baroness de Marty must feel about him—proud because men feared him. But she did not fancy her Jacques fearing any man.

As she turned into the entrance drive of the Matinecock Club she looked at her wrist watch. It was one o'clock, almost time for lunch, which pleased her as she loathed having to sit over endless cocktails. Jacques would have finished his golf and changed. He was probably now on his third martini with Dexter Miller and Fanny Farnsworth, who were lunching with them, along with Evangeline and young Billy Locke. The parking areas on each side of the drive before it reached the clubhouse were filled with shining expensive cars. She drove on past the entrance and parked on the side of the road as it dipped downhill towards the golf course. Before getting out, she looked in the rear view mirror for a final inspection of her face. She was satisfied with what she saw. At forty-three she was handsome. There were almost no lines on the smooth freckled skin of her face, and no grey strands had yet appeared in the natural curls of her thick brown hair, which was cut in a writhing Medusa bob. Moreover, she was well turned out—something she had learned to do in recent years to please Jacques—in her brown felt hat, with a blouse of knitted wool to match, and her well-cut tweeds. The only unsporting touch which was allowed, even commanded, by the dictators of fashion was a mass of gold bracelets on her right wrist hung with coins and charms and baubles, which tinkled as she moved like the anklets of an Indian temple dancer.

Doris found her guests in the far room at the right of the patio. Her daughter was with them, dressed in ratcatcher—jodhpurs and whipcord jacket—with her long brown curls held away from her face with a bow of velvet ribbon. They had made a circle of chairs around a low cocktail table.

"Fanny darling, and Dexter! Such fun having you here. I hope I haven't kept you waiting," Doris said, making the kissing gesture with Fanny of touching cheeks so as not to impart lipstick.

"We came down early as Dexter wanted to take a walk before lunch," Fanny Farnsworth said. She was a hothouse, molasses blonde, separated from her husband and reputed to be angling for Dexter Miller. Her right arm carried twice as many bangles as Doris'.

"I'm glad you ordered cocktails," Doris said, sitting down next to Dexter. "Where's Jacques? Hasn't he appeared yet?"

"He was just called to the telephone," Dexter said. "Here, why don't you take his drink? He hasn't touched it." He picked up a full martini glass and handed it to Doris.

"No, thanks. I'm going to have a sherry if I can catch a steward's eye," Doris said, then looked at her daughter. "Evangeline, sweetie, are you going to have time to go home and change before getting your train at Manhasset?"

"I'm not going to change, Mummy," Evangeline said. "I have my bag here, and Billy is going to motor me to Penn Station in time to catch the four-thirty to Washington."

"What will Miss Charlotte say if you arrive at school in that outfit?"

"As long as it's riding clothes Miss Charlotte doesn't mind," her daughter answered.

"How right you are, Evangeline," Fanny Farnsworth said. "At Foxcroft a horse is a horse is a horse."

"Which reminds me, Doris," Dexter Miller said. "Have you heard the one about the cab horse in front of the Plaza?"

"If it's suitable for jeunes filles, I haven't," Doris replied.

Dexter looked at Evangeline and winked. "Do you classify yourself as a *jeune fille?*" he asked.

"I decline to answer on the grounds that it might incriminate and degrade," Evangeline answered soberly.

"I'm saying she is," Doris announced.

"You'd be the last to know," Fanny said.

"Here's Pa now," Evangeline said, happy to get the conversation on cleaner ground. Among the things she disapproved of in her parents' generation was their preoccupation with smut.

Jacques came bustling up. He was a tall, lean, aristocratic-looking man, immaculately turned out in a very bright tweed jacket and grey flannels. Doris noted that his face was paler than usual and that his expression was not the gay carefree one of Sundays at Matinecock. He sat down next to his wife and patted her knee as he tossed the warm martini down in one gulp. Then he motioned to a steward and ordered another round and a sherry for Doris. Evangeline was drinking orange juice and she gave a negative nod to the steward to indicate that she did not want another.

Jacques got up. "Here, change places with me," he said to his daughter. "I want to sit next to Fabulous Fanny." His English was fluent with only a trace of an accent, and that more British than Swiss. It showed, to those who had been around, his schooling at Zuoz.

"You look as if you'd had a jolt," Fanny said to him as he sat down beside her. "I hope it wasn't bad news."

He had not wished to tell them and thus spoil the light forgetfulness of the luncheon. They would know it soon enough. Why hang crepe on a nice cosy party? He almost answered with a lie but thought better of it, knowing that they would catch him out before the day was done. The smile he had forced left his face. "It *is* bad news, about the worst you could imagine."

Doris' heart stopped. She thought at once of Robert at New Haven.

"My God, Jacques, Hitler hasn't attacked Switzerland, I hope," Dexter said anxiously.

"Worse than that, the Japs have attacked Pearl Harbor at Honolulu and destroyed the Pacific fleet," Jacques announced. He had spoken in low tones so that his voice would not carry to the near-by tables.

"Jacques, you're not kidding, are you?" Fanny gasped.

Doris said nothing. She knew he was not kidding. She thought of Robert again, this time as a pilot in training.

"The Pacific fleet destroyed! Good God, that's terrible!" Dexter said, all the color having left his ruddy fat cheeks. "Where did you get this, Jacques?"

"From an unimpeachable source," Jacques said gravely. He was not in the habit of disclosing his lines of communication, which in this instance happened to be Hans Bürli, the Washington correspondent of the *Neue Zürcher Zeitung.* "As far as is known, many squadrons of carrier-based Jap planes came over Pearl Harbor and Honolulu at dawn, leaving the place a shambles. With the exception of one or two minor ships, the whole fleet was in the harbor and not one was saved. Furthermore, every plane on Hickam Field was shot up and put out of action."

"This means war," Dexter said, rising.

"It *is* war," Jacques said. "The President will announce it to Congress tomorrow morning."

"Order me another drink, Jacques," Dexter said. "I'll be back in a minute. I've got to make a telephone call."

Doris shivered with the fear that settled around her heart like a coating of ice. She looked at her husband and saw that he too was uncertain and afraid. The big room with its stewards and smoke and shrill babble of alcohol-raised voices suddenly struck her as an alien place where she and Jacques were like strange, lonely refugees. Then she heard her daughter's voice putting her own thoughts into words.

"Will Bobby be called up?" Evangeline asked her father.

"Eh? Bobby?" Jacques said, startled by the idea. "No, I shouldn't think so. Not, at least, until he has graduated."

"Poor Bobby, it may be over by that time," Evangeline said with a sigh.

The steward brought the second round of drinks and Jacques ordered a third round.

"Why, those dirty little bastards!" Fanny said indignantly. "Sneaking up on us like that without a warning. I hope we catch that Tojo and geld him."

"So do I, Fanny," Jacques said. "But this isn't going to be easy. This attack will give them a big jump on us."

"I wonder what your father will say," Doris said to Jacques.

Jacques looked at his wrist watch. "He'll know any minute now. I got to Miss Schrader and told her to cable him at once. Yes, I'd like to hear his reaction. I think I can imagine what it will be."

"That this will hand Europe to Hitler on a platter?" Doris asked.

Jacques shook his head. "No, I don't think so. If I know Grosspapa, he will figure that this is where the Axis lost the war. He has infinite faith in the power of this country."

"Do you think that, Jacques?" Fanny asked.

Jacques emptied his martini. "Yes, I do," he said firmly.

A young man came up to the table. It was Billy Locke, who apologized profusely for being late, saying that he had had to shower and change after riding.

"You're for it, Bill," Evangeline said to him.

"For being late?"

"We've gone to war, soldier," Evangeline said. "The Japs have knocked out the Pacific fleet at Pearl Harbor."

"Don't kid me, Lina, I'm sore in every bone as it is."

"Tell him, Pa."

"It's true, Billy," Jacques said. "By noon tomorrow we will be at war with the Axis powers."

Billy's eyes grew round and his mouth opened. "Golly!" was all he could say.

Dexter returned, looking pale and worried. He quickly downed the martini waiting for him and turned to Jacques. "There will be a lot of selling on the Exchange tomorrow," he said quietly.

Jacques made no comment. Dexter Miller was a broker.

CHAPTER VI

"DEAR ROBERT," Yvonne de Marty said after the embrace of meeting, still holding him by the shoulders and gazing at him with rapt devotion. "Oh, what a relief it is to see you looking well and strong! When I read the *Journal de Genève* this morning, I knew why you telephoned last evening that you were coming today to Geneva, and it frightened me that the news might have been a great blow to you."

"A good blow, Yvonne," he said, smiling and patting her cheek. "Come, we must drink to it."

He sat down by the fireplace in which small pieces of wood were burning brightly, casting a dancing light on the crystals of the chandelier which in turn flashed like fireflies on the green-brocaded walls. It was an eighteenth-century salon which had remained as it was since the days when Voltaire had held court at the Château de Ferney, and it suited Yvonne's flowing gown of ivory satin as it had probably once suited Madame de Staël. At a side table she poured the cold champagne into two glasses, bringing one to Robert Eggli and with the other sitting down to face him at the opposite side of the chimney.

"Let us drink to America's entry into the war," Robert said, lifting his glass.

"Gladly." Yvonne acknowledged the salute and sipped from her glass. "But why is this a matter for rejoicing? I would have thought that their troubles in the Pacific—"

The old man wagged a finger at her. "Now you must not talk like my son Walter."

"God forbid!"

"He tried to advance the same argument with me, that the

54

entire American effort will be directed toward the defeat of Japan, thus leaving Hitler free to conquer all of Europe."

"That was also Gerald Blythe's argument."

"Who is Gerald Bly?" He pronounced it as she had, unaware of the spelling.

"An Englishman who lives here in Geneva. He and his wife have been very kind to me."

"A friend of your family?" The old man was suspicious of all people with whose names he was not familiar.

"No, not at all, though of course they know who I am."

"What does he do here in Switzerland in wartime?"

Yvonne laughed—a low throaty rippling laugh. "Mercy, Robert, but you are suspicious! Or is it jealousy? Have no fear, my dear, he appears to be devoted to his Daphne and I fancy thinks me—what shall I say?—a bit too international."

"But what is he doing?" Robert repeated impatiently.

"Oh, something to do with the League of Nations. One of those bureaus that go on in a vacuum, war or no war—narcotics or labor or something like that."

"Where did you meet him?"

"What an inquisitor you've become, Robert! I've never seen this side of you. Not that I mind telling. Everything I do or think or say is yours on an open page. Where did I meet the Blythes? Let me see. I think it was in October at a luncheon at Lucy de Weck's."

"So! They go out in Genevois society."

The evidence of the snob coming out in him amused her. She realized that what had amazed and pleased him was that *she,* not Gerald and Daphne Blythe, had crashed the pre-Calvin aristocracy. "Yes," she said casually, to impress him the more, "one meets them everywhere. They are quite charming, and I might say almost excessively cultivated."

Robert Eggli took another sip of champagne. Her guess had been right: he was both pleased and flattered that she was received in Geneva society. Unquestionably they were aware—

everyone in Switzerland was—that she was his mistress, so it was
to the credit of the good Genevoises they had accepted her for
what she was, a distinguished and witty woman. But the English
couple still bothered him. If they were also accepted, they also
knew of her lover. And if they were in any way interested in
her lover's activities as a banker, they might be trying to use
Yvonne as a wedge.

"You saw this Bly today, then?" Robert remarked.

"I had tea with them."

"And the news worried him?"

"Very much. England, he said, cannot hope to hold out without American aid."

"He is quite right."

"He seemed to feel that the United States would now need
all its production for itself."

"Bah! That is what Walter said, and he should know better
than this English friend of yours. The Americans can and will
produce enough for two wars—one in the Pacific and one in
Europe. When I pointed this out to my son, he saw of course
that I was right. And then the fool cracks himself up in his car
going back to Baden, because he is so angry I had to tell him
that when the Japs attacked Pearl Harbor they sealed the doom
of Hitler."

"It's a pity Gerald Blythe can't hear you say that. It might
cheer him up. He seemed very discouraged."

Robert snorted. "Surely he would like to hear it, and from me
of all people! That is what London would like to know—what
is Eggli going to do now?"

Yvonne smiled. That was what she loved about this staunch
little man—he knew precisely the degree of power he wielded
in the world. He knew that he could not sway or alter the course
of the war, but that he could, in the long pull—after the guns
were silenced, when governments emerged from their bomb
shelters to survey the wreckage—have an influence on the grand
strategy, the alignment of forces.

He waited for her comment, but as she remained silently

gazing at him, the smile still hovering at the corners of her lips, he went on. "The English have maintained their position of authority in the world by the judicious handling of the pound sterling. It has been the tangible thread which has held an empire together and has persuaded other nations to follow England's advice. On a relatively small island, having no resources other than coal, she has been able to maintain and employ a population of fifty million. Again, the pound sterling made this possible, bringing in as it did raw materials and food out of profits from investments all over the world."

"Like Switzerland," Yvonne commented.

"But with one important difference. . . ."

A maid entered to announce that dinner was served. The Baroness nodded to her, then looked again at Robert Eggli, not wishing to interrupt the thread of his exposition.

Eggli rose to his feet. It was his rigid canon that no meal should be made to wait on talk, no matter how important. Yvonne led the way into the dining room, which was more somber than the salon, paneled in dark wood and lit only by the candles on the table. A place was set at each side of the long narrow table so that they could look at each other at close range and without the obstruction of the pair of silver candelabras.

Yvonne picked up the napkin on her plate and extracted the small bread secreted in its folds, before spreading it on her lap. "Now tell me the important difference between England and Switzerland," she said.

"You keep me on the tracks," he said, smiling. This attentive interest she displayed in all he said was one of her attributes he most admired. "The difference is this. In addition to using its external investment for acquiring food and raw materials for its population, Switzerland also performs the function of repository for the capital of foreigners, keeping it safe from the forces of war and internal upheaval. Like a good vault, it holds this capital with no questions asked and no policies demanded. England, on the other hand, is forced by the circumstances of her position to use her money power for political ends. Good ends, mind you, ends which are primarily directed towards preserving peace under a balance of power."

The Baroness sighed. "Poor England! With all her pounds, she has twice failed to keep Germany from starting a war."

"Not altogther her fault, though it might have been different had she had a Castlereagh for a Lloyd George and a Palmerston for a Chamberlain."

"Has it never occurred to you, Robert, that perhaps the United States is to blame?" She felt a need to defend the country of her birth.

"You mean that if they had told Bethmann-Hollweg in 1914 and Hitler in 1939 they would be with England if war was declared, these two wars would never have happened?"

"Exactly."

Robert Eggli helped himself to a piece of pink tail meat from the boiled ombre chevalier, then covered it with the sauce mousseline which the maid held forth in a silver boat. "Ah, that is possible, but it is quite wrong to blame the United States. You must remember their form of democracy is more Swiss than that of England or France. It is government by the consent of the governed, which was an idea they borrowed from Jean Jacques Rousseau. You may be sure that both Woodrow Wilson and Franklin Roosevelt would have gladly given the pledge in advance, but they were powerless to act under their Constitution until the people had expressed a will to act."

"Well, it seems to me that this second time Roosevelt might have led them on the right course. They knew from experience what a danger to Europe and the world Germany could be."

Eggli shook his head sadly. "I discussed this with the President in the spring of 1938. I told him what was going to happen here. The seizure of Austria was a clear signal, to any man who could weigh facts, that Hitler would not stop."

"Was it clear to him?" Yvonne asked skeptically.

"As clear as crystal. But he was helplessly bound on all sides. The American people were in no mood for any more foreign commitments. The Senate would never have given him the authority. All he could do was to prepare his forces quietly, without arousing public suspicion, for the day when the citizens would demand intervention. In a democracy, my dear, statesmen may not always exercise their own judgment."

"Yes, yes, of course," the Baroness said sadly. "It was the same with poor England. Dear God, do you remember the cheers Chamberlain received when he returned from Munich? 'Peace in our time.' What a bitter memory!"

Robert Eggli took a sip of champagne and dabbed his lips with a napkin. "Do you know why I came to Geneva today?" he asked.

"You told me on the telephone that you had some business to attend to."

"And it concerns you, Yvonne."

Her heart beat a little faster. She wondered if she was going to be asked to leave Switzerland, but she let nothing show on her face as she sliced a piece of breast from the poussin on her plate. "Indeed!" she said. "What is it?"

"I was not sure how you would receive the news of the Japanese attack. I wanted to reassure you."

"That is sweet of you, Robert. So thoughtful, so typically thoughtful."

"And I wanted your presence. I can think better with you near me. It must be a sign of old age, Yvonne, this need for the comfort of someone you love."

"Dear Robert, don't, please. You're going to make me weep."

"There are times when I feel very much alone in the world," he said in a harsh voice, trying to camouflage his emotion. "There are matters, family matters, which I used to discuss with Matti. She was not a clever woman like you, but in her simple way she had a great deal of common sense. She would always defend her children with me, seeing good points in them which I was prone to ignore. Since her death I have no one with whom I can talk over these problems."

"Not even your sister?"

"*Ach*, Vicki! She is a sharp-tongued gossip. Whatever one says to her is known to all Zürich within an hour. No, most certainly

I cannot discuss Walter and Jacques and Lucy with her. She would repeat to them everything that I said. These matters I have to keep in here." He tapped his head. "And they worry me, Yvonne. They worry me increasingly as time goes on and I approach the day of my death."

Yvonne de Marty laughed lightly. "Oh, Robert, death has long given you up as a lost cause! Look at you, with your cheeks as fresh and pink as a child's, eating poussin and drinking champagne."

"Let us be sensible," Eggli said sternly. "I am eighty years old. The machinery"—he tapped his chest this time—"is, to be sure, of the best Swiss manufacture, but even that cannot last forever. One of these days it will stop very suddenly, the way a good watch will after a certain time, and then . . ." He put down his knife and fork and looked at her with his piercing blue eyes. "Who will carry on? Who will make the decisions which your friend Bly would so like to know about?" He stopped as if he expected an answer, but there was none. She just waited, believing the question rhetorical, requiring no more than her attention. "You don't know my sons. . . ."

"I know Jacques," she put in quickly. "I met him and his American wife at a dinner party in Paris. You remember. I told you how charming and clever I thought him."

Robert waved his hand in a gesture of dismissal. "He's an American. Even if there were no war, it would be difficult for him to return to Zürich and take command. Now of course it is impossible. That leaves Walter." He stopped as if to imply that the prospect could not be more forlorn.

Yvonne had no wish to be caught up in any appraisal of a man whom she had never met. What she had heard from her acquaintances in Geneva was none too reassuring. They had given her to understand that Walter Eggli was an earnest, humorless fellow who was frightened out of his wits by his father and traduced by his wife. She thought for a minute before speaking, searching for the frame of generality which would at once be harmless and comforting.

"Did it ever occur to you, Robert, that fathers, in their desire to see their sons develop into perfect specimens of wisdom and energy, are often blinded by the memory of youthful failings? When one has nursed a plant from a seedling, it is difficult to look on the full-grown flower without seeing evidences of the once frail little plant that drooped in the sun and shriveled in the cold."

Eggli smiled. "You talk as Matti used to."

"Your son Walter is afraid of you, isn't he?"

"For good reason. He is a fool and I am impatient with him."

"Have you ever given him his head, let him take a fence without your weight on the reins?"

"And risk the money of my clients? No, surely not. It is my judgment they depend on. The reputation of the bank has been built on that."

"And yet the day will come—you have said it yourself—when you will no longer be here to exercise that judgment. The bank will carry on, Robert; don't worry about that. It will carry on in the same way, following the pattern which you have so deeply engraved on it. All these years your sons have been absorbing your splendid example. Consciously and unconsciously they have been learning the methods you use to arrive at decisions. If they seem dull and hesitant to you, it is because they so admire your ability that they are afraid to voice their true thoughts in your presence."

Eggli grunted. "God help the bank!"

"God and the United States," Yvonne murmured softly.

"Ach, that is true enough. If Hitler should win this war, it would be the end of Switzerland." He took another sip of wine. "Oh, yes, about that English friend of yours—what was his name?"

"You mean Gerald Blythe?"

"Yes, yes. The League of Nations fellow who was so discouraged by the attack on the American fleet. He knows, of course, of our friendship."

Yvonne smiled. "I should doubt it. He's not a gossip."

It was Robert's turn to smile. "One of the nicest things about you, my dear, is your belief in the innocence of people."

"What possible difference can it make if he knows or not?"

"A good deal more than you would suspect," Robert Eggli said quietly. "If his wife calls you tomorrow and suggests tea or lunch, or even a stroll on the Quai de Mont Blanc, you may be sure that he knows of our relationship."

"Why, Robert, are you trying to suggest that he is a spy?" Yvonne asked in a shocked voice.

"My dear," Robert said gently, "you should know better than I that in times of danger every Englishman is a spy for his country. I do not say that he has been planted here by some British Intelligence Agency like the M.I.5. He is undoubtedly no more than he says he is, a man on the permanent staff of the League. But nevertheless his country will use him, and he will serve his country for any mission they require at a time like this. The English are like that, they are the most rigidly loyal people on earth. 'For King and Country,' they say, and I have often thought that their placing of the monarch first is the answer to their unswerving devotion."

"But what would Gerald Blythe wish to learn from you?" Yvonne asked, still puzzled.

"Not he, dear, but the War Office and Number 10 Downing Street would like to know what my reactions were to this news. They would like to know if I have shifted funds from Switzerland and New York to places like Johannesburg and Buenos Aires."

"What good would it do for Blythe to pump me? I don't know what you do with the bank's money, and I don't want to know."

Robert Eggli smiled. He liked her indignation. She was not going to be involved in any intrigues which were disloyal to him. "My dear Yvonne, I am quite aware that you know nothing about my affairs, and that you would never seek to find out." He chuckled. "You have never even asked what I have done with your own money, and you had every right to do that."

"I trust you," she said sharply.

"Thank you. I appreciate that." He raised his head, watching the maid take their empty plates and go out into the pantry. "Does Marie understand English?" he asked.

"I shouldn't think she understood a word."

"Well, to be safe I shall change the subject when she is in the room."

"You're not going to tell me bank secrets?"

"Just one."

"I don't want to hear it, Robert."

"I want you to know it, because I want you to repeat it."

"To Gerald Blythe?"

"Yes."

"Now really, Robert, whatever is this? It's so unlike you."

Robert heard the pantry door swing as the maid entered with the sweet—two little pots of *pot de crème chocolat*. "This is no time for people to be discouraged," he said. "What looks like bad news is often the reverse. This evening there is undoubtedly great gloom in many places. Pessimism is apt to feed on itself until it becomes despair, and despair is usually accompanied by paralysis. I doubt if either of us would like to see that happen to our friends."

"God help us if it comes to that," the Baroness said.

"Then you must help me to give them encouragement."

"Gladly, Robert, but who am I . . . ?"

The pantry door closed as the maid returned to her province.

"You are the one who can carry the message of my optimism."

"To Gerald Blythe?"

"Naturally. I particularly wish him to know that Eggli and Company are making no changes in their accounts because of the Japanese-American situation. But I want no one else to know it, not even Mrs. Blythe."

Yvonne looked across the table at him in astonishment. This was the first time in their friendship that he had ever spoken to her of his affairs. Now he had not only disclosed the bank's position but had asked her to act as his agent. It was fantastic, like some silly story of international intrigue. "Robert, are you being serious? Or are you just pulling my leg?" she asked.

"I do not go in for jokes. You know that well enough," he answered crossly. "I would do this myself but for a very good reason. If the information comes from me or through my agent in London, the British Government would at once suspect it was the direct opposite of the truth, purposely given in order to screen my actions. On the other hand, if Blythe should learn it casually from you, knowing you are a Britisher, he will believe it, and so will London."

Yvonne nodded her head thoughtfully. "I understand your purpose now. Of course if you wish me to, I shall try to do it. It's not going to be easy. I have never discussed matters of this kind with . . . Robert, what makes you think that Blythe will report my statement to London?"

"If I were not sure, I would not ask you to do this."

"Then you knew all along who he was—what he was."

"I was aware that he has tried to get information on account movements from some of my Geneva colleagues."

"Oh, Robert, why did you pretend that you did not even know his name?" She was shocked at finding a duplicity in him which she had never suspected.

"I was not deceiving you, Yvonne," Robert answered with a frown. "When you said his name was Blythe, you pronounced it English fashion, without the 't-h-e.' My friends have always referred to him as 'Mr. Blite.' It only occurred to me during dinner that it must be the same man. However, my dear, if you have any doubts or fears about this, I shall explore other means of letting the British Government know. Shall we leave it this way? If his wife calls you tomorrow or Wednesday to arrange a meeting, then you may be certain that he is the man, for he will have known of my arrival this afternoon and my departure for Zürich tomorrow at noon."

"Is this the real reason you came to see me, Robert?"

"No, it is not. When I called you on the telephone, no such thought had entered my head. Then, just as I was leaving for the *bahnhof*, my sister caught me in the hall and tried to tell me that you were a British spy."

"What crazy nonsense!" the Baroness said indignantly.

"Like everything she says. I asked her where she had picked up such a stupid story, and she answered that Marie Rappart had told her of meeting you at the house of an English couple. This was enough for Vicki, who must imagine you as some sort of *femme fatale.*"

"How awful!"

"It is beneath notice. It means nothing. Just the bile of a disappointed old maid. But it gave me the idea of how to send my message to Winston."

"Then it is true what you wish me to tell Blythe—that you are not really shifting your accounts?"

"As true as my love for you, Yvonne. But do not imagine that it is pure altruism. I like England and wish her to survive, but above all I am a Swiss who wishes this Confederation to remain as it is. If Hitler conquers England, then all of Europe will be his sovereign territory. Switzerland will be swallowed up, as it was swallowed up by Napoleon. We would be the last to fall, but when we did, we would disappear as a nation."

Yvonne pushed back her chair and stood up. "We shall have our coffee in the salon," she said and led the way out of the dining room. She waited for him to pass through the door, then put her arm through his and said in a low voice, "I shall try to deliver your message as discreetly as possible."

"I am sure you will do it cleverly, so that he will believe it to be the truth."

She laughed softly. "Don't forget that I was the wife of a diplomat. I know something of how these things are done, how to make him ask the question so that I can answer reluctantly." She released his arm and went to a cabinet on a console at the side of the room from which she extracted a box of his special cigars.

He took one, cut off the band with his fingernail and took a gold clipper from his waistcoat pocket. "You are a great comfort to me, my dear Yvonne," he said warmly.

CHAPTER VII

ON FRIDAY afternoon, the nineteenth of December, 1941, young Robert Davenport Eggli arrived from New Haven at the apartment of his parents in Park Avenue with three bulging suitcases, an immense duffel bag, golf clubs, tennis rackets and a pair of skis tied together with sash cord. Over his tweed jacket and grey flannels he was wearing a polo coat, and on the back of his head was a battered brown felt hat. He was a fine-looking specimen, tall, broad-shouldered, with alert, searching, light blue eyes, unruly brown hair which, like his mother's, had a tendency to curl, and a smooth pink complexion like his grandfather's.

The elevator man carried his baggage into the foyer of the flat, which was the only one on that floor, and pushed the bell while Robert let himself in with a key and yelled, "Hi!" in a loud voice. Nora, one of the maids, came darting out of the door that led to the kitchen and pantry.

"Anyone home, Nora?" Robert asked.

"No, Mr. Robert," Nora replied. "Your mother and Miss Evangeline went down to Brookville after lunch. I was to tell you that your father will be fetching you here in his car about half-past five. You'll be going down to the country with him." She saw the mass of luggage in the foyer and tried to edge past him.

"Never mind that stuff," Robert said. "I'll take it to my room. It's too heavy for you."

"Don't you bother, sir. I'm as strong as can be." She started to pick up one of the suitcases.

"Now, mind what I say, Nora, you're not to lift those bags.

66

They weigh a ton." He took the bag away from her, grabbed another and walked down the hall to his room.

"You're to bring a dinner jacket with you," Nora said, running ahead of him to open the door. "Will you have a cup of tea, sir, while you're waiting for your father?"

"Make it chocolate, Nora, with plenty of whipped cream."

When all the luggage was in the room, he heaved one suitcase onto the bed and threw out all of its contents—shirts, underwear, suits, and quantities of books. Then he opened the other suitcase and the duffel bag, which were on the floor, and started to repack the empty suitcase on the bed, selecting the clothes he wanted from the bed, the floor, the other bags, the dresser and the closet. He tossed things in with abandon, knowing that Morton would straighten them out when he unpacked and press the things that needed pressing. It took him about three minutes to complete the job, then he locked the suitcase and brought it out into the front hall, leaving it beside his coat and hat which Nora had placed neatly on a bench near the entrance. Going back to the library, he picked up a copy of *Esquire* from the magazine rack and sprawled into one of the deep chairs, his long legs extending far out on the green carpet. He was gazing appraisingly at a double-page spread of a semi-nude blonde when Nora brought in the tray with the hot chocolate and sugar bowl. She put it on the table by his elbow.

"I'm sure it must feel good coming home for the holidays," Nora said, beaming down at him.

"You said it! This is the life, Nora—nothing to do but drink chocolate and look at pictures of beautiful girls."

" 'Tis good to enjoy it while you can. According to the papers, they'll soon be drafting all the men from twenty to forty."

"Not me, Nora. They won't catch me. I'm allergic to drafts."

Nora put one hand on her hip and with the other stroked her chin, with a look of pained surprise on her face. "But how can you do that, Mr. Robert? There's no way of dodging it unless you be a cripple, which the Lord knows you're not!"

He put down the magazine and looked up at her with a broad grin. "If I tell you how I'm going to dodge it, will you promise not to say a word about it?"

"Oh, I wouldn't want to be knowing a thing like that."

"Don't kid me, Nora, you're dying to know. And what's more, I'm going to tell you. I've already joined up."

"A volunteer?"

He nodded his head. "But not a word, Nora. Remember, it's top secret."

"Glory be! Mr. Robert, your mother is going to be very upset when she hears it. When will you be going?"

He pulled a paper out of his pocket and consulted it. "On the third of January," he announced.

There was the rattle of a key in the front door. "That'll be your father," Nora said, hurrying out to the hall.

Robert tossed the magazine on the floor and stood up. He listened to hear if Nora was telling his news to his father. She didn't. She only said that Mr. Robert had arrived and was in the library. He stepped forward just as his father appeared at the library door.

"Well, Bob, my boy, how are you?" Jacques said, taking his son's hand and patting him on the shoulder. "I don't know when your mother and I have looked forward so to a Christmas holiday."

"And me! Nora tells me we're going to Brookville for the week end. Fine stuff!"

"Any minute now. I see your bag is all ready." Jacques went to the corner of the room and opened a panel which disclosed a bar lined with glasses and bottles. "How about one for the road?"

"No, thanks, I'm drinking cocoa."

"Cocoa? For God's sake, Bob, you in training?"

"Yep."

"Well, thank God I'm not," his father said, pouring himself a scotch on the rocks. "Tell me, how did the term go?"

"As well as can be expected. Nothing startling one way or the other. Marks safe, but not spectacular. Thanks for calling me on the seventh. The news rocked dear old Yale right down to its foundations."

"I can well imagine. It rocked the entire country. The America Firsters are as dead as Wilhelm Tell. But you're safe for the time being, Bob. I hear on the best authority that R.O.T.C. men at college will not be taken until they graduate."

"So they say. Have you heard from Grosspapa?"

"Yes, indeed."

"How did he take it?"

"His reaction was curious, Bob. He was jubilant, thought this signed Hitler's death warrant."

"How does he figure that?"

Jacques looked at his drink and smiled. "Mind you, I agree with him. I said the same thing when I heard the news that Sunday. But that Grosspapa should see it that way really does not astonish me. All his life he's been a pessimist and made money out of it. He was one of the few who predicted the crash of '29 and ordered me to get out of the market. He foresaw Hitler's game in '37 and saved fortunes for our clients in Eastern Europe. And now when on the face of it things couldn't look worse, he's predicting the defeat of Germany and Japan. That's how smart he is."

"He's sure a seven-day wonder, Pa. Sometimes I think that Grosspapa has more on the ball than all these hot-shot politicians. If he's cheered, I'm cheered. Just give us a few months, Pa, and we'll have those bastards on the run."

Jacques' smile broadened. He was proud of his son, proud of the freewheeling, uninhibited Americanism he displayed with his father. How different it was from the relationship between himself and his own father, the Grosspapa whom Bob so admired and so closely resembled. There had been—Jacques could always feel the rattle in his backbone when he thought of it—that awesome parental fear, that patriarchal domination, exacting, unbending, which had survived since the days of the Alemans. He thanked God as he looked at his son that the boy had been brought up in the gentle, lenient matriarchy of the United States. Bob could state his views honestly, forthrightly, even though they were sparked by juvenile optimism, and he, Jacques, would listen as if the words were worthy of consideration, the way other American fathers did. Loving his son, he felt instinctively that it was the better way, yet reason made him wonder if the result would be as solid, as dependable, as thoughtful as the product of the Swiss method.

"That's the right spirit, Bob," he said. "It's the spirit that will bring us eventual victory. I think I ought to tell you, however, that you and I and Grosspapa seem to be a very small minority. I happen to know how they feel about the situation in Washington and I can tell you that they are very gloomy indeed about our chances."

Robert put down his cup of chocolate. "Is the President gloomy?" he asked.

Jacques waved his glass in a gesture of dismissal. "*Ach*, Bobby, what can you expect from that man but smiles and soothing syrup? He sees himself as some sort of invincible prophet before whom the enemy will kneel in fear and gratitude, so that he and Stalin can remake the world into socialism."

The young man's face flushed with anger. "Let's drop it, Pa," he said crossly. "There's no sense in you and I getting into that argument again. I like Roosevelt, and that's that! What's more, I'll bet Grosspapa likes him too."

Jacques smiled. "Okay, son, we'll forget it, but if you want to know, Grosspapa does like Roosevelt—he calls him Franklin."

"I'm sure glad to hear that," Bob said and drained his cup of chocolate rather than add another rude remark.

Jacques put his empty glass on the bar. "Well, if you are ready, we might as well start for Long Island."

"Just a minute, Pa. There's one thing I want to tell you."

"What's that? You're not engaged to Emily, are you?"

Bob snorted. "Not me. I'm not getting hooked to any girl until this war is over. What I wanted to tell you is that I'm not going back to New Haven after the holidays."

His father's face went white. "Why, Bob, what has happened?"

"I'm transferring from pre-flight to flight training with the Army Air Force."

"Wait a minute, Bob. You don't have to do that," Jacques said quickly, visibly upset by the news. "The Army doesn't even want you to do it. They prefer that you finish college, then take your officer's training."

"They seemed to be mighty glad to take us."

"You mean you've done it, you've signed up?"

"On the dotted line. Every pre-flight man in the Junior class is joining."

"Why didn't you— Did you consult your mother about this?"

"No, sir. I wanted to tell you first."

Jacques walked over to his son and patted him on the back. "If it's done, it's done, and there's no use arguing about it. Of course we realized that it would have to happen sooner or later, but that doesn't ease the shock."

"I understand, Pa," Bob said, rising slowly to his feet. "But just think how you'd hate my guts if I hadn't done it. Picture me sitting on my behind in New Haven after those little yellow bastards kicked us in the behind when we weren't looking."

Jacques gave the boy a final pat and walked out of the room toward the elevator. Bob picked up his hat, coat and suitcase and followed his father. They did not speak to each other until they were at the curb and the chauffeur had brought the car up. When the doorman opened the rear door, Bob suggested that he drive and that his father sit beside him on the front seat. The chauffeur got out and sat down in the back.

They were on the East River Drive, headed for the Triborough Bridge, moving slowly along in the solid line of Friday-afternoon Long-Island-bound traffic when Jacques said, "Why don't you switch to infantry, Bob? They'll allow you to do that. I can pull some wires. . . ."

"Because with my twenty-twenty eyes and pretty fair co-ordination the air is the safest place to be."

"There will be plenty of staff jobs in Washington, and . . ."

"Don't insult me, Pa. I'm not that kind of a rat."

"But you're my only son. You've got to think of that."

"I think of it often. That's why I joined up, so that you and Ma can be proud of me. Christ! You don't think any of us like this having to go and fight! We're not that soft in the head. We know they're using real bullets."

"But a man of your background and education has more responsibility than just being cannon fodder. They are going to need brains, good brains to direct this show."

"Don't think it doesn't take a fairly active brain to fly a B-17. Come, Pa, let's forget it until we get to Brookville. We're going to have to go over the same ground again with Ma."

Jacques conceded, but they could not keep their talk off the war. No matter what subject was brought up—Evangeline's beaux, Bob's hockey, the parties arranged for Christmas—it had a way of turning corners until it found the war again. The dark shadow of war was too insidious, too pervasive to be thrust aside. It had become the dreadful, dominant factor of their lives, and there was no evading it.

When the car rolled onto the gravel of the circular drive in front of the house, old Morton opened the door and came forward. "You're lookin' fine, Master Robert," he said, with a broad smile. If he had a favorite in the family, it was the son whom he had known since birth.

"You're not looking so bad yourself, Morton," Bob said, shaking the old butler's hand.

"I've no complaints," Morton said. "Ever since your father retired me here to the country, it seems like I'm getting younger."

"And how is Maggie?"

"She's fine, sir, and waitin' for a sight of you."

Doris ran down the circular stair and across the tiled entrance hall to greet her son. "Bobby, dear Bobby!" she cried as she hugged him. The emotion she put into her words was unlike her. It was as if he were the prodigal returned after a long and unfortunate journey instead of the student at Yale whom she

saw almost fortnightly during the term. She was aware that it
was the news of the war that made her behave this way. Her
heart told her that he was a soldier, and from the way he answered her embrace with a kiss pressed hard into her cheek, she
could tell that he knew it too and was eager to go. "Come," she
said, taking his arm, "we'll have one little welcome-home drink
before we dress for dinner." And she walked with him towards the
library, followed by Jacques.

As in the apartment in town, there was a completely equipped
bar concealed by a panel of woodwork. Jacques opened it. "A
sherry for you, dear?" he asked his wife.

"No, indeed, not tonight," Doris answered, sitting down on
the couch. "I'm going to have a martini."

"How about you, Bob?" Jacques asked.

"A coke," his son answered.

"Bobby!" Doris exclaimed. "What's the matter with you? You
haven't caught something, I hope?"

Bob laughed. "I sure have."

"Tell her what it is, Bob," Jacques said, pouring gin into a
glass pitcher.

"Hang onto your hat, Ma," Bob cautioned.

"Don't tell me, Bobby," Doris said quickly, with a frightened
face. "Wait till I have a drink in my hand."

"You'll need it," Jacques mumbled into the bar.

There was a silence while Jacques stirred the martinis and poured
out two glasses. Then he opened a Coca-Cola bottle and poured
the contents into a highball glass. When he had given them each
their drink, he picked up his own and looked at his wife. She was
gazing transfixed at her son.

Bob lifted his glass. "Well, folks, I want you to drink to the
Army Air Force."

"I knew it. I knew it," Doris whispered.

Evangeline rushed into the room, looking very chic in tweeds
with her hair wind-blown. "Hi, Bobby," she said. "What's all
this about the Army Air Force?"

"Salute when you mention that name," Bob said.

His sister clicked her heels together and brought her hand to her forehead in a snappy salute. "Okay, flyboy, but this is the last one until you get your wings." She went over to her brother and, rising on her toes, pecked his cheek. "Good boy, Bob. Wait till Hitler hears this. He'll shake in his red flannels."

Doris drank her martini in one gulp. "Come and sit here," she said to Bob, patting the couch. When he had sprawled his bulk in the seat beside her, she took his hand. "I'm proud of you, my son."

"Good old Ma," Bob said, grinning.

"When do you go?" Jacques asked.

Bob took the paper out of his pocket and held it out for his father to see. "The invitation reads 'From six to eight on the afternoon of January third at the Army Air Force Training Base, Albany, Georgia.'"

Doris dabbed her eyes with a handkerchief. "That's enough of this. Let's talk about something jolly. Did you see that stack of invitations on your bureau in town?"

"Gruesome!" Bob replied. "I'll let you open them for me, Lina. You can rate them like Baedeker—three stars for the really hot ones."

Evangeline stood in the middle of the room, studying her brother with her head tilted. "The hot ones will be the parties I'm going to," she said pensively, and then she laughed quietly at some private joke.

"What's so funny, Lina?" her father asked.

"I was just thinking that Emily will have to change the Christmas present she bought for Bob. It won't be much use to him now."

"Tell her to make it diapers," Bob said gruffly. "I might need them before I'm through."

Doris held out her empty glass. "Is there some left in the shaker, Jacques?" she asked, with two little rivers on her cheeks where the tears were falling.

CHAPTER VIII

AS SHE turned the corner of the Uto-
quai to cross the Quaibrücke, Hélène had to hold her umbrella
firmly over her right shoulder against the slanting, stinging rain
that was blowing in cold gusty blasts up the Limmat from the
north. The view of old Zürich with its arcades facing the river,
surmounted by the graceful towers of the Grossmünster on one
bank and the Fraumünster and the St. Peterkirche on the other,
were thus blotted out. All she could see were the scudding white-
caps on the lake, making waving lines on the dark water, and
the elephant-grey clouds that were hurtling overhead, hiding the
Uetliberg and the Albis and near enough, it seemed to her, to
touch. She thought of the Engadine, probably now above all this
storm, shining white in the winter sun, and of Lugano sheltered
from this north wind by the Lepontine Alps, and wondered why
anyone with money enough ever spent winters in this cold
and clammy city. Yet she did it—she of all people—who prided
herself on her independence of mind. To be sure, in the days of
peace she had spent every winter holiday at the Suvretta in St.
Moritz and every Easter she had gone alone to Lugano for a
fortnight. But that spring excursion had not been for any warmth
other than the adoration of Tony Venturi.

Those days and the few—too few—surreptitious nights with
him had given her the strength to meet her responsibilities as a
mother and a wife without bitterness. In Zürich she had always
tried, though she realized that she had only been partially successful, to behave as she was expected to. She had striven valiantly
to make sure no one could say of her that she neglected her
obligations as the wife of Walter Eggli. Her house was efficiently,

spotlessly run in the accepted manner of the well-to-do Zürich-
oise. Her food was recherché, expensive and commented on by
gourmets. Her children were strong, handsome and well man-
nered. In her clothes alone did she rebel. She refused to abide
by the Zürich rule that dowdiness was an evidence of respecta-
bility. She always dressed in the height of fashion, and having
an exceptionally good figure, with well-shaped legs tapering to
thin ankles, she was the envy of and the irritant to most of the
women she knew, bar Lucy Waldmann, who admired her extravagantly.

She had walked this morning because she did not want to be
seen in a tram. If someone she knew saw her tramping the streets
with raincoat, umbrella and sturdy rubber-soled shoes, there
would be no comment. That was an acceptable picture. Ladies
were expected to do their errands on foot in defiance of the
weather. Those who feared to face the *Foehn* were considered incapable weaklings and shiftless wives. Even had it not been the fact
of her assignation with Tony, she would have walked, because she
wanted, needed the strain of her body against the wind, the feel
of the cold air in her lungs in order to set things straight in her
mind.

Ever since the night of the accident her relationship with
Walter had deteriorated. Not on his part. On the contrary, he
had been more humble and obsequious than ever. He seemed
incapable of understanding why his fawning efforts to win her
back disgusted her to the point of nausea. Yet as she had totalled
the sum of him while walking down the Seefeldstrasse, there had
been only that one item on the debit side—the cringing insecurity. She knew the source of it. She needed no psychologist to
tell her that his father had from the earliest days filled him with
a fear and resentment which had thrown him into the soft bosom
of his mother. Now as a man of middle age he sought in her
what he had found in his mother—encouragement, sympathy,
belief in his powers. Had she given him this? Would he have
changed? Would he have in time been able to stand up to Gross-

papa Eggli and assert himself had she done so? Perhaps. She did not really know about these things of the id and the ego. It may have already been too late when she married him. On the other hand, if she could have saved him, made him into the man she could have respected and loved, then the fault was hers.

She crossed the Bürkliplatz and entered the Fraumünster-strasse. She had seen no one she knew. Most of the people who had passed her were businessmen and working girls, all hunched under their umbrellas, walking quickly, purposefully. There were no cars parked in the Münsterhofplatz, which she crossed diagonally, headed for a narrow medieval lane that led up to the Peterkirche. Her thoughts had put her in the wrong mood for her meeting with Tony. On the previous day when he had telephoned to say that he was in Zürich, stopping at a small hotel in the Augustinerstrasse, and suggested the lunch, she had been thrilled. All night, alone in her bed—for Walter, mended and well, had returned to his regiment at Baden—she had thought of this meeting, imagining all of it from the drink in the bar to the final glorious oblivion of his lovemaking. Now, chilled by the wind and rain, worried by the thought of her own failure as a wife, she almost hated herself for this duplicity. She suddenly saw the whole affair as something noxious and unclean. In the sun of the Tessin there may have been the excuse of atmosphere and animal spirits, but here in a dark, narrow alley, in a second-rate hotel, on a cold winter day, there could be no justification other than great love. And that, Hélène knew, she did not feel.

She liked Tony. He was amusing, flattering and, in contrast to the men of Zürich, completely lacking in ambition or moral sense. His father had been a dealer in incunabula, with a shop in Lugano—a scholarly product of the Tessin whose beautiful catalogues were known to every rich collector in Europe and the Western Hemisphere. His mother was a Vaudoise who, after the death of her husband, had settled in Ouchy with enough of a fortune to live comfortably, if not extravagantly. Tony was dependent on a monthly allowance from his mother which allowed him to paint pictures which were clever imitations of Matisse. There was no question that he had a certain talent. He painted with great facility the sort of pictures his friends could hang without being accused of bad taste. He had a flair for what was in the mode, but he was no artist. In Lugano where he lived and worked when he was in need of a little extra cash, he was immensely popular with the lotus eaters and lonely widows. His manners were elastic enough to be suited to the occasion; he dressed more like an Englishman on holiday than a Swiss painter, and he spoke English and German fluently and Italian and French without accent. He understood *Schweizerdeutsch*, but refused to admit he could speak it.

He was no more in love with Hélène Eggli than she was with him, but he enjoyed making love to her because the conquest of attractive, dissatisfied women bolstered his ego. Furthermore, he was, for a man, peculiarly possessive about his conquests. He demanded fidelity and devotion. It was having them under his thumb, obeying his commands, ready to risk the pale for his affection that really delighted him. That Hélène had never succumbed to this extent infuriated and baffled him. She would yield to his embraces with a passion that was almost nuclear in its intensity, and yet he knew, he could sense that it was only a physical response to the adroitness of his performance. He knew how to achieve the release which she could not obtain with her husband, and because of that, she would risk much to come to him when he called. Her body he could have, but her heart was withheld and it annoyed him and piqued his pride. Outwardly they used between them the words and gestures of lovers. Their moments alone together were embroidered with all the little gentle endearments associated with true love. Yet he knew that they meant no more than the patterned behavior of good society. They were part of the act, stimulating its performance as the right background music stimulates an emotional scene in motion pictures.

That he had failed to capture her heart was undoubtedly the

reason why he had continued his pursuit of her for three years. Failure had made him stubborn and determined. He was not used to it. In most cases—and there had been many—he had brought women to the point of abject, groveling devotion, then dropped them to weep their bitter tears alone.

Tony Venturi got down from the high bar stool when he saw her come through the door, shaking the drops from her dripping umbrella. At first glance one would have said he had a strong face with its high cheekbones, prominent cleft chin, and large, intense black eyes, but then, on closer scrutiny, the mouth gave the secret away. It was thin, cynical, rising at the corners, one side slightly higher than the other. His jet black hair had been allowed to grow just long enough to accomplish well-trained swirls above each ear. He looked even younger than his thirty-five years.

"My God, Hélène, you're soaked," he said in French, the language they always spoke together. "Don't tell me you've been walking in this downpour."

"I can't imagine why anyone in his right mind would leave Lugano to come to this Godforsaken town in January," Hélène said while he helped her off with her raincoat. "Yes, I walked— all the way from the Zollikerstrasse."

"Why? Have you no gasoline?"

"Not for coming to the Augustinerstrasse," she answered. Although they were alone in the bar, nevertheless they avoided any expression of affection. It was their public behavior, which had been agreed upon long since. "Besides, I like to walk in the rain. It's like a cold bath, it stimulates the blood and the mind."

"A good drink will do it better. What will you have?"

"A dry martini. Can they make them here?"

"I'll tell the Fräulein how to mix it." He banged on the counter with his fist and a girl in a white smock appeared from a door at the end of the bar. "Can you make a dry martini?" he asked in high German.

"Naturally," the barmaid replied haughtily, stressing the Swiss pronunciation of the word.

"Three parts gin to one of vermouth," Tony said. "And a twist of lemon peel."

"Two?" the barmaid asked.

"No, one," Tony replied. "I'll have a Cinzano." He did not believe in alcohol as an apéritif for love.

Tony and Hélène sat down at a small table in the rear of the barroom. Hélène took out her powder box and lipstick to repair the damage of the wind and rain. She wanted to compose her nerves. In spite of all the doubts and fears which had assailed her during the walk, she felt the old quiverings in her stomach and the tickle on the roof of her mouth now that Tony was beside her.

"What are you doing in Zürich?" she asked.

He smiled at her and whispered, "Need you ask?"

"Don't be silly, Tony. There must be some other reason."

"I spent Christmas and the New Year with Mother at Ouchy, and now I'm on my way back to Lugano."

"By the Great Circle route."

"I wanted to see you in your own surroundings. I wanted to find out if you change your coloring when living among the bumblebees." He looked at her smart tweed suit, the double row of pearls around her neck, and the yellow knitted silk blouse.

"Well, do I?" she asked.

"Not in appearance—now that you've discarded the raincoat. Where is Walter?"

"With his regiment. Why aren't you with yours?"

"I will be in February, and God how I hate it! I was never built for the life of a chamois."

"No truer words were ever said. But it will do you good, raise your ambition to higher things."

"Ambition? What a horrible word, and so unlike you to use it, Hélène! That is the Zürich coloration showing through."

"You ought to be ashamed to say it, Tony. What is it you want out of life?"

Tony laughed. "A large soft bed and a few tubes of paint to fool with when I'm not in it."

She shrugged her shoulders. "At least you're honest about it."

The barmaid brought the drinks and put them on the table.

"Tell me," Hélène went on, "have you never considered marriage as a state which might give you some peace and security?"

"Is this a proposal?" Tony asked, smiling.

"God forbid! A month ago, when Walter was in the hospital, I did speculate on what your reaction would have been had he been killed in the accident."

"And what conclusion did you come to?"

"Not any, really. I just wondered."

"If I would propose?"

"Yes. I wanted to be prepared with my answer."

"Which would have been 'no.' "

"How did you guess?"

"Because I know you, know how you think."

Hélène laughed softly and sipped her martini. "How well we do know each other, Tony! I knew also that I would never have to say that 'no,' because you would never ask."

"But of course I would never ask you to marry me. Can you imagine anything more likely to destroy our friendship than marriage?"

"Nothing," Hélène said, and stood up. "Come, let us have lunch. I'm famished after my walk."

The dining room of the little hotel was small but clean and tastefully decorated in Swiss mountain style, with pine-paneled walls and chairs carved in elaborate scrolls. The tablecloths were of red and white checked cotton, giving the room a bright appetizing air. Only three tables were taken, and these by solemn-looking men reading their newspapers. Tony led her to a table under a window of small leaded panes. Hélène ordered bratwurst and spinach and he an omelet. They talked little during lunch. A pall of doubt and misgiving seemed to have fallen between them after the talk of marriage. The mere thought annoyed Tony, and he wondered why she had brought it up.

Hélène had regained her stability, and just as when she had been walking in the rain, she was able now to see their relationship in its proper perspective. She was more than ever determined not to go to his room after lunch. Not that desire for him had left her, but because she felt that it could not be other than sordid and disappointing in this bystreet atmosphere. Furthermore, there was too much at stake here in her home city—the children, Grosspapa Eggli, her position in the oligarchy. She cared about that. It was important to her. One had a certain obligation to one's class, and her class had ruled here since the Reformation. Walter did not enter into her calculations. She realized this and was not astonished. What did surprise her was her inclusion of old Robert Eggli. Why should she consider him? Had he not himself defied the rules by keeping a mistress?

"How did your father-in-law take the news of America's entry into the war?" Tony asked.

Hélène looked up at him, startled. Had he read her thoughts? "Why do you ask?"

Tony shrugged. "No particular reason. He's such a wise old fox I wondered what he would do when something happened that he had not predicted."

"He didn't have a stroke, if that's what you mean."

"Took it in his stride, eh? Got his money out of New York before the others knew what had happened?"

Hélène stirred her coffee as she examined Tony's face carefully. This was the first time she had ever heard him remark on money or banking. "Why should that interest you?" she asked.

He lit a cigarette and grinned at her. "Personally, it interests me less than anything I can think of. I don't care a centime what the old miser does with his money, or anyone else's money."

"Then it was just conversation?"

"I have a friend who would give a lot to know."

"I imagine there are many who would like to know."

"Does Walter ever tell you about the bank's business?"

"Of course not!" she answered indignantly.

"Was the old man frightened or happy?"

"At the news? Tony, what are you getting at? Why do you ask me such questions?"

"I told you, there is a friend of mine who would give a lot to know." He leaned towards her and whispered, "He'd give it to me if I could tell him."

Hélène was appalled by this cynical announcement. She knew that Tony had no morals whatever, and yet in spite of this knowledge she found it hard to believe that he would ask for information concerning Robert Eggli which he could sell for cash.

Tony saw the shock and incredulity in her eyes and smiled. "Why are you so squeamish?" he asked. "What's wrong with that? A man is willing to pay me ten thousand francs for telling him whether old Eggli was stunned or pleased when he heard that Japan had attacked the United States. Of course I think he's a damn fool, but that's his business. I can't see that any vital secrets are betrayed. It's quite simply a little social gossip between friends. I ask you how Eggli felt when he heard the news. You tell me quite innocently that he was downhearted or elated. I happen to mention this to a friend, and for this bit of idle comment I am given enough to see me through the winter and maybe into the spring. Where's the harm?"

"Tony, Tony," Hélène said sadly, shaking her head to indicate her feeling of hopelessness. "Have you really no sense of right or wrong? Don't you see that what you are asking for is information which could be used for political ends? And to tell me straight out that you want to sell my answer! It's incredible! Why try to involve me in your spying? If you had brought up the subject casually, I might even have told you Robert Eggli's reaction in all innocence."

"Don't be silly, Hélène. You are mine. We belong to each other. I'm not pulling tricks like that on you. You ought to know me better than that. For three years now I've devoted my life to your happiness. I've never lied to you. I've opened my mind to you like a book. You may not approve of what you've read there, but it is not as bad as your Zürichois mind would have it. You think of me as having no morals, but I notice you don't worry about morals when I make love to you. You like that, all right. You can't wait for me to hold you in my arms and kiss you behind the ear. For that, for an hour of that delicious . . ."

"Stop!" she commanded, her face flushed from the excitement his words had provoked.

He put two francs on the table and motioned to the waitress. "Fräulein, put this on the bill of Room Number 24," he said and stood up.

Hélène picked up her raincoat and umbrella from the chair beside her and walked out of the restaurant into the narrow lobby of the hotel. Her will, her resolution had dissolved. She followed him silently up the stairs, down the corridor and into the room which he unlocked with a key.

It might have been an hour later that she saw him emerging from the bathroom in a robe of bright green silk. Time, thought, everything had eluded her since she had entered the room. Now as she sat there on his couch, one arm behind her head, she felt only a great emptiness, as if all sensation had been drained from her, leaving her mind as calm and clear as the water of the Türler See.

"Who is this man who wants to know how Grosspapa Eggli reacted to the Pearl Harbor news?" she asked in a quiet, measured voice.

Tony came to the couch and smiled down at her triumphantly. "You wouldn't know him, my dear," he replied.

"Is he Swiss?"

"He is a German poet who lives in a small château near Lausanne."

"A Nazi agent."

Tony shrugged his shoulders. "Probably. Otherwise he would not offer money."

"You know him well?"

"Fairly. He has come to Lugano every winter for years. He's one of those romanticists who find me fascinating."

"Do you like him?"

Tony laughed gaily. "Frankly no. I find him extremely boring."

"If I said that Robert Eggli was pleased by the news, what would that mean to your pansy friend?"

"That the old fox knew it meant victory for the Axis."

"Did he say that?"

"Sure, he said it. He told me quite frankly that that was the word Goering was hoping to hear."

This was precisely what Hélène had hoped he would say. Sitting there while Tony had been in the bathroom, she had decided to find out who wanted the information and how they would evaluate it. If it was the Axis—she had suspected that it was the Italian Government because of Tony's acquaintanceship with many of the Ciano set at Cernobbio—she was going to give him a story, true or not, which would give them false courage. Now he had made it easy for her. She could tell him the truth. Tony could get his money which, in her state of bliss, she felt he was entitled to, and Hitler's stupid sycophants would believe what she wanted them to believe. They would believe in their victory because they had heard that Robert Eggli believed in it, and Eggli was never wrong. It amused her to think that she, Hélène Eggli-Sieber, in a second-rate hotel in the heart of Zwingli's Zürich, her lover looking at her, would give the Nazis the false confidence that would lose them the war.

"Well, Tony, I'll tell you. He was pleased, very pleased," she said.

Tony looked at her skeptically. "You are sure?"

"Quite sure. Walter was with him and told me that his father was delighted."

"I would have thought . . ."

"Walter was surprised too," she interrupted.

Tony sat down on the edge of the couch and lightly stroked her tousled hair with his thin, nervous hands. "My wonderful, my beautiful Hélène!" he whispered.

CHAPTER IX

HOW brave of you to walk here on a day like this!" the Baroness said.

Mrs. Blythe laughed, a pianissimo twitter in a high key, like a skylark at its ceiling of altitude. "You've been too long away from England. This *bise* is a trifle compared to an east wind on the Cambridge fens. Just look at Gerald. He fairly revels in it."

Gerald Blythe had gone at once to the fireplace where he stood now, feet apart, his face pink from the cold wind, warming his hands behind his back. "What I really revel in is a jolly good fire when I come indoors," he said. "A hearth and a cup of tea— the two blessings England has given the world." His eyes turned toward the tea table all set with cups, silver kettle sitting over its alcohol flame, teapot covered with a cosy of padded silk, a rack of toast, slices of thin bread, and a plate of little cakes. "We do it well, we English, and we're properly smug about it."

"I fancy we are quite the most rigidly conforming race on earth," Yvonne de Marty said, sitting down at the tea table to commence the ritual of brewing. It was the day following Robert's visit and as he had predicted, Mrs. Blythe had telephoned suggesting tea. "We never change our habits no matter where we live."

"You illustrate that statement to perfection, Baroness," Daphne Blythe said. She had seated herself in the *fauteuil* which Robert Eggli had used two days before. "Until now I found it hard to believe that you were born and brought up an English girl. Hearing you chatting away in French with the ladies of Geneva, you seemed so thoroughly Continental. Every word and gesture, and your lovely clothes, and the way you do your hair— not a single clue, that is, not until I walked into this room."

"Don't forget that I had a French mother," Yvonne said.

"A good mixture," Blythe commented. "The French blood supplies the taste for the beautiful and exotic, while the English blood preserves the balance by insisting on the sensible things like tea, hearth fires, and woolies."

"Tea and fires, yes, but in the matter of woolies the French blood won out," the Baroness said.

"You mean to say, in this climate?" Daphne Blythe started to ask.

"I wear silk," Yvonne stated. She made a shivering gesture with her shoulders. "I could never abide the feeling of wool on my skin, not even as a child when my nanny insisted."

"I should have a chill on the liver straight off," Gerald said.

"Like the Eskimos, when I leave my igloo, I cover up in furs," the Baroness said.

"Well, I must say you keep your igloo nicely warm," Mrs. Blythe remarked. "Our flat is like a refrigerator in comparison. It has built-in drafts that are unpredictable. The moment you think you have one properly trapped, another springs up from the opposite direction. And as for the central heating, it would scarcely melt an ice."

"My dear, you exaggerate," Yvonne said. "Last week when I had tea with you, I thought how nice it was that I could put off my fur coat, a thing one can never do in other Geneva houses."

"You'd have jolly well kept it on today," Gerald said. "Knowing what I do now about your underthings, I'd have insisted."

"But that is not the reason I made you come here," Yvonne said. "It was rather rude of me, changing your nice invitation like that, but as a matter of fact, I was about to call you to ask you both for tea when you telephoned. There it is, Mrs. Blythe."

"I say, do call me Daphne," Mrs. Blythe said. "We poor exiles should put off formalities."

"Splendid thought! Hereafter I'm Gerald," her husband echoed.

"How nice! And I shall be just plain Yvonne."

"Yvonne, yes, but never plain," Gerald said.

"You've been picking up Continental phrases," Yvonne said, smiling at him. Then to Daphne: "How do you like your tea?"

"As it comes, cream and one of sugar."

When the cup was ready Yvonne handed it to Gerald who took it to his wife.

"And mine the same," Gerald said.

"The good old English mixture, black as coffee," Yvonne said. "It used to horrify my French friends. Gerald, bring Daphne the toast and the bread and jam."

The Blythes ate heartily, with that special ravenous delight which the British reserve for tea. Yvonne, on the other hand, ate only one piece of toast. She believed in the ritual but could not afford to make a meal of it. Proud of her figure, she knew that it could not be indulged.

"Are you still so pessimistic about America's war with Japan?" Yvonne asked Gerald.

"I've heard nothing which would change my views," Gerald answered. "I should not care to have it repeated, but I must confess to you that the situation seems very black indeed. Even the Swiss I've talked to are a bit windy."

"What Swiss have you talked to?" Yvonne asked.

"Oh, some of the chaps at the League. I fancy they are beginning to wonder if Hitler isn't planning to march this way. Have you that same impression?"

"That the Swiss are worried? No doubt some of them are. One can hardly blame them, surrounded as they are by Axis armies. The newspapers and the wireless are not giving out much cheer these days."

"You're talking about the Swiss in general," Daphne commented.

"Yes," Yvonne said. "Isn't that what you meant, Gerald?"

"I suppose I did," Gerald replied. "On the other hand, I am quite certain that what people in general are thinking is scarcely of much value. As you say, they are guided by what is given them by the press and the wireless. What would be interesting to know is the conclusion reached by one of the more astute Swiss observers of international affairs."

"I don't quite see how anyone, no matter how clever he is, can foretell what will happen," Daphne said. "Even if one knew what was in the minds of Hitler and Mussolini and Tojo, one would be no better off. It is perfectly clear that they want to conquer the world. But who can tell if they will or not?"

"Quite right, my dear, there are no clairvoyants," Gerald said. "But there are in this little country a few men whose business it is to study the course of world politics objectively, never allowing themselves to be swayed by any prejudice or emotion."

"You are talking about the bankers," Yvonne said.

"Primarily," Gerald said. "They are the ones whose existence depends on guessing correctly."

"Their existence also depends on keeping their conclusions a secret," Yvonne said with a smile.

Gerald Blythe laughed in a high falsetto. "Oh, I dare say you'd never get one of them to divulge a thing. They're as tight-lipped as a Somerset farmer. Ah, well, the human animal never changes, and I'm a very human animal, with an itching curiosity to know the future."

"What good would it do us if we did know it?" Yvonne asked.

"We would be prepared to meet it," Gerald answered.

Yvonne looked up at him with a sly smile. "What you really mean is that we might be able to alter it. That, of course, is cheating, for it would not be the real future at all."

"I fancy Yvonne has you there, Gerald," Daphne said.

Gerald laughed and took a cigarette case out of his pocket which he opened, offering it to Yvonne. "You are far too clever for me. No doubt of it, if we foresaw a future that was wicked and oppressive, we would—it's the old instinct of self-preserva-

tion—do everything in our power to change it to our benefit."
Yvonne declined his offer of a cigarette, so he picked one out
of his case. "May I?"

"But of course," Yvonne replied. "Daphne, there's a cigarette
in that box by your elbow."

Gerald lit a cigarette for his wife and returned to his post in
front of the fire. "Wishing is one thing, but the power to act
is another," he went on. "A lowly civil servant messing about
with the cultivation of poppies is in no position to mould the
course of history."

"You are too modest, my dear," Daphne said. "The work
you've done has had profound effects. Just look at Turkey and
Egypt. You have given them a proper moral outlook on opium
and heroin, and straight off they have become more responsible
governments. I am convinced that had it not been for your education in the field of narcotics, the Turks would have embraced
the Germans as they did the last time."

Gerald bowed to his wife. "A flattering view, my dear, but a
bit farfetched."

"You must not belittle Daphne's theory," Yvonne said. "It is
splendidly loyal and no doubt truer than you think. If Turkey
continues to remain neutral, I am going to boast that it was
the doing of my friend, Gerald Blythe."

Gerald took a deep inhale of his cigarette. "Bless me, I wonder
how long our luck will last! How long will it be that we can
continue to behave like civilized human beings, drinking our tea,
warming ourselves by the fire, and talking delightful nonsense?"

"Gerald frets because he's not at home, dashing about in a
uniform," Daphne said to Yvonne.

"Yes, yes, of course," Yvonne said sympathetically, then turned
to Gerald. "But you have the consolation of knowing that your
government has kept you here because they wish to."

"Quite," Gerald said. "Our dear old government persists in
maintaining all these minor international activities as if the ship
were merely going through a stiff blow and all would be calm

again when we wake up in the morning. They refuse to regard it for what it is—a devastating mortal typhoon."

"Perhaps they are wiser than you imagine," Yvonne said.

"More likely I am just a small part of a valiant face they are putting on," Gerald said.

"If they have to have a face, it might as well be yours, dear," Daphne said. "It's the sort of role you perform rather well. Don't give him away, Yvonne, for having dropped it this afternoon. It is because you are one of us."

"But I don't really believe that keeping up these League activities is part of a face," Yvonne protested. "I think that Churchill is certain this is only a bad storm, and that every part of the ship must be kept functioning in order to make headway in calmer seas."

"For the life of me, I cannot see what can give you a grain of optimism," Gerald said. "The whole place is full of signs and portents. Who should suddenly show up in town yesterday but that shocking young German, Graf von Orb? You know, the one who writes decadent poetry and lives in Lausanne. We met him at the Berliers' and for a tuppence I'd have smashed his face in. He pranced around as smug and self-satisfied as if Geneva were already a province of the Reich. Sickening, I tell you. And on top of that, old Robert Eggli of Zürich came racing over here to see his banking friends, his wind up as high as Mont Blanc."

Yvonne could not help smiling. It had come out at last, and Robert—wise Robert—had been proved right once more. He had said that if Gerald Blythe should ask her to tea within twenty-four hours of his departure, it was because Blythe wanted to learn of his attitude toward the new war development for the purpose of advising London. When Daphne had telephoned as predicted, she had purposely changed the tea to her own house. Ever since they had arrived she had tried to thread the talk so that it would disclose a motive, if there was a motive. Gerald had skirted it skillfully, building up the picture of his frustration over an enforced isolation on a job that had no bearing on events. He had wanted her to believe that any curiosity he had about the conclusions of the bankers was purely personal, based on this frustration. Finally, seeing that he was getting nowhere, he had come out with Robert's name, admitting that he knew of his presence in Geneva. The time had come for her to plant the seed.

"Robert Eggli is a very dear old friend of mine," she said quietly.

"To be sure," Daphne said. "Someone told me—I forget who it was—that you used to know him in Paris."

"That is where I first met him," Yvonne said.

"Very keen chap, I hear," Gerald commented.

"One of the brightest minds I've ever met," Yvonne stated.

"Did you run into him by chance the other day?" Gerald asked casually.

"He dined with me here," Yvonne said, then looked at Daphne with a smile. "I would appreciate it if you would not repeat that. You know what gossips the Genevoises are."

"You may be sure that I shall not breathe a word of it," Daphne said.

"He is held in high esteem here," Gerald said. "Which is quite an admission for this city. You know how they are about the *bourdons*. But he must be getting on. In his seventies, isn't he?"

"He is eighty, but one would never think it to meet him. A really remarkable man," Yvonne answered.

"So they say," Gerald said. "One of the keenest bankers. Never gets caught out with funds in the wrong spot. No doubt he is switching money about this very instant, getting out of Wall Street and into some safer territory like Rio."

"Who knows? That is his secret," Yvonne said.

"Quite," Gerald agreed. "Bankers don't talk about their affairs to anyone, bar other bankers."

"I doubt if he even tells them what he is doing," Yvonne said. "He forms his own judgments and goes his own way."

"I dare say," Gerald mumbled. "Lets the other chaps do the talking. Clever that. Rushed over here to find out what his Suisse Romande colleagues were going to do, and let them assume he was following their lead. Pity he looked so worried. That gave the show away."

"Worried?" Yvonne exclaimed. "That's odd. To me he seemed quite the opposite. I never saw him more relaxed and content."

"Really!" Gerald said, raising his eyebrows. "Odd how people gain wrong impressions. Wishful thinking, I should judge."

"It was not quite like that, Gerald," Daphne said, then turned to Yvonne. "The remark was made at the Berliers' and I told Gerald about it. Madame de Tessier happened to mention that she had seen Herr Eggli in town and that horrible German poet smirked and said, 'Sans doute il a des soucis en ce moment.' "

"Sorry. I got it wrong," Gerald said apologetically.

"Indeed you can put your mind at rest on that point," the Baroness said. "Robert Eggli showed no signs whatever of being worried."

"Of course he is a German Swiss," Gerald said, as if weighing the matter in his own mind. "They say that many of them—you know, association of language and culture—are inclined to favor the Nazis."

Yvonne's face flushed red. "Gerald Blythe, if you wish to remain my friend, never say that again or think it. Robert Eggli despises Hitler and all his cohorts as deeply as you and I do. On most matters of international politics he tries to maintain a rigid attitude of neutrality, but on that subject he is clear and outspoken. Do you think for a moment that I, who am half English, half French, would let him set foot inside this house if he had one ounce of sympathy for the Nazis?"

"I do apologize, Yvonne," Gerald said, blushing. "I did not mean to imply that I thought Eggli pro-Nazi. Quite naturally you would not see him if he were. It's just the whole bloody war and the worry and confusion. . . ."

"I must say, Gerald, it's quite unlike you to speak so stupidly," Daphne said crossly. "You had better give up going out if you cannot control yourself better than that."

"I understand how disturbed you are," Yvonne said, smiling at him pleasantly in an effort to ease his chagrin. Yet she felt it necessary to rule out doubts that might lurk in his mind. "But remember what I said and put it down in your book— Robert Eggli is heart and soul on our side."

"Jolly comforting to hear it," Gerald mumbled. "And knowing it, to hear that he is not worried."

Daphne stood up. "Well, my dear, this has been a lovely tea. Just like old times. I do envy you the delicious bread. The muck we get from our baker is inedible."

"My one indulgence," Yvonne said, rising. "I hoard my flour and my cook bakes it for me. Your coat and snow boots are in my bedroom. Do look around. I'm quite proud of my little house."

"*Little* house? It seems positively regal to me," Daphne said as Yvonne showed her to the door which led to the bedroom.

The Baroness closed the door carefully and came back to where Gerald was standing. "Gerald," she said in a low voice, "it bothers me seeing a countryman of mine as low in spirits as you."

"It was wrong of me to have said that about Eggli," Gerald said humbly.

"It was a symptom of your despair. I understand that and am not angry with you. But I don't want you despairing. Listen, if I tell you something, will you promise never to repeat it, not even to Daphne?"

"If it concerns England, I cannot promise anything," Gerald said gruffly.

"Will you promise, then, never to repeat it here—and I still include Daphne?"

"Yes, that I will do."

Yvonne hesitated. "I don't want you to think that I am betraying a friend. In a way I am, but it seems to me that it is the sort of betrayal that may even reinforce his plan of action. I want you to believe that I am telling you this for the good of England and Robert Eggli. Listen, Gerald, he told me the night before last that in his opinion this attack on the United States by the Japs has sealed Hitler's doom."

"I hope he is right."

"What is more, he is so firmly convinced of the power of America that he is leaving all his funds in New York."

"He told you that?"

"Yes."

"Why? I thought he never discussed his affairs."

"Because he handles my money and I asked him."

"You believe it then?"

"Believe it? Look, Gerald, I have only one faith and that is in Robert Eggli."

"Quite, quite. I shouldn't have questioned it."

"Oh, yes, you should. You should question everything. You know, of course, what we are to each other."

"Ah—er—just what one hears about—the sort of idle gossip."

"Well, it's true. He has been my lover for years, and I'm proud to have his love."

"I like you for that, Yvonne. You're a good girl."

"I am what I am. But enough of this, Daphne'll be coming. Remember your promise."

Gerald took her hand and patted it. "I have every reason to keep it," he said, smiling.

CHAPTER X

"CUTE little place you have here,"
Jacques said, looking around the small living room which was on
the ground floor, facing the garden in the rear of the house.
The French windows which led to a flagstone terrace were open,
for the air was warm, drifting into them scented with roses.
The room might have been in London's Chelsea with its English antique furniture and its hunting prints on the walls. "How
did you find it?"

"It belongs to Bob Sever," Dexter Miller answered. "He's a
classmate of mine, one of those nuts who picked up the New
Deal religion at Harvard Law School after he left Princeton. He
has been down here for the past four years running errands for
the Great White Father. He was sent to London a few months
ago on this Lend-Lease deal, so he let me have this bandbox
of his in Georgetown."

"Georgetown? Is that what they call this part of Washington?"

"It's the oldest part of the city. Went through its bad times
when the colored folks took over most of it. Only a few of the
old families stuck to their mansions on N Street. Now of course
it has come back into its own—the chic place to live. The New
Deal intelligentsia rushed into it like rabbits into a warren. You
know how they are, those long-haired pedagogues—anything for
atmosphere, to hell with the plumbing as long as it's quaint."

Jacques laughed. "I never thought to find you living in the
middle of them. What are you doing, spying on Francis Biddle
and Archie MacLeish?"

"Funny, isn't it?" Dexter said, shaking up a second batch of
martinis. "That's what the war will do for you. Here I am play-

96

ing on the same team with them. You'd get a laugh seeing me
on a Sunday morning buying my *Times* at Morgan's Drugstore,
rubbing elbows with the lot of them."

"It's a wonder they ever gave you a job."

"Oh, look, that's all changed now. Party politics is on ice for
the duration. Did you ever hear of Skull and Bones?"

"You mean that club at Yale? I think I've heard Bobby speak
of it. Why?"

"Well, it constitutes the Rock of Gibraltar, the bastion of good
old private initiative. Just to show you what a smart fox F.D.R.
is, the minute the flag was raised for war, what did he do but
demote the Harvard Law School boys and recruit Skull and Bones
for the top jobs."

"Princeton doesn't figure, eh?"

"We fill in here and there."

"And do these Yale men live in Georgetown too?"

"Oh, sure, but in the N Street mansions where the quality
used to live."

Jacques laughed. "That's wonderful, Dexter—the quality re-
turns to claim its own."

"You're damn tootin'! When it comes to the pinch, it's the
quality that knows how to perform. Those intellectual dreamers
who sound off about the common man are so impractical they
couldn't organize a game of slapjack. They are theorists, Jacques,
not administrators."

"I'm lucky. I've never met one. You don't run into them in
Wall Street."

"Except in S.E.C."

"We leave that to our lawyers."

"Jenny!" Dexter called in a loud voice. A Negro woman in
black uniform with white apron appeared at the door.

"Yes, sir. You want sumpin'?" she asked.

"Jenny, I think it's warm enough to eat in the garden," Dexter
said.

"I done already set the table in the dinin' room like you said, Mr. Miller."

"Would it be too much trouble to change it?"

"No, sir, not for me. It all depends on when Martha's fixin' for you-all to eat. She's makin' a soufflé as won't want to wait on no one."

"Okay, Jenny, we'll leave it to Martha. If she says you have the time, we'll eat in the garden. Otherwise it's the dining room."

"Yes, sir," Jenny said and went out.

"Did the servants come with the house?" Jacques asked.

"Yes, and as good a pair of girls as you'd want to find. They take wonderful care of me."

"With Fanny's help?"

"Not a chance. That whirl has run its course. Ever since they tapped me for this job down here I haven't seen a peep of her. Called her twice, but she was out both times and never bothered to call me back."

"That's too bad. Doris and I had figured that you and Fanny were practically hitched."

"There was a time when I thought so too. But with Fanny Farnsworth absence makes the heart grow colder. She likes her man where she can touch him."

Jacques walked out on the flagstones and looked at the little garden with its square carpet of lawn bordered with shrubs and roses. It was seven o'clock, but the light was still strong in the western sky. A great tulip tree in the garden beyond shaded the rear wall. It was a peaceful little haven which reminded him of Berne and Lucerne. The rumble of traffic on P Street was only faintly heard. In the tulip tree a mockingbird tried a few tentative cadenzas, then stopped, as if the hour were too late for practice. The song was followed by the tinkle of ice in the shaker.

"Your glass," Dexter said and filled it as Jacques held it out. "I don't know how I would have stood it here this summer without this garden."

"Romantic spot, I must say." Jacques was about to pursue the subject of Dexter's love life when he saw that Jenny had emerged from the house and was setting the glass table at the side of the terrace.

"So we can eat here, Jenny. That's fine!" Dexter said.

"Yes, sir, in ten minutes that soufflé'll be raidy," Jenny said.

Dexter turned again to Jacques, still holding the shaker in one hand and his glass in the other. "What news have you of Bobby?"

"Very good. He finished his basic training up at the top of his class. Starts advance training next week. He seems to be a natural-born flyer."

"Is he going for fighters?"

"No, he wants to fly a B-17. I'm glad in a way. I like to think of him having a copilot and a crew around him. Those fighter boys, alone in their cockpits, are at the mercy of everything— enemy, weather, and mechanical failure."

"He's a good lad."

"Yes, he's all right—tough like his grandfather."

"And Evangeline?"

"She starts at Bryn Mawr this month."

"Pretty kid."

"A handful."

"I'll bet. Don't let her get married until this is over."

"She doesn't want to, thank God. Neither Doris nor I could stop her if she did."

"Your glass?"

"No, I've had enough. Tell me, Dexter, what is this all about? Why did you want me to come down here to talk to you?"

"You've guessed, haven't you?"

"This thing you are in? What is it, O.S.S.?"

Dexter nodded his head toward Jenny. "We'll talk about it later, over a highball."

"Doris didn't want me to come. She smelled a rat."

Dexter chuckled. "You can tell her for me that there are no more rats in Georgetown. It is strictly a high-class community nowadays with modern plumbing and Ph.D.'s."

Throughout dinner the talk was perfunctory, even slightly strained, with Jacques impatient to learn why Dexter Miller had urged him to come to Washington and Dexter seeking to avoid the subject until Jenny had left them alone. They spoke of the war mostly, for that was the dominant cloud which shaded everything. Dexter inserted a few items of gossip, chiefly about his Georgetown neighbors, many of whom were old friends who like himself had responded to the call of duty, some to don uniforms over their middle-aged figures and sit in the Pentagon or the Navy Building, others in mufti, scuttling about the innumerable, newly created alphabetical agencies engaged in the various non-military aspects of all-out war.

Night had fallen, enclosing the circle of light made by the candles in hurricane glasses on the table, when Jenny took away the coffee cups and said good night. Dexter Miller waited until he heard the door in the living room close before he burst out laughing.

"Good old Jacques!" he said, slapping the table. "Fit to be tied! I think if Jenny had stayed a minute longer you would have burst an artery with curiosity."

"Well, Dexter, what is it all about?" Jacques said, not seeing the humor of the situation.

The smile gradually left Dexter's face, followed by a frown of earnestness. "I wanted to know if you would consider joining us at O.S.S.," he said.

"In what capacity? To do what? What is it all about?"

"You know what the Office of Strategic Services is, don't you?"

"Only vaguely."

"Well, let me state it briefly this way. In the past military intelligence has been run by the Armed Services; the Navy had its own, so did the Army and the Army Air Corps, and on top of that the State Department operated a separate branch for political intelligence. There was supposed to be an interchange of information among them all, but it never worked satisfactorily. Each service was jealous of the other and either didn't tell the full story of what it had or discounted what it got from the others.

A real shambles. So General Donovan—you know, Bill Donovan, the New York lawyer—goes to the President and sells him the idea of a separate agency to handle the entire intelligence problem, that is, everything but immediate tactical intelligence in the field. F.D.R. bought the idea and Donovan was supplied with the funds to set it up. Furthermore, the services were ordered to cooperate. They did it by assigning officers to duty with O.S.S. In this way the President and the Joint Chiefs of Staff get a unified intelligence report on enemy activity every day. It makes sense, doesn't it?"

"The way you tell it, it does. What do you do in this organization, or can't you tell me?"

"I'm in the administrative end of it and one of my jobs is to recruit the kind of men we need."

"So the telephone call and the offer of a bed and a good dinner was recruiting."

"Yes, Jacques. You're just the man we want."

"Very flattering, Dexter, but it depends on what you want me for."

"Before we go into that, just tell me this—if you felt the work was the kind you could do, would you join up?"

"That's a difficult question to answer."

"You're a citizen, Jacques, with a boy in the Air Corps. This is a life-and-death war. Each of us has a responsibility."

"Yes, I'm aware of that, Dexter. I want to do my bit, but I don't want to dash into something for the glory of it. I want to know I can do a job that is really useful, not just shuffling papers so that I can tell my grandchildren I was in it. When you get to be my age, which is a couple of years more than yours, you try to face things sensibly."

"That's why I put the question that way. I said, would you join if the work was what you felt you could do well?"

"And I answered it. If I was offered a post wherein I could be of real service, I would not hesitate."

"Are you talking about rank and title?"

"No, damn it, I'm talking about how I can serve—really serve."

Dexter Miller stood up. "Okay, Jacques, that's all I wanted to know. I'm going to call a chap who lives around the corner and ask him to drop in here for a few minutes. He can tell you about the particular job we have in mind for you better than I can. It's in his division."

"How do you know he's at home?"

"He's waiting for me to call."

Jacques laughed. "It looks as if I've been framed."

"Help yourself to brandy. I'll be back in a second."

Jacques poured some more brandy in his *ballon* and held it in both hands, rotating it slowly. He was more pleased and excited than he had let on to Dexter Miller. Ever since that day in December of the year before when he had heard the news of Pearl Harbor he had held a strong urge to offer his services to his new country, but the fear of rejection because he was only a naturalized citizen, born and brought up in German-speaking Switzerland, had prevented him from making any overture. He had not even mentioned his desire to Doris. It was something that had burned inside him, becoming more painful and urgent as Bobby progressed in his training. And now the weight had lifted, leaving him lightheaded with zeal. He was being asked, being sought after, being cajoled. It was more than he had hoped for.

Dexter returned to the terrace and picked up his glass and the brandy bottle. "Let us move into the living room," he announced.

Jacques followed him. "Who is this man who is coming to sell me a bill of goods?" he asked.

"Commander Stevens. Jim Stevens, a Naval Reserve officer. Very able chap."

"Jim Stevens? Not the Jim Stevens from Philadelphia!"

"Yes, a partner of Smith, Penfield and Stevens. Do you know him?"

"Very well. We do business with them."

"Good! That makes the whole thing easier."

"Does he know that I'm here?"

"No, I didn't tell him the name—just said I had the man he was looking for."

"You should have tipped him off, Dexter. If I'm not the man he wants, it's going to be damned embarrassing for him."

"Don't worry about that."

When the front doorbell rang, Dexter jumped to his feet to answer it for the maids had gone home. Jacques could hear the familiar authoritative voice of Stevens in the hall. Then he appeared at the door, resplendent in white uniform, a big powerful man with close-cropped sandy hair and a ruddy face. He strode in, then stopped suddenly when he saw Jacques, hesitating amazed before he burst into a loud booming laugh.

"My God, Miller, why didn't you tell me it was Jacques Eggli?" he roared.

"I told him he should have," Jacques said. "Jim, you look good in that uniform—like an old sea dog."

"What a surprise!" Stevens said. "I can't get over it. Tell me, why did I have to get Miller to find you when I could have done it myself by lifting the telephone off the hook? It just goes to show how dumb I can be. Wonderful, wonderful! Just the man we're looking for!"

They sat down in three deep chairs around the fireplace. A glow of purpose and hope and dedication spread over them, emanating from Stevens, sparked by his oriented vitality. He had taken command of them, and they were willing and ready to submit to his orders.

"Jim, let me start this off by saying that Jacques is willing to join up provided the job is one in which he believes he can be of real service," Dexter said. "I told him that you could explain better than I just what the job was."

Jim Stevens leaned back in his chair and gazed at the ceiling for a time before he spoke. "Jacques, this puts me in a difficult spot," he said finally, speaking slowly, thoughtfully. "The very nature of the job I have in mind for you is such that I cannot disclose it without knowing in advance if you will take the oath with no mental reservations. All I can say is that it is of the utmost importance, and that it requires the services of a man of the world—someone who can move in cultivated circles without arousing suspicion, someone who speaks French and German fluently. I can say this at least. The assignment will be overseas and will involve a certain period of preparation and indoctrination."

Immediately Jacques's mind formed a picture of himself being dropped in a parachute into Germany or occupied France where he would play the role of a rich dilettante collaborationist. The idea of physical danger, of reliance on his own skill and cleverness to save his skin and aid his country appealed to him, made his heart beat faster as it used to in his younger days when in an Alpine hut he thought of the final ascent of the peak at dawn.

"Jim," he said, "you know me, know my antecedents and background, therefore you must be the best judge of my fitness for the job you have in mind. If you say that it is important, that it will involve a real and definite service, I'll take your word for it and sign up. But I think you ought to know that I am forty-eight, and outside of a little golf and some very unenergetic bird-shooting I have taken no strenuous exercise in ten years."

"Anything wrong with you, Jacques?" Dexter asked. "Ticker, or ulcers?"

"I'm as sound as a dollar," Jacques answered confidently. "Only a little flabby."

"Aren't we all?" Jim Stevens said. "If I could pass the physical, I guess you can."

"Okay, what is it, Jim?" Jacques asked.

"Your father, the grand old man, is still living, isn't he?" the commander asked, ignoring the question.

"Very much so," Jacques replied with a sinking heart, fearful that the family, the bank, the German accounts would be the stumbling block. "He will be eighty-one in November, but he is still as active as ever."

"Wonderful man," Stevens said pensively. "I met him in Paris in 1936. You remember, you gave me a letter to him."

"Yes, I remember. That was during the São Paulo traction deal."

Stevens chuckled. "He advised me to lay off. How right he was! Tell me, how does he feel about this show?"

Jacques frowned, wondering if Stevens was using his position to get banking information. "What do you mean?" he asked.

"Quite frankly, Jacques, I mean are his sympathies with the Nazis?"

"Good God, no!" Jacques exploded. "He hates their guts."

"Sorry, Jacques, I'm not trying to be rude," Stevens said. "It's just that we have to be sure of our ground. You have a brother, haven't you?"

"Yes. Walter. He's two years older than I am."

"In the bank?"

"Yes, a partner, next in seniority to Father."

"Does he hold with your father about the Axis?"

"Entirely."

"The bank's position, then, is pro-Ally?"

"The bank's position is strictly neutral. You asked me about my family's sentiments, not about the bank. The bank, like any good bank, has no sentiment."

"Stout fellow!" Stevens said with a laugh. "In the future I'll listen to you and your old man when I want investment advice."

"I've told you that for years," Jacques said.

"I've never lost any money following him," Dexter said to the commander.

Stevens leaned back and studied the ceiling again. "Jacques, do you know a chap named Werner von Orb?" he asked finally.

"Never heard of him. Who is he?" Jacques answered.

"Never mind," Stevens said. "One more—does the name Antonio Venturi mean anything to you?"

"Do you mean the fellow from Lugano? The artist?"

"He lives in Lugano all right. I didn't know he was an artist. Do you know him?"

"Yes, I know him. He's one of those gadflies you run into at resorts."

"You mean he's one of those?"

Jacques laughed, thinking of Hélène. "His reputation is strictly heterosexual. The gossips have it that he has had more ladies than any man since Casanova."

"Nice work if you can get it," Dexter remarked.

"Why do you ask me about Tony Venturi?" Jacques asked.

"Because he is a friend of Werner von Orb," Stevens answered.

"I gather that von Orb must be a Nazi. Is that it?" Jacques said.

"You're catching on quickly, Jacques," Stevens said with a smile. "So quickly in fact that you have probably already surmised the job we want you for is in Switzerland."

"In Switzerland!" Jacques exclaimed, thrown completely off balance. "But my dear man, everyone knows me there!"

"Exactly," Stevens said calmly. "That's why we want you there, because your presence will be accepted as entirely natural and proper."

"Not to my father," Jacques stated.

"We are going to help you with that problem," Jim Stevens said. "We'll fix you up with a story that will even fool him."

"It will have to be good."

"Granted. Arranging foolproof cover stories is our business. I wouldn't worry about that if I were you."

Jacques stood up. "Where's your scotch, Dexter? I need a drink."

"Here. Right over here," Dexter said, jumping up and going over to a chest of drawers. "How do you want it, with water or soda?"

"Don't you bother," Jacques replied. "I'll mix it myself."

"How about you, Jim?" Dexter asked.

"A light one," the commander replied. "Then I must run along. I have a tough day ahead of me."

When they were seated again with their drinks, Dexter turned to Stevens. "If it's all right with you, Jim, I'll bring Jacques down to the shop with me in the morning to meet the boss and General Magruder."

"You'll process him at the same time?" Stevens asked.

"That's up to Jacques," Dexter said. "Can you stay over another day? It will take that long."

"I suppose I might as well," Jacques said resignedly. "I'll call Doris in the morning and tell her I won't be back until Thursday." He took a deep drink of his highball, then drew in his breath. "I have the impression you fellows have put one over on me."

"What do you mean?" Dexter asked.

"Well, Switzerland was the last place on earth I thought you had in mind for me," Jacques answered. "I've given you my word and I'm going through with it. Don't worry about that. But if I had known, I doubt if I would have joined up."

"I thought you might feel that way about it," Stevens said.

"It would have suited me a lot better if you had said you were going to parachute me into Germany," Jacques said.

"We have youngsters for that job," Dexter said.

"You are going to a spot where you can do infinitely more for us," said Stevens. "Switzerland is the key point, the listening post where you learn the important trends, not just the order of battle. We need men there with brains and capacity. You said you wanted to be of real use, Jacques. Well, you've got the one job in the world where you can be."

"I was thinking of the family," Jacques muttered.

"I know, you're afraid they will suspect," Stevens said. "I told you we'll fix that."

"Oh, I don't doubt for a minute that they can be thrown off the scent. That's not the point. I've never deceived them, and I don't like starting now."

Commander Stevens sat up straight in his chair and leaned toward Jacques with a stern expression. "Look, Jacques, would you lie to your wife if you knew that lie would help us to win the war?"

"Obviously I would," Jacques replied.

"Well, that is just what you are going to have to do, lie to her and your kids and your friends and your family in Zürich. You can put the lie down to sacred, patriotic duty, and if that doesn't salve your conscience, nothing will."

"Jim's right, Jacques," Dexter said. "You'll see it that way when you have a chance to think it over."

"I know, I know," Jacques said wearily. "It's the shock. I've got to get used to the idea. By the way, what will I tell Doris tomorrow?"

"Let's see," Jim Stevens said, studying his glass. "You might tell her that you are having talks with B.E.W. Tell her you are listening to their offers, but making no commitments."

"What is B.E.W.?" Jacques asked.

"The Board of Economic Warfare," Dexter said. "They send people abroad to do pre-emptive buying of strategic materials."

"Such as watch movements and industrial diamonds," Stevens added.

"Will that be my cover, as you call it?" Jacques asked.

"It might well be. I'll have to think it over," the commander said, then drained his glass and stood up. "Jacques, I put this down as a good evening's work—thanks to Dexter Miller. We're delighted to have you aboard. You are going to do a grand job, I know that."

Up in his chintz-draped bedroom that looked out on P Street, Jacques sat on the edge of the bed thinking. They were so sure, Jim and Dexter, that he was the right man to do spying in Switzerland. They were so confident that they could invest him with a story which his father would swallow without suspicion. They did not know—how could they?—that his children were translucent to the old man, that they were incapable of fooling him with any story. Well, he had cast the die. There was nothing to do but make the best of it, do it with all his heart and soul for his country, for Doris, for Bobby and Evangeline. He would lie to them all, as Jim Stevens had said, lie with a straight face, lie till it hurt. Yes, lie to Grosspapa even when the old man laughed and told him off, as surely he would. That would be the hardest part of the job, but he would go through with it.

CHAPTER XI

THOSE men and their secrets, phah!" Tante Vicki said as the maid took her coat and umbrella. "They behave like little children. As if we could not keep our mouths shut! Besides, who is interested in what they do at the bank? Money, money, that is all they talk about! Shylocks, all three, gloating over their pound of flesh. Is Lucy here yet?"

"Not yet," Hélène said as she followed her aunt-in-law into the drawing room. "She will be here by twelve-thirty. You know Lucy, always fifteen minutes late."

The three women were lunching at Hélène Eggli's because old Robert Eggli had summoned Walter and Hans Waldmann to lunch with him at the Sudstrasse. It was a dull November day, almost a year since Walter's accident. Because it was a business meeting, Robert had ordered Hélène to invite his sister. The idea of including Lucy had been Hélène's inspired means of avoiding the intimate, searching questions about her personal life which Tante Vicki would surely pose if they were alone. Now of course her scheme had been partially defeated by the early arrival of the old lady (the hall clock showed ten minutes past twelve) and the inevitable lateness of Lucy. Her only hope was to launch immediately on a topic which could be counted on to absorb twenty minutes.

"What do you think of the exciting news?" she asked Tante Vicki who was progressing slowly around the room, taking a quick mental inventory of each object with her darting birdlike eyes.

"What news? Are you going to have another baby?" the old lady asked without stopping her inspection.

"Of course not," Hélène answered impatiently. "I mean the war news—about the Americans landing in Morocco."

"Oh, that. It surprised you no doubt. What is this? You never had this here before." Tante Vicki picked up a small easel frame which held a brilliantly illuminated page from a thirteenth-century manuscript.

"I found it in Lugano when I was there in October," Hélène answered.

"Found it? Hah! That's good. I can imagine where."

Hélène blushed. It had been a present from Tony, one of the few items remaining from his father's collection which had not been sold at auction after his death. The fact that it was the only present he had ever given her lent it significance, for his habit was to receive, not give. She realized that it had been a gesture of appreciation for the money he had received—thanks to her—from his German friend.

"That sly fox Darlan has capitulated," she said, hoping to get the talk away from the illuminated page. "But if I were an American, I wouldn't trust him. He is a Vichy man through and through."

"Old Venturi's shop used to be filled with things like that," the old lady said, still holding the frame and looking at the page with her head cocked to one side. "Pretty. Prettier than the daubs that shocking son of his paints. How much did you give him for it?"

"Really, Tante Vicki, can't we discuss something more important?" Hélène said, exasperated.

"Of course we could talk of something else," the old lady said, putting the frame back on the table and continuing her tour of the room. "But it happens that I consider the subject of young Venturi very important. I've been meaning to speak to you about him for some time. A lot of people are talking about you and him. It has become an open scandal, and I don't think it fair to Walter or my brother."

Hélène was trembling with anger. This snooping old aunt of

her husband's was a trouble-maker, a gossiping old harridan who had nothing to occupy her mind but the personal affairs of others. She would have liked to blaze out at her, tell her once and for all that what she did and whom she saw was her own business and no one else's. But she could not. The instinct of family, of tradition, of acceptance of the right of age to criticize was too firmly imbedded in her. "I cannot prevent people from making up stories to suit their dirty minds," was all she could say.

"If you didn't see so much of Venturi, they wouldn't talk," the old lady said tartly.

"I hardly ever see him. Only once a year when I go to Lugano."

"Then you are with him all the time."

"So is everyone else. That's all he does. That's his silly life, chasing about with the crowd that goes down there. Don't think for a moment that I'm the only woman he sees."

"Hah! Don't I know it! He's after them all—a regular gigolo. But you have Walter and your children to think of."

"Has Walter complained to you about my friendship with Tony?"

"Walter? Gracious God, no!" Tante Vicki uttered a dry harsh chuckle, like pebbles rattling in a tin. "Walter would be the last to mention it. He has too much silly pride. He wants the world to think him irresistible to ladies. Poor Walter, what a fool he is!"

Hélène lit a cigarette and sat down, trying to calm her nerves. "You have no right to say that, Tante Vicki. Walter is not a fool. He is a serious, conscientious man."

"Bah! He's my nephew and I say he's a fool. It's his father's fault. He bullies him too much. He has made him afraid of his own shadow."

A maid entered the room with a tray on which were three glasses, a decanter of sherry and a plate of nuts. She put it on the table near Hélène.

"Will you have some sherry?" Hélène asked.

"You know perfectly well, my dear, that I never drink before meals," Tante Vicki answered crisply, sitting down on a couch, having completed her tour.

Hélène poured herself a glass of sherry and took a sip of it. "Let me say this, Tante Vicki, and I hope it will ease your mind. I am not in love with Tony Venturi, nor have I ever been. As far as I am concerned, he is nothing more than an agreeable dancing partner during a holiday."

"He is the kind of snake who can be dangerous."

"In what way?"

"You know, I suppose, that he is crossing the border all the time?"

Hélène shrugged her shoulders. "What of it? He has a great many friends in Como and Milan."

"And in Rome," Tante Vicki stated, bobbing her head emphatically so that the wattle of skin which hung over the band of grey ribbon worn tightly around her scrawny neck waved back and forth. "He's a pet of that Fascist crowd, those awful Ciano people."

"They amuse him, I suppose."

"And they use him. I have no doubt of that. He keeps his eyes open for them."

Hélène said nothing, remembering the time when Tony had asked her for Robert Eggli's views of the war so that he could sell the information to the German poet. She realized that the old lady's surmise might well be correct. There was no sense in trying to defend him.

"That is why I say it is not fair to Walter and Robert that you get your name linked with his," Tante Vicki went on. "What is it that people will say? Naturally, that he is getting bank secrets from you which he can pass on to Ciano."

"That's silly. I don't know any bank secrets."

"That may be, but other people don't know it. They think that, Walter being married to you, it is only natural he tells you in the confidence of the bedroom what position the bank is taking."

The front doorbell rang, followed by the steps of the maid in the front hall.

"That's Lucy," Hélène said with a sigh of relief. She got up and went to the door.

Lucy rushed in, pink in the face. "Mercy, am I late?" she gasped.

"Yes, by fifteen minutes," Tante Vicki announced.

Hélène gave her a peck on the cheek. "You forgot to take off your rubbers."

"*Ach,* so I did!" Lucy exclaimed. "Here, Emma, take these." She steadied herself with one hand on the back of a chair while she ripped off her rubbers.

"And your hat," Hélène added.

"*Gott in Himmel,* I'm losing my mind," Lucy said and took off her hat, handing it to the maid who walked out with the three objects. "So!" Fluffing out her hair, she walked over to her aunt and leaned over to kiss her cheek. "How are you, Tante Vicki?"

"Hungry," her aunt replied. "Where have you been, watching the gulls on the lake?"

"Hans insisted on bringing me, and lunch at Grosspapa's is only at twelve-thirty," Lucy said, smiling brightly.

Hélène was about to pour a glass of sherry for her sister-in-law when the maid entered and announced that luncheon was served.

Tante Vicki bounced to her feet as if released by a spring. "Thanks to God!" she exclaimed, hurrying out the door.

"That is all she has to think about," Lucy whispered to Hélène.

Hélène gave a short bitter laugh. "Don't you believe it. For the past twenty minutes she has been dissecting my private life."

"Poor Hélène, I'm sorry," Lucy said. "It's my fault for being late."

The dining room, like the rest of the big house, was correct in every detail, yet impersonal and undistinguished. It was the product of a perceptive interior decorator who had supplied Walter and Hélène with the surroundings he considered appropriate for a ménage of substance, after discovering that the lady of the house had no decorative convictions of her own. Like many women who have an innate sense of costume, Hélène had no interest or taste in furnishings. She was content to hire the taste of experts. The result was a photogenic interior of proper period pieces, properly arranged and upholstered, which would have received top marks from an editor of a household magazine. And in that sense the house suited her.

The table too was unassailable, displaying a rich and highly polished collection of silver pieces surrounding a bowl of tawny chrysanthemums. Hélène sat at the head of the table, facing the pantry door, with Tante Vicki on her right and Lucy on her left. She had ordered the old lady's favorite meal—*kaespastetli*, followed by creamed chicken with rice and an *apfel strudel* for dessert. The white wine was from Neuchâtel, properly iced.

"I'll say one thing for you, Hélène, you have a good cook," Tante Vicki said, quickly devouring her first cheese tart.

"A kind word from you means a great deal, Tante Vicki," Hélène said pointedly.

"Have you heard about Jacques?" Lucy said, sensing danger.

"What has he done now?" the old lady asked.

"He has taken a job with the Government," Lucy replied.

"With Bruggmann in Washington?" Tante Vicki asked.

"No, no, with the American Government," Lucy explained.

"What sort of a job?" Hélène asked.

"Something economic. Ask Walter, he can tell you," Lucy said.

"But in New York," Tante Vicki insisted.

"No, in Washington. He is there all week and only comes home for the week ends," Lucy said.

"That's hard on Doris," Hélène remarked, "now that young Bobby is with the Air Force and Evangeline away at college."

"I have no doubt that she can find amusement," Tante Vicki said cynically. "Probably glad to get rid of him. I hear that the way young married women carry on in New York is a caution. No morals whatever. It's the cocktails. They pour pure alcohol into an empty stomach and before they know it they're in bed."

"With a headache," Hélène said.

"I don't think Doris is that kind at all," Lucy stated decidedly.

"Neither do I," Hélène agreed.

"She is probably doing some kind of war work herself," Lucy added to the defense.

"Jacques is a fool," the old lady announced, bound to find fault with the whole affair. "He should be watching his father's money, not strutting about in Washington with a fancy title just as if he were a real American. That's the trouble with Jacques. He was like that ever since he was a little boy. Always trying to be like someone else. No character of his own. Remember when he was here last, those bow ties and the laugh and those silly jokes? Wanted everyone to think he was an American. Why, he even talked Zürichdeutsch with an accent."

"I wonder what Grosspapa will say about this," Hélène said.

"It seems he told Hans that he thought Jacques had been too hasty," Lucy said.

"Gotteswillen! Your father is right," Tante Vicki said. "Of course he was too hasty. That is just what I have been saying."

"He thinks that if Jacques had used a little influence in the right direction, he might have been given a better position— Under Secretary or something," Lucy went on, ignoring her aunt.

"Robert will cable to Roosevelt, you watch," the old lady said.

"Has he no title, then?" Hélène asked Lucy.

"Apparently not," Lucy replied. "Just a sort of economic adviser."

"Better that way," Tante Vicki announced. "Give him an important title and it would go right to his head like a cocktail. It would make him sillier than ever. He might even lose the war for them."

"I suppose that was out of the question at his age," Hélène said. "One must remember that he did his military service here."

"Where did you get this chicken?" Tante Vicki asked Hélène.

"At Bianchi's, I imagine," Hélène answered.

"It must have cost a fortune," the old lady commented. "I

refuse to buy it at these prices. Robert complains, but I tell him that I'm not going to make a pauper out of him just to satisfy his appetite."

"Oh, Tante Vicki!" Lucy exclaimed. "I think that is mean of you. Poor Papa, he is going on eighty-one and he has the right to be spoiled a bit."

"Ach, he never spoiled you or your brothers, or me for that matter," Tante Vicki said. "To be sure, he spoiled Matti and I suppose he spoils that woman in Geneva, but on the whole he likes people who speak their minds and watch the bills."

"Oh, that reminds me," Lucy said suddenly, putting down her knife and fork and looking up brightly. "Hans and I met her last week in Geneva."

"Met who?" the old lady asked.

"The woman you just spoke of, the Baroness de Marty," Lucy answered.

"Aha! So! Hansli has been doing some more of his spying, eh?" Tante Vicki said, her wattle shaking with excitement. "How did it happen? Did you call on her?"

"It was at the Tessiers'," Lucy explained. "We were asked for tea. I'm sure Madeleine did it purposely. She could not wait to drag us across the room to present us. I must have blushed deep red with everybody watching the performance."

"I hope she had the decency to blush too," Tante Vicki said.

"Indeed she did not," Lucy said. "She was as composed and gracious as a queen."

"Queen, bah! Queen of cocottes!" Tante Vicki exploded.

"Did you have an opportunity to talk with her?" Hélène asked.

"Naturally. I wasn't going to let a chance like that slip by," Lucy said. "I pulled a chair up and sat right down beside her. Hans was furious with me. He went stalking off to talk to old Emil Schwarz."

"How was she dressed? Loaded with jewels, I suppose," Tante Vicki asked.

"Not at all," Lucy replied. "That is what surprised me. She

had on a very chic tailleur, grey, like the one O'Rossen made for you, Hélène. You know, with a long jacket trimmed with matching braid. And her blouse was a dream, dove-grey marocain, with a collar that tied into a bow at the side of her neck. She wears her hair short, not too short, with the front waved off her forehead so that it curled over the brim of her small grey felt hat. I tell you, with those large black eyes of hers and her black hair with just a few streaks of grey in it, she is a striking woman."

"How old?" Hélène asked.

"One can't judge," Lucy said. "She is one of those women on whom age doesn't show. She might be fifty, but she does not look more than forty. Beautiful skin, smooth and white as ivory."

"What about the jewels?" the old lady asked impatiently.

"A short rope of pearls, tight around her neck so that they were almost entirely hidden by the collar of her blouse," Lucy answered. "Oh, yes, and a darling little diamond clip on her hat."

"On her hat?" Tante Vicki asked, incredulous.

"That's the very latest thing," Hélène explained. "I'm going to have that old brooch made over into a clip that I can wear on my hat."

"No lady wears jewels on her hat," Tante Vicki announced with finality. "What did you talk about? Not Robert, I hope."

"Really, Tante Vicki, what do you take me for?" Lucy said in a shocked voice. "We talked about the war. She seemed very sad about France. I gather she has no use for the Vichy regime. Her French is beautiful to hear—such a real Parisian accent—and her voice is very low and musical."

"You liked her then," Hélène said.

"I thought her absolutely charming," Lucy replied emphatically.

"Lucy, my child, you amaze me," the old lady said. "How can you speak of being charmed by a designing cocotte who will end by getting all your inheritance? You have fallen into her trap, just as your father has. That is exactly what she wanted, to get you on her side so that when Robert dies she will have a fifth column within the ranks of the family. I have no doubt that she engineered the whole thing, made Madeleine Tessier invite you to her house. Madeleine is such a fool that she would never realize that she was being used. *Ach*, what is the world coming to when a young lady has tea with her father's mistress!"

"The world understands that a widower has the right to fall in love," Hélène said.

"Love? You call that love?" Tante Vicki exclaimed, outraged. "Hah! Rutting around like an old billygoat is not love. When a man loves, he marries."

"Maybe she refuses to marry him," Lucy said. "I'm sure I would if I were in her shoes. Can you imagine what an awful life she would lead here in Zürich with everyone out to cut her throat?"

"If Robert ever brought her to the Sudstrasse, I would move out at once," Tante Vicki announced.

"I should hope so—for her sake," Lucy said.

"Well, of all things! Is that the kind of thanks I get for devoting my life to the care of your father?" Tante Vicki exclaimed indignantly.

"I'm sorry, Tante Vicki, but you brought it on yourself," Lucy said stubbornly. "You insist on insulting a lady you have never met. Well, I have met her, and I know now that she is not at all what you imagine her to be—not at all. She is no more a cocotte than Hélène is."

"*Ach!* That's good!" the old lady exclaimed with her rattling caustic laugh. "Next time you might find a better comparison."

"Now, Tante Vicki, I won't have you saying such things in my house," Hélène stated, crimson with rage.

"Don't be so touchy," Tante Vicki said. "After all, being a cocotte has become fashionable, like wearing diamonds in your hat. My trouble is that I grew up in the wrong age. I never had the chance that you girls have had. Oh, I would have been a good cocotte, don't fret about that. I've had my chance, but fashion was against me."

Both Lucy and Hélène burst into uncontrolled laughter, releasing the tension, dissolving the bitterness.

"Oh, dear, it's like that story of Jacques'," Lucy said, wiping the tears from her eyes with her napkin. "Nice work if you can get it."

That set them off again. This time even Tante Vicki, succumbing to the infection, giggled so hard that her wattle trembled like an aspen in the wind.

"Oh, you naughty girls, you make me misbehave!" the old lady said when the laughter had subsided. "Hélène, tell your Emma to bring back that apfel strudel. I can eat another bit of it. The pastry is perfect, just the way it used to be at Sacher's in Vienna."

Hélène tinkled a little silver bell. "I didn't know that you had ever been to Vienna," she said to her aunt-in-law.

"*Ach, Gott,* that was over fifty years ago when Walter's grandfather and grandmother took us on a trip to Austria," Tante Vicki said wistfully. "Robert and I were just at the age to enjoy all the silly goings-on. We even went to a ball at Schönbrunn and saw the Emperor. He was not so much to look at. But the young officers of the guard—mercy me, but they were handsome! *Ach,* how they could waltz in those beautiful uniforms! You won't believe me, I know, but I was a real beauty at twenty-three and I could dance all night without getting tired."

"Is that where you got the story you used to tell me when I was a child? The one about the handsome baron who drove the young lady home at dawn and gave her a pearl as a pledge?" Lucy asked.

The old lady picked at her *strudel,* tears forming in the corners of her eyes. "You remember that, eh?" she muttered.

"It made a deep impression on me. It was so romantic," Lucy said. "She never saw him again after that night, as I recall the story."

"Never," Tante Vicki said stiffly, then cleared her throat. "He was an aide to the Archduke Rudolf and had to flee the country." She put down her fork and fingered the large pear-shaped pearl which hung from her neck on a small platinum chain. "It was on the following night that the tragedy occurred at Mayerling."

"Why, my dear Tante Vicki, I never realized!" Lucy exclaimed.

"Well, now you know," the old lady said. "I was the girl and this is the pearl."

"And you never heard from him?" Hélène asked.

"Oh, yes, I received two long letters from Peru before he was killed in an accident there," Tante Vicki answered. "After I'm dead maybe you can write a story about us, Lucy. I'm leaving the two letters to you, and also the one from the Austrian minister at Lima telling about his death and his last words."

"What were they? Do you mind telling us?" Hélène asked.

Tante Vicki sniffed and cleared her throat. "It seems he said, 'Tell Victoria that I will be waiting for her,'" she whispered in a cracked voice, then dabbed her eyes with her napkin.

Hélène reached over and patted the old lady's withered, clawlike hand. There was nothing she could say.

CHAPTER XII

THE old man looked at his wrist watch as Walter and Hans Waldmann entered the library together. "Five minutes late," he said.

"I had to drop Lucy at Hélène's," Waldmann explained apologetically.

"So Lucy is lunching there too," Robert Eggli said. "I have no doubt that those two young ladies will supply Vicki with a fresh crop of gossip." He snorted. "Perhaps it is just as well. What she has is becoming very stale."

Hans would have liked to say that Lucy would undoubtedly tell her aunt about meeting the Baroness de Marty in Geneva. It was one of those flashes of perversity which came to him occasionally but which he was able to suppress.

"It is more likely that Tante Vicki will be doing the talking," Walter said boldly. "Hélène is not what one would call a gossip."

The old man eyed his son appraisingly, wondering if he was aware of his wife's interest in Tony Venturi. He, Robert, did not approve of that liaison, not because it was adulterous (he understood that a girl as attractive as Hélène could never be satisfied with the love-making of his wooden, hesitant son) but because he suspected the lover of being involved in nefarious schemes. He had heard rumors which led him to believe that young Venturi was peddling information for cash. It was fortunate, he said to himself, that Hélène, as Walter had said, was not a gossip. Still, one never knew what a clever rascal might be able to squeeze out of a woman who was attracted to him. Not that Hélène would have any secrets of value, but she was smart enough to learn from her dull husband the general trend of the bank's thinking.

"We shall dispense with sherry and go right in to lunch," he said, not wishing to bring up the question of his daughter-in-law at this moment.

The old man led the way into the dining room and when they were seated—Walter on his right and Hans at his left—he announced that the conversation was to be in English for obvious reasons. He turned to Waldmann. "Now, Hans, you may tell us your news."

Hans cleared his throat, wiped his mouth and said, "You will please to pardon my English. It is not being as fluent as yours, Grosspapa. I am not having as much opportunity to practice, since wartimes keep me within the boundaries of Switzerland."

"I did not ask you to make a speech," Robert Eggli said impatiently. "Out with it! What did your friend from Berlin tell you?"

"That it is the deciding . . ."

"Decision," Walter prompted.

"Ach, yes, the decision of the Nazi Reich to occupy all of France, moving at twelve hours this night," Hans said. "The fact of American and English soldiers in Morocco and Algeria is presenting a threat to the Riviera. This is making a necessity for Germany to have defensive places on the coastline of the Mittelmeer from Italy until Spanie."

"Such a move was already foreseen by the Anglo-American high command," Robert Eggli said brusquely. "The point is, what do they intend doing with Pétain and his government at Vichy?"

"No change there," Hans replied. "The decision of the Fuehrer is that nothing shall be changèd at Vichy. The employment of General Pétain and his cabinet is important with the people of France and with the men in Africa who are in faith with Vichy."

The old man snorted. "Yes, like Darlan. They are finished— old Pétain and all of them. They will be kept alive like monkeys in a zoo, to be looked at and laughed at. What does he say about Spain?"

Hans bobbed his head to signify uncertainty. "Hitler is always having the hope to bring Franco to action."

"Il Duce has sent Franco some very strong messages about Morocco," Walter put in.

"Which have had no effect, except to make Franco talk bigger," Robert Eggli said. "You mark my words, he will not lift a finger to help the Axis unless he is attacked, and that is out of the question, even in Spanish Morocco. The Americans are not here to pick a fight with a bantam cock. What did he have to say about Rommel's position in Tunis and Libya?"

Hans scooped up the last spoonful of soup and wiped his mouth. "It is at the moment disfavorable, but not without hope. The matters of most worry are petrol and ammunition. If these can continue to be coming from Sicilia, it is the belief that Rommel can be reaching the Suez while he is holding his rear against the Americans."

The old man laughed. "The Anglo-Americans will kick his rear so hard that he will fall flat on his face."

"If Rommel is falling," Hans went on, "the Reich armies will be moving faster, with double strength, to the Caucasus and Baku. The problem is petrol. It is recognized that the last decision remains with the power which is having enough of it."

"It is now almost two months that the Germans have been halted at Stalingrad," Walter commented.

"Yes, Hans, it is winter in Russia," Robert Eggli said. "The German Army, with its camions and tanks and motorized artillery, cannot fight a war of motion in the snows of the Caucasus. They will learn the lesson that was taught to Napoleon—that a Russian winter can defeat any Western invader, no matter how strong. The problem of supplying an immense army across two thousand kilometers of snowbound roads is too much. It cannot be done. That crazy fool Hitler has *la folie de grandeur*, and it is at Stalingrad that he will fall, just as Napoleon fell at Moscow.

He does not have the mind to see that the pact of non-aggression made between Von Ribbentrop and Molotov was the ace in his hand of cards. With that ace he could have played for Egypt and Turkey and Arabia and had his petrol and been the dictator of the Western world. But no, he had to attack Russia because he hates Bolshevics. That is childish. It is the thinking of a fanatic, not of a good general. And the consequences may be very bad for everyone. For when the Bolshevics start to push him back, they will not stop. They will come into Europe and they will stay here. Ach, he should have left those Slavs and Asiatics alone!"

"Hitler is still filled with much hope," Hans said.

"Because he is a fool," the old man retorted. "Just the same, Hans, keep your line of communication open with your friend in Berlin. It is always useful to know the dimension of Nazi stupidity. And you, Walter, have you any news?"

"Some of the Geneva houses are continuing to make loans to certain French industries," Walter replied.

"Yes, yes, of course," Robert said. "Why not? Business is business. If the company has good orders and is making money, why should it not have a loan?"

"There is always the question of the value of the French franc," Walter said.

"They have an exchange guarantee from the German control in Paris," his father said. "For short-term commercial loans, that will be safe enough. But if my good friends in Geneva let any commitment in France run longer than six months, they are not as clever as I think them."

"The American invasion of North Africa has given them a great deal of optimism," Walter said.

"Optimism and money have never been friends," the old man stated. He waited until the two maids had passed the veal and noodles for the second time before going on. "Now I have something to tell you. It is about your brother Jacques. He has taken a position with the American Government in Washington."

"With the Board of Economic Warfare," Walter added.

"Don't interrupt me," his father scolded. "Let me finish what I have to say. That is what he writes, that he is with the Board of Economic Warfare which is concerned with buying up raw materials in many countries for the use of American industry and to prevent them from being bought by the agents of Germany. That is good. It is proper work for him to be doing. But I have certain intimations from sources in Washington that he has been seen with General Donovan."

"Who is General Donovan?" Hans asked.

Robert Eggli looked at his son-in-law in astonishment. "I am surprised that you should ask that," he said. "You are a lawyer. I thought that all lawyers knew of Bill Donovan."

"I have never heard of him," Hans admitted meekly.

"Isn't he the American who came to see you in 1939? The one who stopped at the Dolder?" Walter asked.

"In 1938, 1939, and in 1940—that was the last time," his father replied. "He has come to call on me for years. He is a very old friend. For an American he has a remarkably good ear for the harmonies of international politics. Unofficially he has been a sort of sub-rosa ambassador for President Roosevelt."

"Why is it strange, then, that Jacques should talk with him?" Walter asked.

"Because Roosevelt has recently made him the head of a new Bureau of Secret Service," his father answered. "The question that I ask myself is whether Jacques is also working for Bill Donovan."

"Why should he not?" Hans asked.

"No reason, no reason in the world," the old man replied. "It is only that I do not like it that my son does not tell me frankly what he is doing. He represents the bank in the United States. His first loyalty is to the bank—to me. It is as if Hans should be giving information to the Gestapo without my knowledge."

"That I would never be doing," Hans protested.

"And if you did, I would know about it," Robert Eggli said. "I am not accusing you, Hans, but a little warning does no harm. Be careful what you say when you talk to your Nazi friends. Remember that Eggli and Company can live and prosper without German accounts—particularly the individual accounts. Listen to them, but tell them nothing beyond what I have told you to tell them."

"Never, never!" Hans exclaimed.

"That is what I mean in connection with Jacques," the old man said. "If Donovan should ask him about affairs of the bank, he might out of some silly sense of duty tell things that are of no concern to Donovan or his government."

"Is he having the key to the numbers?" Hans asked in surprise.

"Don't be stupid. Of course he hasn't," Robert Eggli stated.

"Then what can he say?" Walter asked.

"Ach, you are both so dumb!" his father shouted. "He can tell where we are investing, can't he? He knows about the shift of funds from B.A. to Mexico, doesn't he? He has been handling the financing of watch movements and rapid-fire guns, hasn't he?"

"Only those to the United States," Walter said.

"And to Cuba and Panama. Where do you think those are going?" the old man asked.

Hans Waldmann shook his head reflectively. "I am seeing what your meaning is. It would not be a good affair, having Jacques speaking about the business of the bank to the American Gestapo."

"Very good," Robert Eggli said. "As long as that is clear you will both take note of my instructions. The New York accounts are to remain as they are, invested in accordance with the decisions of Spears, Wetherell. However, no instructions concerning accounts in other countries of the Western Hemisphere will be sent through Spears, Wetherell, nor are they to be informed of such instructions until the war is over. Is that clear?"

"How shall they be handled, then?" Walter asked.

"Don't be so impatient," his father snapped. "I was coming to that. I do not wish any shipments, except those directly to or from the United States, to be financed through New York. All bills involving any Latin American country will either be discounted here in francs, or by Huber, Barros and Company in *cruzeiros*."

"There are certain clients, particularly in Cuba and Mexico, who demand dollars," Walter said. "Only the other day, when Da Costa was here, he made a point of that."

"Da Costa will have to take *cruzeiros* on all shipments out of Cuba," the old man stated. "Only shipments from Europe will be financed in francs."

"He will not like it," Walter warned.

"He will have to like it, or go to some other bank," Robert Eggli stated firmly.

"What shall Huber, Barros be doing with the dollars in number *neun und* . . ." Hans started to ask.

"English, English!" the old man shouted.

"*Natürlich*, I am forgetting," Hans apologized. "It was of thirty-nine I was speaking. The dollars they are receiving from the selling of airline shares."

"You may instruct Huber, Barros to either hold the dollars or invest them in American shares in the Rio market," Robert Eggli said.

Hans Waldmann shook his head doubtfully. "*Ach*, but *neun und* . . . thirty-nine is ordering us that they are to be employed for the buying program," he protested.

"Thirty-nine can use *cruzeiros*, or Argentine *pesos*. They have plenty of them," Robert said.

"I am fearing they will be commanding us to use the dollars," Hans said, still shaking his head.

Old Robert Eggli, who was sipping the last of his wine, spluttered, slamming his wine glass down on the table and flushing with anger. "They can command your friend in Berlin and his agent von Orb, but they cannot command Robert Eggli," he shouted. He rose to his feet. "You have heard my orders. Come now, we shall have our coffee in the library."

Hans and Walter followed the old man out of the room and into the paneled library. Hans, his mind still on the problem of how to placate the powers in Berlin, stopped before the fireplace and looked up at the portrait of a Milanese lady by Ambrogio de Predis. "That is a picture which Goering would like to own," he said in Swiss German.

The old man wheeled about to face his son-in-law. "Goering?" he asked gruffly. "How does he know about my picture?"

"Word has come to me that he would appreciate it if you would allow him to buy it," Hans said. "Of course I told my friend that it was not for sale."

Robert Eggli smiled but his eyes were hard and cold. "The impudence of that fat pig knows no bounds," he said icily. "But he cannot treat me the way he treats Mussolini and Ciano. I know what he forced them to let him take last year—the Tintoretto 'Leda,' the Veronese 'Nymph and Satyr'—fat naked women. That is what he likes. And now, only two weeks ago, he goes back to Germany with that wonderful Rubens 'Judith and Holofernes.' Ciano's orders. They are packed and put on his train—no inspection, no tax. The Belle Arti are told to shut their mouths and look the other way. Hah! He can't do that here, not to me." His steely eyes bored into Hans. "You did not answer me. How did he know I had that Ambrogio?"

"That I was not told," Hans said, his face pale.

"You bought it from Corradi, didn't you?" Walter asked his father.

"Ah, yes, that is who told him," Eggli said, nodding. "Corradi of Florence, of course. It is from him that Goering is buying his pictures, with the help and advice of Hesse." He chuckled. "Prince Philip knows my picture also. He was here once about ten years ago. He looked at it and said, 'That is a Leonardo which I do not know,' and I told him that it was by a pupil of Da Vinci. He wished to know where I had bought it, but I did not tell him. He had no right to ask the question. Typical German arrogance. Now he knows. Corradi has surely told him. As a matter of fact, I did not buy it directly from Corradi. I had seen it in his villa, but it was old Venturi of Lugano who arranged the deal."

"Hitler too has taken his share of pictures from the Fascists," Hans said.

"Not alone pictures," the old man growled. "He has stolen the real prize—the Lanceolotti 'Discobolus'—and on top of that the Corsini Memling. Mark my words, he will get other treasures before he is through with Il Duce. He will rape the Uffizi, you wait and see."

A maid brought in the coffee, placing the tray on a table next to a row of decanters. She left the room and Walter went over to the table to pour the coffee. He brought a cup to his father, saying, "There is one for you there, Hans."

Hans stepped across the room to pick up his cup. "Will you have a cognac, Grosspapa?" he asked.

"In the middle of the day? Of course not. You know that," his father-in-law said gruffly as he walked over to the humidor and picked out two cigars, one of which he handed to Waldmann. "What do you know about this man, von Orb?" he asked his son-in-law.

"Nothing, nothing whatever," Hans replied.

"If you mean the poet who lives in Lausanne, I know him, Papa," Walter said.

"Where? How?" his father asked.

"I met him first in Lugano two years ago," Walter answered. "Again I ran into him in Geneva last week. A harmless little chap."

"You think so, eh? Well, you're wrong," the old man said, clipping the end of his cigar. "I have reason to believe that he is far from harmless. He is a Nazi to begin with, and he asks questions which have no bearing on poetry or the arts."

"You think he might be an agent?" Hans asked.

"I am convinced that he is," Robert Eggli stated.

"I shall inquire of my friend in Berlin," Hans said.

"*Gott in Himmel*! Don't do that, you dumbhead!" the old man exclaimed. "Do you think for an instant that they would tell you if he was? They would deny even knowing his name, but they would realize at once that we were suspicious of him. They think he has the perfect disguise—a silly effeminate who writes verses and has lived here for ten years prior to the war. I want him to stay in Switzerland. He can be useful to us."

"In what way? I don't understand," Hans said.

"Never mind. I may tell you when the time comes. In the meanwhile forget that you even know his name. Don't speak of him or think of him." Robert Eggli turned to his son. "He is an intimate of young Venturi, is he not?"

"I believe he is," Walter said hesitatingly.

"You know he is," his father snapped. "And if you don't know, Hélène does."

Walter flushed. "You are referring to that silly gossip?"

"I am stating a fact," his father announced. "Hélène is a friend of Venturi and Venturi is a friend of Graf von Orb. I am not censuring your wife. She can have what friends she chooses. That is her affair. But she should know—she should be told—that both of them are seeking information for the benefit of the Axis."

"What could Hélène tell Tony?" Walter asked. "She knows nothing. I never discuss the bank's affairs with her, and she never asks about them."

"It is not details of accounts or shipments that they want," the old man said. "They know all that. What they do not know is the attitude, the position we are taking with regard to the ultimate outcome. Oh, that is what they would like to find out! They would give a great deal to learn how our colleagues in New

York and B.A. and London are feeling about the situation. They gather up all those bits and pieces and put them together like a picture puzzle until they can see a definite design."

"You would prefer that I order Hélène to see no more of Tony?" Walter asked hopefully.

"On the contrary," his father replied, "I should prefer that she continued the friendship as if she were unaware of his activities."

"I am glad you realize, Papa, that this friendship is quite innocent—not at all what the gossips say it is," Walter said.

Robert Eggli shrugged his shoulders. "Hélène is no fool if that is what you mean. Just tell her what I said about Venturi. She probably knows it already, but it will do no harm to make her aware that I know."

"Yes, Papa, I shall do that at once," Walter said.

Hans Waldmann had been filled with embarrassment at having to listen to all this. It was the first time, to his knowledge, that the names of Tony Venturi and Hélène had been coupled in the presence of Walter. He had been afraid for a moment that he was going to be an unwilling witness to a scene of parental wrath and denunciation, and he had been greatly relieved when no such outburst had occurred. He wondered why it had not. It was unlike the old man not to upbraid his son for allowing his wife to be talked about. Maybe it had been his, Hans's, presence which had prevented it, but that too was unlikely. Old Robert had never been bothered by the presence of others when he had scolded his children. Hans had seen him do it many times in front of the whole clan. It occurred to him that it might be a sign of age, a mellowing at last, now that he had passed eighty. Either that or the old fox had some plan up his sleeve.

"So you and Lucy had a good time in Geneva," Robert Eggli said to Hans, changing the subject abruptly.

Hans blushed, thinking of the tea at Madeleine Tessier's and meeting the Baroness de Marty. "Ach, it was work we went there for, not a good time," Hans said, frowning.

"It was work, was it, going to tea at the Tessiers'?" the old man asked, smiling at his victim.

"I had an opportunity there to talk to Emil Schwarz about the shipments of movements and jewels," Hans replied.

"Business is best talked in an office," Robert Eggli said. "Von Orb was there, trying to listen to your conversation."

"Von Orb? I told you, I do not know this von Orb," Hans said stuffily.

"Perhaps Madeleine Tessier did not introduce you but he was there all right, standing only a meter from you when you were talking to Schwarz," his father-in-law said. "You see what I mean? One has to be careful in wartimes. One does not talk about shipments of watch movements at tea parties. That has always been your trouble, Hans. No light touch, no small talk. No wonder they call us bumblebees. Talk to the pretty women sometime, it will do you good."

Hans was on the point of asking whether it had been Lucy who had told her father about von Orb. Then he realized that it must have been the Baroness. Had he made a mistake, after all, in not talking to her? That, it appeared, was what the old man was driving at. "It is a question of language," he said, trying to excuse himself. "My French is not as fluent as yours or Lucy's."

"It is fluent enough to inquire about many things which are of no concern to the bank," the old man said pointedly.

"I have other clients," Hans protested huffily.

Walter could not help smiling. It was such a relief to have his father's rapier pricking someone else. He knew what the old man was getting at, as well as Hans. Somehow he had learned about Hans's inquiries into the past of the Baroness. That would be something to really anger him. He felt sorry for Hans, but his pity was secondary to the excitement of witnessing a real explosion in which he was not involved.

"Oh, no doubt you have," Robert Eggli said, sitting down in an armchair and inspecting his cigar reflectively. "Among them,

of course, would be Vicki and Lucy and Walter here. As a good
family lawyer you would have to make sure that their interests
were protected."

"Only in occasional matters of minor importance do I ever
give them legal advice," Hans said pompously. He was furious,
believing Tante Vicki had told her brother what he had said
almost a year ago about pursuing an inquiry into the life of the
Baroness de Marty in order to safeguard the family inheritance.

The old man chuckled softly, passing the lighted end of his
cigar under his nose in order to savor the aroma. "You are frightened, all of you. Oh, I have known it for a long while, and it
has amused me to observe your creeping fears. Vicki has been
the only one with courage enough to mention the subject. The
rest of you make a secret of it, like some dreadful skeleton in
the closet. Well, don't expect me to set your mind at rest, Hans.
You are a successful lawyer, with a good practice. What should
it matter to you if Lucy inherits nothing? As for you, Walter,
and your brother Jacques, there is always good money to be
made with the name of Eggli to trade on. The two of you could
start a shop selling golf clubs." He chuckled again. "Yes, that
would be good—'The Eggli Brothers, Everything for Sports.' You
could also sell skis and tennis racquets and croquet sets, and
have succursales at St. Moritz, Lugano and Long Island. I am
sure that some of our good banking friends would lend you a
little capital to get started. Jacques, with his flashy tweed jackets,
would make an excellent salesman."

"Is this a joke, Papa?" Walter asked. "I don't quite understand what you are trying to say."

"If you don't, then you are even duller than I suspected," the
old man said gruffly.

"You started by making some cryptic references to inquiries
that Hans had made," Walter protested, "and now you are intimating that the bank is to be liquidated. How should I know
what you are suggesting? Is it your opinion that Hitler will seize
Switzerland and with it the bank?"

"Ask your lawyer Hans. He will tell you what I am talking about," his father said.

"This is really preposterous," Hans blustered. "I cannot imagine how I should come to be involved in this matter. I can only guess that it must be Tante Vicki who has said something. . . ."

"She has said plenty," the old man cut in. "That is her best feature—no thought in her mind can escape from passing over her tongue. She thinks me a senile old rake, and she says so. Well, that is her privilege, just as it is my privilege neither to confirm nor deny it. When I am dead you will learn the answer soon enough. Until then I shall have the pleasure of watching all of you squirm with uncertainty."

"It is not for ourselves that we think of these things," Hans protested. "It is the bank and its clients, its reputation."

"*Gotteswillen!* If that were true, I could meet death with a calm spirit," Robert Eggli said.

"Hans speaks the truth, Papa," Walter said. "The bank is our only concern."

"*Ach*, don't tell me fables as if I were a child," his father growled. "I know you better than you know yourselves. You—both of you, and Jacques too—think of money as something personal, something to keep and hoard, something to insulate you from the mass of honest hard-working little people. You think it is your own, to wear like your clothes. Well, let me tell you, it is not that. It is a trust, a public trust. It is credit and valuta, both of which are needed to protect our little country against the ravages and competition of bigger, richer states that have *matières premières*. We have no coal, no iron, no petroleum, no copper. We could not exist on the sale of cheese and kirschwasser. It is on money that we survive—my money, your money, the bank's money—invested in every part of the globe, creating a favorable balance of payments with which to import the *matières premières* that our industries must have in order to give employment to good Swiss workmen. What have riches given me? A nice house, a few pictures and objets d'art? Yes, but much more. It has given me the satisfaction of knowing that I have been able to help my country to prosper, to live in peace, to preserve its precious neutrality." He sat up straight in his chair and waved his cigar at his son and son-in-law. "Go, now. Run along back to the bank. Execute my instructions, Walter. I shall come along later. I wish to rest awhile. And remember what I have told you."

CHAPTER XIII

THE grim changes that war can make on any scene it touches were never more forcibly impressed on Jacques than by the picture of the Clyde as he stood on the deck of the tender, which was edging its way from the towering side of *H.M.S. Queen Mary,* headed for the port of Greenock. The town lay huddled: lines of grey stone buildings, their slate roofs glistening in the rain, beneath the rolling moors of Renfrew. Everywhere on the waters of the wide river were grey menacing ships at anchor—cruisers, destroyers, corvettes, and their flocks of dirty, battered freighters, empty now, awaiting their signal to dash the Atlantic. Across on the other shore the highest of the hills, masked now by low clouds, were in Argyllshire, framing the Kyles of Bute, that neck of land which protects the entrance of the Clyde's mouth. The hills looked dun and somber, like the purposeful ships, like the oily waters of the Clyde, like the mass of officers and G.I.'s who packed the tender's deck, watching in silence the shores of Scotland. It was mid-May, yet nothing in the picture gave a clue of spring, of hope. The drizzle of cold rain and the low dark clouds were not the only reason for the drabness of it all. Jacques had been in Scotland before, and he knew that it could be a country of friendly warmth even in the rain.

Standing on a tarpaulin-covered hatch in the lee of a ventilator, he looked at the heathery hills of Dumbarton and recalled his last visit to the Lowlands in August of 1939. His father had leased Gifford in the Lammermuirs, those rolling hills, like the ones he could see across the Clyde, which made the watershed between the Forth and the Tweed. It had been a gay carefree shooting

136

party of sixteen people, eight guns with seven wives and Tante Vicki as chatelaine—a mixed bag of Swiss, French, Scots and English. For two weeks politics had been banished, and the ugly evidence of Poland's disaster, heralded by the Danzig crisis and the Hitler-Stalin pact of non-aggression, was not discussed— that is, not on the hill or in the presence of the ladies. To be sure, his father had kept the wires to London, Paris, Zürich and New York humming with instructions, but he had never displayed a sign of worry or distraction. With a pony to take him to the line of butts, the old man had shot surprisingly well, better in fact than some of his guests, and at dinner he had been a witty and gracious host.

That glorious holiday, Jacques thought, had been the final stanza, the epilogue to a peaceful world. Only a few days after he and Doris had returned to London the storm had broken, Hitler had invaded Poland, and England and France had declared war. Here, then, was a different Scotland, with the keepers, stalkers and ghillies marching in uniform after German and Italian game on a far-off blazing desert, while the grouse and deer and salmon were left to the mercy of poachers and vermin. Only a few rooms of the great houses would be open, just the small ones which could be kept warm for the old and the indigent. He pictured Gifford House, that gem of the Adam brothers, in its policies of towering limes, muffled in silence, the great rooms covered against the dust, and the elderly Lord Drem reading *The Scotsman* by the fire in his little study, with a woolen scarf around his neck. He wondered if those glorious days would ever return, or whether Scotland, England, the whole of Europe might fall under the command of strutting, officious *gauleiters*. It was a sickening thought, but then his eyes swept over the flotilla of fighting ships in the stream, and he remembered the voyage with the *Queen Mary* packed to its limit with serious, tough G.I.'s, and he became confident and glad that he had joined to do his bit.

Yes, he was happy to be finally on his mission after almost a

year of training and indoctrination. That year, now gratefully
ended, had been one of frustration and boredom. Nothing that
he had been taught had seemed to him applicable to the work
for which he had been selected. He had gone to clandestine
schools where, with younger men of many races, he had learned
all manner of techniques more fitted for thugs and burglars than
a drawing-room spy. He had listened to endless lectures on the
habits and behavior of European nationals, concerning most of
which he knew more than the lecturers. Only during the last
month had he been briefed by the Board of Economic Warfare
so that he would be able to assume his cover with credibility.
Then, at long last, his orders had come to proceed to O.S.S.
headquarters in London, and with them a glorious two-week
leave with Doris on Long Island. The year had been long and
dull, but it was behind him and he was impatient now to be at
the center of activity.

Not that he was too happy about the uniform they had made
him wear. At first, on board ship, he had been embarrassed by
his lack of insignia of rank and the shoulder patch with the
letters "B.E.W." In the cabin which he had shared with five
other men, he had been the only one not in some branch of the
military service. He had felt like a slacker in the presence of
these officers, but they apparently did not share this feeling. They
had accepted him without question or distrust as a middle-aged
man who was serving his country for the duration. Then, too,
he had not been the only one on board in rankless uniform.
There had been a score or so of correspondents, Red Cross
workers, U.S.O. entertainers, and non-military civil servants who,
like himself, wore hermaphrodite tunics. By the second day out
he had recovered from his sense of shame and had entered into
the life of the officers' quarters. This had been chiefly an earnest
attempt on the part of all to defeat boredom. Bridge and gin-
rummy games for stakes of an altitude that only the devil-may-
care atmosphere of war can produce went on in the lounge from
early morning until early morning. Cabin parties, with whisky

and gin procured from the chief steward, went on nightly, producing a minimum of inebriacy but a universal comparison of hang-overs at the breakfast table. Jacques had slipped easily into the general camaraderie. He was jolly, cheerful and undaunted by the overhanging fear of U-boats. The young officers liked him; he was catalogued as a "good Joe." The field and flag ranks, having heard the scuttlebutt that he was a rich Wall Street banker, treated him deferentially. The U.S.O. actresses thought he was cute and called him "Bew," after the letters on his shoulder patch.

Now that interlude was over. With the entry of the Queen Mary into the mouth of the Clyde, the laughter and the kidding and the games had ceased. The voyage had been the last respite. It was over, and the panorama of the grey ships, their blinkers signalling to each other in the drizzly dawn, made it clear that they had reached their destination—the war for which they had been trained. They were ready, if not eager, for the business at hand.

Jacques, feeling the engines slow down, turned to face the town. The dockside was only a few yards off and he could see that the railway station was virtually there, separating the town from the quay. Three long trains were waiting under the shed. He wondered if they were to take the full cargo of twelve thousand men. Taking the card which the transportation officer had given him out of his raincoat pocket, he looked at it and read for the fourth time: "Compartment 46, London Train." The engines of the tender reversed and she swung into a perfect landing. Jacques picked up the small suitcase that held his toilet kit, pyjamas, a clean shirt and a bottle of scotch whisky, and stepped down from the hatch cover, hoping that his duffel bag would eventually turn up, if not in Compartment 46, at least in King's Cross Station.

The casual officers and civilians were the first to disembark. M.P.'s guided them across the wet pavement to a stairway which led to one of the station platforms. On reaching it, Jacques looked around for a sign which would indicate which of the two trains on his platform was destined for London. There was no sign. Then he saw a cart carrying a percolator and a steaming metal box that was attended by two pretty young girls in Red Cross uniform. He asked them if they could tell him which was the London train. One of the girls was about to answer when her jaw dropped and her eyes widened in astonishment.

"Why, Mr. Eggli! Fancy meeting you here!" she exclaimed.

He recognized her then through the disguise of her uniform. It was Joan McCabe, one of Bobby's friends who lived at Oyster Bay. "What a blessing to find you on this bleak platform, Joan," he said pleasantly.

"Mary Lou, this is Mr. Eggli, the father of the boy I was telling you about," Joan said to her companion. "Or should I say Colonel Eggli?" She gave him a ravishing smile as she handed him a mug of coffee and two hot doughnuts.

"No, it's still plain mister," he answered, putting down his suitcase in order to take the coffee and doughnuts. "I'm a civil servant now, Joan, bound for London. That is why I wanted to know what train to take."

"You have to read the tickets on each car. They tell you where it is going," Joan said, and added, "Where is Bobby?"

"Somewhere on this island, I should gather from his A.P.O.," Jacques told her.

"Really! How exciting!" Joan squealed. "Oh, Mr. Eggli, if you should see him, please tell him I'm at Greenock and hope to be transferred to Rainbow Corner in London soon. What is his rank?"

"First Lieutenant," Jacques said proudly.

"Golly! I'll bet he looks cute with his wings."

Jacques was forced to step aside, as a solid mass of officers and soldiers were crowding around the portable canteen, clamoring for coffee. They all had a kidding, flirtatious word for the two girls, who took it laughing, giving back as good as was tossed them. He noticed that the porcelain mug was a special dispensation for Bobby's father. The others got paper cups. When he had emptied his mug, feeling better for the warming liquid, he pushed his way through the crowd and handed it to Joan. "Good-bye, my dear Joan," he said. "I hope I run into you again."

Joan took the mug, smiling sweetly at him. "Don't forget my message to Bobby," she said.

"Look, sister, you can tell me direct, I'm Bobby," a voice in the crowd called.

"He called her Joan," another voice said. "Hey, Joan, how's about a doughnut for your Bobby?"

"Hell, Joan, he ain't Bobby. He's Pussyfoot. I'm Bobby," still another G.I. called.

Jacques took his bag and walked along the platform, reading the small placards on the carriages until he finally found one marked "London" which had a compartment numbered "46." The only other occupant when he entered was a colonel he had met on board, but whose name escaped him. He greeted him pleasantly and put his suitcase on the rack over a seat by the window, then took off his raincoat and sat down. The colonel had settled himself in a corner by the corridor.

"Dismal looking place," the colonel said.

"Rain doesn't help," Jacques commented.

"Is this what they call a Pullman?"

"Not exactly. It's a first-class carriage."

"You mean it's the best they have?"

"In peacetime when they are heated and kept up, they are pretty comfortable."

"You've been here before?"

"The last time in 1939."

"Business?"

"No, pleasure. I came over for the shooting."

"Man! What a hell of a place to come to on purpose! What did you hunt?"

"Grouse."

"You mean like our partridge?"

"Yes, much the same, only a little bigger."

"How many did you kill?"

"There were eight of us and we killed eight hundred and sixty brace—that's seventeen hundred and twenty birds—in two weeks."

"Wait a minute, wait a minute! How many did you say?"

"One thousand seven hundred and twenty grouse."

Two more officers entered the compartment, a lieutenant colonel and a major, and threw their shoulder bags and brief cases on the rack. They greeted the colonel and Jacques like old friends.

"Do you think we'll ever see our flight bags?" the major asked.

"I should think it improbable," Jacques said, laughing.

"The transportation officer said we would find them in our compartment," the lieutenant colonel said.

"It's the old snafu," the major wailed. "Three hundred dollars' worth of uniforms gone for the duration. Just my luck to buy a new set and have the old ones show up the next day. I've never seen it fail."

"Maybe you won't need any more than what you're wearing," the lieutenant colonel said. "Maybe your number is engraved on a Kraut bomb. Then they can exhibit those uniforms in the Smithsonian Institution."

The colonel, who had been scribbling in a notebook with a small butt of pencil, looked up at Jacques. "Look here, Mr. Bew, either you were pulling my leg or you're the biggest liar in the civil service. You said you were eight guns. Am I right?"

"That's what I said," Jacques agreed.

"And you hunted for two weeks?"

"Twelve days, to be exact," Jacques said. "It's against the law to shoot or fish in Scotland on Sunday."

"Oh, boy, that makes it even worse," the colonel said, scribbling again in his notebook. "Just listen to this, you, McManus and Klotz. Stop worrying about your bags and listen to this. Mr. Bew, our stable mate in this cattle car, has the nerve to tell me that he and seven other fellows killed seventeen hundred and twenty grouse in this Godforsaken spot in twelve days. Do you realize what that means? It means an average of one hundred and forty-four birds a day, or eighteen per man per day."

"What did you use, gas or d.d.t.?" the lieutenant colonel asked.

Jacques laughed. "Just ordinary old-fashioned double-barreled shotguns," he answered.

"Don't kid me," the colonel said. "Why, that's more grouse than are killed in all of New England in a year."

"So what, Colonel?" the major said. "It's Bew's story, so let him stick with it. You can't prove he's wrong and he can't prove he's right."

"Oh, yes, I can," Jacques said, smiling.

"How?" the colonel asked. "How can you prove a thing like that?"

"All you have to do, Colonel, is to go to the stationmaster's office at the end of the platform and ask to use the telephone," Jacques said. "Tell the operator you want to make a trunk call to . . ." He took a small address book out of his pocket and consulted it. "Here it is—to Haddington 62-34. When you get it, ask for Lord Drem and when he is on, tell him that you are a friend of Jacques Eggli and that you don't believe his story that he and his father and their friends killed eight hundred and sixty brace of grouse on Gifford Moor in August, 1939."

"Suppose he said you did," the colonel insisted. "How would that prove it?"

"Because he is the owner of the house and moor that my father rented. His game book shows the bag for every day's shooting on that property since 1880. Of course, Colonel, if you're not willing to take the word of Lord Drem on the telephone, you can run over there in a staff car and read the entries in the game book yourself." Jacques pulled out his wallet and extracted five twenty-dollar bills. "I've got one hundred smackers here that I'll put up to your fifty the book will show I'm within ten birds of being honest."

"Put up or shut up, Colonel," the major said. "Looks to me as if Bew here ought to be in antiaircraft instead of economics."

"By God, Mr. Bew, if I ever get the chance, I'm going to call on this Lord Drem. Not to check you, but to try and wangle a little of that grouse-hunting," the colonel said. He took out his notebook and the stub of pencil again. "How do you spell Drem?"

"D-r-e-m," Jacques replied.

"Any pretty daughters, Bew?" the lieutenant colonel asked. "I want to meet Lord and Lady Drem and all the little dreams."

"What's the address?" the colonel persisted.

"Gifford House, Bolton, East Lothian," Jacques answered. "It's not far from Haddington."

The colonel wrote it all down carefully, then put the book in his pocket and leaned back in the corner. "I'll tell him I'm a friend of yours, but I've got to remember that it's Eggli and not Bew."

"Saints in Heaven! Look what's here!" the major shouted.

They all looked out on the platform where three G.I.'s were dumping duffel bags in front of the door. "Lieutenant Colonel J. F. Klotz?" one of them asked, reading the name stamped on the bag.

"I thought you'd thrown it overboard," the lieutenant colonel said.

It took thirteen hours for their carriage to reach London. It had seemed to Jacques during the long and tiresome journey that they had been shunted about on every siding south of the border. At first there had been a great deal of talk among the officers, speculative talk about their probable assignments and duties, where they would be billeted and whether or not there would be any night spots after the severe bombing raids. Not one of the three had ever crossed the Atlantic, so they had plied Jacques with endless questions about London. His answers had been qualified by the statement that the city they would find would have probably little relationship to the city he had known in peacetime. The small parcels of sandwiches and crackers which had been doled out to them on the *Queen Mary* to serve as food for the journey had soon—all too soon—been eaten and forgotten. They had staved off hunger during the long day with snacks at station platforms, elbowing their way through crowds of soldiers in British uniforms, many with "Poland," "Australia," "Canada" embroidered on their shoulder patches. Civilian clothes were in the minority, even with the women. Between them they had had enough whisky to counteract the chill of the unheated compartment. When darkness had made it impossible to watch the unfamiliar landscape, the alcohol had made them drowsy until all four of them had finally made nests for themselves on the cushions and gone to sleep.

It was midnight when their train rolled to a stop at King's Cross. There were no porters, so that each of them had to carry his own bags to the long queue of passengers waiting for taxis. The lieutenant colonel and the major had orders to proceed to a staff headquarters in Putney and were lucky enough to find a U.S.A. staff car going there. The colonel wanted no part of any military installation until he could get his bearings. Standing in the taxi line, he asked Jacques what hotel he was going to. Jacques told him Claridge's and added that the Embassy had engaged a room for him there.

"Do you know it? Is it any good?" the colonel asked.

"It's among the best," Jacques told him. "I've stopped there for years and they know me."

"Well, if you don't mind, I'll go along with you. I can spend a day or two there and look around."

"They might be full up."

The colonel grunted. "Don't give it a thought. I'll throw rank at them if I have to."

The ride to Claridge's was an experience they had not counted on. The darkness outside the station was impenetrable. It was as if the taxi were trying to crawl through a tunnel of coal dust.

Every so often a pair of faintly glowing eyes would come at them, passing, to the colonel's horror, on the wrong side. He kept his hand on the door, ready to leap out when the crash came. But it did not. They bowled along, around corners, swaying first one way and then the other until the brakes went on with a squeak before a luminous column of dark blue light.

Jacques, remembering the brilliantly lighted canopy of the entrance to his favorite hotel, made no move to get out.

"Where are we?" he asked the driver.

"Claridge's, sir," the man replied. "That blue light marks where the door is."

The Swiss night clerk greeted Jacques deferentially, asking after his family and hoping that he had had a good voyage. There was nothing in his manner to indicate that war had in any way altered the dignified opulence of the hotel, or that he found it strange that Mr. Jacques Eggli should arrive at midnight in an outlandish non-military uniform, with a duffel bag instead of matched luggage by Vuitton.

"I'm giving you the suite your father always has," the clerk said. "Number 20. Thinking you might be late and hungry after the journey, I've instructed the kitchen to have a snack sent up to you, sir."

"That's very good. I can do with a bite to eat," Jacques said.

The colonel, who had been waiting impatiently beside Jacques spoke up. "You can do the same for me," he commanded.

The clerk looked at him coldly, noting the rank. "Are you a guest of the hotel, Colonel?" he asked stuffily.

"No, but I expect to be," the colonel stated peremptorily. "I want a room with a bath."

"Sorry, sir, but we have nothing available," the clerk said, then turned to Jacques. "I shall show you to your suite, Mr. Eggli."

"See here, young man, I'm Colonel Baxter of the U.S. Army Staff Headquarters," the colonel said angrily. "I have just arrived here on duty and I insist on having a room. For the past twelve hours I've been travelling around your country in a filthy, unheated train. Either I get a room at once or you will hear about it in the morning."

Jacques let him sound off, knowing that no rank below two stars would pull any weight with a Swiss clerk at Claridge's. It amused him to witness the wing-clipping of this pompous colonel, those bright eagle wings which he wore as if they had been conferred on him by the angel Gabriel.

"There is no room for you at Claridge's, Colonel," the clerk said acidly.

"Now don't give me that applesauce," the colonel stormed. "You know damn well you always have an extra room for officers of rank."

With a look of infinite boredom, the clerk picked up a slip of paper on the desk and glanced at it. "As a matter of fact, we are holding a room for Field Marshal Sir Gavin Brakethorne who is expected to arrive at five this morning."

"Look, Colonel," Jacques said, feeling that his travelling companion had received enough squelching, "you can put up for the rest of the night on the couch in my sitting room, if you don't mind the inconvenience."

"Is the Colonel a friend of yours?" the clerk asked suspiciously.

"Yes, we came over from the States together," Jacques replied.

"Ah, well, if that's the case, I think I can find an empty maid's room for the night," the clerk said with sudden affability. "Tomorrow I shall ask the Cumberland for a room. They are very good about taking American officers for us."

The colonel's face was crimson with rage and chagrin. He turned to Jacques. "Who the hell are you, Bew, anyway, the Secretary of the Treasury?"

Jacques laughed. "After you get settled in the maid's room, come down to Number 20 and have something to eat. I'll tell you all about it."

"Porter, take the Colonel to 362," the clerk commanded, handing the night porter a key. "This way, Mr. Eggli."

CHAPTER XIV

Being no longer subject to command regulations of the military, Jacques put on a grey suit with ebullience. Until he looked at himself in the tall mirror on the door of the wardrobe, he did not realize the extent of his loathing for the uniform, the color of rotting algae, which he had been forced to wear during the voyage. Now, with white shirt, neatly checked tie, and black shoes, he regained confidence in himself and his mission. He could meet the eyes, those cold appraising eyes of the reception desk, with that degree of hauteur which only a Swiss hotel clerk understands and respects. Of course the problem of a hat still confronted him. The supple Borsalino which he had had to carry rolled up in his duffel bag was hardly appropriate for Grosvenor and Bond streets—a fact which the eyes at the reception desk would detect at once, giving them a psychological upper hand. He would have to hide it under his folded topcoat until he had gained the street, then as soon as his preliminary skirmish with the O.S.S. office was over, he would go straight to a hatter and procure a suitable black Homburg. And, ah, yes, an umbrella. Jacques believed in protective coloration, except of course in Zürich where it tickled him to flaunt his wildest Long Island concoctions just to impress them with the fact that he had become an American. Here, in London, it was wiser to dress like an Englishman. The English had a way of judging a man by the cut of his clothes. They were the tag which indicated the drawer into which he could be filed. For that reason he refrained from sticking a pearl pin in his tie, a Continental touch which would have been detected at once.

He looked at his watch. It was half-past nine. By the time he had walked to headquarters it would be the proper, the dignified moment for him to make his appearance. He must not give the impression of being an eager little drone, waiting on the doorstep to insure good marks in his personnel dossier. He glanced at the breakfast tray on the table in the living room and thought of the ridiculous colonel who had shared a bottle of champagne and cold chicken with him at midnight before going to his maid's room in the attic. Jacques hurried out the door and down to the lobby, hoping to escape before the colonel attempted to renew the intimacy of the night before.

Aside from the boxed-in entrance to the hotel, Grosvenor Street in the delicate morning sunshine gave no evidence of hostilities, which was a surprise to Jacques, who had pictured the city in partial ruins. Later, of course, when he had seen the corner of Bond and Bruton Streets and other gaping holes with gay Regency rooms hanging naked over a pile of rubble, he had changed his view, but at this moment, feeling confident in his grey suit and seeing the stately houses erect and haughty, he imagined the City of Westminster to be, like himself, spruce and in order.

O.S.S. under the command of Colonel Bruce had taken over two of these stately houses in Grosvenor Street and turned them into a labyrinthine rabbit warren of little rooms and narrow corridors in the best secret-service tradition. A young lady in a cubicle in the front hall took down Jacques' name and asked him to wait while she disappeared into the maze of the warren. It was at least ten minutes before she returned with the announcement that a Mr. Holden would see him. He followed her through a narrow hall, up a narrow staircase, down another narrow hall until they reached a door which she opened, standing aside so that he could enter a bare little room containing a metal flat-top desk, two metal chairs and a man with thick brown hair, horn-rimmed spectacles and a pipe in his mouth.

"This is Mr. Eggli, Mr. Holden," the girl said and darted off. Mr. Holden got up from the desk and held out his hand.

"Good morning," he said noncommittally. "Did I understand Miss Ambrose to say that your name is Eggli?"

"That's right, Jacques Eggli. Washington has advised you, I presume, that I was to arrive on the *Queen Mary*."

"May I see your travel orders?"

Jacques extracted a sheaf of copies of his orders from his wallet, picked one from the clip and handed it to Holden.

Holden glanced at it, then looked up. "Have you your passport?"

"Yes, here it is." Jacques handed it to him.

Holden turned to the photograph and studied it. "Hmm," he said. "I thought you would be in a B.E.W. uniform."

"I was until one o'clock last night."

Holden smiled. "Couldn't wait to shed it, eh? Well, I don't blame you. Sit down, Mr. Eggli." He opened the folder on his desk. "You understand we have to be very sure that you are the man you profess to be, and not someone who has taken his papers—or forged them."

"I quite understand. One can't be too careful. By the way, is Colonel Bruce in? I was told to report to him personally."

"He is out of town at the moment. You say you arrived on the *Queen Mary*. When, Mr. Eggli?"

"She dropped anchor in the Clyde about eight-thirty yesterday morning. The train left Greenock about eleven and reached London about midnight last night." Jacques could see Holden's eyes ticking off data from a paper in the folder while he was reciting.

"What was your cabin number on board ship?"

"A-18."

"And where did you sleep last night?"

"At Claridge's."

"Would you mind raising the trouser of your right leg?"

Jacques lifted up his trouser leg, undid his garter and pulled down his sock. "There it is," he said. "The old skiing scar."

Holden peered at it, then reached out and felt it gently with a stubby, hesitant finger. He looked up at Jacques and laughed. "If you are not Jacques Eggli, you're the best imitation of him I've ever seen. Why, you would even fool your son Bobby."

"You know Bobby?" Jacques asked, incredulous.

"I was his history instructor at New Haven."

"My God! You're not Dr. Alan Holden?"

"The very same."

It was Jacques' turn to laugh. "Pity I don't know your identifying mark or I would ask you to show it. From what Bobby has told me it is probably a naked houri tattooed on your chest."

"On my buttocks, Mr. Eggli, the most exercised portion of my anatomy." Holden leaned back in his chair and applied a match to his pipe, giving the impression that he could relax now in the presence of a colleague. "What do you hear from Bobby?"

"Precious little since he arrived here in England."

"Oh, so he is over here, is he? I remember when he left for his Air Corps training. I suppose you will be looking him up."

"That would seem to depend on when you fellows are sending me off on my assignment."

Dr. Holden smiled. "You'll have plenty of time. Things don't move at such a rapid tempo around here. There will be a lot of planning and briefing before we can send you out."

"I thought I had done all that in Washington."

"That's what they all think when they get here. The answer is that there are many details, little corrections and perfections which we have learned to superimpose on the basic training which our home office gives. We have learned a great deal, largely through trial and error, which means that our operatives have to be re-indoctrinated before they are sent out. In your case, for example, there are many little refinements we have developed concerning the nature of contacts and how they may be exploited." He glanced down at the paper in the folder. "Yes, Mr. Eggli, you are to have a rather special assignment, one that differs radically from the general run of work in our Berne office."

"In what way will it differ?" Jacques asked.

"I'd rather not go into that now. As a matter of fact, I believe that Dave Bruce would like to brief you on that himself." He looked at the calendar on his desk. "In the meanwhile—let's see, this is Friday and Dave will not be back in London before Tuesday—why don't you locate Bobby and look in on him?"

"There is nothing in the world I would like better, but how do I go about locating his squadron?"

"I think we might be able to do that for you." He handed Jacques a pad of paper and a pencil. "Here, write down his rank and serial number and the designation of his outfit." While Jacques wrote he said, "Drop by this afternoon and I'll tell you where he is and when you can see him."

"This is very kind of you, Dr. Holden."

"Give Bobby my best and ask him if he remembers what Talleyrand said at Vienna."

"What was that?"

"*La paix n'existe que dans l'équilibre des forces.*"

"I will ask him." Jacques got to his feet. "Now, about my cover story while I'm here in London—"

"No change. You are a representative of the Board of Economic Warfare—or is it 'Office' now?—on temporary duty with the London Embassy. Incidentally, I will arrange for you to go around there and meet some of your B.E.W. colleagues. They are going to brief you on their Swiss activities."

"Is there any objection to my looking up some of our banking connections in London?"

"None whatsoever. It's all straightforward and aboveboard. In fact, I would rather like them to know what you are doing, or should I say, what you are supposed to be doing, so that word will reach Swiss banking circles and set their minds at rest."

Jacques's heart missed a beat and he could feel the blood draining from his face. "Their minds are never at rest."

Holden puffed on his pipe for a moment before saying, "So I am told. That is why your assignment will be a special challenge."

Walking down Grosvenor Street toward Bond Street, Jacques

thought about that statement of Dr. Holden's. Why should the restless, suspicious minds of Swiss bankers be a special challenge to him? There had been no inkling in Washington that his work would be connected in any way with bankers or banking circles. With cold horror he wondered if Holden and Bruce had cooked up some cockeyed scheme, some plan to have him find out the nature and extent of Axis accounts in Switzerland. If so, they were barking up the wrong tree. They would have to find that out through German and Italian sources. No Swiss, least of all Grosspapa, would divulge that information. They would rather die first. Then he wondered if Walter was privy to the locked code book in the bank's vault. Probably, now that the old man was in his eighty-second year.

Jacques's thoughts were interrupted by the appalling evidences of German bombing which now met his eye. A building which had once housed the gallery of an art dealer where he and Doris had bought two drawings by Gainsborough had virtually disappeared. A great gaping hole, filled with pools of water and wallflowers sprouting from ragged stalagmites of brick masonry, was all that remained. He felt suddenly furious, as if the damage had been a personal affront to his amour-propre. Sons of bitches, he said to himself and quickened his pace down Bond Street. When he reached the hatter's where he had always dealt, he found it too had suffered. The shop front was battened down with hoardings on which he found a small sign directing customers to a temporary abode in Pall Mall. This increased his fury and he strode on, crossing Piccadilly and heading down St. James's Street.

"What the devil are you doing here, Jacques?" a voice beside him asked.

He wheeled about abruptly to find a smartly dressed British officer with a scarlet band around his cap standing on the steps of Black's Club. He had to stare for a second or two before recognizing the face in its unaccustomed frame. "Michael!" he exclaimed. "What a piece of luck! What am I doing here? I don't really know yet—some sort of economic mission. Just got off the boat. I was on my way to Smythe's to buy a decent hat."

"The one you have on is very dashing. Just the thing for an air raid. Come in and have a drink with me," Michael Hoy-Babbington said.

"Thanks, I will. Imagine my finding you, of all people, the first moment I step out in the street!"

"Walking in St. James's Street, my dear boy, is the certain method of running into a friend."

They walked into the club, hung their hats on hooks in the foyer and went on to a little wicket in the rear of the hall.

"What will it be?" Hoy-Babbington asked.

"A martini for me," Jacques replied.

"It won't be what you are used to," Michael said. Then to the man behind the wicket, "Two gin and its."

They took their drinks—gin and vermouth out of the bottles, warm and potent—and went into the lounge.

"What are you, anyway?" Jacques asked when they were seated in worn leather armchairs. "I've never learned to decipher your insignia of rank."

"Colonel, if you must know, but it's bloody unimportant. I'm just an old crock from the City doing a bit of staff work at the War Office."

"Who is running the banking business?"

"Old Fothergill goes down a few hours every day to read the *Times*. There is no banking any more. How is your father? Still going strong?"

"The last I heard he was. He's almost eighty-two now."

"Wonderful old chap. What is his attitude about all this?"

"About the war? He's optimistic."

"For what side?"

"Ours, for God's sake! He hates a Nazi as much as you do."

"Stout fellow! I always said he was the cleverest man on the Continent. Now about yourself, are you going to be stationed in London?"

"For a few weeks at least."

"If I'm on the wrong wicket you don't have to answer, but is it on this Lease-Lend business?"

"No, though I wish it were. I wouldn't mind having a post here."

"Wait till the Hun starts dropping things."

"If you can take it, I can. I'm with an agency they call the Board of Economic Warfare. Our job is to purchase strategic materials wherever we can find them."

"Before the Nazis get them."

"Exactly."

"Ah, yes, we have a show like that too."

"You have indeed. We work more or less together."

"How is that lovely Doris of yours?"

"Fine. And Gladys?"

"Thriving. We have taken a little place in Wiltshire for the duration. She's down there now. You must come and have a week end with us. We have about a mile of the Kennet that goes with the place. It's stiff with huge educated trout."

"Educated by you?"

"By the chap who owns the place. He must have gone out of his way to teach them the difference between an artificial fly and the real thing. Are you a fisherman?"

"A very bad one."

"Splendid! Then you shall learn how humiliating it can be to have a trout cock a snook at you."

"I have no tackle with me."

"We have masses."

"Nor any waders."

"We'll fix you up with a pair. You can't wriggle out of this, Jacques. Those trout are pining for a good laugh, and you are the man to give it to them. Besides, Gladys would never forgive me for not bringing you down. She's forever talking about those days at Gifford. How about a week from today?"

"I will have to ask my colleagues at the Embassy."

"Imagine Jacques Eggli having to ask if he can leave the room! Marvelous the miracles that war can produce!"

"Have you no boss at the War Office?"

"Have I not! A cranky old general who is forever ticking me off. But we are raised to that sort of thing. Our bosses are supposed to be livery, violent and abusive. You Americans are in the habit of doing what you will without asking."

"You forget that I was born a Swiss."

"Quite. I had forgotten. Yes, that could make a difference."

"A hell of a difference. Where are you living in town, Michael? The house in Charles Street?"

"Heavens no, it had a direct hit. I've a little flat in Carlos Place—Number 10, first floor."

"How about dining with me this evening?"

"Sorry, but I promised Tania I would trot her out for a meal."

"That's your youngest daughter, isn't it?"

"Yes, she's a WAAF in the Air Warning. This is her only evening free in the week."

"Then I ask you both."

"Jolly decent of you. Tania will be thrilled. Why don't you come to the flat around six and we can have a proper martini?"

"I shall be there. How old is Tania now?"

"Nineteen, and an absolute raving beauty."

"And Etheldred, who married Lord Stockton? How is she?"

"She and her baby are with Gladys in Wiltshire."

"And Stockton? A soldier, I suppose."

"Oh, haven't you heard? The poor chap was killed at Dunkerque."

"How awful! I didn't know. . . ."

"He was magnificent, Jacques. Died holding the line so that those on the beach could get off in the boats. What about your kids?"

"Robert is here somewhere, as an Air Corps pilot. I hope to see him this week end if I can locate his squadron."

"If I can be of any help . . ."

"Thanks, but the Embassy is finding him for me." Jacques got to his feet. "I really must go and buy that hat."

"Nonsense," Hoy-Babbington said, rising also. "You are lunching with me right here. Besides, as I told you, the hat you have is quite the thing."

They went upstairs to the dining room which was stark and depressing with its black-out curtains and the dusty markings on the walls where pictures had once hung. Michael noticed Jacques' quick scrutiny of the room and said, "Dismal, isn't it? Rather like eating in an abandoned schoolroom. It was the hit across the street that did it. Blew all the windows in and knocked the pictures down. The committee has decided to leave it as it is until the Luftwaffe have been taught a lesson. No sense in giving them rather nice portraits to shoot at. Take my advice, Jacques, and have the sole. Everything else is filthy."

"For the first time since 1939 I'm beginning to think that the old man is right," Jacques said when they had ordered the sole and a bottle of hock. "We are going to win. You will be redecorating this room sooner than you think."

"The African news is good, there's no denying that," Michael said. "But I'm none too keen about the dose your man Roosevelt wants to prescribe. Frankly, Jacques, our staff chaps are rather worried about it. To them this unconditional surrender appears to lack an understanding of the German mind. Like most brutes, they are sentimental, given to elated ideas of glory—dying for the fatherland and all that. Why is it they worship this little bounder Hitler? Because he feeds them all this Wagnerian rot that they cherish. And they'll stick to him, you mark my words, even if he decrees that the whole ruddy Reich has to perish in some sort of flaming Valhalla. What worries me is that the statement of the Casa conference is going to put more iron in their backbones."

"Have you read this morning's paper?" Jacques asked.

"You mean about the final surrender of the Afrika Korps? We knew that the day before yesterday. Oh, I agree that it's highly important. With all of North Africa and the Middle East in our hands we can begin the job of sticking in the knife. Only don't let this bit of news deceive you into thinking that the Hun is beaten. Look at the show he's putting on at Kharkov."

"I know he isn't beaten," Jacques said. "But he has just suffered a second major defeat in six months. Psychologically that is bound to make a deep impression on the German mind. I know them. They are full of fight and swagger when things are going their way, but they are bad losers. Once they begin to lose faith in their invincibility, they get panicky."

"I hope you are right, Jacques, but notwithstanding I don't like this business of unconditional surrender. It shuts us off from trying a bit of footsies with some of the unhappy generals of the old Junker General Staff. However, we've talked enough about this bloody fracas. Let us put our minds on Wiltshire and the Kennet. A week from today you and I will be taking the train from Victoria, unless of course you can wangle one of those lovely staff cars from your Embassy."

"I shall first have to see how I rank in Grosvenor Square."

"You'll wangle one, I've no doubts on that. I know the reverence your civil servants have for Wall Street bankers."

Jacques laughed. "Those were the old days. Roosevelt has changed all that. We sit below the salt now."

CHAPTER XV

JACQUES saw his son standing in the door of the waiting room eagerly searching the faces in the carriages as the train pulled into King's Lynn. His heart beat faster with pride at the sight of the tall young man, strikingly handsome in his uniform. He waved and Bobby saw him and rushed forward, loping along the platform until the train stopped. Jacques noted the double silver bars and, grinning, put a finger on his own shoulder. "Since when?" he called.

"Last week," Bobby answered. "Pretty sharp, eh?"

Even before the wheels had ceased to turn Jacques undid the door and jumped down to the platform, carrying his suitcase, which Bobby immediately took from him.

"Gee, Pa, this is great!" Bobby exclaimed. "When Colonel Byers told me yesterday that you were coming up to see me, I couldn't believe my ears. I thought he'd made a mistake."

Jacques stood looking at his son, waiting until he could be sure that his emotion would not crack his voice. "Captain Eggli," he said finally. "Captain Robert Eggli! Have you written the news to your mother?"

"The very day it came through. But tell me, Pa, what are you doing over here?"

"An economic mission," Jacques answered, brushing the question aside as if his work were unimportant compared to that of his son. "What does this promotion mean? Are you in command of your squadron now?"

"This way, Pa. I have a jeep waiting for us." Bobby led the way through the milling throng of soldiers on the platform to the exit where the guard took their tickets. "What is your mission, Pa? Hush-hush stuff?" he asked when they had reached the street.

"Economic warfare, temporarily attached to the Embassy in London," Jacques answered.

"Gee, that's fine! Right up your alley." Bobby threw the suitcase into a jeep that was parked at the curb.

As they drove off down a quaint and quiet street flanked by low brick buildings, Jacques said, "You never answered my question about your promotion."

"Innate modesty."

"Well, what does it mean?"

"Command of a squadron. You know, like the lead gander in a gaggle of geese."

"Have you flown a mission yet?"

"Lord no, we're only just getting acclimated, learning to fly English weather, how to rendezvous, how to come down through the soup and find home plate."

"Where are you taking me to?"

"Right here," Bobby answered, stopping in front of a low rambling hotel. "At the King's Arms. I've booked a room for you, as they say in this land of overcast and partridge."

"Of course. We're in Norfolk, aren't we?—best partridge county in England."

Bobby grabbed the suitcase and swung over the side. "You're telling me! We've got them right on the airdrome. Chuck Taylor —he's a pal of mine, bomber-navigator on my ship—and I walk 'em up on Sundays. All we have is a couple of lousy pump guns they use to train waist gunners, but we manage to get enough for the colonel and our crew."

They walked into the hotel, which was attractive with its low-beamed ceilings and chintz curtains. A florid, bosomy woman behind a narrow counter greeted Bobby pleasantly and turned the register around so that Jacques could enter his name.

"You the captain's father?" she asked.

"Yes, indeed," Jacques answered proudly.

"Dearie me, you don't look old enough," she said. "Now, sir, I'm afraid I'll have to ask you for your passport. War regulations, you know. The police has to know who's who and who's where. I'll have it back for you in the morning, or maybe even tonight." She turned around and picked a large key from a board on the wall behind her which she handed to Bobby. "Will you be taking your father up, Captain? It's the room I showed you—Number 19."

The bedroom was cheerful in spite of the faded wallpaper and the rings from wet glasses on the dresser and table. Bobby put the suitcase on the bed. "How long are you staying?" he asked his father.

"I've got a compartment on the night train tomorrow," Jacques replied. "I hope your colonel will give you a little time off."

"I have no duties until eight o'clock Monday morning. The colonel handed me that on a platter. 'I don't want to see your face around here until Monday,' he said. 'Take good care of your old man, and if you want to, bring him around to my quarters for Sunday dinner.' You could have knocked me over with a feather. That from Colonel Plimpton, the toughest, hardest driving C.O. that ever came out of Kelly Field. Whoever it was who sent the word from London that you were coming must have had plenty of stars."

"Now prepare yourself for a real shocker," Jacques said, grinning. "Do you know who it was who arranged my visit here? Dr. Alan Holden!"

"Not Doc Holden from New Haven?" Bobby asked, incredulous.

Jacques smiled at his son and nodded assent.

"Well, for crying out loud! What in hell is he doing over here?"

"Like me, a desk job in London. He sent you his best regards."

"He's a great guy, Doc is, even if he did damn near flunk me."

"He told me to tell you to remember what Talleyrand said at Vienna."

Bobby let out a whoop. "He would. That was one of the questions I got wrong in the exam and he was forever ribbing me about it, said it was something no man with Swiss blood in his veins should forget."

"What was it?"

"Gee, I thought you would know it."

"Maybe I did once, but I've forgotten. What was it?"

"*La paix n'existe que dans l'équilibre des forces.*"

"The balance of power."

"He's a funny guy. I see what he's driving at. He wants me to remember that when I take the ship over Germany I'll be giving Hitler the old equalizer, putting him back where he belongs. Good old doc, he would be over here in the thick of history. It's his passion. According to him it's all old stuff, all happened before. The only difference is that the cavalry now fly and the sabers are ten tons of TNT." He stopped suddenly with a look of dismay. "Golly! The sight of you in King's Lynn was such a shock that I clean forgot to ask you about Ma. How is she?"

"She's all right, Bobby. Keeps her chin up and doesn't complain. War is harder on the women than on us."

"I guess you're right—they worry."

"She made me promise we would not dine together in London. She said there was no point in her men making a double target."

"Not much chance of my getting to London until this training is over."

"If you ever do, you might drop around at the Red Cross."

"Why?"

"Because you might find Joan McCabe. I bumped into her in the railway station at Greenock when I got off the boat. She was serving coffee and doughnuts to the soldiers. She sent her love to you."

"Good old Joan, she passes out the kisses like doughnuts to anyone who'll take them, and plenty do. Thanks for the tip, Pa. I'll sure look her up. I might as well have my share."

Jacques opened his suitcase and took out a bottle of scotch. "We might have a drink before we go down to dinner."

"Save it, Pa. Give it to the colonel tomorrow. I'll buy you a drink at the bar. I'm lousy with pounds, shillings and pence."

The bar was crowded with officers, the majority Americans with a sprinkling of RAF, but the noise created by their voices was neither high-pitched nor alcoholic. It was a steady drone created by earnest conversations and occasionally punctuated by staccato quips or insults. Most of the glasses held beer, and those that did not were noticeably in front of tunics which held no pilot's wings. Bobby and his father found two chairs at a table already occupied by an Air Corps lieutenant and an RAF squadron leader. They greeted Bobby casually, like old friends, and exhibited no surprise when he introduced them to his father. Jacques sat down while Bobby went to the bar in the corner to fetch the drinks.

"We were just remarking what a bloody dull part of the world this is," Squadron Leader Hankey said. He was a dark, wiry little man with eyes like a terrier. It was not easy to judge his age. His small body in a tight-fitting tunic and his dark brown hair, which was wavy and worn longer than that of the Americans, gave the impression of youth, say middle twenties; but his black, darting, button eyes were marked at the outer corners by a group of little lines, as if they had been etched there to draw attention to the intensity of the pupils, so that looking only at them, he seemed in middle age.

"It's years since I've been in Norfolk," Jacques said noncommittally. "The last and only other time I came up for the partridge-shooting. It occurred to me when I looked at my railway ticket that the name of this town rang a bell. Now I recall that the place I stayed at was near King's Lynn. Perhaps you've heard of it—Hadley Hall?"

"I know it," the American lieutenant said eagerly. He was a kid, even younger-looking than Bobby, with a round baby face on top of which was a bush of sandy hair, crew-cut. "It's about ten miles east of the field. We use it as a marker for the hundred and eighty degree turn when we're coming in for a landing on number two runway."

"It used to belong to Sir Isaac Schonheim," Jacques said. "I wonder if he still owns it."

"The banker from the City?" Hankey asked.

"Yes. Do you know him?"

Hankey gave a dry laugh that sounded almost like a cough. "I know him right enough, though he wouldn't know me from a pillar box. I used to work in the City, clerk in a stockbroker's office. Many a time I've delivered shares to Schonheim and Company. I've even stood by the old man's desk while he signed a chit for me. Very smart dresser, old Schonheim. Always a flower in his buttonhole."

"We used to do quite a lot of business with him," Jacques said. "That's why he asked me up here to shoot."

The squadron leader's terrier eyes flashed at Jacques for a fleeting instant. "You a broker, sir?" he asked.

"Well, banker-broker," Jacques replied pleasantly.

"But you're not an American, are you?" the young lieutenant asked, having noted Jacques's accent.

"Sure Pa's an American," Bobby boomed, putting a double whisky and soda in front of his father and a beer at his own place. "He's as American as you are, Olsen, you precious Swede. Your father was naturalized and so was mine. So what?"

"It's okay by me," Olsen said apologetically.

"Well, sir," Hankey said. "Sir Isaac's partridges may be all right for a day or two, but as for me, I fancy the partridges you flush in Streatham. Nice plump little birds that squeak when you pinch their fat breasts."

"I must explain Squadron Leader Hankey to you, Pa," Bobby said. "He's a fighter jockey. One of those lone birds who darts about the sky with no companion but his own livid imagination.

When he lights after an hour or two of mental and aerial acrobatics, he's hungry for women, women, women!"

"Your son is building me up to divert attention from his own shortcomings," Hankey said, his terrier eyes focused on the dregs of his beer. "If he don't get a flying mission soon, there'll not be a virgin left in the county."

"I wouldn't worry, Mr. Eggli," Olsen said. "Norfolk isn't so big. Just about the size of Rhode Island."

Jacques smiled, happy to be treated as an equal in the leg-pulling. "I'm glad you're keeping your eye in, Bobby."

"His eye? My eye!" Hankey said.

"He's jealous," Bobby said to his father.

"Bloody right I am," Hankey said. "You Yanks get all the breaks. You have the local partridge eating out of your hands." He turned to Jacques. "Do you know why, sir?"

"Don't say it, Hankey," the lieutenant said. "Because we're over . . ."

"Not that rot," Hankey interrupted. "That's a line one of your own chaps thought up to give him a shot of courage. Look here, Mr. Eggli, as long as you've come all this way to see your son, you might as well know the worst. It isn't his eye, or his manly fuselage. It's the uniform, that fancy dress costume he wears, all covered with clips and pins and bangles. It's hardware the girls are after. Think of it, sir, just for one little wing over and a short flip on their backs, they get a shiny, solid silver pin to wear on the new frock."

Jacques laughed and looked at his son. "You seem to have all your insignia intact, Bobby."

"And why shouldn't I?" Bobby said. "The only girl in town that you could kiss without being blindfolded is the exclusive property of Squadron Leader Albert J. Hankey, D.S.O."

"Exclusive?" Hankey said bitterly. "She's exclusive with the 507th Fighter Wing."

"I'll say she is," Olsen said sadly. "The other day I asked her to have a drink with me, and she said"—he pursed his mouth and lifted his nose in the air—" 'I don't drink with bloody bombers.' "

"Right she was," Hankey said. "Bombers are not to be trusted with women. Flying level all day makes them restless. Oh, Katie knows her flyers from nose to stabilizer."

"Speaking of angels," Bobby said, looking at the door.

Jacques followed his son's gaze and saw a pretty redheaded WAF with freckles and grey eyes, in a uniform that demonstrated a well-developed figure. She was with a tall blond RAF officer and they seemed to be searching the room for a place to sit down.

"And see who she's got," Lieutenant Olsen said, "Cecil Pyne. What good will that do her?"

"Katie doesn't want to be done good," the squadron leader said. "If that was what Katie was after she'd be with the WRENS, or sitting around the Ritz bar with a couple of silver stars on her garter. She's a serious girl, Katie is. Likes to talk highbrow. That's why she has picked on Master Pyne for the evening. She knows she can trust him not to make a pass, as you chaps would say." He turned to Jacques. "Flight Lieutenant Pyne crawled out of the woodwork of Oxford to split his ruddy cocoon and grow wings—from don to D.S.O. in two short years."

"He's terrific!" Bobby said admiringly. "But so is our friend Albert J. . . ."

"Steady on, Captain!" Hankey interrupted, frowning at Bobby. "Keep the talk clean." He drained the dregs from his glass and stood up. "If I were you I wouldn't worry about your son, sir," he said to Jacques. "We'll keep him in formation. Cheerio." He walked out through the tables, nodding to Katie and Flight Lieutenant Pyne as he passed them at the door.

"What makes him so bitter?" Jacques asked.

"The fact that he's alive," his son answered. "He's one of the real heroes of the Battle of Britain, the only one of his flight who survived. Now he's assigned to this Wing that flies escort for us, and he hates it. To him it is like being nursemaid after you've won the welterweight championship."

"He wears no ribbons," Jacques commented.

"He won't wear them," Olsen said. "He won't even talk about them, and he has every one they hand out."

"Pa, I think it's time you and I were eating," Bobby said. "On a Saturday night the dining room fills up early."

Lieutenant Olsen jumped to his feet when Bobby and his father got up from the table. "It has been a pleasure meeting you, sir," he said respectfully.

Bobby waved to Katie and Pyne to indicate that there were vacant places at their table, then followed his father towards the door. As he passed them Katie smiled sweetly and Pyne muttered, "Thanks awfully."

When they were seated at a small table for two in the far corner of the oak-beamed dining room, Bobby asked, "What news do you get from Switzerland?"

"Little," Jacques answered. "Your Uncle Walter is on duty with his regiment a great deal of the time. Otherwise life goes on as usual, although they are short of many items of food."

"And Grosspapa?"

"When I left New York he was just the same as ever."

"Great guy, that," Bobby said admiringly. "Smart as they make 'em. I'll bet he hasn't got a dime of the bank's money in Germany."

"Indeed not. That would be the last place to invest at this time. It is more likely to be the other way round."

"What do you mean—that he is holding Nazi money?" Bobby asked, shocked at the thought.

"Not necessarily Nazi accounts," Jacques said guardedly. "But it is more than possible that many German banks and industries are holding funds in Switzerland."

"I can't picture Grosspapa holding that sort of money."

"He is a banker. Bankers can't throw out old customers just because of sentiment."

"But he hates the Nazis. You told me that yourself."

"That is quite right, he does hate them; but that is his personal feeling in the matter. A bank has no personal feelings."

"You mean to say that he would take their money even though he hated them?"

"Listen, Bobby my boy, you must remember that Switzerland is a neutral country. It can't afford to take sides, that is, officially."

"I realize that, but Grosspapa's bank is not official. It's his own. He can do what he likes with it. He could tell the Germans to go to hell if he wanted to."

"And I'm sure he does whenever he gets the chance. But the matter of clients is another thing. A banker may not approve of some of them, but he cannot suddenly refuse to continue their accounts for that reason. A banker is a trustee who builds up the confidence of his clients by never letting politics or sentiment sway his judgment."

"But, Pa, holy smoke! This is an all-out war, an ideological war. It's freedom against tyranny. You are either for them or against them. If you touch their money, you've soiled your hands. You can't deal with crooks."

"I'm sorry we got into this, Bobby. I know how you feel, and in a way, I'm inclined to agree with you. The trouble is that like so many people in a time like this, you oversimplify. Right now every German is a crook in your eyes."

"Well, isn't he?"

"Not necessarily. Let's take the hypothetical case of a manufacturer with a good business, who has no interest whatsoever in politics. Suddenly the Nazis tell him what he has to make and to whom he has to sell it. He resents the whole thing and decides he is better off to get as much of his loose capital as he can out of Germany, in some spot where it will be safe. He doesn't trust Hitler or his gang and thinks the whole regime is doomed. Now if you were a Swiss banker like Grosspapa, would you refuse to take his money?"

"I would want to be damn well certain he was on the level."

"Look at it this way, son. Isn't it presumptive that any man who wants to get his money out of Germany has no faith in Hitler?"

"Maybe so. Maybe you are right, Pa. Maybe there are a few smart ones who see the writing on the wall. Christ! Wait till we get through with them—the RAF by night and we by day. We'll wipe the place off the map."

"Good boy! You can write my name on the first bomb you drop."

A waitress put a plate with a metal dome in front of each of them. Before lifting off the covers, she put a finger to her lips to indicate no comment.

"I brought them over from the mess—special dispensation," Bobby whispered.

The waitress lifted the domes, disclosing broiled steaks surrounded by roast potatoes.

"Okay, Emma," Bobby said. "Now you can bring in that bottle of claret Mrs. Tingle has been saving for me."

It was almost eleven o'clock when Jacques returned to his bedroom after Bobby had left for the B.O.Q. at the airdrome. He poured himself a stiff drink of scotch and sat down in the one upholstered armchair. His son's words about Grosspapa and the bank disturbed him. Perhaps it was his own fault for never having taken the pains to explain to Bobby the exact nature of Eggli and Company in its relationship to European, even world economy. Had the boy been carefully indoctrinated with the basic philosophy of Swiss banking as an integral characteristic of neutrality, he would not have been shocked to learn that the bank received accounts impartially, not questioning the client's political views any more than a doctor would question the politics of a patient. Bobby would then have taken for granted that among the clients there would be Germans, Austrians, even Bolshevics, and that the handling of those moneys would have no more effect on the beliefs and convictions of Grosspapa Eggli than the snowfall in Glarus. He should have started earlier with that education. Now it was in a way too late. At least it would have to be postponed, held in abeyance until the Germans were defeated and the value of the assets held in Switzerland could be used to demonstrate the need for an invulnerable safe deposit in the Alpine center of Europe. Then Bobby would be able to see, to comprehend that this valuta—for it was valuta, gold or Swiss francs or dollars, and not ephemeral currencies of sick and weakened states—would pour back from the Alps to their surrounding lands like glacial rivers to reconstruct and revive a stricken civilization.

"You are either with them or against them. To touch their money is to soil your hands." When he had said that, Bobby had meant his grandfather and that was the pity. Robert Eggli— Grosspapa to them all—had always been more than the head of the bank, the guardian of the family fortune, and the venerable chieftain of the clan. He had been a symbol of unity, of strength, of purpose and direction. That he had been venerated more than loved was the inevitable lot of symbols and he had preferred it that way. This veneration had reached beyond his own blood to his in-laws, his associates, his competitors. Nothing had affected or weakened it, not even his long affair with the Baroness de Marty, which had only served to color and strengthen the aura of his invulnerability. To Jacques it had always been taken for granted that Grosspapa would appear to his children, Bobby and Evangeline, in the same light—the light of awe—that he appeared to himself. Without ever saying so, he had believed that his attitude towards the old man, which was one of respect, complete faith, and admiration tinged with fear, had been imparted to his children. That had obviously been a wrong assumption. He had forgotten that Bobby was a pure American who based his judgments on his own prejudices and not those of others. "A youth who bore 'mid snow and ice a banner with a strange device," Jacques recited to himself, thinking how like his son that youth was. "Excelsior!" had been the burden of Bobby's announcement. To touch their money was to soil your hands.

The ideal, the clean and noble ideal, the white and black of good and evil, was what he would carry with him on his missions over Germany. He would give the order for "bombs away" with the zeal of certainty that he was carrying a banner for all that was decent and right. There would be no qualms, no sympathy for the victims, for they were evil and must perish lest they soil more hands.

Yes, it was a pity that the boy had lost faith in his Grosspapa because of those German accounts. The old man had ceased to be a symbol to him. He had sensed that when Bobby had spoken. It had been implicit in his words, in the tone of his voice, and in the expression of his eyes. The veneration had dissolved, leaving only a shrewd, crafty banker who said one thing and acted another. Well, time would mellow the picture—time and experience. The old man could not live much longer—he might not even see the end of the war—whereas Bobby would come to maturity in the aftermath when the rubble was being cleared away and the gaunt survivors would be peering from their bomb shelters. That would be the moment for Bobby to begin his apprenticeship with Eggli and Company in Zürich, where he could watch the funds flow out to perform their work of rebuilding. Then he would learn that "Excelsior" could mean many things. "Higher, always higher" could also be the motto of those who saw beyond the immediate struggle and strove to hold intact some part of what would otherwise have vanished.

For a fleeting moment Jacques thought of the possibility that Bobby might be killed, and he felt suddenly cold, as if a draft of icy air had swept through the room. Then he tossed off his whisky and laughed out loud. Ridiculous! he said to himself. Bobby is an Eggli, a Robert Eggli, and like his Grosspapa the air of invulnerability shines out from him. It will take more than the Luftwaffe to bring him down.

He got to his feet and took off his coat. I must tell him tomorrow, he thought, to christen his ship "Excelsior!"

CHAPTER XVI

WHERE Hélène was seated she could look at a mirror panel which reflected the image of the dining-room door behind her. In it she saw Tony enter with Werner von Orb and dropped her head instantly, as if engaged in attention to the food on her plate. She had no desire to be greeted by her lover in the goldfish bowl of the Hotel Beau Rivage. Particularly she did not wish to be seen talking with von Orb, whom she loathed as much for his perversity as his politics. He was a cold, bloodless worm who made her shiver with distaste. She knew why Tony cultivated the German poet and the knowledge angered her. It was a blatant illustration of his complete, unabashed immorality. Tony had no conscience, no ideals, no beliefs other than hedonism, which required money, and for that he would do anything, betray anyone. Momentarily she was ashamed of herself for ever having had an affair with him, and was pleased that now in the autumn of 1943 a year had passed since she had last seen him at that little hotel in the Augustinerstrasse.

If only Walter had been able to lunch with her, she said to herself, there would be no danger of recognition. Her husband had told her that he was engaged for a men's luncheon at some cercle, and she had not called one of her friends because that would have meant an invitation and more food than was good for her figure. So she had decided to lunch alone at the hotel, then do some shopping before meeting Walter for tea at the Emil Schwarzes'.

She raised her head cautiously for a quick glance in the mirror in order to locate the table which the two men had taken. Her eyes met those of Tony, who must have been staring at the back of her head. He jumped to his feet and came over to her table.

"My dear Hélène," he said, smiling at her, "how wonderful to find you here in Geneva! And alone! Why should we not sit with you? You know my friend Werner of course."

"No, Tony," she said sharply. "I don't want either of you to sit with me. I'm expecting my husband."

Venturi winked at her. "I understand—too many eyes to watch us. How about a quiet cup of tea this afternoon? I have a friend who has a charming little flat."

"I don't doubt that. Walter and I are having tea with the Emil Schwarzes'.

"*Allora*, that is perfect. I shall see you there."

"Have you been invited?"

"*Ma certo!* Werner and I are going together."

"Then why did you ask me to have tea with you in some friend's flat?"

"Pleasure before business is my motto," Tony replied, grinning down at her.

"Please, Tony, go back to your Nazi friend before all Geneva starts talking," she pleaded.

He took her hand and kissed it ceremoniously. "*Più tardi, eh?*"

When Hélène and Walter arrived at the Schwarzes', Venturi and von Orb were already there. The German, a thin, sallow young man with a surly mouth, wearing a tweed jacket and grey flannel slacks, was standing in a corner of the salon talking to a ruddy-faced man whom Hélène did not recognize. Their host Emil Schwarz, the banker, greeted them effusively.

"Have you seen your brother?" he asked Walter.

"My brother? You mean Jacques?" Walter said, puzzled.

"Yes, Jacques," Schwarz said brightly. "He is here. He called me on the telephone only an hour ago. Just flew in from Lisbon. I asked him to come for tea, but he said a car was waiting at the airport to take him to Berne. I told him that you and Hélène were in Geneva and were coming here this afternoon. He said to tell you both that he would see you in Zürich." He turned to greet a new arrival. "Ah, my dear Baronne, what a pleasure to see you! You know, of course, Walter Eggli and his wife. May I present the Baronne de Marty?"

They shook hands politely, the Baroness exhibiting no impression beyond mild cordiality. Walter was less constrained. For a long time he had wanted to meet this woman who had captured his father's heart. It had piqued him that Jacques and Doris and Hans and Lucy could speak of her as a person they had met and talked with. Of all of them, he was convinced, he was the one who carried the least prejudice. He was if anything inclined in her favor, never having really feared that his father had left her his sole heir. It had been Hans and Tante Vicki who had promoted this preposterous idea—the one because he was incapable of understanding the deep sense of continuity which motivated the old man, and the other because, like most old maids, she fancied all women who carried on affairs not sanctioned by matrimony to be heartless, designing gold diggers. So he smiled warmly as he gave her hand a special vigorous shake, looking into her eyes in a friendly, sympathetic way. The words he spoke were unimportant, the usual greeting given to a stranger in the French language. It was the manner and intonation which conveyed his pleasure, his desire to become a friend and not just another social acquaintance.

Hélène, like the Baroness, was more formal, less obvious, even though her greeting was pleasant. Her eyes, however, missed nothing. She noted all details instantly in one swift appraisal— the smooth ivory skin, the sensitive mouth, the large honest, trusting eyes, the un-Swiss, even un-English figure which was Gallicly female, the perfectly fitted *tailleur de fantaisie* which could have been made only in Paris, the choker of large pearls, and the hat which, adorned with a diamond clip, became part of the asymmetrical though precisely placed whorls of her dark brown hair. The picture was better, more pleasing than Hélène had imagined. Seeing beyond the Baroness, in the corner of the salon, the figure of Tony Venturi talking animatedly with one of the Tessier girls, she felt that there was a bond between them. Both she and the Baroness had been able to flout the puritanism of Zwingli and Calvin without losing their positions in the social stratum to which they belonged.

"Come, let us sit down over there," Yvonne de Marty said to Hélène. It was a command—the older woman to the younger, assuming her authority as a right. And Hélène accepted it as such without question, without the slightest annoyance.

"So, your brother-in-law Jacques Eggli has arrived from the United States," the Baroness said when they were seated. "A most charming man. I met him and his wife in Paris in 1939."

"What is this? Jacques has arrived?" It was the voice of Tony Venturi behind them.

"So it seems," Hélène said. "It is a pleasant surprise. Baroness de Marty, this is Monsieur Venturi."

"Oh, we are old friends, are we not, Baroness?" Tony said, holding the backs of their chairs and leaning forward between them.

"As old as the war, which is too old for my liking," Yvonne de Marty said.

Unfazed by the rebuff, Tony turned to Hélène. "This is interesting about Jacques. What brings him to Switzerland?"

"How should I know?" Hélène answered. "Emil Schwarz said that he called from the airport. That's all I know. I had no idea that he was coming."

"Then we shall see him here this afternoon?" Tony asked.

"No, I believe he is motoring directly to Berne," Hélène answered.

"Aha! Berne, and by motor. Sounds official," Tony said.

"You are old enough to know that bankers always sound official," the Baroness said.

Tony darted across the room to greet a pretty young girl whom Hélène recognized as Lise de Muralt.

"He is a busy butterfly," Hélène commented.

"And an inquisitive one," Yvonne said. "He makes a point of knowing what is going on."

"Society and gossip are his vocations," Hélène said.

The Baroness glanced at Hélène out of the corner of her eye as if she wondered how much this woman from Zürich knew about the young man. "Perhaps that is it. Do you know him well?"

Hélène was startled by the question, but then she recovered when it occurred to her that had the Baroness really known the truth, she would not have asked it. "Off and on for years," she answered casually. "Everyone who ever went to Lugano knows Tony Venturi."

"In recent months he has been spending a great deal of time in Geneva and Berne. One cannot help wondering how he can afford it. Certainly not by the sale of his pictures."

Hélène realized that the comment was purposely pointed, and speculated as to how much the Baroness knew about Tony's activities. "His kind always seem able to raise enough cash to appear at the right place at the right time."

"Yes, but Switzerland in wartime with only the Swiss as clients is hardly good hunting ground for a gigolo."

"There are always a few foreigners."

The Baroness smiled. "I at least am not among his supporters."

"I didn't mean to imply that."

"Then do you suspect, as I do, that he has supporters other than women?"

"You mean fellows like that Graf von Orb?"

"Horrible man! They came together."

"Did they? Then he's that too."

"I don't think he's like that," the Baroness said, then waved to the ruddy-faced man who had been talking to von Orb when Hélène and Walter had entered the salon.

The man walked over to them and Yvonne de Marty introduced him as Gerald Blythe. "Dear Gerald," she said in English,

"I thought you ought to meet the daughter-in-law of my old friend Robert Eggli." She turned to Hélène and asked if she spoke English.

"The Baroness was saying that the war had taken all foreigners from Switzerland," Hélène said in English, by way of answering the question. "But both of you contradict that statement."

"In war or peace Switzerland is very hospitable," Gerald Blythe said graciously.

"That is all very true," the Baroness said. "Switzerland is neutral and hospitable, but you and I are not supposed to be neutral, Gerald."

"Nor are we," Blythe said.

"Then how can you think of talking to the enemy as I saw you a minute ago?" the Baroness asked sharply.

"Good manners, quite simply," Blythe replied. "As a guest of Switzerland I must, at least outwardly, behave as a neutral. As a guest of Monsieur Schwarz I must be polite to those I meet in his house."

"Then your manners are better than mine," Yvonne de Marty said. "I could not trust myself with that young man. I should tell him straight out what I thought of him and his Fuehrer."

"I quite understand, my dear Yvonne," Blythe said wistfully. "It would be a great satisfaction to tell him off, though it would hardly affect the outcome." He turned to Hélène. "Is it true that your American brother-in-law has just arrived?"

"So I am told," Hélène answered, wondering why this Englishman should be interested.

"Well, I hope I shall meet him," Blythe said. "It would be interesting to hear what they are saying in New York."

"If you will be in Zürich—" Hélène started to say.

"I rarely get that far," Gerald interrupted. "Berne is about the limit of my excursions, and that only rarely."

"Mr. Blythe is with the League of Nations," the Baroness explained, then turned to Blythe. "If he should come to Geneva, I shall see that you meet him—a most charming man."

"He has become very American," Hélène said.

"But he is an American, is he not?" the Baroness asked.

"Yes, an American citizen," Hélène replied. "I believe he is now even working for the American Goverment."

"Really," Gerald said.

"Something to do with economics," Hélène added.

"I've no doubt he's clever at it," the Baroness said. "That is, if he takes after his father."

Then other guests came up to greet the Baroness and Hélène, and the conversation was interrupted; typical of the weaving pattern of tea and cocktail parties, partners were changed and new groups formed and other dialogues begun. It was like a square dance except that no music imposed the changes. Hélène found herself again with Tony Venturi, against her will and wish. During the weaving he had appeared at her side.

"Had you met her before?" he asked.

"Who?" Hélène demanded.

"Madame la Baronne de Marty."

"Never."

"How did you find her?"

"A very attractive woman."

"Clever, too."

"Without a doubt."

Tony leaned closer to her ear so that he could lower his voice. "She knows a great deal, a great deal that I might find useful."

"Then why don't you make love to her?"

"Nothing doing. I've tried every gambit I know. She is too clever. She knows what I'm after."

"What are you after?"

"Momentarily, a little ready cash. When I have that in my pocket, I'm after you."

"So what you said at the Beau Rivage is not true. It is business before pleasure."

"Only because you insisted in coming here instead of meeting me at my friend's flat."

"See here, Tony, you might as well know it. I cannot stomach your 'business,' as you call it. I'm through with you, and that's final!"

Venturi smiled at her. "You think I'm working for the Axis."

"I know it. You told me so yourself."

"That was almost a year ago. Things have changed."

"I wouldn't believe you under oath. Now run along to your friend von Orb. I'm going to talk to Jacqueline."

"Adieu, my sweet and petulant Hélène. I love you most when you are righteous and angry."

Hélène left him standing there and went in search of Jacqueline Tessier.

Tony was not disturbed. He knew that he could trust Hélène Eggli to keep her mouth shut. He also knew that when he wanted her again, when the time returned for pleasure, he could have her back. The campaign of the moment was the conquest of Yvonne de Marty. He was convinced that she was supplying Blythe with information which she obtained from Robert Eggli. He could use that information in his own way. The problem, the difficulty, was that she was doing this out of patriotic fervor. Had money been her motivation, the solution would have been relatively simple, but she was rich and money was the last thing that interested her. He had already tried his standard approach, that of the irresistible lover who could satisfy her lonely yearnings, and had failed. That had annoyed him, piqued his pride. On the evidence it should have been an easy conquest—a widow, patently passionate, rich, mistress of an octogenarian who rarely came to Geneva. What could be easier for a man who had been pursued by rich widows? But this one, so much more attractive and desirable than the others, had rebuffed every advance, had in fact given him to understand that she was not interested in him from any standpoint. There seemed to be only one possible avenue, that of her consuming devotion to the Allied cause. He had, and could get, information which was worth money to the Combined Chiefs of Staff. The Britisher, Blythe, he felt sure, had some of that money to dispense. He could of course attempt a direct contact with Blythe, but that might be dangerous. One breath of suspicion and his source, Werner, would dry up. It was better that he stick to the women. That was expected of him. Futhermore, he had the future to think of. Old Robert Eggli was in his eighties. He could not live many more years. Once free, the Baroness de Marty would make a suitable, perhaps exciting companion and could support him in the luxury to which he was unaccustomed.

He met her in the foyer as she was putting on her coat. "May I drop you home?" he asked. "I am about to engage a taxi."

"Thank you, but I shall walk," Yvonne de Marty said. "I don't approve of using taxis in wartime."

"Then I shall accompany you."

"There is no need," she said coldly.

"But there is the honor and pleasure of walking with you, my dear Baronne," Tony insisted.

She did not answer, but her face showed displeasure at the prospect. He noted the expression but appeared oblivious. Once in the street he dropped the false gallantry.

"I am quite aware that you prefer not to be seen walking with me," he said. "But there seemed no other way for me to explain to you that your prejudice against me might be founded on a false assumption."

"I have loyalties, young man, and not prejudices," she said sharply.

"Precisely. You have loyalties to France and you suspect me of Axis leanings."

She gave a short mirthless laugh. "Now you are going to tell me that being a good Swiss, you have to maintain strict neutrality."

"Superficially only. At heart I am as anti-Nazi as you are."

"Have you told that to your friend von Orb?"

"I would not dream of telling him."

"Then you are as false as I thought you were."

"There are times when one can be of more service by not admitting one's beliefs."

"Service is a strange word for you to be using," the Baroness said bitterly.

"You think so because you do not know me."

"Quite right. I know very little about you, but what I do know is sufficient."

"Would you care to know more if it would be of help to your cause?"

"My cause?" she asked sharply. "What do you mean?"

"I mean France."

"Pétain is not my cause, I'll have you know."

"I meant Free France—the Allies."

"They seem to be doing very well as it is. I am afraid there is nothing you or I could do to help them," she said sarcastically.

"There are always little things that they would like to know, things that would affect their plans."

"I don't doubt that, nor do I doubt that they have the means to find them out."

"They try, but not always successfully."

"Just what are you trying to say to me, Venturi?"

"That I should like to be your friend, to help you and the Allied cause."

"Being a friend has nothing to do with helping the Allied cause," the Baroness said impatiently. She was quite aware of what he was aiming at and determined to give him no opening. "If you have any information that might be of value to the Allies, the British Legation at Berne or even the Consulate here would undoubtedly be happy to hear your story."

"I am surprised, my dear Baronne, that you would recommend me to do such a thing," Venturi said in a hurt voice. "You must realize that my sources would immediately learn of it and I would be of no further help."

"Are you trying to say that I should act as your messenger?"

"You wish the Allies to win, do you not?"

"Naturally."

"Then you should be willing to help them."

"It is perfectly ridiculous! Even if I were willing to take your stories to the consul, he would not believe them."

"There are others beside the consul."

"What others? Not people whom I know."

"Are you so sure?"

"Quite sure. I do not count spies and agents among my friends."

Tony looked at her and smiled as they walked along. "Perhaps I have misjudged you. Perhaps you are not as observant as I had imagined."

"I am observant enough to find the people who think as I do, who are true and honest." She stopped. She had reached the door of her house. "You have selected the wrong person, Venturi, but I am sure that a fellow as clever as you are will have no trouble finding someone to carry your messages. Good-by." She opened her purse and took out a key.

"Then all this talk about loyalty was just words," he said, standing there, watching her putting the key in the lock. "I would never have mentioned all this had I realized."

"With all your successes, you have a lot to learn about women," she said as she opened the door and went in.

After closing the front door she stood in the foyer revolving the conversation in her mind. He was, she thought, exactly what she had always suspected, completely without moral sense. His proposal was to supply her with information which she in turn would pass on to—whom? Gerald of course. Werner von Orb had undoubtedly told him that Gerald was a British agent. That Venturi had been supplying von Orb with bits and pieces of intelligence concerning Anglo-American plans was a certainty. That would account for his recent affluence. And now, not content with the sums he was receiving, he was willing to double-cross the Nazis and sell in the reverse direction—juggling two balls at twice the profit, having his cake and eating it.

She suddenly remembered her talk with Frau Walter Eggli and her face flushed with the shock of her own stupidity. Slowly she walked up the narrow staircase and entered her bedroom where she threw off her coat and sat down on the foot of the chaise longue. She tried to recall exactly what she had said to Frau Eggli about Tony Venturi. The words escaped her, but she remembered having made some disparaging remarks about the source of his income, implying that he must be selling information. At the time she had completely forgotten the old rumor that Frau Eggli was or had been Venturi's mistress, and that was why she had spoken out so clearly. It had been a warning which she had hoped the woman would repeat to her husband and her husband would repeat to his father, so that Robert would be put on his guard. She wondered now reflectively if what she had said had been really indiscreet. Perhaps it was fortunate that she had forgotten the rumor and had spoken as she had. In view of what she now knew for a fact about Venturi's activities, it was signally dangerous for this daughter-in-law of Robert's to be in liaison with this scamp. Could it be that much of the intelligence that he was selling to von Orb came from Robert, through the media of Walter and his wife? If so, it would be a mortal blow to Robert to learn of it, of deceit within his own family circle. She could not tell him, even hint to him of such a possibility. Yet it must be stopped. The danger was too great, not alone to the Allied cause but to Robert's solid reputation.

She hesitated, then picked up the telephone from the reading table at her elbow and dialled the Beau Rivage. When the hotel operator answered, she asked to speak to Madame Eggli-Sieber.

"This is Yvonne de Marty speaking," she said in French to Hélène. "I hesitated to disturb you, but I have a matter of such vital importance to discuss with you that I have taken this liberty."

"I am flattered that you have called," Hélène said.

"It is something that I cannot speak about on the telephone. Is there a way which you could suggest whereby I might see you before you return to Zürich? Perhaps tomorrow morning?"

"I am afraid that would be difficult. You see, my husband and I are leaving on the early train."

"This evening, then?"

"We are dining with the Berliers at seven."

"Their house is only a step from mine. Could you come to me at a quarter to seven? Ten minutes would be enough."

"One moment, Baroness, let me speak to my husband."

Yvonne could hear her speaking to Walter in *Schweizerdeutsch*, of which she understood nothing.

"If you say it is important, we shall stop at your house at six forty-five," Hélène said.

"Thank you. It is indeed important. My house is at 24 Rue de Glacis de Rive," Yvonne said, then hung up.

It was not quite as she had planned. She would have preferred to speak to Frau Eggli alone. Now she would have to phrase the story differently, in a way that would assure Walter Eggli that she was not interfering in their married life.

"It was very kind of you to do this for me," the Baroness said as Hélène and Walter entered her little salon. She had changed into a house dress of flowing black velvet which set off her white skin and her *collier* of large pearls. "Do sit down for a moment and I shall go directly to the point in order not to keep you from your dinner with Thérèse Berlier."

Hélène was busy noting all the details of the salon, thinking it exquisite and done in a taste which she herself could never equal. The beauty and grace of the Baroness impressed her more forcibly than it had during the tea, accentuated as it was against the background of her Louis XVI furniture.

Walter noted these outward things only vaguely, his curiosity over the reason for the summons being so great that all other appraisals were shut from his mind. He thought of course that he was about to hear something concerning his father and the settlement of the estate, perhaps even that this woman was his stepmother.

"I don't have to tell you," the Baroness began at once, looking at Walter, "that your father and I are very old and very dear friends. I wish you to know that I value his friendship beyond anything. It is because I value it so highly that I wish him to know what occurred this afternoon. I could have written him, of course, but with things as they are in wartime one never can be sure that letters, particularly letters of foreigners, are not opened and read, either by your authorities or by foreign agents. So I shall ask you to repeat to him what I am going to tell you.

"As I left the Schwarzes' house this evening, that young man Venturi insisted on walking with me to my door. I tried to get rid of him, but he was persistent. Without any preliminaries he proposed that I act as a go-between to relay information concerning Nazi plans to the British authorities. It was quite obvious that his interest in this arrangement was financial. He wishes to be paid for what he delivers. When I protested that I would have nothing to do with such machinations and suggested that if he had any intelligence which might be of interest to the Allies he take it directly to the British Consul in Geneva, he argued that such a course would be discovered by the Nazis and he would be denied any further information."

She was seated on a small chair, her back straight, her hands resting limply in her lap, her eyes never wavering from Walter. "It is quite plain to me what he is up to," she went on. "He has been acting as a spy for von Orb, the German agent in Lausanne with whom he came to the Schwarzes' party, and is on von Orb's payroll. In order to get more and better information, he wished to involve me in the hope that thereby he could get firsthand news of the views and operations of the Eggli bank. To do this, he would bait me with information on Germany which I was to get the British to pay for. In this way he would not only get a new source of income but also better the source he already has. His mistake was in not knowing me or he would never have proposed anything so outrageous, and furthermore, he would have known that I know nothing and care nothing about the operation of your father's bank. In all the years I have known him he has never once vouchsafed any information concerning his affairs, nor have I ever questioned him about them. What is more, I have never even asked him what he does with my own small fortune which he has handled since the death of my husband.

"The important thing—and this is why I asked you to come here—is that Robert Eggli be made aware of this effort of the Germans to find out about the bank's operations. I don't think Venturi suspects for a moment that I realized what he was up to. He still hopes that out of my love for England and France I might yet agree to carry his messages. But once he finds out that I am not going to play his game, he will look for other sources." As she said that she turned her eyes for a brief second on Hélène. "Robert Eggli should be put on his guard."

"I shall repeat to my father exactly what you have said," Walter said stiffly. "It is very kind of you to take this trouble."

Hélène said nothing. Her admiration for the Baroness had risen to a new height. The woman's honesty was apparent in her candor, but beyond and beneath that there had been, as Hélène realized, an intensely clever effort to establish two points —a warning to Hélène that for her father-in-law's sake, she should drop any friendship with Tony, and a clarification for the Eggli family of her position with regard to Robert Eggli, both financial and sentimental. The Baroness wanted to impress on them that her loyalty to the old man was the equal of theirs, that she expected Hélène to join them in a unified defense of the bank, and that as far as money was concerned, she would never make any claim on the estate because old Robert had so guided her affairs that she was adequately taken care of.

"It is not kindness, Monsieur Eggli," the Baroness said, nettled by the stiffness of Walter's statement. She had hoped that her meaning had carried to him. The Venturi part was for his wife, and *that*, she could tell by Hélène's attentive silence, had gone home. It was the other message, the one that had to do with her loyalty to Robert, which she wanted him to get. Against her better judgment, she felt the urge to drive it home. "Kindness is a sentiment to be used for those we pity. I do not pity your father. I admire him, respect him—yes, you might as well know. I love him and would do anything to protect him."

Walter flushed, realizing that he had been scolded for treating her gesture so coldly. "It was the language, my dear Baroness," he said apologetically, not wishing that she report to his father that he had been rude. "I used the wrong word. I am not so expert as you are in French. We Zürichois are not clever at expressing ourselves where matters of sentiment are concerned. But I understand what you wish to say, and I thank you for it. My father, in his way, is an important figure. He could not choose his children who admire and respect him as you do, but in the choice of his friends he has always been right. You, my dear Baroness, are proof of this point."

Yvonne de Marty stood up, smiling at him. "That was nicely said, and disproves your criticism of the men of Zürich. Just remember this, you of the family, you will never have a stauncher friend. That is the least I can do for Robert Eggli. And now you must run along to Thérèse Berlier."

CHAPTER XVII

THE old man sat motionless at his desk, looking out on the Schanzengraben where a mother swan and five grey cygnets were swimming slowly against the current. His face was a frozen mask, indicating nothing. Every word that Walter was saying was taken in and digested. At first he had been annoyed that Yvonne had taken it upon herself to interfere; then as the whole recital unfolded, he perceived the motivation and his feelings towards her softened. Whether or not she had been right in doing it, there was no question that love for him had been the compelling reason for sending this message by his son. She had acted impulsively, something one should never do, which was the French blood; but the impulse had been loyal, protective. She had no need to warn him about young Venturi. He knew all about that fellow's work for Ciano and the Nazis. Furthermore, he had never doubted that Venturi had tried his best to get information of the bank's operations from Hélène. That he had not succeeded, the old man was equally sure. Hélène might enjoy the excitements of a lover, but she was no fool, and in her independent way was loyal too. Besides, what could she know? As dull as he was, Walter was security-conscious.

"She ended by saying that the Eggli family had no stauncher friend," Walter said in conclusion. He was sitting by the side of his father's great flat-top desk with his back to the window.

The old man smiled, but it was not what his son had said that caused him to do so. The swan had stretched her neck out and given one of her offspring a sharp peck, a reminder that it was still under parental command. The old swan was right, he thought, discipline never hurt anyone, not even a cygnet. The teachings of Freud and Jung had persuaded young mothers that it was harmful, with the result that his own grandchildren had developed like little egocentric savages. Yet here in the dark waters of the Schanzengraben was proof that nature, ignorant of psychoanalysis, pursued the course of education in the fundamental, effective way. It pleased him to discover that despite the disapproval of the women—particularly his daughters-in-law —the swan and he agreed. Walter was a case in point. Had it not been for his father's constant vigilance and strict commands, he would have turned into a lazy, thoughtless playboy. As it was, he was a plodding, sober, and reliable son even though he lacked initiative.

"Of course none of this is news," Walter went on when his father remained silently gazing out of the window. "Months ago you warned Hans and me about Tony Venturi."

"Yes, and I told you to warn Hélène," Robert Eggli said, without moving.

"Which I did at once—that very day."

"What was her comment?"

"She laughed and said that I was not to worry, she knew what Tony was after and that he would get nothing out of her."

"You know why Yvonne told you this?"

"As she said, to warn you."

"Not to warn me, but to warn Hélène."

"Hélène sees no more of Venturi. That is over. She told me so."

"Bah! How do you know whom she sees?"

"I believe her."

"A clever woman is truthful about everything except her lover."

Walter flushed. "That is silly gossip. He was never her lover."

The old man turned his head slowly and regarded his son. He was silent for a minute, then said, "Your brother Jacques is in Berne."

"Ah, so you know. I was about to tell you that he called Emil

Schwarz from the airport at Geneva. He had just arrived from Lisbon."

"He called me this morning from the Bellevue-Palace."

"Is he here officially?"

"How else could he get here as an American? Why else does he go first to Berne and not to Zürich?"

"Naturally, his economic job."

"Then don't ask silly questions. He says that he must report to his minister first, then he will come here on Saturday for two or three days."

"Hélène and I can put him up."

"He will stop with me in the Sudstrasse. You and Hélène will come for dinner on Saturday night. I shall also expect Hans and Lucy to be there."

"*Ach*, that is the night we are to dine with Rüdi Hüppli."

"You can change that to some other night. Saturday you dine with me."

"Very good, Papa."

The old man turned his gaze back to the window and the swans. "Well," he said slowly, "what did you think of the Baroness de Marty?"

"I thought her very elegant and very clever," Walter answered.

The edges of Robert Eggli's eyes crinkled with the trace of a smile. "She is too elegant for Zürich," he said.

"Not for Hélène. She admired her greatly."

"Hélène would. In some ways they are much alike."

"She said that you had done well with her fortune, which surprised me. I don't recall having seen her name among the accounts."

"You did not see it because it is not there," the old man lied. It was one of his crotchets that no one, least of all any member of the family, should know the identity of the account until he was dead. They would find it then in the locked drawer of his desk in the Sudstrasse. The answer was in a little book in which was explained that an account in the name of Liebermann was in reality that of the Baroness de Marty, and that its ramifications through New York and London ended at the Banque de la Suisse Romande in Geneva, which credited the checking account of the Baroness with uniform monthly sums. "She has her account with a bank in Geneva. I merely advise on the investments."

"She is obviously a rich woman," Walter hazarded.

"Rich? What does that mean, rich? You as a banker should have learned at your age that 'rich' is a comparative word. To Georg, the gardener's helper, Tobald is rich. To Tobald, Uster, the grocer, is rich. But to me the Baroness de Marty is not rich. She has a modest little fortune which I have been able to improve by some judicious investing. It is enough for her—all that she will ever need."

"I am glad to hear that," Walter said, thinking himself very clever in having extracted a confirmation of the Baroness' statement.

"You are glad, eh? Don't think for a moment that I do not know why you are glad. It is not for Yvonne de Marty that you are glad. Why should you be? You hardly know her. No, Walter, you are glad because you imagine that there will be no need for me to leave her anything in my will as long as she has all she needs."

"I assure you, Papa, that no such thing ever crossed my mind."

"Then you are more stupid than I thought you. It has crossed Vicki's mind, and Lucy's and Hans's and I suppose Jacques', too. So why should it not cross yours? It has, of course. I know that. You say it has not because you have not the courage to acknowledge it."

"There was a time, naturally. . . ."

"And that time was yesterday in Geneva. *Ach*, you make me sick with your scheming little fears." He nodded his head vigorously. "Well, you will all learn the truth in good time—when

the will is opened after my death, and not before. Now tell
Frau Bonstetten to come to my office. I have some letters to
dictate."

Walter walked slowly down the carpeted hall of the bank's
first floor which was devoted to the offices of the partners and
ranking staff. Stopping at the door which led into the room of
typists and secretaries, he opened it and called in, commanding
Frau Bonstetten to go at once to the office of Herr Doktor
Robert (the "Doktor" was a legitimate degree in jurisprudence
which was, however, only used at the bank). Having discharged
this commission, he went on towards his own office which was
at the other side of the building, looking out on the Bleicherweg.
He was not as disturbed by his father's outburst as he would
have been ten years earlier. There had gradually grown within
him a protective cartilage against the old man's scoldings.
They no longer threw him into fits of despondency and belief
in his inadequacy. True, his outward reaction remained as it had
always been, one of meek contriteness, but it was a response
that not only helped to maintain the inner coating of impervious-
ness but also served to lessen the period of his father's anger,
which was bad for his aging heart. There had been moments
when, at the goading of Hélène, he had contemplated self-asser-
tion and remonstrance, but he had never tried it and was content that he had not. Patently it would accomplish nothing. One
could not change a father like Robert Eggli, and according to
all natural law—that is, natural law as good Swiss conceived it
—it was quite right and proper that sons be scolded and told
they were fools even though they had reached middle age.

He considered his father's statement that the Baroness had sufficient money to care for her needs. In spite of the old man's
defiant secretiveness concerning the terms of the will, it would
appear that she was not to be a beneficiary. Of course this was only
conjecture. He might well leave her something of value—a sum
of cash, his mother's jewels, the Ambrogio, the pair of Lancrets
or the Hellenic torso—just to spite them. If, however, he was

guided by his usually sensible approach, unswayed by any poison of sentiment either of affection or resentment, he would leave his fortune intact so that his heirs could carry on the affairs of the bank without altering the quality of its liquidity. His annoyance at Walter's use of the word "rich" had been another clue. He remembered now having heard the old man say on more than one occasion that anyone who lived as he wished to live, without envy or ambition, was rich. Had he not said of the Baroness that she had all she would ever need?

On opening the door of his office, Walter found Hans Waldmann, hat on his knee, seated by the desk reading the *Neue Zürcher Zeitung.*

"Grüezi, Hans," Walter said cheerfully. "What brings you here?"

"*Ach,* Walter, have you read this? The Anglo-Americans have crossed the Straits of Messina and have landed in Italy," Hans said, folding the newspaper and putting it back on Walter's desk.

"You are not surprised, are you?"

"Not in the least. As a matter of fact, the reason I came over to see Grosspapa concerns the situation in Italy." He stood up. "Now that you have finished your talk with him I shall go to his office."

"You had better call first. He just asked me to send him Frau Bonstetten as he had some letters to write."

"Yes, yes, I know how he is." Hans lifted the telephone and asked the operator for Herr Doktor Robert. "Ah, grüezi, Frau Bonstetten, will you ask Doktor Robert if I may see him? I am in Herr Walter's office. What? In half an hour? Good, good." He put his hat on the desk and sat down again. "You have heard. Not for half an hour."

"Just as well. He was in a bad humor when I left him. Maybe the letters will calm him down."

"So he is angry, eh? I suppose because Jacques goes to Berne without seeing him first."

"How did you know that Jacques was in Berne?"

"I have friends there who told me."

"Friends or spies, Hans?" Walter asked jokingly.

"It does not matter what one calls them," Hans answered huffily. "They tell me what is going on—which is good for the bank, for you."

"What are they telling you about Italy?"

"It is very confidential."

"I understand. What is it?"

"That negotiations are under way between Badoglio and the Anglo-Americans. There will be an armistice. The Italians will withdraw from the war."

"Quite frankly, Hans, I'm not surprised. When they threw out Il Duce, it was clear that they had had a bellyful of his nonsense."

"Hitler is furious. He intends to occupy Italy as he did France."

"What good will that do him?"

Hans shrugged his shoulders. "He will send many new divisions into Italy to stop the Allied advance."

"Which will weaken the defenses of Norway and the Channel."

"The General Staff are aware of the Allied plans for invasion from the north. They will be able to concentrate their forces at the right place."

Walter let out a snort of derision. "They will probably be as wrong in the north as they were in the Mediterranean. It was you who told Grosspapa they had positive information that the attack should be on Sardinia and Greece, and then it came on Sicily and they were quite unprepared."

"That was a mistake, a bad mistake. Canaris has suffered for that one."

"Ach, Hans, everything they do is a bad mistake. Look what is happening right now at Kharkov and Rostov—they are being beaten by those Slavs and Cossacks. And the bombings of Germany, how can they stop it? They need the Luftwaffe in Russia."

"Yes, that is bad." Hans shook his head. "It is very bad. The destruction is interfering with transportation."

Walter twisted the *Neue Zürcher Zeitung* around so that he could read the headlines. "Funny, isn't it, having Jacques' boy Robert as one of the bomber pilots? It is a good thing the Nazis don't know that! They might make a special effort to shoot him down."

"Why should they care particularly about young Bobby?"

"Just to prove to you how clever they are."

"They have more serious things to occupy them. It is more likely that he might land in Switzerland. Two more did yesterday."

"Forced landings, eh?"

"That is what they said. We shall know the truth after our air force has inspected the airplanes. One came into Dübendorf and the other at Burochs."

"American bombers?"

"The very latest models. Very fine, I am told. Better than the British. Everything went well in Geneva?"

"As usual, Schwarz is very cooperative. We are handling all the advances on watch movements and jewels through him."

"All?"

"That is, to the West."

"Any parties?"

"Just one. A tea at Emil's."

"Hmm. Well, Lucy will hear all the gossip from Hélène."

"Without doubt." Walter was determined not to discuss his meeting with the Baroness de Marty with Hans. On the way home he and Hélène had agreed that only his father should know about it.

"If you are busy, I shall read the paper," Hans said.

Walter laughed. "Busy? Who is busy at banking these days? If it were not for Grosspapa, I would be playing golf."

"I presume that Jacques has called his father on the telephone."

"This morning. He is coming to Zürich for the week end. We are all to dine at the Sudstrasse on Saturday."

"Ach, so! That is too bad. Lucy and I are spending the week end at the Türler See."

"Not this week end. You had better call Lucy and tell her that she is dining with Grosspapa."

"Did he tell you that we were expected?"

"He gave the command—you and Lucy and Hélène and me."

Hans shrugged. "There is nothing to do. Do you mind if I use your telephone?"

Before Hans could lift the receiver, the phone rang and Walter answered it. "Good! Thank you, Frau Bonstetten," he said and hung up. "Grosspapa wishes to see you at once."

Hans Waldmann grabbed his hat and darted out of the room as if the old man's command had been issued directly into his ear.

Walter picked up the newspaper that Hans had been reading and leaned back in his chair. He looked at the article about the Allied invasion of Calabria, but his mind did not take in the meaning of the words. It had returned to the Baroness de Marty and the comments of his father. He reviewed the dialogue until he came to that part where the old man had implied that Hélène was not telling him the truth about her relationship with Tony Venturi. That was a matter he had never liked to dwell on. It was an old habit of his to close his mind to any subject that was disagreeable. He knew that Hélène and Tony were old friends, that they saw each other constantly on her visits to Lugano. He had been kidded about it enough by his friends to realize that they were trying to tell him it was more than mere friendship and that he should put a checkrein on her; but he had purposely shut out the realization, obliterated it, consoling himself with the belief that his friends in fact knew no more than he did. Hélène had never been caught *flagrante delicto* or he would have known about it—all Switzerland would have known about it. So what proof did they have to substantiate their gossip? Nothing more than the fact that Tony had been her tame cat during those holidays in Lugano, and those holidays had not been repeated now for almost a year and a half. Yes, the last time had been at Easter of 1942, and it was now September of 1943. Where else could they have seen each other? Tony never came to Zürich, and it was hardly likely that they could have arranged an assignation at Zug where she occasionally went to visit Elsa von Beckenreid, or at Lucerne where she went once or twice a year with the children, or at Geneva where they always went together.

Besides, he believed Hélène. The one thing you could say of her was that she had the courage of her convictions. She was not afraid of the truth. When he had cautioned her a year ago to be careful about Venturi, that he was probably getting information for his Axis friends and that he might well try to pump her about the bank's position and Grosspapa's views of the war, she had replied with frankness that she knew all about Tony's "spying" (that was the word she had used) and that he would never get anything out of her. She had not said she would not see any more of him. She had given the impression he continued to amuse her, though she was fully aware that he was completely unprincipled. Now at Geneva, however, her tone had been different. After leaving the house of the Baroness she had stated flatly that she was through with him and wished never to lay eyes on him again. Grosspapa thought that she was lying. He himself was convinced that she was not. As for the past—well, that was the past and there was no sense in digging into it.

He picked up the telephone and dialled his house. One of the maids answered and he asked to speak to Frau Eggli.

"Well, did you tell him?" Hélène asked.

"Everything, exactly as she told us."

"What did he say?"

"That it was no news to him, that he knew all about the activities of our friend."

"He was annoyed with her for speaking?"

"Oh, no, not at all. On the contrary, I had the impression he felt that she had done the right thing. He said that it had been given as a warning to you."

"To me?"

"Yes, to you."

Hélène laughed softly. "What a smart old fox Grosspapa is! He is quite right of course. I realized that at once."

"You never said so."

"Why should I remark on something that was obvious?"

"I see your point now. Only it never occurred to me until Grosspapa mentioned it."

"It wouldn't occur to you, dear. Your mind is above that kind of gossip."

"Then there was some truth to it."

"Naturally. You know that as well as I do. He was a friend, and when a married woman has a man friend, people will talk. In the old days before the war it did not matter. I knew they were talking and I didn't care. It was something which concerned you and me and no else. Now of course it is different with him behaving as he does."

"Then you meant what you said, that you would see no more of him?"

"Absolutely! I told him so."

"At the Schwarzes' tea?"

"Yes. You may have seen him come over to talk with me. I told him then in no uncertain terms that I did not wish to see him again."

"That's good, Hélène. You have acted wisely."

"For a change. I shall see you at lunch. I must run now."

"Just one thing—you will have to call Maria Hüppli and tell her that we cannot dine with them on Saturday. Grosspapa wishes us to dine at the Sudstrasse. Jacques will be there."

"Now, really! That is asking too much. Must I make enemies of my friends just to please your father?"

"I'm sorry, my dear, but you know how it is."

"Oh, I know. But I can't help being annoyed just the same. Adieu." And she hung up.

Walter swung his chair around and looked out of the window. The Bleicherweg was not crowded as it used to be in the days of peace when financiers and merchants from every country came to Zürich on matters of international trade. The few pedestrians he saw were housewives carrying string bags in search for a decent meal to put before their men, and youngsters in uniform sauntering idly, looking into shop windows. The blue and white trams still rattled by on their way to and from the Enge, but they, too, except in the morning and evening, were sparsely filled.

He wondered how Jacques would find this somber wartime Switzerland, confined to its little problems and squabbles. He would of course have plenty to occupy him with his official duties, which would probably keep him in Berne for the greater part of the time. He remembered his father having said that Jacques was with the Office of Economic Warfare which was an agency engaged in pre-emptive buying. As far as Switzerland was concerned, this would mean watch movements, instrument jewels, and antiaircraft guns. If Jacques was hoping to corner the market on those items so that there would be none for the Axis, he would have to have more than dollars. Swiss manufacturers did not fancy turning down orders from old customers, even if the new one would pay higher for their entire output. They thought in long-term cycles, remembering the days when orders were scarce, when competition from other countries and tariff walls made it difficult to keep their workmen, their skilled workmen, on the payroll. In those days it had been the orders of shrewd old customers, who could foresee the days ahead when they would need Swiss sources, that had kept them going. Those days were likely to come again, so they preferred to spread their sales among as many customers in as many countries as possible.

He supposed that it was for this reason that the United States Government had selected Jacques to come to Switzerland, believing that he, because he spoke the languages and knew the mentality, being in essence a good Swiss, would be able to persuade the manufacturers to drop their German and Italian customers and sell their entire production to America. The British, he knew, had been toying with the same idea for some time, but so had the Germans, with the result that each had bid the other up, to the delight and profit of the Swiss. Jacques was coming in late in the game and would find it an expensive one. Well, so much the better for Switzerland.

Walter turned his chair so that it again faced his desk. He laughed to himself. If Jacques was counting on help from Grosspapa, he was backing the wrong horse. The old man was strongly pro-Ally, believed in their cause as fervently as he loathed the Nazi-Fascists, yet he would never lift a finger to disturb the delicate balance of Swiss trade.

CHAPTER XVIII

JACQUES had purposely not told his father on the telephone what train he was taking on Saturday morning. He wanted if possible to avoid any fuss and ostentation. To be met at the Bahnhof by Tobald and the Rolls would have excited all kinds of comments which might reach enemy ears. Not that he could keep his visit a secret. That, he realized, was quite out of the question. Berlin had probably known of his presence in Switzerland within an hour of his arrival at Cointrin Airport, confirming what they had already learned of his departure from Lisbon. But it would be wiser just the same to keep his movements in a prudent low key. The red-carpet greeting accorded V.I.P.'s would be sure to excite questions and speculations which would impede the work in hand. It were better that his return to the city of his birth be as unobtrusive as possible. For that reason he had taken a third-class carriage at Berne, bringing along only a small suitcase, and had decided during the journey to take a tram from the Haupt Bahnhof to the bank. He had even remembered that the number of the tram which took one to the Bleicherweg was 13:23.

His timing was precise. He reached the bank at exactly eleven forty-five and as he entered, his father, grey Homburg on his head, grey gloves in his hand, was descending the curved marble stair at the rear of the main banking floor. Jacques put down his bag and waited. The old man traversed at least half of the floor before he recognized his son. The only sign he gave was a slight raising of the eyebrows. He walked toward Jacques without changing the measured dignity of his pace.

"Grüezi, Papa," Jacques said, smiling at his father.

"I did not expect you so early," the old man said. "Vicki will not have prepared lunch for you."

"I can probably lunch with Walter and Hélène if they are back from Geneva. If not, I shall go to the Baur-au-Lac."

"No, no. You shall come with me. Vicki will have to find enough food for the three of us. Take your bag. Tobald is waiting for me across the way in the Claridenstrasse."

Tobald saw them as they emerged from the bank and darted across the street to take the suitcase from Jacques, greeting him effusively as he did so and complaining that he could have fetched Herr Jacques at the Haupt Bahnhof had anyone let him know.

When they were seated, Robert Eggli instructed Tobald to close the sliding window which separated the chauffeur's seat from the tonneau.

"You look well, Papa," Jacques said.

"There is nothing wrong with me," his father muttered.

"Vicki has written that Dr. Huber insists you take it easy."

"I am not as young as I was, though I feel no differently. Dr. Huber is afraid of losing a valuable patient. How are things in London?"

"You knew I was there?" Jacques asked in surprise.

"It was no secret, was it?"

"Not especially, though it is better that my movements are not too well known."

"Then you should avoid fellows like Hoy-Babbington."

Jacques smiled. "Of course! I might have known that the news would reach you."

"Just what is it you will be doing here?" the old man asked, turning his head as he did so, spearing Jacques with his agate-blue eyes.

"Chiefly purchasing," Jacques answered casually, feeling cold in his stomach from his father's gaze. The task that he had been assigned—the real task—had been disclosed to him in London and confirmed in Berne only the day before in a long talk with

John Margett at the Legation. He had pleaded the almost insurmountable difficulties to all of them, to Holden and Bruce in Grosvenor Street and to Margett yesterday in the Alpenstrasse; but not one of them had appeared to believe him, laughing it off as if they thought he was trying to build a case for himself that would call for a citation when he pulled it off. They seemed to assume that a son of the house, a partner, could ask for the combination, go to the vault, take out the account code and examine it at his leisure. They had even implied that he should be able to do it without exciting the least suspicion. He had argued that his father and his brother were the only two who had access to the book and that any attempt on his part to get it in his hands would be fatal. They had smiled at him knowingly. "We are not telling you how to get the names," they said. "That is your job. Get them any way that seems best to you, even if you have to burgle the safe. The important thing is to get them, and in such shape that we will be able to identify the accounts by their numbers. Naturally you must not arouse any suspicion which might cause the family to change the code before we could trace them."

His father's next remark made the chill within him almost choke his breath.

"You will be trying to find out about Hitler's resources, I suppose," his father said.

"Naturally we want to know all we can in order to embarrass the Nazi war effort."

"It is in plenty of trouble right now. How is Doris?"

"Oh, worried, I think, at having both of her men overseas."

"Where is young Robert?"

"In England. I went to see him there at his airfield."

"He is bombing Germany?"

"By this time I suppose he is. When I saw him his squadron was in training."

"That is how you will defeat the Nazis. They cannot support heavy destruction of their factories and railroads, not while their

armies are being beaten in Russia. With the invasion of Italy
and the surrender of Badoglio, you have the Nazis in a precarious
situation. The German people are beginning to see it, to realize
that they are facing another disaster. The old Junkers are fed up
with the stupidity of Hitler. They would get out of this mess if
they could, but they cannot as long as Roosevelt and Churchill
insist on that 'unconditional surrender.' That was very short-
sighted of your President. I thought he was cleverer than that.
He does not know the Germans. Such a demand encourages
their silly 'will to die.' "

"You still get news of what is going on there, I gather."

"Naturally. Hans has his contacts."

"So?"

"You will see him tonight at dinner, but I doubt that he will
give you any information."

Jacques smiled. "Because I now work for the American Government? Neutrality! Good old Swiss neutrality!"

"It is not something to laugh at."

"Who else will be at dinner?"

"Walter, Hélène, Lucy, and of course your Tante Vicki."

"How is Tante Vicki?"

"She does not change, always complaining, always gossiping."

"Wonderful! It will be good to see them all."

"They will be curious to see you in your new role. What is
your title anyway?"

"Economic attaché, that is all."

"You should have demanded the rank of minister. After all,
you are an important banker and in your fiftieth year."

"In war every citizen does his bit without asking for titles."

"Nonsense. Look at the friends of mine who have left Wall
Street to become cabinet members and ambassadors."

"They were known to Roosevelt."

"Am I not known to Roosevelt?"

"Yes, Papa, but it does not always follow. . . ."

"You are too modest. It is not dignified that you, my son, a partner of Spears, Wetherell, should come to Switzerland as a little agent to buy watches."

"It is important work for the war effort. Which reminds me that I want to have a talk with you, Papa, on that subject. Some of these manufacturers here are being very pigheaded."

"You can talk as much as you wish, but don't expect me to interfere. I don't tell my clients to whom they should sell."

"It is a question of their own interests, their profits."

"Hah! No one is going to tell a Swiss about his profits. That is a subject that is his own business and no one else's."

"I was counting on your help, knowing how you feel about this war," Jacques said, trying hard to convince himself now that his father believed in his cover.

"How I feel about this war and helping you buy watch movements and guns are two different things which have no relation to each other. You forget that you are in Zürich now and not in Washington. By the way, where will you be living? Here or in Berne?"

"I don't know yet." Jacques saw a crowd of people streaming in front of the car. "What is that? What goes on?"

They were circling the Bellevueplatz where people were racing to the quayside, looking up in the sky. Tobald who had slowed the car was leaning forward, trying to see what it was that the crowd was watching. The old man knocked on the glass partition and shouted a command for the car to stop. The chauffeur drew up to the curb and Robert Eggli jumped out, followed by Jacques. The two of them walked quickly from under the shade of the plane trees to the edge of the quay, where they could get a clear view. Coming down the lake at an altitude of about two thousand feet was a trim Swiss fighter plane with its red tail, on which was a white cross, shining in the sun. Behind it a chunky, clumsy-looking bomber spluttered along, smoke pouring from one engine, the propeller of which was feathered. As it passed overhead Jacques could see clearly the blue and white insignia of the U.S. Army Air Corps on its khaki-colored fuselage. Three more Swiss fighters followed on behind and above the crippled bomber. They were leading it in to Dübendorf Airfield. Jacques' heart tightened with fear until he saw from the double tail that it was a B-24.

"Is it British or American?" his father asked.

"American. A Liberator. It has been badly shot up. I saw a hole in one wing."

"Lucky boys! They will now be interned here. It would be good news if that was your Robert's airplane."

"It isn't. He flies a different model."

Robert Eggli turned and walked back to the car, but Jacques waited by the lake, watching the four planes until they disappeared over the Dolder, praying that the bomber would make it.

"One of those Swiss pilots is probably the Schweizer boy," the old man said when they were seated again in the car. "They use him on this work because he was brought up in America. He knows what to say to the American and British pilots over the radio."

"I know him. A fine young man. As a matter of fact, he is an old friend of Bobby's. They went to prep school together."

"His father did the right thing to send him here to the university. Now he does his military service in a Swiss fighter instead of being shot up over Germany."

"Bobby was determined to go to Yale," Jacques said with a note of regret in his voice.

"He could have come here for his military service just the same."

"In theory, yes, but morally he could never have done it, not with his classmates joining the service to fight for their country."

"Just so, that is why you should have insisted that he go to the Universität, or the Technische Hochschule. If you expect him to be a good banker, he should have a European background of education. Look at young Schweizer. When he goes back to New York after the war, he will have a head start as an engineer."

"I'm not so sure, Papa. He is apt to have a difficult time explaining why he was not fighting."

"Nonsense! He has the best excuse in the world. He was here at school when his country went to war, but as he was born a Swiss, his father's naturalization is not accepted by the Swiss authorities as a reason for the boy not doing his military service here. That is clear. No one can object to that."

Jacques had no desire to pursue the argument. In his heart he agreed with his father, but the one element which the old man could not possibly comprehend was the relationship between father and son in the United States. How could he explain that he could not have insisted Bobby go to Zürich University and not to Yale? Such a statement would be unthinkable to any Swiss parent and, above all, to Robert Eggli, who could not conceive of a civilization which was not based on authoritarian patriarchy. Suppose he had insisted. What would have happened? Bobby and Doris would have turned against him, accusing him of being unreasonable and unfair. He would have been ostracized and hated at home. The serene course of family harmony would have received a blow from which it probably never would have recovered. Was that worth the satisfaction of seeing his son a Swiss pilot over the Dolder? The answer was clearly no. Bobby was too good a boy, too fine a boy, to be denied the right to go to the school of his choice or to fight for the country of his birth. Yet he envied John Schweizer whose boy was probably now coming in for a landing at Dübendorf.

"How is the business?" Jacques asked. "I have been out of touch now for months."

"*Ach,* business!" the old man snorted. "When one considers the state of the world, it could be worse. These are times when one has to think of conserving funds, not increasing them."

"Yet the discounting of bills must have been profitable."

"A little here and a little there. Nothing to boast about."

"Why did you take the Latin American business away from Spears, Wetherell?" Jacques asked.

"Because Huber, Barros can handle those matters under the circumstances."

"To keep New York from knowing about those shipments?"

"You are in the American Government now. When you go back to Spears, Wetherell, I will discuss the bank's affairs with you."

"I am still a partner, Papa."

"And you still ask too many questions."

The car stopped in the driveway and Jacques waited until his father had descended before climbing out. When Tante Vicki, who was sitting in the sunroom which looked out over the lawn, heard voices in the hall she jumped up. She thought at first that it was Walter talking to his father, then she detected the slightly American inflection of the *Zürichdeutsch* and walked quickly to the door.

"Grüezi, Tante Vicki!" Jacques exclaimed and hugged the wiry little old lady.

Vicki held him at arms' length and looked at him. "Well, Jacques, what is this I hear about you? You are a big official for the Americans, eh?"

"He is nothing at all but a petty attaché at Berne," Robert Eggli said, moving past them into the room. "But he is having lunch with us, so you will have to tell Frau Maur to cook enough for three."

"We did not expect you so early," Tante Vicki said. "I shall have to see what can be done about lunch. *Ach*, with that suit you do not look as American as you used to. He is a real Zürich-looking banker, eh, Robert?"

"He looks like every attaché in London or Paris," Robert grumbled.

"I must go and speak to Frau Maur," Vicki said. She started down the hall, then stopped. "Will you be wishing a cocktail, Jacques?"

"That would be wonderful," Jacques answered. "You still have some gin?"

"Robert, find that bottle of gin in your cupboard," she called. "I shall tell Anni to bring the shaker."

"One should not drink alcohol in the middle of the day," the old man grumbled, but he went to the cupboard in the library and brought back a bottle of English gin and one of French vermouth. "I do not approve of this," he said sternly as he put the bottles on the table, "but as you have been away for a long time, I shall make this exception."

"Thanks, Papa. I need a martini after that train trip."

"What was wrong with the train?"

"Nothing unusual, but two hours on a hard wooden bench that bounces like a trotting horse is quite a punishment."

"You have grown soft like all Americans. Our trains are good enough for us."

Anni, the maid, came into the sunroom carrying a tray on which were a silver shaker and a dish with two small pieces of ice. When she saw Jacques, she grinned broadly, saying, "Grüezi, Herr Eggli-Davenport. It is wonderful that you could manage to come home in these bad times."

"It is good to be here, Anni," Jacques said. "Like Herr Robert, you don't grow any older."

"We are not allowed to grow older in this house. It is against orders," Anni said, nodding towards her employer.

"Run along!" Robert commanded gruffly. "Like all the women in this house, you talk too much."

With a wink at Jacques, Anni left the room.

"Can I make one for you?" Jacques asked his father.

"*Gott in Himmel!* I should say not! That stuff is poison. One might as well put cyanide in one's stomach. And in the middle of the day! It is a crazy American habit which you will have to forgo while you are in my house. Oh, today I will allow it because you come here after three years, but after this, no more cocktails. A glass of sherry before meals is good enough for us and it will have to be good enough for you."

"Yes, Papa," Jacques said, thinking that he would have to connive with Anni to get one in his bedroom before he came down to dinner.

Vicki came bustling into the room, breathless and flushed from the excitement of having had to change the luncheon order. "Well, we have managed it. There will be enough. Have you everything you need for your cocktail, Jacques? It is something we are not used to. You know how your father is about cocktails. That bottle of gin has been here since an Englishman came to dinner in 1939. Robert heard that he liked his cocktail, so Walter brought us the bottle. Who was that man, Robert? I think you said that he was a chess player."

"The Chancellor of the Exchequer," Robert Eggli snorted.

"I follow in distinguished company," Jacques said, revolving the shaker in his hands.

Vicki sat down on the edge of a chair. "Now I want to hear all your news," she said. "Your father tells me that you have come to Switzerland to buy things for the American Army. Well, I am sure that you will find plenty of people ready to sell. You know how we Swiss are—always ready to overcharge the Americans. And you have so much money over there. Robert tells me that everyone is rich."

"I never said any such thing!" Robert stated angrily.

"You said that all the money gravitates to New York. Now don't deny that. I heard you say that to Hansli in this very house," Vicki went on.

Jacques smiled. "What Papa meant was that money goes to New York for safekeeping. It does not belong to us."

"Some of it does," Vicki insisted. "Didn't you tell me, Robert, that most of my money was in Wall Street?"

"Oh, Vicki, why do you talk of things you know nothing about?" Robert Eggli complained. "Certainly your money is in New York but that does not make all Americans rich."

"Don't be so cross. How am I know these things?" Vicki said. "Poor Jacques, what a greeting for you, hearing us squabble!"

"Just like old times," Jacques said, drinking his martini.

"*Gotteswillen!* I wish it were like old times," Vicki said with a sigh. "Those were good days before the war when we had plenty of sugar and butter and coffee, and you coming here every summer with Doris and the children. Now your visit only unsettles Robert. He is forever worrying that you will be trying to spy on German secrets."

"Vicki, you are out of your mind!" Robert shouted. "What makes you say that I think Jacques is a spy? That is preposterous!"

"Now don't excite yourself, Robert," Vicki said. "Remember Dr. Huber told you that it is bad for your heart. I know that you have been worrying about Jacques and his work here. Only the other day when Lucy was here she said, 'Hans tells me Grosspapa is worried that Jacques might suddenly appear in Switzerland.'"

"Don't listen to her, Jacques," his father said in a tone of disgust. "She makes all this up in her mind. She has missed her vocation. She should have been a writer of detective stories. Of course I was worried that you might come here. That is only natural with the dangers of wartime travel."

Jacques laughed. He realized that his Tante Vicki in her scatterbrain way had probably hit the nail on the head. Ever since he had met his father at the bank he had had the uneasy feeling that the old man was skeptical about the true nature of his son's assignment in Switzerland. The fact that he had made it plain that as long as Jacques represented the United States Government he would be barred from any information concerning the bank's activities was an indication of suspicion. This, Jacques thought, was going to complicate greatly the execution of his primary mission. In fact, it might make it altogether impossible. His only course now was gradually, painstakingly, to erase that suspicion from his father's mind by convincing him—the whole family, in fact—that his sole interest was the buying of strategic materials.

"Oh, I shall be doing some spying, have no fear of that," Jacques said, quite seriously. "That will be part of my job here. Not only must I buy for my country but I must also find out, if I can, what the Germans are buying. But you must never mention this, Tante Vicki. It is something I am not supposed to talk about. I would never have mentioned it had you not brought up the subject."

The old lady raised her eyebrows conspiratorially. "I would speak to Hansli if I were you," she said in a loud whisper. "He should know what the Germans are buying."

"*Ach*, you would get nothing out of him if he did know, which I doubt," the old man said.

"Oho! Hans knows a lot," Tante Vicki said. "He does his own little spying." She winked at Jacques.

"About matters which do not concern him," Robert Eggli said. "He is not as smart as he thinks he is."

"Well, I'm not the one to tell tales about him," Vicki said knowingly.

"Hah! You are the one to tell tales about anyone, even your own brother," Robert scolded.

Vicki turned to Jacques. "He says that because I have the courage to tell him the truth sometimes. He is just like your grandfather, he cannot take criticism."

Anni appeared at the door to announce that lunch was served. Vicki jumped to her feet and darted towards the dining room. Jacques, waiting for his father to precede him, drained the last of his martini.

"Be careful what you say to her," the old man whispered as he walked out of the room.

CHAPTER XIX

Good night, Vicki," Robert Eggli said as they were standing in the hall after the departure of Walter, Hélène, Hans and Lucy. "You run along to bed. Jacques and I will have a little talk in my study."

Jacques gave his aunt a peck of a kiss on her wrinkled cheek, then followed his father into the somber panelled library—the room that the old man always referred to as his "study."

Robert Eggli looked at his watch. "It is late and you are probably tired after your trip in our uncomfortable train, so I shall not keep you long. Sit down." He sat down in a deep leather chair and motioned to his son to sit near him.

"I'm really not tired, Papa," Jacques said, aware of the dig about his criticism of the Berne-Zürich journey, which he had expressed merely to justify the cocktail before lunch.

"It is a long time now since you have paid us a visit," the old man went on, his sharp blue eyes focused on his son, demanding concentrated attention. "Since you were here the world has been thrown about in the earthquake of war. Your new country has become a belligerent in two hemispheres and naturally that has made all of you forget many things, because, like all youthful people, you enter into the battle with impulsive enthusiasm, thinking only of the defeat of the immediate enemy. That is all right. I don't criticize it. It will bring you history, as I have said from the beginning—history that is now coming true just as I predicted. What is of interest to me is the effect on you. As far as I can judge from this brief half-day, you have caught the contagion. You have entered the battle like the rest of the Americans, with a mind closed to everything but victory. Now that is fine for a boy like your Bobby. I admire that he wants to be a pilot and bomb Germany. But you are a banker, and a banker may not divide his loyalty. He must never let his mind become so inflamed that he loses his power of inductive thinking. He must always keep his mind clear enough to think ahead, to be able to plan for the day when the shooting stops and the world has to resume its business.

"What I am saying to you, Jacques, is a repetition of what I told you when you proposed to me to become a citizen of the United States. Do you remember my words?"

"Yes, Papa," Jacques replied dutifully.

"Well," the old man went on, "it will do you no harm to hear them again. I told you that citizenship is merely a recognition of abode, of responsibility to pay taxes and to abide by the laws. Waving flags and singing songs and shouts of 'My country, right or wrong' are devices used by demagogues to anesthetize the ignorant so that they will follow wherever they are led without question or thought. One sees a perfect example in the theatrics of Hitler. Sentiment, which is the basic ingredient of loyalty, has only one place—in the family. There it is acceptable, and there alone. Not only is loyalty within the family acceptable, it is an absolute requirement. Family first; state second.

"That is what I told you, and I say it again because I wish you to hold it well in mind now that you are back among us. Do your job here as well as you are able, outbuy the Germans wherever you can, find out all you can about their plans, like your clever Mr. Dulles in Berne. But never forget that you are an Eggli, that your first loyalty is to me, to your brother and sister, and to the bank. I am getting on in years. Though I feel strong enough, I am well aware that the time is not far off when I will cease to be the head of the family, but until that day comes I will remain in command."

He smiled, chuckling to himself. "Don't think for a moment that I do not know how much Hélène and sometimes Hans resent what they consider my tyranny. *Ach,* and Doris would too if she lived here. In their secret thoughts they probably pray for my death so that Hélène can strut about as the wife of the new dictator and Hans will have Lucy's fortune to squander on silly modern pictures. They think that I have been too severe with my children, too critical, that I have cowed you and Walter to the point where you are afraid to express an opinion or even have one. That of course is rubbish. I only reprove you when you wish to do something stupid. That is the duty of a father. Imagine the mess you would have made had I not held a strong hand on you both!"

Robert Eggli looked at his watch again. "Aha! It is already midnight. That is enough talk." He stood up. "Remember what I have told you. You are still my son, no matter what passport you carry."

"Yes, Papa," Jacques said.

"Good night then." Robert Eggli shook his son's hand, a good Swiss gesture which Jacques had all but forgotten. "Go to bed and rest that soft behind which has been beaten on a wooden train seat."

"May I be allowed a whisky to take to my room?"

"Whisky! Gin! Alcohol! Is that all you Americans think of?" Robert Eggli went to the cabinet in the corner and brought out a bottle of Scotch whisky. "Here, take this to your room. If you must rot your insides, do it where I cannot watch you."

"Thank you, Papa."

In his room Jacques poured a stiff shot of whisky into the glass by his bedside, filling it up with water from the thermos jug, then went over to the bureau, put the glass down and looked at himself in the mirror. What he saw was to his mind the face of a once handsome weakling: slightly pudgy, jowls beginning to appear, pouches under the eyes, and a mouth that was facile, too facile, too prone to laugh, to speak before thought. He was far from proud of the reflection. It seemed to him standing there in that room in the Sudstrasse—his room, the room of his earliest

memories—that whatever authority of mind or decision he had
been able to acquire since going abroad had vanished the moment
he had met his father at the bank. At the very first keen piercing
look of those china blue eyes into his, the years had fallen away
and he was again the frightened, dominated youth of earlier
Zürich days. He no longer had a will, or courage, or the power
to ratiocinate.

He took a drink of whisky, then sat down in a chair by the
window with the glass in his hand. The shutters had been closed
and the heavy curtains of faded green stuff—the same curtains
which had been there when he had been a student at the university—were drawn, shutting out the night, making the room
a claustrophobic cell. The whisky tingled within him as he began
to review what his father had said. The words had been—he saw
that plainly—a warning, a reminder that he might seek information concerning German affairs anywhere in Switzerland except
at the bank. To report to his government anything which had
to do with the bank's accounts or its movements of funds would
be considered a treasonable act, a disloyalty to Robert Eggli and
the family. And yet his government had commissioned him to
do that very thing. They had, in fact, selected him for this
mission because he was in a better position to obtain the information than any other American. They had made that clear in
London, even in Washington for that matter, although Jim
Stevens had avoided disclosing the exact nature of the particular
job; but he had said, "You can be of unique value to us, Jacques.
With your background and associations you can perform a service
to your country which no one else could accomplish." He had
come back to Switzerland determined to do it, filled with zeal
to execute a really brilliant coup which would have given him
the satisfaction of having performed a major service in the fight
against tyranny.

Now all that zeal had vanished. His father had exposed the
whole problem in a different light. It was as if the old man had
wiped the quicksilver from the back of the mirror, allowing him

to look through a clear pane and observe the true consequences of this mission of folly. His first loyalty was to the family, his father had said. He could not argue with that. It was a principle which motivated the entire world. The joker was that by "family" the old man meant the bank. That was the family in his eyes. It was their fortune, their bond, their grave responsibility. To tamper with the bank was to tamper with the very loyalties which held them together, the source of the clan's strength. Though he had not seen it when he was fired by the fervor to enter the ranks and fight for his new country, he saw clearly now that in stealing the bank's secrets for the benefit of Washington, he would be destroying the unity of the family, cutting the throats of his father, his brother and sister, and committing himself to permanent and irrevocable disinheritance, not alone of money— that was the least of his fears—but of the right to consider himself a member of the clan.

As he finished his whisky he looked about the room. The brass bed on which he had slept for over twenty years, the great oak wardrobe, its elaborate and deeply incised panels of cherry and pear wood polished so that they glistened like burnished bronze, the big, ugly Victorian dresser with its oval mirror which could be tipped to suit the gazer, the row of eighteenth-century prints of Swiss soldiers in the uniforms of various regiments—all were there unchanged, as precise as his memories. This was where he had dreamed and planned, where he had fought the resentment of his father's harsh treatment, where he had learned to accept it, to believe that it stemmed from justice and wisdom and to realize that respect and admiration were worth more, perhaps, than the softness of affection. His eventual escape to the United States had been an endeavor to find within himself an identity which was not wholly controlled and submissive. As the second son he had been allowed this dispensation, but with the understanding that he was to remain an integral part of the family, the bank, and that if anything should happen to Walter, he was to return to his place on the right hand of the throne.

The room, the memories, like his father's eyes, were all too compelling. He could not be a traitor to them, surely not as long as his father was alive.

He got to his feet and started to undress. In growing panic he cast about frantically for ways in which he could be of service aside from divulging the account names. There were sources to be tapped which might well be more fruitful for victory than the mere blocking of German funds. Tony Venturi might be one of them. He remembered that Jim Stevens had asked him if he knew Tony. In London, too, Holden had told him that the leading agent of the Nazis in Switzerland was a chap named von Orb, whom Stevens had mentioned, and that he was suspiciously friendly with a Swiss named Antonio Venturi. The last time Jacques and Doris had been in Zürich there had been a lot of gossip about Venturi and Hélène. Apparently she had had quite a buzz with him in Lugano. He must have a talk with her. Maybe she could give him a line on Venturi's activities. He would have to sound her out first to see where her sympathies lay. If Tony had brought her into the Nazi camp, then he must not disclose his hand. The more he thought of that, however, the more he thought it unlikely. Venturi, as he remembered him, was a man without convictions beyond money and women. He would call Hélène in the morning to see if he could work out a date to see her alone. He could use as his excuse a desire to hear the latest about the Baroness de Marty who was now living, he had heard, in Geneva. That approach, one of straight family gossip, would be natural enough to disarm her. And even if she told Walter and Walter told his father that he was asking questions about Tony Venturi, the old man would be relieved to learn that his spying did not concern the bank.

"This is positively romantic," Hélène said, standing in the window of Jacques' sitting room in the Bellevue-Palace in Berne, looking out on the swift waters of the Aare.

"Don't put ideas in my head," Jacques said, bringing her a

martini. "It was just my luck that you came up to Berne this week."

"As I told you on the telephone, I had promised Margi she could visit her cousin Elaine before taking her examinations. Besides, I love these visits with Dora and Karl. They are such fun. We laugh so much. It is a relief from the solemnity of Zürich. They were unhappy that you wouldn't lunch with them, but I explained that you wanted to have a family talk with me."

"You can tell the von Graffenrieds that I should love to lunch with them some other time. It was only today that I wanted to see you alone."

"Oh, they understood."

"You say that Margi is a cousin of their daughter Elaine. How is that?"

"Dora von Graffenried's grandmother was a Sieber from Winterthur."

"Oh, I see. Then there is no connection with the Egglis?"

"Not until I married your brother," Hélène said with a mischievous smile.

Jacques laughed. "Thus raising the social standing of my family." He enjoyed talking with his sister-in-law. She had a nice wit and a cosmopolitan point of view which he found particularly agreeable because it was so untypical of Zürich. As he looked at her now, silhouetted against the light from the window, her trim figure and her perfectly coiffed head in its becoming toque made her appear feminine and desirable. He did not blame Tony Venturi for making a play for her. He would like to himself. A pity, he thought, that she is Walter's wife. But it was out of the question. The country was too small and the watching eyes too many and too alert. "Tell me," he said, "have you been to Geneva lately?"

She turned her gaze from the Aare and looked at him with a smile. "You mean, I suppose, have I met the Baroness de Marty?"

"You have read my mind."

"It's an open book, Jacques. I was wondering what you wanted to talk to me about. It seemed to me that there were only three subjects on which I might have some information and which you could hardly discuss with Grosspapa. One of them was the Baroness de Marty, and the minute you mentioned Geneva it was clear."

"What were the other two?"

"Never mind about them. Let me tell you that Walter and I were in Geneva last week—Emil Schwarz told you that on the telephone—and we met her at tea."

"What was your impression?"

"Oh, I completely succumbed to her charm."

"A clever woman."

"And a nice one, I should judge. She seems truly devoted to Grosspapa."

"What makes you think so?"

"Well, she did something, something she needn't have done, which proved it."

"What was that?" Jacques asked, made curious by her use of the word "did" rather than "said." "Did she give you her pearls?"

"No, silly, it was something more significant. She asked me to her house, which is a little *bijou*, by the way, to warn me that a certain man was trying to get information about the bank."

"Why should she warn you? Why did she not go directly to Grosspapa?"

"It's a long story. This was a man I used to know quite well, an old flirt of mine before the war. The Baroness saw me talking to him at the Schwarzes' tea. She probably thought I was still intimate with him, and she knew what he was after because he had tried to get her to join him in a scheme to get Grosspapa's bank secrets."

"What you tell me is fascinating," Jacques said, which was the truth. The situation seemed to be playing into his hands almost too neatly. He was sure that the man would turn out to be Tony Venturi. "This fellow really made a proposal to the Baroness?"

"Apparently. According to her story, he came right out with

the statement that he could supply the British with valuable information, for which of course he wanted to be paid."

"Oh, he was selling German information. I thought you said that he wanted the Baroness to get facts about the bank."

"That is right. It was her idea that his real purpose was to find out what Grosspapa was doing. The sale of information to the British was only a blind to get her confidence."

"My God, Hélène, this is fantastic! Who is this man? Is he a German?"

"His identity is unimportant. The point of interest is that she asked Walter in my presence to tell the whole story to Grosspapa, because she did not dare send it by mail to Zürich and she thought he ought to be warned at once."

"Walter was with you at her house?"

"Yes, we went together."

"What makes you think, then, that she was warning you?"

"Because as I told you, she had seen me talking to him and she knew he was an old beau of mine."

"Had you been seeing him of late?"

"Not for quite a while, but she didn't know that. How should she? She wasn't taking any chances. She wanted me to know in front of Walter that this fellow was the sort who would use any means to get salable information. Her one idea was to protect Grosspapa. Now you know why I think she is all right."

Jacques looked at his watch. "It is already a quarter to one. I think we had better go down to lunch."

"Afraid of the gossips?" she asked, her eyes crinkling with laughter.

"Afraid of myself."

Hélène picked up her bag from the table and gave his cheek a pat as she passed him. "You're amusing, Jacques. Too bad I married your brother."

"I was thinking the same thing."

"Well, put it out of your mind. I've given up flirting for the duration."

As they walked down the hall with its carpet of deep Turkey-red pile, Jacques made up his mind that he would have to pursue the subject in the dining room. It would have to be done tactfully so that the waiters caught no inkling and in tones so low that they could not reach an adjoining table. Hélène's disclosure had opened up many avenues of possible operation. He had to explore these tentatively, making sure where his sister-in-law's true sentiments lay. He reminded himself that she was a clever woman who might well be trying to set his mind at rest to the point where he would disclose his hand.

Jacques insisted on a table in the far corner of the room near the windows which looked out on the terrace and the river. He wanted to limit the number of eavesdroppers by insuring at least two sides without adjoining tables.

When they had ordered *truite au bleu*, which was one of the few items of good food that the war had not denied the Swiss, and a bottle of white Neuchâtel, he waited until the waiter had left the table before speaking to Hélène in a voice so low that it was almost a whisper. "Has Walter told this story to Grosspapa?" he asked.

"Yes, on Saturday, before you arrived."

"What was his reaction?"

"Walter was surprised that he took it so calmly." She laughed softly. "He is really a clever old man. He saw at once that it was really aimed at me."

"Did he say that to Walter?"

"Straight out. You know your father; he never minces words."

"Then Grosspapa must have known about this man, this friend of yours."

"But of course! He knows everything."

"I admire you, Hélène. You don't seem to care that they should suspect you."

"What would you have me do, go into mourning because a man I once flirted with turns out to be a Nazi agent? I always knew he was no good, but he used to amuse me."

"Do you still see him?"

"At Geneva last week was the first time in a year. I told him that I was through with him."

"Because you don't approve of his spying?"

"Oh, I might overlook it if he did it out of dedication to a conviction, a belief. But when he does it just for the money, not caring a damn which side wins, then I'm disgusted."

"I agree that is pretty low. One has to have a firm belief about this war. Neutrality is all right in principle, but each of us, deep down, wants one side or the other to win."

"Naturally."

"I'm glad you feel that way about it. You approve then of my helping—joining my government?"

"I think it is what every man should do when his country is at war."

"Grosspapa is sure we are going to win."

"I hope he is right. He usually is."

The waiter came with the trout, and a bus boy brought the wine in an ice bucket which he put on the table. While they were being served and the wine poured, Jacques talked to Hélène of food and the difficulties the Swiss were having in getting many staples. But he kept the tone of his voice in the same low key in order to give the impression that food had been their sole topic of conversation.

"It is interesting to learn that you are pro-Ally," he said when the waiter had left the table, switching the subject abruptly so that she would notice it.

Hélène looked at him quizzically. "What makes you say that?" she asked. "You couldn't have thought that I would be for Hitler."

"Why not? He seems to appeal to many women."

"Not to me!" she said emphatically. "I think he is the most evil, sinister, dreadful man who ever lived. If I had the chance, I would kill him without the least compunction."

"Do you mean that?"

"Of course I mean it," she said indignantly. "If you knew me better, you'd know that I don't say what I don't mean."

Jacques smiled at her. "Don't get huffy, Hélène. I just wanted to make sure."

"See here, Jacques, tell me the truth—did you suspect that I was working hand in hand with Tony?"

"Tony who?"

"Now don't try to be clever. You know perfectly well that the man I was talking about, the one whom the Baroness warned about, is Tony Venturi."

"I suspected it might be."

"Oh, don't be so circuitous. You sound like Hans Waldmann. Why not come straight out and admit that you knew perfectly well it was Tony Venturi, and that you asked me to lunch in order to find out if I was involved in German secret service work?"

Jacques could not refrain from laughing. "You're a wonder, Hélène. You do my heart good. Only please keep it in a low key. We don't want that couple at the next table sending wires to Berlin."

"I'm sorry if I talked too loudly. I was so annoyed I forgot."

"Okay, Hélène, if you want me to come clean, I will. I did ask you to lunch because I wanted to find out if you were mixed up with Venturi's activities. You see, we know all about him and for whom he is working."

"Is my name in the dossier?" she asked, frowning.

"Not that I know of, and what is more, I have never let on that one of his former lady friends is my sister-in-law. I have a particular reason for keeping that fact to myself."

"To protect the bank," she inserted.

"No, this time you are wrong. It was because I had a secret hope that I might be able to elicit your help."

"Help in what? I don't understand."

"Help in using your friend to our advantage."

"No, thank you. I'm not getting mixed up in that game."

"You said that if you had the chance, you would shoot Hitler. Well, Hélène, if you would be willing to work with me, you might be able to speed his destruction more effectively than with a bullet."

"I thought your work was economic, buying watch movements and things like that."

"It is. What I want you for is a little side line."

She smiled. "I don't believe that, but I'll be a good girl and pretend that I do." She sipped her wine thoughtfully as if waiting for Jacques to say something. When he remained silent, she finally went on. "Just what do you mean by 'working with you'? What have you in mind that I could do?"

"Act as an intermediary between Venturi and me."

"Why do you need me? You know him, don't you?"

"It would be safer." Jacques grinned. "People would scarcely expect me to go to him for watch movements and jewel bearings. I would prefer to have no contact with him whatsoever. Above all, my name has to be kept out of this business."

"Knowing Tony, I imagine his price is high."

"That is no obstacle. If what he produces is authentic and valuable, we will be willing to give him plenty."

"How would you know whether or not it was authentic? I wouldn't trust him for a second."

"We have ways of checking."

"Be sure not to pay before you check."

"I have no such intention. Is it a bargain?"

"The one person who bothers me is the Baroness de Marty. If she should get wind of the fact that I was seeing him again, she would go at once to Grosspapa."

"You must take care that she doesn't hear. In the first place, don't operate in French Switzerland. Perhaps you could arrange your meetings in some unlikely place like Zug or Rapperswil."

"That is easier said than done."

"I leave that to you. As long as there is money in it for him, you can probably rely on him to be discreet. It isn't as if he were having an affair that he wanted to boast about."

"You have such a delicate way of putting things."

"Why fool ourselves?"

"When do you want me to start?"

"The sooner, the better. Tell him that you have an Anglo-American contact who is willing to pay for important and authentic information concerning the plans of the German High Command."

"Anything specific?"

"Troop movements are always desirable. But plans, either for defense or offense, are the most important. For example, plans for the invasion of the British Isles—are they still on or have they been called off? Then there is the secret weapons program that we hear about. Just what are these weapons? Where are they being developed and tested?"

"Suppose he tries to blackmail me for some of your secrets?"

"Fine. Go right along with him. Tell him you will try your best to get some. We will give him plenty."

"Of fake stories, I gather."

"Not necessarily. What we will give him is information that we happen to know they already have. That way their suspicions won't be aroused."

"You amaze me, Jacques. I never thought you were so clever."

Jacques laughed. "That is because you live in Zürich where the opinion prevails that Grosspapa has a corner on Eggli brains."

"It's quite natural when he allows no one of the family to think for himself."

The waiter returned and they talked about their children until they parted.

CHAPTER XX

THE first thing Jacques did when he returned to his rooms at the Bellevue-Palace after dining with the de Graffenrieds was to pull the letter out of his pocket in order to read it carefully. It had arrived just as he was leaving the Legation and he had been able only to glance at it, extracting the mere unadorned kernel of the news. He sat down with the three sheets of airmail paper, covered with Doris's orderly, precise handwriting, and started to read.

My dearest Jacques:

Thanks for your letter of September 6th. It was a blesséd relief to learn that you were safe in the haven of Switzerland at last. Never again will I make facetious cracks about that sturdy little perpendicular country of yours. I'll even consent to tie a bell around my neck and ruminate there with you after the war is over, so grateful am I that you are among its protective peaks. If only Bobby could join you, then all my anxieties would be over. Maybe he will have to make a forced landing there, as I read that so many of our planes have had to do. Wouldn't that be a gift from Heaven!! I can picture him interned in the Sudstrasse, making jokes with his Grosspapa over a breakfast of schapzigger and strawberry jam. I pray for it every time I pass a cup of coffee to an Air Corps officer at the canteen.

I suppose he has written you about his Big Step. I had to learn about it from Ellen McCabe, of all people. She called me last night from Oyster Bay to say that she had just received a letter from Joan announcing her engagement to our Bobby. Well, I was so dumbfounded that, like a silly fool, I burst into tears. I think Ellen McC. was a little annoyed. It must have sounded as if I considered the match quite unsuitable. I tried to explain to her that I was tired and upset, worrying as I do (God help me, I try not to) about you and Bobby, but I don't think that she was altogether mollified. I've just written her a nice note, telling her how pleased I am, and it's the truth. I do think it's fine, though I wish Bobby had waited a little. He's so young and should have a chance to look the whole field over before sewing up his lot for life. But he might have done worse—far worse. Joan is a bright, pretty child, even though she is a bit forward and hard-shelled, like so many of the Long Island youngsters. As for the McCabes, well, we'll simply have to put up with them, but, golly, how they bore me with their endless prattle about boats! He has a Navy commission in Washington now, as you might have expected. I'll bet he's more nautical than the oldest seadog of an admiral. I have asked Ellen to send me Joan's A.P.O. address.

Fancy Bobby turning up at Joan's canteen! Rainbow Corner, Ellen called it, somewhere in the heart of London. The result of that reunion was, I suppose, inevitable in wartime, with bombs falling and the young clinging to each other for comfort and security. They probably bounced right into each others arms, and then felt that they had to sanctify the embrace by making it legitimate. Poor sweet kids, I hope they enjoyed it!

Why don't you send her a nice little wrist watch from Türler's as an engagement present? Something plain and sensible, gold strap and case, suitable for a Red Cross girl. You could send it to Bobby and ask him to give it to her. I haven't yet received her A.P.O. from Ellen McC.

Evangeline is my Rock of Gibraltar. She wanted to give up Bryn Mawr and stick with me for the duration, but I would have none of it—as much as I longed to have her near me. So she left the day before yesterday, putting on a brave Stiff-Upper-Lip act, laughing and wisecracking to cover her tears. She insists on coming home every week end, and I don't say no because I'm weak and silly and miss her very much. Not, of course, as much as I miss you, my dearest, dearest Jacques. Is there anything lonelier than a lone double bed? Or colder? I have taken to sleeping with a bed jacket to keep my lonely shoulders warm. (Do they censor these letters?)

Everyone asks after you. Morton and Maggie beamed when I read them the regards in your last letter. They are convinced that the war will come out all right, now that you are running it. They may have something there. Things have been going much better these past few weeks, what with Patton racing across Sicily and the Russians driving the Huns relentlessly. The Pacific is the worst spot. Those dreadful, endless islands creeping with inhuman Jap monkeys! Thank God they didn't send you there to carry on your economic warfare. I prefer to picture you in Berne, buying shiploads of fat cheeses and tons of pretty wrist watches.

My love to all the family—Tante Vicki, Lucy, Hélène, Walter, Hans and Grosspapa (don't let him bully you!). As for you, my brave and shining knight, good night and may God keep you safe for me!

Your

Doris

P.S. How clever of you to suggest "Excelsior!" as the name for Bobby's plane. I hope he did it.

Jacques folded the sheets carefully and put them back in his pocket. He smiled. The letter had sent a flow of warmth through him. It had kindled the still glowing coals of his love for Doris, making them burst into bright flame. He had missed her during the long months since his departure, but now the realization of her absence became a sharp ache. He wanted her beside him, in his arms, so that he could tell her, confess, that he was responsible for Bobby finding Joan at Rainbow Corner. She would scold him of course, saying, "So like you men to tip one another off about the location of a cute number"; and he would explain his action by telling her that when one is far from home in the fearsome time of war the finding of a familiar face is a bright solace. And he would add what Bobby had said when he had told him of finding Joan on the railway platform at Greenock, that she dished out kisses like doughnuts and he might as well have his share. Doris would understand that that had been the hyperbole of the modern generation, that he had not meant to say that Joan was promiscuous, merely that she was gay, flirtatious, outgiving. He wondered why Bobby had not written to him or to his mother. Maybe he had. Maybe it was only the snafu of army mail which had landed Joan's letter in New York before his. Then there was the other contingency, that on return-ing to his base in Norfolk, he had had to fly off on his first mission with no time to write before take-off.

There was a knock at the door. Jacques got up quickly, taking the brief case from the table and going into the bedroom where he locked it in his suitcase which was on the rack at the foot of his bed. Going back to the living room, he opened the door carefully, holding his left knee against it in case the intruder tried to force his way in. The bulky figure of John Margett, pipe in mouth, curly hair disheveled, was facing him.

"Oh, it's you," Jacques said with relief, opening the door wide. "Come in."

Margett ambled in with the rolling gate of large, stout men. His loose clothes looked as if he had slept in them. His tie was askew and the corners of his shirt collar stuck out like the ears of a white rabbit. "I thought you might have gone to bed. That's why I didn't knock a second time," he said in his rumbling, bass voice.

"I was reading a letter from home," Jacques said. "Sit down while I mix you a highball. What's on your mind at this hour of night?"

"Nothing in particular," Margett said, settling his big frame in one of the overstuffed armchairs. "My room is just down the hall. I thought that if you were up and about, we might have a little talk."

Jacques took a bottle of scotch whisky out of the sideboard and poured two drinks. The glasses and ice and soda syphon were already there on a tray: his standing order with the floor waiter. "Well, I'm delighted you dropped in. I was bemoaning the fact that I would have to drink my son's health all by myself."

"The boy in the Air Corps? What has he done?"

"He has got himself engaged to be married. That's what I was reading about when you knocked." Jacques brought a drink to Margett, then took his own and sat down.

"Here's to both of them—long life and happiness!" Margett said, raising his glass.

"To Bobby and Joan!" Jacques added to the toast, and drank deeply.

"Is she an English girl?"

"No, an old flame of his from Long Island. She's working for the Red Cross in London."

"I can tell by the look of you that you approve."

"As my wife writes, he could have done a lot worse. He's too young, though."

"That's what war does. It's nature's compensation for the destruction of human life. With every war marriages increase and the birthrate jumps. Aside from your boy, have you any news?"

"Not for publication yet, but I've laid some traps that ought to produce."

"Good work. I told Allen that he needn't worry about you. He seemed to have the impression that you were trying to duck your assignment."

"I am on something now which might turn out to be very big," Jacques said, trying to get the subject away from the bank's account numbers which he knew Margett was referring to.

"Both Treasury and B.E.W. have been on our tails about it. I'm glad to hear it is coming along."

Jacques saw now that he could not escape. "Are you talking about the Eggli accounts?"

"Certainly. That's your job, isn't it?"

"It is one of many, John," Jacques said, frowning. "In my briefing in London I was given four or five assignments, the primary one of which was to get information on the secret weapon program. . . ."

"Have you made a careful inspection of this room?" Margett interrupted in a low voice.

"Every inch of the floor and walls," Jacques answered. "That young electronic expert you fellows call 'The Eye' was up here yesterday to check for me. He gave the suite a clean bill of health."

"Okay. Now tell me, do you think you have a ghost of a chance of getting anything on this program you speak of?"

"I'm not yet ready to answer that, but I think I'm on the best lead in Switzerland."

"What is involved?"

"Money—maybe a lot of it."

"Hmm. Does von Orb come into it?"

"Possibly," Jacques answered with a cryptic smile. "Why do you ask?"

"Because M.I.5 are trying that one. The British seem to think he's their special property."

"That's interesting," Jacques said, relieved that he had been able to get Margett safely away from the bank job. "But it doesn't bother me, unless of course we have made some deal with them to lay off."

"There are no deals in this business. It's every man for himself. I just wanted to caution you not to be too optimistic, the limeys may have been there ahead of you."

"Anything is possible. I can tell you this, though. My contact is as close as you can get."

"I wish you luck, but remember the name Gerald Blythe. He's the fellow who will cross you up if he can."

"The M.I.5 chap?"

Margett nodded assent, and added, "A narcotic expert with the League of Nations."

"Thanks for the tip."

"Don't mention it. Now about the numbers game, what have you started on that line?"

"Nothing," Jacques replied, his heart sinking again. "It is a brick wall as long as the old man is alive."

"What about your brother?"

"Nothing on earth could drag it out of him without Father's permission."

"Your father is well over eighty. He can't still be active."

Jacques snorted. "Hah! You don't know him. He is more active than F.D.R. They don't dare go to the can at the bank without his permission. He is the absolute boss, and will be until he drops dead."

"There must be some way. As his son you are closer to the situation than anyone else."

"Don't worry, John, this thing is constantly on my mind," Jacques said, knowing it was a stall and that he had no intention now of turning traitor to the family. "You tell Allen to keep his shirt on. Let me get this other lead started."

"I thought you said it was already started."

"It is, but it hasn't ripened into production yet. It is one of those intricate, delicate lines that take nursing."

John Margett drained the last of his whisky and heaved his great bulk out of the deep chair. "I leave it to you, Jacques, you know what you are doing; only don't forget that the numbers game is top priority." He walked towards the door.

"Higher than the weapons?" Jacques asked.

"I wouldn't say that, but one is easy and the other is pretty near impossible from where we sit."

"You're telling me," Jacques said, meaning the opposite of what Margett was saying.

When he had closed the door and locked it, Jacques put the empty glasses back on the tray and went into the bedroom. It was clear to him that his only hope of dodging the assignment of the bank's secrets was to succeed so well with the Hélène-Venturi deal that it would be sidetracked in the minds of O.S.S. in London. After all, he argued to himself, feeling the cold fear in his stomach again, what effect would the disclosure of German funds in New York and Rio and B.A. really have on the outcome of the war? The amount of pre-emptive buying of scarce minerals and metals and a few end-items which Germany was able to do in South America and Africa could not possibly alter the result. The only dangerous use to which this money could be put was the paying of agents operating in the United States and Mexico, and we had the F.B.I. to keep an eye on them. Was it worth, in terms of aid to victory, the destruction of his family and the bank? He thought not, though he was fully aware that he had thought differently in London. Yes, the establishing of a source of information on German plans and weapons was definitely more important. He would put all his efforts in that direction.

Two weeks had passed since he had talked to Hélène, yet he had had no word from her. Well, he would be seeing her the next day in Zürich, where she would be dining, together with Lucy and Hans, in the Sudstrasse.

He took Doris's letter out of his pocket and laid the sheets on the dresser so that he could reread it as he undressed.

At dinner in Zürich the following night, which was at Walter's because Grosspapa was laid up with a touch of the grippe, Jacques was able to make a date with Hélène for tea the next day. He did it openly, in the hearing of Walter and Lucy and Hans, to allay any suspicion of complicity. He was pleased with himself for having worked it out in a way which had seemed so natural. He had remarked that he yearned to have tea again on the Bauschänzli as he used to as a child. Hélène had echoed the desire, saying that they had all become too sophisticated, thinking only of the garden of the Baur-au-Lac or Sprüngli's. So they had laughingly made a date to meet there at four-thirty.

Hélène was already seated when Jacques arrived. She had selected a small table on the rail by the Limmat where they could look out on the swans and the arcades of the ancient city on the east bank. She had shifted the chairs so that they were side by side, facing the river, with their backs to the garden.

"You were very clever to catch on at once when I mentioned wishing to come here," Jacques said in a low voice.

"I rather fancy my new role," Hélène said. "It relieves the monotony."

"Have you see him?"

"Here's the Fräulein. Let us order our tea first," Hélène said. When the waitress had gone, she went on. "Yes, we made a rendezvous. Don't ask me where. I would rather no one knew."

"Is he willing?"

"Naturally. As I told you before, he would do anything for money. He promises to have something by the end of this week."

"That's fine!"

"Perhaps, but I'm not so sure. You see, he wants full payment before giving me anything."

"But you told him that we would have to check it first."

"Yes, and he told me flatly that he would not play on that basis."

"Does he think we're fools? He could give us any nonsense that he thought up himself."

"That's what I told him. His answer was that if the first delivery did not check, we could call it off. You know what I think? That he needs the money to share with his source."

"You mean that—that his friend has turned his coat?"

"That is my guess. Do you know him?"

"I've never met him."

"Well, if you had, you would understand. He's the sort of weak sister who would play the winning side. He used to have an independent income, but that has probably vanished in Germany and he sees the writing on the wall. This is his chance to build up a nest egg in Switzerland, so that he can continue to live here."

"You don't *know* this, do you?"

"Not actually, but I know the other fellow well enough to figure out his motives."

"What is he asking for the first delivery?"

"Ten thousand."

"Francs?"

"Yes."

The waitress brought them tea with some slices of very dark bread and a tiny pot of honey.

"That is a hell of a lot of money for a cat in the bag," Jacques whispered when the waitress had left.

Hélène smiled. "He said he was letting you off cheap on the first shipment."

"His stuff will have to be sensational if he's thinking in those terms. Did you mention the"—he leaned over until his lips were close to her ear—"the weapons?"

"He seemed doubtful that his friend was in a position to get anything on that, but if he did the price would be astronomical, as there was keen competition for it."

"Did he say who the competition was?"

"No, but one can guess."

"Maybe we are playing second fiddle in this orchestra," Jacques said, remembering what John Margett had said about the narcotic expert.

"I was wondering about that, but I don't see that it makes much difference as long as the first fiddle is a friend."

Jacques laughed softly. "In theory you are right, though I don't like the idea of paying for something that has already been sold."

"Can you find out if it has been sold or not?"

"Not until after the fact—that is, if he insists on payment in advance."

"Suppose I offer to double the figure if it is exclusive."

"You couldn't trust them."

"No, I don't suppose I could."

"We can worry about that when he comes with it."

Hélène sipped her tea, her brow furrowed by concentration. "There is another thought," she said finally. "I might by-pass my friend and go directly to his source."

"I'd be careful how I did that. You would have to be absolutely certain that he had turned, otherwise you would wreck the whole affair. Furthermore, you must consider the reaction of your friend when he finds out, and he is bound to find out."

"I'll think it over."

"I would if I were you. In the meantime let us wait and see what the initial delivery looks like."

"Good. We'll forget the matter for the moment. How do you find Grosspapa?"

"Oh, I don't think it is anything serious, just a touch of flu."

"Dr. Huber always makes such an alarm."

"I think he does it to scare the old man into submission. If he had not done it, Grosspapa might well have come to the dinner last night."

"Tante Vicki can't control him, that is sure."

Jacques laughed. "No one can. That is why I'm not worried about him. He has a will of iron, and he's not prepared to die yet."

Hélène got up, gathering her furs and bag together. "I must be going home. Walter will be waiting for me."

Jacques put his hat on and stood up. "If you are walking, I'll go with you."

"Doesn't the Consulate let you have a car?"

"I thought it better not to use it today."

They walked out between the tables and onto the Stadthaus-quai which was crowded with people returning from work, hurrying to the Bürkliplatz to catch a tram.

"It must have been amusing for you to renew an old friendship," Jacques said as they moved along with the crowd.

"In a way it was," Hélène said. "I took great pleasure in keeping our talk on a strictly business plane."

"That must have annoyed him."

"Not as much as you might think."

"It even annoys me sometimes."

She laughed. "I know, this sort of intrigue should involve a love affair. It always does in novels."

"In a novel we would have concocted our conspiracy in the bedroom of a small hotel instead of at a tea table on the Bauschänzli. Real life is always so prosaic."

"Do you find a hotel bedroom more romantic than the Limmat with its swans swimming in the shadow of the Grossmünster?"

"Poor old Lohengrin and his swan!"

"You are in a bad way, Jacques."

"Thanks to you."

"I'm glad you suggested tea and not a ride in a swan boat."

"Whether here on the Bauschänzli or in a swan boat, I'm sorry in a way that I asked you to help me."

Hélène turned her head slightly, squinting her eyes at him to determine what he meant. She sensed it was a compliment, but the instinct of the flirt made her conceal the knowledge. "I shall withdraw if you wish," she said softly.

"Don't be a fool, Hélène. It's just that you are too attractive to be meeting this way—on the sly."

"The next time I'll wear my oldest clothes."

"It isn't a matter of clothes."

"Tst! Tst! Put me out of your mind. Remember that in all good novels it is thoughts like that which defeat the patriotic spy."

Jacques laughed, swinging along by her side as she increased her gait now that they had left the crowded Bellevueplatz and were starting up the Seefeldstrasse. "Don't worry, my dear, I'm only teasing for the fun of it."

"So that's what it is, only teasing."

"That's what we are going to call it."

When they reached the door of Hélène's house in the Zollikerstrasse, it occurred to Jacques that he might grab a quick cocktail before going to the Sudstrasse where they were forbidden. Walter, who had arrived before them from the bank, was delighted to play the good Samaritan to his thirsty brother. The three of them went into the room which Walter considered his special sanctuary. It was panelled in knotty pine carved in rococo designs, like the *bierstube* of an Alpine inn. Inset in one of the panels was a bar and sink, copied almost exactly from the one in Jacques' Long Island house.

"So you two have had tea on the Bauschänzli. Was it fun?" Walter asked, mixing the martinis.

"It was like old times, sitting there looking over the water and the old houses on the Limmatquai," Jacques answered.

"Tante Vicki just called to say that Grosspapa was going to the Bürgenstock for a week or two to recuperate," Walter said.

"When?" Hélène asked.

"Tomorrow, if Dr. Huber will let him," Walter replied. "I wanted to get him enough gasoline so that he could go by car, but it seems he insists on going by train to Lucerne, then by boat and funicular."

"He'll have Tante Vicki to look after him and see that he keeps a rug around his legs," Hélène said.

"That's just the point, he won't let her come with him," Walter said. "He says that Tante Vicki must stay here to keep house for Jacques, and that worries me. He shouldn't take that journey alone at his age after a bout of flu."

"It doesn't make sense to keep Tante Vicki at home to take care of me," Jacques protested. "Anni and Frau Maur can do it just as well without her. Besides, I'll be going back to Berne in a day or two."

"Of course, and he knows that," Walter said. "I think the truth is that he wants to get away from Tante Vicki for a week or two. She pesters him too much."

"But someone should go with him," Hélène said.

"I could do it," Jacques offered.

"No, it is better that I go," Hélène said decisively. "If either of you two go, he will find fault with you the whole way, and that will raise his blood pressure which is not good for him. In my opinion, he doesn't want Tante Vicki because very probably he has asked the Baroness to meet him there. For that reason I will leave him at the funicular and come right back to Zürich on the next train. I'll call Tante Vicki at once. Grosspapa can pick me up on the way to the Bahnhof." She left them to make the telephone call.

"Maybe that is the best solution," Walter said when his wife had left the room. "Grosspapa likes Hélène. She soothes him."

CHAPTER XXI

THREE days later Jacques was at the Haupt Bahnhof at nine in the morning to catch the nine-fifteen to Berne. He carried with him in his mind—for on his instructions nothing written had been passed—the information for which Hélène had given Tony Venturi ten thousand francs of U.S. Government funds. He was far from happy about the transaction. The intelligence which his sister-in-law had gained seemed hardly worth the price and gave him no encouragement about the future. It was a partial inventory of the German divisions deployed in Italy, the south of France, the Channel and Norway, all of which, Jacques felt sure, was already known to the Allied command. The only scrap which might prove of value was the word that unrest and dissatisfaction were rife within the German General Staff, that the failure of Hitler's campaign in Russia had turned many of the top generals against him, and that there was a growing feeling among a large group of professional officers that the war was already lost. This was all right as far as it went, but as Jacques had told Hélène, it was not specific enough. Hereafter he would insist on having names and dates and direct quotes before any money was handed over.

He was not only discouraged but worried. This first effort to find an escape from the bank mission had turned out to be an expensive dud. As he walked down the platform where his train was loading, he noticed a group of young men in American uniforms. With them were a civilian whom Jacques recognized as one of the American vice-consuls in Zürich, a Swiss officer and two Swiss soldiers carrying rifles. Slowing down as he approached the group, he heard the vice-consul say to the three American officers, "Colonel Sweeney, the Air Attaché, will meet you at the station and take you to the Legation. He'll see that you get everything that you need in the way of clothes and toilet articles."

"Will you be going with us, Lieutenant Schweizer?" one of the American officers asked the Swiss.

Jacques had only seen the back of the Swiss officer, but when he heard the name he edged forward.

"I wish I were," Lieutenant Schweizer said in pure American. "I've got to go back to Dübendorf in case any more of you fellows drop in for a call." He nodded toward the two soldiers with rifles. "Those fellows will go with you but don't let that bother you. They won't shoot unless you try to jump the train."

The American slapped Schweizer on the shoulder. "Sorry, pal, wish you could stick with us. When that red-tailed Messerschmitt started to talk to me in good old American, I thought I was slap-happy from the flak. If you ever get over to this place they call Burn, drop in to G.H.Q. and I'll see that you get a drink of real likker."

"Okay, Captain," Lieutenant Schweizer said. "I'll note that in the log." He clicked his heels and came to a snappy salute. "So long, gentlemen, I hope you enjoy the scenery. It's better than the climate."

As Lieutenant Schweizer turned, Jacques stepped forward. "Hello, Freddie!" he said.

The lieutenant stopped and stared, then burst into a broad grin. "Mr. Eggli! Gosh, I never expected to see you here!"

"Over on a little business for the Government," Jacques said. "You look fine in that uniform. What do you hear from your father?"

"He's fine. Writes that Bobby is also a pilot. Where is he? Over here or in the Pacific?"

"I haven't the vaguest," Jacques lied with a grin.

Freddie Schweizer laughed. "Naturally you couldn't tell me if you did know." He glanced at the suitcase Jacques was holding. "Are you taking this train, Mr. Eggli?"

"Yes, to Berne."

"Maybe you would like to meet these men. We're taking them to our—I should say, your Legation." He blushed as he turned around to face the Americans. "You know Mr. Martin, the vice-consul, I suppose."

Martin extended his hand to Jacques. "I know Mr. Eggli by sight," he said.

Then Jacques was introduced to Captain Ekstrom and Lieutenants Silverthorn and Hirsch. Schweizer explained to them that Mr. Eggli was a fellow-citizen who was also bound for Berne.

Two first-class compartments had been reserved by the Federal Government for the party of interned airmen and their two guards; the three officers and one guard were to travel in one, and the four enlisted men with their guard in the other. The captain asked Schweizer if Jacques would be allowed to sit with them. When Freddie hesitated the vice-consul intervened, explaining that Jacques was an official of the Legation.

"I'm sorry, Mr. Eggli, but I will have to see your passport," Schweizer said, embarrassed. "Those are the regulations."

Jacques produced his diplomatic passport and Schweizer made a pencilled note of the number and date of issue. "It's quite all right, sir," he said, shaking Jacques' hand, then saluting formally.

In the compartment Jacques insisted that the American officers take the corner seats so that they could see something of Switzerland. He explained that the journey would be mostly through the lowlands of northern Switzerland and that it was unlikely that they would see any snow mountains with the clouds closing in as they were. He watched the three of them stowing the odds and ends of personal gear that they had taken from their airplane on the luggage racks and thought that they had the drawn, taut look of men who had lived through a harrowing experience. Lieutenant Hirsch had a heavy canvas zipper bag which he put on the floor between his feet and Jacques could read the legend "Bombardier Case Type E-1" stencilled in black letters on its side. The captain had a brief case, presumably containing the ship's flight log and maps, which he placed beside him on the seat. He was a big rawboned fellow with great hands that would have served well for a heavyweight boxer. Every motion he made was slow and deliberate, like a man in a trance.

Lieutenant Silverthorn who sat in the corner opposite the captain was a sallow young man with dark circles under his eyes. He smoked incessantly, knocking the ashes from his cigarette even when there were no ashes to knock. His gaze darted nervously from the window to Jacques as if he suspected this American stranger who spoke with an accent to be an enemy spy. Hirsch, who was fat with a mop of curly black hair, had a fixed grin on his face. He is still in the euphoria of being saved from the jaws of death, Jacques thought.

"I really thought I'd had it," Captain Ekstrom drawled, turning to Jacques. "When that voice came over the earphones, I was sure a connecting rod had snapped up here." He tapped his blond crew-cut with a finger as big as a banana. "They'd briefed us that a lot of these Swiss pilots could speak English, but nobody said anything about American. 'Welcome to Switzerland, Flying Fort,' this voice says. 'Just stick to my tail like good boys and you'll be sleeping in sheets and buying watches before you know it.' I looked at Slim." He nodded towards Silverthorn. "'Slim,' I says, 'did you hear what I hear?' And Slim starts to blabber, 'It's heaven, Ole. We're dead and we don't know it.' Then after I'd rogered, this voice says, 'Don't look now, pal, but you've got a wheel showing.' So I tried the landing gear and sure enough it was out. Flak must have hit the servels. I couldn't get the other wheel down and I couldn't get that one up. The nose was the only one working. I tell this to the voice and it says, 'Have you any bombs aboard?' 'No,' I tells him, 'left them in Regensburg.' 'Okay,' it says, 'try for a nice easy ground loop and if the wheel collapses, you can cut the grass with your belly. Only get that tail gunner up in the cockpit.' We were losing altitude fast then, with the outboard starboard engine feathered and the inboard hardly pulling at all. Well, before you could say 'over' this Messerschmitt ducks around a hill with woods on it and there is the strip right in front. 'Good luck,' he calls, and does a climbing turn to get out of my flight path. 'Cross your fingers,' I says to Slim, and I put down the flaps and throttled back. Sure enough, when the wheel hit the runway I could feel it was as soft as a drunk's knee, so I swing her off the runway like he said and skidded her onto the lawn. Yes, sir, it was thanks to that Schweizer we made it. He's a good kid even if he does wear the wrong uniform."

Jacques explained to them the circumstances which brought Freddie Schweizer into the Swiss military service although he was born and brought up in New York.

"When I shook his hand and said 'pleased to meet you,' brother, I sure meant it," Lieutenant Hirsch said without dropping the grin. The train was gaining speed as it passed through Schlieren. "Look! Look at it! Nice little houses, geraniums in the windows, everybody doing business just like any other day of any other year." He leaned across the aisle and grabbed the hand of the stolid, uncomprehending guard. "Switzerland, I am glad to meet you. Just stay neutral and you'll have no complaints from me." The soldier jerked his hand away from the lieutenant and frowned.

Jacques explained to the guard in *Schweizerdeutsch* that the lieutenant was expressing his gratitude at being safe in Switzerland. The guard nodded and, grinning, extended his hand so that Hirsch could shake it again.

They all laughed except Silverthorn who continued to stare at Jacques between intervals of looking out the window. He seemed not to have heard what the others had said. This constant staring, whether of inquiry or fear, began to make Jacques feel uneasy. He decided to say something to this furtive, sad-eyed officer if only to relieve his own disquiet.

"What part of the States do you come from, Lieutenant?" he asked Silverthorn, catching a moment when the sad eyes had switched from the window to him.

"From South Carolina, sir," Silverthorn answered respectfully in a soft, musical Lowcountry accent.

"A lovely state," Jacques said, picturing the camellias and the broom sedge. "I've been there often for the quail-shooting."

A trace of a smile flickered across the dark eyes. "Then you likely know my home town, sir. I come from Walterboro. That's in the middle of right good bird-huntin' country."

"Yes, I know Walterboro. It was near there that I used to shoot. Tell me, was the flak bad over Regensburg?"

"Did you ever see a flock of blackbirds over a field of corn stubble? It was like that, sir. The air was full of little black bursts." He shifted his gaze to the window again. "This country ain't much like Norfolk, is it?"

"You mean Norfolk, Virginia?" Jacques asked.

"No, sir, I mean Norfolk, England—the country around King's Lynn," Silverthorn said. "I been wondering ever since that Swiss lieutenant introduced us if you were the same gentleman I saw having supper at the King's Arms sometime back—around May I guess it was."

"What a coincidence!" Jacques exclaimed, smiling with pleasure. "I certainly am the same man. I went up to King's Lynn to see my son, Captain Robert Eggli. Do you know him?"

Both Ekstrom and Hirsch straightened up as if a bolt of electricity had been shot through them.

"You Bob Eggli's father, sir?" Ekstrom asked, his eyes widening with amazement.

Jacques noticed that Silverthorn gave a quick, cautionary glance at the captain and wondered what prompted it.

"Poor old Bob Eggli," Hirsch muttered.

"What do you mean 'poor'?" Silverthorn shot back in an angry voice. "He's the best damn pilot in the outfit and you know it, Max."

"He's good all right," Hirsch agreed, glancing at Silverthorn and then at Ekstrom. "I wasn't trying to disparage your son, sir.

I was just sympathizing with him for not having as good a bombardier as Captain Ekstrom here."

"Don't listen to him, sir," the captain said. "Lieutenant Hirsch thinks he's the only man alive who really understands how to work that gadget he carries in the bag."

Jacques, realizing that these men were a part of Bobby's own group, maybe even of his own squadron, felt a sudden sinking in his stomach. "Was Bobby on this mission with you?" he asked, all the blood having left his face.

Captain Ekstrom opened his mouth to answer, but Silverthorn was too quick for him. "That's classified information, sir," he said.

"You forget that I'm an attaché of the American Legation," Jacques said impatiently, his fears mounting.

Silverthorn nodded his head in the direction of the Swiss soldier. "It's not you, sir, it's on account of him."

"He doesn't understand a word of English," Jacques protested.

"Andy is right, sir, we are not supposed to take any chances," the captain said, picking up his cue from Silverthorn. "Maybe he speaks English as well as that Swiss lieutenant. Maybe they sent him along with us for that reason."

"You, soldier, you with the gun, what time do we get to Berne?" Jacques asked the guard in a loud commanding voice. But the question went unheeded. The soldier sat gazing out the window, as stolid as the Matterhorn. "You see, he doesn't understand a word. But your very refusal to answer is sufficient confirmation. Just tell me one thing please, did he get through all right?"

Captain Ekstrom cleared his throat while Lieutenant Silverthorn returned his sad gaze to the landscape. It was Lieutenant Hirsch, the bombardier, who answered. "We couldn't answer that one for an A-2 Board of Inquiry, sir," he said. "When we got it and had to pull out of formation, we were just finishing the bomb run. As far as we could tell at that moment your son's ship was headed straight on through that flock of blackbirds Andy was telling you about."

"You think he made it then?" Jacques asked breathlessly.

"If anyone in the group could get his ship out of a hole, it's Bob Eggli," Ekstrom grumbled. "But don't let anyone tell you that those krauts are beaten. They've got more ack-ack than a snowstorm has flakes."

"Bastards!" Jacques exclaimed, and heaved a deep sigh.

"You're telling me!" Hirsch said. "Look, Mr. Eggli, I'm Jewish and I know just what variety of bastards they are. Boy! The sweetest sound I ever heard in my life was Ole singing 'Bombs away!' "

"Look here, gentlemen," Jacques said, "as soon as you get yourselves squared away at the Legation, I want the three of you to be my guests for dinner. I'm at the Bellevue-Palace Hotel, Room 64. Come up there first and have a cocktail. This is Tuesday. Maybe we could make it Thursday evening at six o'clock."

"That would be wonderful, sir," Captain Ekstrom said. "Make a note of that, Max."

Lieutenant Hirsch pulled a bent notebook out of the breast pocket of his battle jacket and wrote down the entry. "That's swell, Mr. Eggli. We will drink a toast to Bob."

Lieutenant Silverthorn said nothing. He was still looking out of the window, his face sadder than ever.

It was on the morning of the Thursday that he had invited the three officers to dine with him that Margett asked him to come to his office. It was a small room at the back of the Consulate in the Spitalgasse and Jacques had walked there from the hotel.

John Margett took the pipe out of his mouth and used it as a pointer to indicate the chair in front of his desk. He was leaning back against the wall, his grey suit wrinkled as usual and his shirt oozing out from the belt around the bottom of his protruding stomach. He knocked the pipe stem on the paper on the desk in front of him. Jacques looked over and saw that it was his Venturi report.

"It isn't good enough," Margett said.

"That's what I told you."

"Von Orb is doing the same thing we'd do to him, feeding us stuff he is pretty certain we have already."

"I agree that that is the case on this first delivery, but my contact has reason to believe that von Orb is ratting on the Nazis and is now willing to get us what we want."

"That may be. We have some information which would tend to confirm that, but I don't think that Venturi is going to be in the picture—not for the important dope. Von Orb doesn't trust him, and I don't blame him."

"That had already occurred to my contact, who incidentally knows von Orb and is prepared to deal directly if need be."

Margett took off his horn-rimmed spectacles and grinned at Jacques through watery, myopic eyes. "Too late, I'm afraid, Jacques. Our British friends have beat you to it."

"You mean that they already have the low-down on the secret weapons?"

"Not yet, but they are hopeful."

"If they can get it, why can't we? You said yourself that it was every man for himself in this game."

"Look, Jacques," Margett said after rubbing his eyes and putting on his spectacles, "I did say that, you are quite right, and at the time I meant it. But since then Allen has had word from Dave that the British have asked us to lay off for fear of wrecking the whole deal. They have promised to let us have whatever they get if we will call our people off von Orb. After considering this, Allen thinks it's worth it."

"You are telling me to stop after all the careful work I've put in to develop this?" Jacques asked with a sinking heart.

"In a word, I am," Margett answered pleasantly. "I want you to tell your contact to see no more of Venturi. He can tell him that this junk we paid ten thousand francs for was so much rub-

bish, and that we have no further interest. Let him sell it to the
Russkis if they are dumb enough to buy it."

"But . . ."

Margett waved his pipe for silence. "There is another good
reason for letting the British handle this. We want you to concentrate on your main objective, Jacques."

"The numbers game?"

"Precisely."

Jacques shook his head. "That's a tough one."

"We know that. That's why we brought Jacques Eggli here to
crack it."

Jacques put on his hat and stood up. "Can I have a car to take
me to the Legation, John?"

"You sure can. Take the first one you find out there. And oh,
I almost forgot to tell you, your cover has changed its name.
You are now representing the Foreign Economic Administration.
The Office of Economic Warfare, which was the old Bureau of
Economic Warfare, was absorbed by this new agency on Septem-
ber twenty-fifth by Presidential decree."

"Foreign Economic Administration? I'll have to write that
down and rehearse it," Jacques said and walked out.

As the car moved slowly through the ancient arcaded streets,
Jacques sat back with a frown and thought about his troubles.
He noticed that a cloud bank was moving down from the hills,
settling over Kirchenfeld, and he likened it to his own predica-
ment. Clouds of uncertainty and indecision were closing in on
him. He had sensed it first on the train coming from Zürich
when the three officers had seemed hesitant and embarrassed to
tell him about Bobby's airplane. There had been something
about the manner of Lieutenant Silverthorn which disturbed him.
The young man with his drained, distressed face had suddenly
come to life, taking over the direction of the conversation, giving
his pals the cue so that the captain had echoed the silly excuse
that they were forbidden to talk about other pilots in their group.

Then the clever, articulate Jewish bombardier had told the all too glib story of seeing Bobby's plane going on through the flak bursts as they dropped their crippled ship out of formation. It had not rung true. Why? he wondered. Had they seen something they did not wish him to know? And yet had Bobby's ship not returned to its base at King's Lynn, or any field in England for that matter, he would have known about it within twelve hours, for Colonel Byers had promised that he would send word to Dave Bruce and Dave had agreed to relay the message to Berne.

The clouds in his mind were lifted slightly by this thought, but they lowered again when he remembered that his well-laid scheme for obtaining German plans through the von Orb-Venturi-Hélène route were now cancelled, and with it all chance of diverting his superiors from interest in his basic mission. He would have to continue to give them the impression that he was working on it while hoping that something would arise which would solve the problem for him.

The car drew up at the Chancellery and he got out, directing the chauffeur to return to the Spitalgasse. Inside he climbed the stairs and went down the hall to his little cubbyhole of an office in the rear of the second floor, adjoining the room occupied by the legitimate representative of O.E.W. He thought as he saw those gold letters on the door that they would now have to be changed to "F.E.A." Taking off his raincoat, he hung it with his hat on the tree in the corner by the door, then went over to his desk. There were no letters or papers in the "In" basket, but a small piece of paper on the middle of his blotter had typed on it: "Please call the code room." He picked up the telephone.

"You have a message for me? This is Mr. Eggli," he said when the code room answered.

"Yes, sir, Mr. Eggli," a clerk answered. "If you are in your office, I'll bring it right up."

Jacques hung up and lit a cigarette, wondering what the message could be, thinking it might be Holden impatiently jogging him about the bank numbers. Then the other thought flashed into his mind—the thought that it might be from Dave Bruce about Bobby. His heart faltered for a few beats, then he took hold of himself and inhaled a deep draught of smoke. Don't be an idiot, he said to himself.

There was a knock on the door and Jacques called, "Come in!" The code clerk, a freckled young man with sandy hair who usually wore a grin and dispensed wisecracks, walked over to his desk, looking unnaturally solemn, and handed Jacques an envelope. Without a word he turned and hurried out of the room, shutting the door behind him.

Jacques turned the envelope around in his hands. There was no writing on it and it was sealed. Every code message he had received since coming to Berne had been delivered to him in an open folder. He fought off another onslaught of fear before ripping it open. Taking out the pink sheet, he unfolded it and read:

> FOR EGGLI. SON MISSING. BELIEVED SHOT DOWN OVER GER-
> MANY. ANY FURTHER NEWS AS TO CAPTURE OR ALTERNATIVE
> WILL BE RELAYED AS SOON AS AVAILABLE. BRUCE.

He dropped the message, covering it with his arms as his head sank slowly forward. "Bobby! Bobby!" he sobbed. "They've got you! Those stinking pigs have shot you down!" The words came out in *Schweizerdeutsch*, the language of his earliest memory.

After a time he raised his head and swung his chair around so he could look out of the window at the fruit trees in the garden, now a dark green under the heavy sky. It all fitted together, he thought. Silverthorn staring at him, realizing that he was Bobby's father, hoping that Ekstrom and Hirsch would twig and keep silent. Then when it could no longer be brushed off, Hirsch had told a story which he had hoped would be comforting. He, the Jew, the one among them whose passion for the war was real, founded on a true and justifiable hatred, had had the compassion to try and shield Jacques from the pain of knowledge. It was the act of a gentleman, and he would thank him. Yes, tonight he

would do it. The dinner would go on with Bobby's squadron-
mates around him, to drink with him, to tell him the truth of
what they had seen, to give him—oh, God!—perhaps an ounce
of encouragement. For it was that which he longed for: some
word that Bobby's ship was still flying, even though crippled, or
that they had seen parachutes descending from it in the flak-
strewn sky.

CHAPTER XXII

WHERE are you headed? For the Consulate?" Walter asked as they crossed the small park from the Bürkliplatz to the Bahnhofstrasse. Jacques had telephoned at a quarter to eight to say that he would stop for his brother in the Zollikerstrasse and walk downtown with him.

"I thought I would go to the bank with you for a while," Jacques answered casually. "I have nothing to do until eleven-thirty."

Walter laughed. "There is damn little to do at the bank except read the newspaper. However, you are welcome. You can use Grosspapa's room if you wish."

"I would rather sit down with you and have a talk about the future—that is, if you are not too busy."

"I told you, there is very little to do. What there is, is handled by Keller and the clerks. This morning I was going to lock myself in and do some work on the code book, but I can do that just as well this afternoon."

"You don't have to bother about me. I'll read while you are working."

"No one is supposed to be in the room with me when I take it out of the vault."

"My God, Walter, I'm not the public. I'm your brother, a partner!"

"Just the same, those are Grosspapa's orders."

"Did he include me specifically?"

"No, no, it's merely the old rule that he and I are the only two to see it."

"I don't want to see it. It doesn't interest me in the slightest."

"Don't be angry, Jacques. Only you must promise not to tell Grosspapa if I allow you to stay in the room while I'm working on it."

"I'll guarantee that you can trust me on that."

Jacques purposely had not told his family about Bobby. He did not want them sending messages to Doris, for he had made up his mind that she should be kept ignorant until he had further word. To this end he had wired Dave to intercede with the War Department. There was no point in throwing her into a pit of grief before the facts were known. It was in her character to jump at once to the worst, the fatal conclusion, and the shock of it would be too much for her valiant heart. The three officers had given him one small thread of hope during the dinner in Berne two nights before. Lieutenant Silverthorn had finally come clean after he had learned Jacques had received word that Bobby's ship had not returned. It was he as copilot who had actually witnessed the fatal wounding of the "Excelsior," as he had called it. He had seen a wing tip disintegrate and then the outboard port motor tear off and drop. After that smoke had started pouring from the open cavity of the wing section and the ship had banked into a wide spin. Bobby's voice, it seemed, had come over to them clear and steady saying, "Tell the Colonel we had to jump for it. Good luck and au revoir!" And then just as their own ship had winged over, Silverthorn had seen the first man drop and his chute open. After that he could see no more as they had pulled sharply to the left in a diving turn.

The three boys had stayed until after midnight in his room, the liquor reacting on them quickly with their nerves drawn as taut as piano strings. Jacques had matched them drink for drink, but without effect. He had wanted desperately to get tight, to forget, but it was no use; the whisky had left him only more forlorn and embittered. The picture of his Bobby, charred and unrecognizable, lying in a German field, could not be erased from his mind by alcohol. The more deeply etched this picture had become, the firmer his resolution of dedication to the cause

of victory. That sense of mission which had originally drawn him
to Washington at Dexter Miller's invitation, because Bobby had
joined the Air Corps and he had wished his son to be proud of
him, to know that his father, though born a foreigner, shared
his sense of duty to his country, had been rekindled with a
coruscating flame. Whatever had happened, were Bobby dead
or a captive, he must vindicate his son's heroic performance.
It had been then as the three high-strung flyers were lounging in
his sitting room, talking in voices pitched stridently by whisky
and hysteria, retelling the story of the action from the rendezvous
over the Channel to the final fatal bomb run, that he had made
up his mind that the defeat and destruction of the Nazis was to
be the center, the core of his endeavor, with priority over any sentiment of family or bank. For that is what the shock had done to
him: it had made him separate his father, his brother, his sister
and Switzerland from Doris, his children and his country, which
now was unequivocally the U.S.A. Neutrality, which once as a
Swiss he had valued and understood, had suddenly become in-
comprehensible, an essay in semantics without meaning. Bobby
had completed his mission, dropped his bombs on the factories
of Regensburg, and had faced death calmly, willingly, to do it.
Well, he would face obloquy, disinheritance, complete severance
from his Swiss relatives with equal stoicism and determination in
the performance of *his* mission.

The next morning he had called Tante Vicki to tell her that he
was returning to Zürich for a visit of indeterminate length. He
had also called the consul-general in Zürich, asking that he be
met at the Haupt Bahnhof at four o'clock. Once at the Sudstrasse
which he had reached only at five in the afternoon as the train
had been late, he had gone to his room and stayed there until
dinner had been announced. He had wanted to be alone in order
to plan, to work out his scheme of attack which he had tried to
do on the train; but his mind had kept reverting to that picture
of Bobby, which had ruled out all other thoughts, leaving him
numb with anguish. The gin and vermouth which he kept on

the top shelf of the wardrobe had helped to settle his nerves and allow him to formulate a plan. He had taken his drinks English fashion, right out of the bottle because he had not wanted to be disturbed by Anni bringing him the ice.

With his father on the Bürgenstock, he had an excellent opportunity of scouting the ground with Walter who was not only amiable but inclined to admire his younger, more dashing brother. He had made up his mind to call Walter in the morning and walk to the bank with him. His opening play would be an appraisal of the future of the bank in view of his father's age and recent indisposition. From that point on he would have to play it by ear, making sure that his brother was held in a cocoon of unsuspecting trust and belief that Jacques was merely being a prudent and farsighted partner.

When they reached Walter's room on the second floor of the bank, Walter picked up a copy of the *Neue Zürcher Zeitung* and handed it to his brother. "Here, read this while I go down to the vault," he said.

Jacques took the newspaper and sat down in a chair in the corner of the room, ostentatiously far from Walter's desk. He was reading and smoking a cigarette when his brother returned carrying a small brassbound ledger and carefully bolted the door. His head behind the paper, Jacques listened, hearing Walter's quick footsteps on the soft carpet, the drawing of his chair toward the desk, the rattle of keys in his hand, the click of the lock, the thud of the ledger being laid on the top of the desk, and then the crack of the binding as the book was opened. He waited silently for a few minutes while his brother ruffled pages and scratched with a pen.

"Entering some new accounts?" Jacques asked finally, still holding the paper before him.

"Not exactly," Walter answered. "I'm splitting up some old ones, making two, even three, out of one."

"If any of those are in New York, you will advise us," Jacques said, to give the impression that he was sitting there as a partner of Spears, Wetherell.

"Grosspapa says not for the moment," Walter replied. "He says not to advise our correspondents until he authorizes me."

"That was before he went to the Bürgenstock?"

"Yes. He said there was no hurry about it; it could wait until he returned to Zürich."

"Has it ever occurred to you, Walter, that Grosspapa is getting on? The next bout of flu, even a recurrence of this one, might turn into pneumonia. It is very apt to, at that age."

"Naturally it has occurred to me," Walter answered, without stopping his work. "Why do you ask?"

"Because it was the reason I wanted to talk to you this morning," Jacques said, folding the newspaper and putting it on the table beside his chair. "As the representative of the bank in the United States, it is only proper that I, as your brother, should come to some understanding with you about the bank's affairs in the event of Grosspapa's death. You realize of course that I hope and pray that he will carry on for a long time, but we must not be blind to the possibility. The bank is, after all, the family monument, the structure which he has built up and expects you to maintain."

"What makes you think it will be me? He has never said so. On the contrary, he is always intimating that I have no capacity to run the bank. Maybe he has you in mind as his successor— or Hans."

"I wouldn't worry about that if I were you," Jacques said earnestly. "You are the oldest son, the crown prince. When he scolds the way he does, it is more the habit of the father than any real misgivings about your ability. Remember, Walter, that you and I are no longer youngsters. We are middle-aged men with grown children and a certain position in the community. Everyone—particularly the bank's clients—will expect us to carry on without change, you as the president, I as a special partner and representative in New York."

Walter looked up from the ledger and thoughtfully examined the pen in his hand. "That is all very well for you to say, Jacques, but until the will is read, it is pure speculation. Grosspapa has repeatedly stated that no one will know until he is dead." He shrugged his shoulders and went back to work on the ledger. "Who knows, maybe he will leave his share to the Baroness."

The heavy brass lever of the door handle rattled, followed by a loud knock.

"Who is there?" Walter called.

"Is that you, Walter? It is Hans. I wish to have a word with you." The voice of Hans Waldmann came only faintly through the thick walnut door.

"Just a moment," Walter called, then quickly shut the ledger, took out his keys, locked the brass clasp and put the book in his desk drawer. He walked over to the door, saying to Jacques as he went, "I will talk to Hans in Grosspapa's room. Bolt the door after me."

Jacques bolted the door and waited until he heard their footsteps recede down the corridor before he went quickly to the desk, opened the drawer and took out the ledger. He examined the small brass lock. In terms of his O.S.S. training it was a simple affair, made for a key with a round shank and a narrow flange—a very old-fashioned lock, never designed to protect the ledger against anyone more malicious than a snooper. From his breast pocket he took out the little kit that had been given him at the training school in Maryland. It was a flat leather case, like the ones made to carry keys, with a number of snap hooks hanging from a bar on the inside. From each hook hung a piece of stout wire, the ends of which were bent in varied ways. He selected the smallest, which had only a short right-angle bend, and inserted it in the keyhole. After less than fifteen seconds of manipulation he heard the small bolt click and he carefully pried the clasp from its seat.

The ledger was alphabetically indexed with lettered tabs.
Jacques's heart sank. Without knowing the names, he would have
to go through it page by page and there was not time enough
for that. He lifted the cover and ran quickly through the first
pages. To his immense relief he came upon an index by national-
ities. He ran his finger down until he came to *Deutschland*.
There were at least thirty titles under that heading, and many
were linked by parentheses and given an additional group title.
Most of them, he saw at a glance, were familiar industrial companies with interlocking interests which were cross-indexed to
"Italy," "Holland," "Sweden" and other countries. They were
important, for every dollar and Swiss franc of these companies
anywhere in the world could be and probably were at the service
of the Reich. But there was one grouping which interested him
the most. It was under the general title of *Reichskanzler*. The
individual names under this grouping were simple nouns, obviously code words. Jacques quickly turned to "R" and found that
the general account number for *Reichskanzler* was thirty-nine.
Then he returned to the index and selected the groups of the
major industrial and financial complexes. Five of these he mem-
orized under their headings and numbers. He repeated the list
to himself, including "*Reichskanzler—thirty-nine*," determined
to etch it indelibly on his mind.

All this had absorbed five or six minutes. He could not risk
any more time. Taking the small hook from his kit, he tried to
ease the bolt of the lock so that it would shut. He fumbled for
a minute or two without success, and then he heard voices ap-
proaching in the hall. Putting the clasp as far down as it would
go, he slipped the book back into the drawer and tiptoed back
to his chair, where he opened the *Neue Zürcher Zeitung*, spreading it on the table to give the impression that he had been
reading.

The voices continued in front of the door for some time before
Jacques heard Hans say "Adieu" and walk toward the main staircase. Still Walter did not knock, waiting, as Jacques imagined,

until Hans had disappeared, not wishing him to know that Jacques was in the room. When the soft knock finally came, Jacques rattled the newspaper violently before rising to open the door.

"What is on Hans's mind?" Jacques asked as Walter came into the room and bolted the door behind him.

"He had some news from his contact in Berlin that he wanted me to get to Grosspapa," Walter replied. He stood there, his hand still on the door handle, patently revolving the matter. "Come to think of it, there is no reason why Hans should not go to the Bürgenstock himself," he went on. "He knows perfectly well that I must stay here while Grosspapa is away. I will call him at his office."

"I could take the message for you," Jacques said. "I had in mind going back to Berne via Lucerne in order to see Grosspapa and find out how he was getting on."

"When will you be going?"

"Oh, tomorrow or the next day." Jacques, having failed to lock the ledger, had made up his mind to make no precipitous dash from Zürich. As he had resolved the matter while waiting for Walter to knock on the door, he must, when Walter discovered that the ledger was unlocked, accuse his brother of failing to set the lock properly in his confusion and haste at the sound of Hans's voice. Above all he must vehemently deny that he had ever left his chair or attempted to look at the ledger. As a proof of the guiltlessness of his conscience, he would stay in the room with his brother until eleven and would dine that evening with him and Hélène as had been agreed on the telephone that morning.

"Well, I'll think that over," Walter said. "It is rather interesting news and I don't like to keep Grosspapa waiting. You know how he is about being *au courant* with every international development." He still stood by the door, weighing the problem in his mind. "Of course I could write it out and send it by one of the bank's messengers. . . ."

"It is best not to write if one can avoid it," Jacques said.

"Oh, I agree. We never do, except in cases like this where we have to reach Grosspapa somewhere."

"Can you tell me what the information is?"

Walter thought for a while. "You want it for your government, of course."

"Naturally."

"And they will know where you got it."

"Indeed they will not. I will tell them that I got it through one of the firms who are selling bearings to Germany."

Walter walked slowly back to his desk. "Don't talk so silly, Jacques. Of course they will know it came from us. They know you are in Zürich, seeing me and living in the Sudstrasse. Besides, they are aware—and don't you forget it—that Eggli and Company knows a great deal that other people do not. They have tried—your own people—time and again to pump information from us."

Jacques shrugged his shoulders and went back to his chair. "Suit yourself, Walter," he said casually. "Getting enemy secrets is not really my business. There are others who handle that. I only thought that if I could help, I should."

"I know. I know how you feel. In my heart, Jacques, I am with you. I would give a lot to see that Fuehrer and his gang defeated. Only you have to remember that our position does not allow us to take sides. You know that. You've heard Grosspapa say it a thousand times—one's own sentiments must never enter the bank. The strength of Eggli and Company is that it remains rigidly neutral in political affairs outside the borders of the Confederation. We must know what is going on everywhere on the globe, but that information is to be used by us only for the protection of our clients' accounts. To use it for the benefit of others is to destroy our usefulness. Does that sound familiar?"

Jacques laughed. "It certainly does. Forget it, Walter. Forget that I ever asked you."

Walter opened the drawer of his desk and took out the code

book, at the same time fishing in his pocket for the keys. Jacques saw him give a start as he realized that the clasp was not locked and held his breath, reaching over to pick up the newspaper from the table.

"*Gotteswillen!* That is very strange," Walter said gazing at the ledger in his hand.

"What is strange?" Jacques asked lightly.

"This code book is unlocked."

"You mean the drawer of your desk?"

"No, the book; it has a lock."

"You had opened it before, hadn't you? Why should it be locked now?"

"Because I locked it when Hans knocked."

"You thought you did."

"Oh, I distinctly remember. . . ."

"So do I. When Hans knocked I saw you take out your keys and fumble with the book, like a child caught stealing the jam. Then you pushed the book into the drawer. I thought you were going to lock the drawer, but you didn't. I figured that you had forgotten to in your nervousness—not wanting Hans to know that I was here while you were working on the codes."

"By God, Jacques, I could have sworn that I . . ."

"Well, you didn't. There's the answer in your hands."

"You could have read this while I was out of the room," Walter said, horrified at the thought.

Jacques chuckled. "I most certainly could have if I were that sort of fellow."

Walter placed the ledger on the desk and took out a handkerchief to mop his forehead. He looked as white as a sheet, and Jacques felt sorry for him but he was not conscience-stricken over what he had done. The thought of Bobby brought down somewhere in Germany sustained him with a sharp pain. Nothing could make him waver in his duty now, not even the distress of his brother. The lies had come to his lips without compunction or remorse. That he could utter them so glibly, so plausibly, amazed him, for he had never since childhood consciously lied to anyone.

"Look, Jacques," Walter said in a quavering voice, "I don't mean to question your statement; but do you mean to tell me that knowing the drawer was unlocked, you resisted the temptation to glance at the book?"

"I never was tempted. Such a thought never occurred to me."

Walter sighed. "I must believe you."

"Of course you must."

"The secrets in here"—Walter tapped the book—"are the very heart of the bank. If they are known, we are finished."

"Who knows that better than I do? Don't excite yourself, Walter. You are talking to your brother, not an enemy agent."

"There was a time when Grosspapa worried about that."

Jacques smiled. "Did he think I came here as a spy?"

"I think he did. He got word that you had been seen in Washington with General Donovan."

"Now really! Of all the silly things I've ever heard! Certainly I saw Bill Donovan. Everybody sees him. He is a very well-known person. The reason he wanted to speak to me was on account of Grosspapa. They are old friends. He wanted to know how the old man was."

"Mind you, Jacques, I don't think that he disapproved of you being a spy. On the contrary, I think the idea rather appealed to him, gave you some stature in his eyes. But he warned us to take care what we told you. He had no objection to your getting information as long as the bank was not involved."

"What a marvelous father we have, Walter! He doesn't trust anyone, not even his own sons."

"His sons least of all," Walter mumbled sadly.

Jacques stood up and went over to the leather couch where he had thrown his overcoat and hat. "Well, I suppose that is the secret of his greatness as a banker." He said this with sincerity. It delighted him, made him proud to think that the old man had been smart enough to penetrate his disguise.

"You are going now?" Walter asked.

"Yes, I must. I've bothered you enough for one morning."

"And tonight you will be dining with us?"

"But of course! I shall be at your house at six-thirty."

"Before you unbolt the door I want you to come here and watch me."

Jacques picked up his hat and coat, walked over to the desk and watched, amused, while Walter took his keys out of his pocket, selected a small one and carefully locked the clasp of the ledger.

"There! You have seen it. It is locked," Walter said, prying the clasp with his fingers to illustrate the statement.

"This time you did it," Jacques said, laughing. "Adieu, Walter."

Walter put the ledger in the drawer and walked with Jacques to the door. "Remember now, no word of this to Grosspapa."

CHAPTER XXIII

THE Consulate had a car going to Berne, so Jacques arranged to have the use of it for his trip to the Bürgenstock, which was on the way. He had called his father, saying that he would arrive in the afternoon and asking him to engage a room for the night. At first the old man had demurred, protesting that there was no need for Jacques to visit him, that his recuperation had been rapid and satisfactory. But when Jacques had explained that he was coming in a Legation car, only to stop off on his way to Berne, his father had agreed to the visit though with patent reluctance, which Jacques attributed, recalling Hélène's shrewd guess, to the fact that the Baroness de Marty must be with him.

On the way, sitting alone in the back of the sedan with a rug around his legs to keep out the damp, chill air which had come suddenly with the month of October, Jacques gazed out of the window at the familiar countryside: the plow with a blush of green from the sprouting winter wheat; the orchards, bare now of fruit, leaves sodden and listless in the rain; and the dark majestic stands of pine—communal forests which stood out in bold relief against the fields and farmhouses. It made him think of his youth, of days such as this when with his father and Walter he had stood at the edge of a wood, gun poised, waiting for the pheasants and hares to be driven out. It was all part of him, this scenery, as familiar, as taken for granted as the furniture in his house on Long Island. Yet it was this ambivalence which disturbed him. He had ordered himself to take sides, to resolve the conflict, yet the dichotomy remained, oblivious to his will. It was not enough to say, "I am an American, married to an American, with a son who has been shot down, perhaps killed, in defense of America." The statement rang true, had no arguable faults, yet behind it, echoing like a distant obbligato of cowbells, was the sensation of being Swiss, of having feeder roots into this land which had not, could not be severed. In his mind's eye he saw, taking shape in a forest glade dappled with sunlight, the head of a roebuck, ears forward, nostrils scenting the still air, carrying such a majestic pair of three-pronged horns as he had never seen, not even in the hall of his father's house. The picture faded and another replaced it, of Bobby as a child in shorts and fleece-lined jacket raising his gun at a squawking cock pheasant as it sailed over the scrub oak of a wood near Islip. The moments that remain, he thought, that come back unsought, are the ones on which our pattern of behavior is based. And there in those two pictures was the root and reason of his schizophrenia.

He shook his head as if to rid his brain of these irresolute thoughts. This was no time to weaken, to be sucked back into the soft womb of his origin. Bobby, his splendid, sterling Bobby, the intrepid pilot who had led his squadron through the spotted sky and had been shot out of the air with a calm message to his colonel on his lips, the lad who had killed that pheasant, his first live bird, with an unerring eye, must be the sole commander of his action. Jacques must, as he had so properly resolved in his bedroom in Berne, perform his mission undaunted by his past, shutting out all influence of this land and of his father from whose subjugation he had escaped. And he had done it exactly as he had resolved. The numbers were securely in his mind, while Walter, good, dull, trusting Walter, had no suspicion that his brother had seen the code.

The clerk at the Grand Hotel greeted Jacques obsequiously, as hotel clerks treated members of the Eggli family everywhere in the world. He said that Herr Doktor Robert Eggli had left word he would receive his son in his suite at five o'clock. Jacques looked at his watch. It was four-thirty. He was grateful for that half-hour in which to steel himself. He would have time to wash up and have a drink in the bar to brace him against the influence of the old man, which he feared might once again bind him by an umbilical cord to the Swiss family.

After washing and changing his shirt, he came down to the bar and ordered a double scotch and soda, which he drank standing while he recited in his mind the titles and numbers from the code book to make certain that he had not forgotten them and that tomorrow, in Margett's office in Berne, he could speak his piece with pride. That was all that mattered now—that and the fate of Bobby. Walter, he felt sure, had been convinced in the end that he had made no effort to look at the ledger. No further word had been said about the matter, either at dinner that night or on the following day, when he had dropped in at the bank to pick up the sealed envelope which he was to give to his father and which was now in his coat pocket. It may be months, even years, he consoled himself, before they learn that the Americans have broken the code. By that time his father might well be dead, which would be a blessing.

The whisky warmed him, gave him courage, lent him the optimism to believe that it would never be discovered he had been the culprit, the spy. Only one person in the family knew his work was other than economic, and that was Hélène. He had contrived a moment with her alone before dinner, before Walter had come down for cocktails, to tell her that the whole operation with Venturi was off because the information had been worthless. She had not appeared disappointed. On the contrary, she had seemed to be relieved to be out of it. And he had echoed the same sentiment, saying that he could now devote all his energies to his proper mission of buying.

At five minutes to five he left the bar and walked up the stair to the second floor. He knew his father's suite well, a grand-ducal affair reserved for potentates and Robert Eggli. The old man was sitting by the window of his sitting room where he could look down on the lake a thousand feet below.

"You needn't have come, you know," Robert Eggli said. "I'm quite recovered though since two days this damnable autumn weather has kept me indoors. Besides, Yvonne de Marty is here to look after me. Look!" He pointed to the window where Jacques could see a thick blanket of mist rolling in from the direction of Lucerne. "The clouds are coming again. In a minute we will be in the middle of them."

"Lucerne was on my way," Jacques said, taking the sealed envelope out of his pocket and handing it to his father. "Walter asked me to bring you this."

His father took it, put on his gold-rimmed spectacles and examined the seals. "If your people opened this, they did a good job," he said.

"I'm not in the spying business, Papa."

"You are not, eh? Just the same, Walter should have had more sense than to let you carry confidential papers."

"That isn't fair, Papa. I'm his brother. He trusts me even if you do not."

"Never trust a man who works for his government. He lies and calls it patriotism. Sit down while I read this." He tore the envelope open, took out a sheet of paper and studied it.

Jacques settled in the corner of a couch, facing his father. He noted that the old man appeared frailer, older than when he had last seen him in Zürich. He seemed to have shrunk, and did not sit rigidly upright as he always had but was slumped in the chair, his once straight back curved as he read the letter with his hands resting on his knees. Jacques was also aware that it was taking him longer than usual to absorb the contents of the message. He sat there motionless, gazing at the sheet of paper as if hypnotized by its import. Then the color mounted slowly in his cheeks, starting with little pink spots on his cheekbones and spreading until his entire face had, chameleon-like, changed its hue. Jacques was worried. He thought it might be a recurrence of the fever or a sudden violent beating of the heart. Before he could speak, the hectic flush faded and Robert Eggli turned pale as he slowly took off his spectacles and looked at his son with hard bright eyes.

"Did Walter speak to you about the accounts when you were in Zürich?" the old man asked.

"Only in a general way," Jacques replied, wondering what Walter could have written that would have provoked the question. "We talked vaguely about the future—when the war would be over."

"When I would be dead."

"The war will end long before that, Papa."

"With your help, I suppose. Did your brother tell you that he was making some changes in the code?"

"I think he did mention something about splitting some accounts. I suggested that he advise Spears, Wetherell, but he said you had instructed him to do nothing until your return."

"Did he say what accounts were to be split?"

"No, and I didn't ask him."

Robert Eggli gripped the arms of his chair and straightened his back as if with a great effort. He turned his head toward the window where nothing was visible any more except the cotton-wool mist. The clouds had eaten up the last of the fading daylight, so that the room had become somber, all objects reduced to black and grey, the figure of the old man a mere silhouette against the mist.

"At a time like this," the father said slowly in an incisive voice as if he were delivering a lecture, "the world beyond the borders of the Confederation is apt to regard our country as inhabited by an immoral, materialistic group of mountain bandits who use the opportunity of war to gain wealth while others bleed. Americans think that; so do the British, the French, the Germans. They loathe us Swiss because we do not take sides in their quarrel.

They would praise us if we committed suicide, saying, 'See what those heroic martyrs have done! They have inherited the spirit of Arnold von Winkelried! They have taken the enemy's spears and thrust them in their breasts!' Yes, and they would wake up after it was all over to curse us in a different way. They would then complain that we had been stupid, idealistic fools, a bunch of dull, heavy-witted mountain farmers who had sacrificed ourselves to no purpose. And of course the second time they would have been right. It took the Napoleonic Wars to prove that, to show them that their only hope of continuity was the bastion of the Alps sticking up in the middle of them, keeping them apart, checking the flow of their forces, making it difficult for them to pit one power against another. Metternich saw that, and so did Talleyrand, and that is why they persuaded Castlereagh and the Czar Alexander to agree to the imposition of neutrality on Switzerland—in perpetuity! Many Swiss will tell you that it was our own idea. They probably taught you that at Zuoz. That is nonsense. In 1815 there was no spirit of neutrality in the Confederation. It was a country divided, still remembering Napoleon's armies. Neutrality was imposed on us by three of the greatest statesmen Europe has ever produced for a very sound reason—a reason which Sir Harold Mackinder would have understood, although the science of geopolitics was not known in those days."

The old man turned his head from the window and Jacques could tell that those piercing eyes were fixed on him, although it was too dark for him to see them. "You are wondering why I am giving you this schoolboy's lecture on history. Well, I am giving it because it is good sometimes to sit back, away from the fire, and look at things in true perspective. When a country goes to war, it is necessary to work up a pitch of emotion among the people, so that they will accept wounding, death, privation, all sacrifices gladly, without question. You can see that now everywhere within the belligerent countries, except in France where the will to fight and resist is confined to a few intelligent patriots who do not need the lash of propaganda to make them behave like Frenchmen. In this way the flame of passion, the blind hatred, so consumes the individual that he loses his capacity for reason, his ability to think in long-range terms. Americans are perhaps the most easily caught up in this mass emotion. They jump at once to the barbaric pitch, calling for annihilation, for silly things like unconditional surrender. That is because you do not think in terms of history. The British do because for hundreds of years they themselves have made history. Look at Churchill, he knows what he is about. He urged Franklin Roosevelt at Casablanca to attack from Greece and Yugoslavia. Why? Because he sees clearly that if it is not the Anglo-Americans who capture and hold the Balkans, it will be the Bolshevics; and no greater misfortune can befall Europe than to have this war end with the Bolshevics controlling the Danube. That would be suicide, for they do not give up what they have taken. To them liberation means communization. They are fanatics—Slav fanatics who believe that they and they alone possess the solution of man's salvation."

The old man grunted, tapping the letter on his knee with his spectacles. "You think that I am wandering down side streets like a garrulous old man who cannot stick to the subject. Don't fool yourself, I am still smart enough to know what I am saying and why I say it. You have allowed yourself to be drawn into this American mass hysteria. You fancy yourself as a noble crusader, going out to battle the Hun singlehanded: It is quite right that you should aid your country so that it may win, but if you start losing your head and mistake Switzerland for the enemy, then you can do more harm to your own people than all of Hitler's divisions. Metternich and Talleyrand ordered us to remain neutral because it was necessary if a balance of power was to be maintained in Europe. There had to be one place, one central place for the safekeeping of Western culture and capital during the upheavals which will always occur on this continent. And what better place than this mass of granite which sticks up impregnable in the very center of Europe? The powers gave us a responsibility, a trust. We were to cease supplying the armies of our neighbors with fighting men and devote our energies to peaceful pursuits, among which was the operation of a world-wide safe-deposit vault. Since that date, except for the stupid Sonder-bund War which the powers quickly put a stop to, not wishing Rome to upset this neutrality by having control of us, we have performed our assignment soberly and well. As long as we do this, as long as we are allowed to do it, it will be possible to restore Europe to equilibrium after the war. . . . I hope you understand what I am saying, Jacques."

"I understand perfectly, Papa," Jacques said. "But why should you tell it to me?"

"Because Americans do not understand the point," the old man almost shouted. "They are so involved in the emotion of war they cannot see that this neutrality, which they regard as wicked, almost treasonable, is in reality something they need, something that will be of vast service to them when they finally emerge victorious and as the only power strong enough to stop the spread of communism." His voice was rising now, always more heated, more strident. "That is why I tell you this, because you are an American who has lost his good Swiss heritage of sober thought. You think it clever and modern to run with the mob, repeating slogans like a parrot. 'Stalin is our brother! He will help us to wipe out the German race!' That is the sort of tommyrot your people are shouting. Defeat Hitler you will, there is no doubt of that. He is, in fact, already defeated. Then hang him if you wish, along with those other stupid pigs like Goering and Goebbels and Hess. But the German people will be an asset after this war, more than they have ever been before. You will have need of them as friends and allies, for if you don't, you will have to keep your armies on the Oder-Neisse for fifty years. And how are they to be revived to the point of being useful allies? How are they to gain true democracy and the respect of their conquerors when they have nothing but debts, rubble and reparations? Your new country will have to foot the bill for this recovery, for if you let them starve they will become Communists, and that will be the end of Europe, the end of Switzerland, and your soldiers will have died in vain. You will have destroyed one dictatorship for the benefit of another, a more dangerous one."

His voice was now cracking under the strain of his vehemence. Jacques started to protest, knowing that his father should not become so excited, but his effort was drowned by the voice of the old man.

"That is where Switzerland can help," he went on. "When the Germans are defeated, when that idiot Hitler is dead, then the money which German industries and banks have placed here for safekeeping will go back to help them rebuild. The bank—my bank—has some of those funds. I guard them as I would my own fortune. That is my duty, my responsibility." (Jacques could hear the paper of Walter's letter rattle as his father pounded the emphasis.) "That is my contribution to the Government of the United States. The day will come when those funds will be used to prevent the Slavs from taking over Europe. Then your people will thank God for Robert Eggli, for Switzerland!"

"Please, Papa. . . ." Jacques tried to plead.

"You can tell that to Leland Harrison and your boss, whoever he is. Tell them that the nature of those accounts is none of their business. Tell them that spying on the banks is cutting their own throats. Tell them that I know damn well why they sent my son to . . ." Robert Eggli's voice ceased suddenly, with a faint gasp, and his body leaned forward as if he were trying to pick something up from the floor.

Jacques waited for his father to straighten up and resume his harangue. Then he realized with a shock that the old man had collapsed. He sprang from the couch to his father's side, calling, "Papa! Papa! What is the matter?" But there was no answer to his question. No sound or motion came from the limp body. Leaning over, he gently raised his father's shoulders until they rested on the back of the armchair. Then he put his hand inside the old man's waistcoat, over his heart. He could feel no pulse.

Quickly he ran to the switch by the door and turned on the lights. His brain was alert, clear, not stricken into paralysis as it had been when he had learned of Bobby's fate. He moved precisely, efficiently, picking up the telephone, telling the operator to send the house doctor to Room 18 at once as Herr Robert Eggli was gravely ill. Going back to his father's chair, he saw clearly from the waxlike pallor of his skin and the blue lips that the old man was dead. It amazed him, even shocked him slightly, that he had no feeling of sorrow or loss. It was like looking down at the death mask of a great figure whom he had admired and respected and who had passed on as even the great must do in old age. The eyes stared straight out, but they had lost their fire, their power to frighten, to demand obedience. The once noble head was a little silly now with its lower jaw hanging open.

Jacques saw the sheet of paper which had provoked the fatal scolding lying on the carpet below the hanging, lifeless hand. He picked it up and read it. It was in Walter's handwriting and told that the German High Command was developing a new weapon with which Hitler hoped to turn the course of the war to his favor. The Fuehrer had, it seemed, given the project priority over all other arms, including airplanes. But the answer to Jacques's curiosity was in a final brief paragraph which read: "Because of suspicious circumstances relating to the vault, I would ask your permission to give new numbers to all accounts in the code book."

Jacques folded the paper carefully and put it in his coat pocket.

Good old Walter, he thought, shaking his head in admiration, you are neither dull nor trusting. You knew what I had done, yet you never let on. All the time while I was blithely assuring you that you had left the clasp unlocked and that I had made no effort to pry into the bank's secrets, you knew that I was lying. And this was your way of telling Grosspapa, knowing full well that having accomplished my mission I would be sure to deliver the message of Hans without tampering with the seals, which might have aroused the old man's suspicion. Walter could trust his father to read the cryptic message correctly. Obviously Grosspapa had been revolving it in his mind, searching for Walter's true meaning, and coming to the eventual conclusion that for "vault" he should read "Jacques." It was then that he had started his lecture, firm in the conviction that he could dominate his American son, as he had in the past, by the force of his wrath, the power of his reasoning, the rightness of his cause.

Well, his father had won, the numbers he had in his brain would be worthless now, for Walter would act instantly on hearing of the old man's death.

The creak of a door hinge and the rustle of silk made Jacques turn quickly. The Baroness de Marty had entered from an adjoining suite. She seemed surprised to find Jacques standing there.

"I'm sorry to have disturbed you," she said in French. "I ask your pardon, Robert. From the sudden silence I had thought you were alone."

"I regret to tell you, my dear Baroness, that my father is no longer with us," Jacques said in a low, gentle voice.

"What? What do you mean?" The Baroness clutched the pearls at her throat. She took a deep breath, then ran forward to the chair. When she saw the body of her lover, sightless eyes staring at nothing, head hanging back, she let out a sharp little cry of pain and sank to her knees, clutching the cold limp hand that hung over the arm of the chair.

To Jacques it seemed a long time that she knelt there, motionless, not sobbing, no tear on her cheek, just holding that dead arm tightly to her breast as if she would go with him, rejecting any parting. When the doctor knocked on the hall door, Jacques left her to answer it.

"Please come in," he said, "but I am afraid it is too late." As he turned to lead the doctor to the body of his father, he saw that the Baroness had risen and was biting her lip in an effort to control her emotion.

There was no need for an examination. It was all too evident that Robert Eggli was no longer alive. The doctor shook his head sadly and extended his hand to Jacques. "You are his son, are you not? My sympathy. I have known him since he first came to the Bürgenstock many years ago. A great man. A credit to Switzerland. Now, if you will allow me, I shall ask the porter for two men to carry the body to the bedroom."

"By all means. Thank you, Doctor," Jacques said. He hesitated for a moment, then leaned over and put his hand in the inside pocket of his father's jacket from which he took a wallet of alligator skin, edged with gold. "I had better take this," he said apologetically. "There might be important papers in it."

"You have only to speak to the manager and everything will be arranged as you wish," the Doctor said and went over to the telephone.

The Baroness had stood there by the chair, biting her lips, twisting a handkerchief in her fingers without looking at them or greeting the doctor. Now she took a deep breath and turned to Jacques. "You had better come to my salon while they are doing this," she said coldly.

Jacques followed her through the door which connected the two sitting rooms. "What happened?" she asked after closing the door behind him. "He was excited. I could hear him shouting." She looked at Jacques accusingly, her dark eyes full of grief and anger.

Jacques felt a sudden pang of sorrow for her which he had not felt for his father. It was obvious that she was the one who would feel the loss most deeply. The mourning of the family would be sincere but perfunctory, something that was expected of them, like going to church on Sunday. They would not be plunged into grief. How could they be? Grosspapa had demanded obedience and respect of them, but never love. Love was something that this woman alone had received from him. He knew it now, looking at those dark, revengeful eyes. "He lectured me," Jacques said in a low voice to indicate his respect for her distress. "I tried to stop him, but he would go on."

"Had you done something to hurt him?"

Jacques flushed. "I suppose so," he answered hesitatingly.

She looked at him long and intently, as if to find the truth in his eyes. "I have lost a great and noble friend," she said slowly, "a man whose honor was above reproach, a man who was faithful and true to his principles, his country and those whom he loved. To betray him would be to betray oneself."

She did not go on, so Jacques said, "As it happens, he has not been betrayed."

"He must have feared that you might."

"Perhaps he did."

"How could you? How could you think of it?"

"Because a few days ago I learned that my son had been shot down over Germany."

She gave a little start. "Oh, merciful God! You poor man! The one whose name was Robert?"

"Yes. Perhaps now you can understand how I felt—that no sacrifice could be too great in the cause of victory."

"Was this the news that you brought?"

"No, I purposely did not tell him, thinking it might upset him."

Heaving a sigh, she turned her head away. "That boy was his hope, his favorite grandchild," she said softly, as if to herself. Then, with her large eyes looking searchingly into his, "Is it the worst? Is it known that he died?"

"Only that his airplane was shot down."

"Then he may be alive—a prisoner."

"Pray to God that he is, but I wanted to avenge him . . ."

"Of course, of course."

"But I didn't."

Her head turned quickly, her eyes probing his again. "Did your father know that you had not done it?" she asked.

"I think so. He always knew when he had succeeded in imposing his will."

Her eyes filled with tears and she dabbed them with the little ball of handkerchief which she held crumpled in her hands. "You must excuse me," she said, with a catch in her voice. "You see, I loved him very much." She waved toward the telephone. "Sit here and do whatever is to be done. I shall go to my bedroom for a little while." She walked out of the room slowly, breathing deeply, holding her head high against the pain in her heart.

When the bedroom door had closed, Jacques went to the telephone and put in a call for Walter in Zürich.